The Medicine Man

IVAN SHAFFER

THE MEDICINE MAN

LESTER AND ORPEN LIMITED, TORONTO

Also by Ivan Shaffer

BUSINESS IS BUSINESS?
THE MIDAS COMPULSION
THE STOCK PROMOTION BUSINESS

ISBN 0-919630-67-7

Printed in Canada

For Anita

Author's Note

Although the characters in this story are fictional and bear no resemblance to anyone living or dead, the essential details of the lobbying and other activities of the international pharmaceutical industry are accurate. Parts of this book are based on *Hansard*, the Canadian parliamentary record, transcripts of committee hearings, documents and letters from the files of various pharmaceutical firms and their industry association, and discussions with officials and scientists both within the industry and governmental regulating bodies. To the extent, then, that it is ever possible to distinguish between history and fiction, the story is rooted in actual happenings that occurred in Canada, Europe, and the United States during 1966 and 1967.

Ivan Shaffer
San Patricio, Mexico, 1975

"In this society, the productive apparatus tends to become totalitarian to the extent to which it determines not only the socially needed occupations, skills and attitudes, but also individual needs and aspirations. . . . There is only one dimension and it is everywhere and in all forms."

Herbert Marcuse

"Even-if-I-know-who-I-am, I-have-no-significance. I am unable to influence others. The next step is apathy. And the step following that is violence. For no human being can stand the perpetually numbing experience of his own powerlessness."

Rollo May

"Medicines that often do more harm than good are being manufactured today by so-called ethical pharmaceutical firms,
stocked by drug stores, and prescribed by doctors. Some of these
drugs can turn your life into a living horror. Some can kill. How
can this be possible in this day and age, in these wondrous
sixties. . . ."

As he watched and listened to Grant MacDonald on television,
it seemed to Joseph that Grant was speaking directly to him.
Joseph realized that this was the way it must appear to all of
Grant's viewers. On television Grant had the power of sincerity.
Anyone would believe what that face told him. Wide set eyes,
high cheek bones, a well-formed face. He inspired trust.

Besides appearing on a five minute network television commentary following the 11:00 P.M. news, MacDonald was also a
political columnist, published in most leading Canadian newspapers and several key American ones as well.

" . . . how is it, you ask yourself, that with all their vaunted
scientific know-how, drug manufacturers continue to market
products that have absolutely no proved value?" MacDonald
continued, naming several drugs that had recently been removed from sale by the Food and Drug Administration in the
United States, but were still being sold in Canada and other parts
of the world. "If they're harmful or not efficacious there, surely
the same holds true here."

In his hotel suite, Joseph Adam Mann stretched his long

frame between the sofa and stuffed chair and listened with mounting dismay as his best friend attacked the pharmaceutical industry — the industry he, as a management consultant, had been sent from New York to defend. Across the room, leaning against a wall and cradling a scotch, the same Grant MacDonald was studying Joseph. Although acutely aware of this, Joseph forced himself not to react. He fixed his eyes on the set, on the pre-taped Grant. He kept his face a mask. Although the two men affected a civilized, courteous, and friendly manner, they both were discomfitted by feelings of tension, wariness, and hostility.

On television the scathing denunciation of the industry continued. Grant claimed that whatever laws existed to protect the public had come about not as a result of industry concern, but through government action following major tragedies. "Scandalous and adulterating contamination and misbranding of food and drug products brought about the first American Food and Drug Act in 1906. The sulfanilamide tragedy, in which a drug maker dissolved the new wonder drug, sulfanilamide, in toxic diethylene glycol and marketed it without testing it for safety, resulted in death to one hundred and seven people, mostly children. It also resulted in the U.S. Food, Drug and Cosmetic Act in 1938. Included is a provision that prohibits traffic in new drugs unless such drugs have been adequately tested to prove they are safe. And yet years later we had the thalidomide tragedy — and others I will tell you about in future programs. The average person is still not safe."

Although Joseph considered Grant's presentation a dangerous oversimplification, he knew enough about audience response to realize that his method of delivery, with its understated moral outrage, made his charges sound reasonable. As a result the viewer would feel terribly threatened. Grant's tendency to pontificate, his very preachiness, was transformed by television into a compelling intensity.

"I'm shocked at your overstatement, Grant," Joseph was forced to comment. "You know the situation is light-years more complex than you describe."

"Let's wait until the program is over before we get into it."

2

Grant was obviously annoyed.

At the interruption, Joseph wondered, or at having his ideas questioned? How much of an ego trip was he on? It was now clear to Joseph that when Grant had called that afternoon and suggested a late drink, it was for the sole purpose of watching this particular program together. Obviously Grant wanted a confrontation — and much sooner than Joseph had intended.

After demonstrating that Canadians paid more for their medicines than the citizens of any other nation, Grant closed the program with a fervent appeal. "A special committee of Parliament has been appointed to probe the question of unsafe drugs, high prices, and their relationship to patent protection. Those hearings begin tomorrow.

"This will be the third such enquiry by various government bodies in the last ten years. Each time the international lobby has been able to prevent action. Clearly, the only way to bring down drug prices is to stop protecting American and other foreign companies. To do that, patent laws must be changed. Canada must then build its own industry and research capability.

"I urge every one of you to find out about this committee and in the interest of your health, of the health of your children, and of your country write to your Member of Parliament. All you need say is, 'I'm in favour of lower prices for drugs. End patent protection now.' Thank you for listening. Good night, and keep well."

Grant switched off the television. "There it is, Joey. You've read my columns on the prescription drug industry, I'm sure, and now you've seen me on television so you know exactly how opposed I am to the drug people you represent."

Joseph was perplexed. It had never been Grant's nature nor his journalistic style to be so biased. Further, he had not been prepared for a confrontation. As it was the first time he'd seen Grant since arriving in Ottawa five days ago, he had looked forward to a quiet evening of scotch and reminiscing.

"Look, Joseph, straight out, I'd like you to drop this project and go back to New York. You're into more than you know."

"Why are you so dead set against the industry? In preparation

3

for this assignment I've studied so much material I think I could pass an examination in pharmacology. I see it completely differently."

"Come on Joey, be real. I can't get it through my head why you were sent. Or maybe I just don't want to. I mean I'm morally certain Pharmpress has a dossier on me. Yes" — he responded to the look of surprise in Joseph's eyes — "I know all about them. Undoubtedly they know we've been buddies since we were ten and assumed you could influence me. Fair game. But what's really bugging me is that you would accept the assignment knowing that. That you would come up here to use me."

"You were never discussed." Joseph forced himself to look straight into Grant's eyes. It was a direct lie. Grant's name had come up at the first conference in New York when Joseph had been assigned to the project. Present were Robert Heister, chairman of Heister Pharmaceutical Laboratories Inc., the man the largest pharmaceutical companies of the world had selected as chief strategist for the lobby against the Canadian parliamentary committee, and Dean Sorenson, president of Heister International. During the briefing, Heister distributed clippings of articles attacking the industry. "Look at these. Then you'll understand what we're up against, and these are only a random selection sent by Pharmpress."

With a sick feeling in his stomach, Joseph saw that many of the clippings were of articles written by Grant MacDonald. He quickly glanced at some, thinking it curious that a massive multinational industry would be so concerned about one newspaper writer.

As if reading his mind, Heister leaned across his desk. "This man can be critical. Articles like MacDonald's condition politicians and public alike and with the competitive nature of media, start other journalists along the same lines of attack. It has to be more than coincidence that a month before the special parliamentary committee was announced, a man who has never written a word about our industry, let alone a bad word, suddenly attacks us. Without doubt the Canadian government is using him to brainwash the public."

4

It didn't seem possible to Joseph that, because of his relationship with Grant MacDonald, he was being chosen for this assignment. And yet clearly, Pharmpress — a sinister sounding private investigating outfit — had ferreted out that he and Grant had been friends since childhood. He couldn't help but admire their efficiency.

"Mr. Heister, Mr. Sorenson, I think you should know that Grant MacDonald is my closest personal friend. If I am being retained because you think I can influence him, then you are making a mistake. He is a very stubborn man. I doubt that I could change his mind, if I wanted to. Or that I would automatically try. I want that understood."

They nodded at what they knew to be a hollow gesture. Meaningless words. Professional role-playing. In a key position, watched by the heads of the giant corporations of the world, this was a chance of a lifetime. Of course he would try to influence Grant. But it wouldn't be easy. Grant was Grant. Stubborn as they came. He remembered at university when, for a short time, Grant had been a card carrying member of the Communist party. Nothing Joseph had said could change his mind. And he certainly hadn't been able to talk him out of marrying Thelma.

As he remembered the meeting in New York, Joseph was satisfied that he had covered himself. "Grant, even if I had known of your involvement, I would have had to come to Ottawa. I had no choice. What could I have said to the managing partner of the firm I work for? That I turned down a very important assignment because I might lose a friend?" He paused. "It's a very big opportunity for me. It could jump me right up there."

"Joey, you can't win. There's more stacked against you than you know."

"What do you mean?"
Grant shook his head. "Let it go. I shouldn't have said that."

Passing off the remark as typical of the inflated opinion he felt columnists had of themselves, Joseph said, "Look, we go back a long way. Let's not fight about this tonight. Besides, I've been working eighteen hours a day. I'm too tired. I haven't even seen my mother."

"How's she been?"

"I don't know. I dropped in twice but both times she was taking a nap. It's not like her. I sent her flowers and I'm having dinner there on Sunday."

Grant walked toward the door. "Give her my love."

"What about a nightcap?"

"I better run along. It was good to see you Joey," Grant said warmly. "And don't forget the party Thelma and I are throwing Saturday. You be sure to come. Okay? No matter what happens in this drug thing."

"Wouldn't miss it," Joseph responded, wondering uneasily what Grant was getting at.

"See you. And Joey, give a thought to what I've said."

After Grant left, Joseph poured himself another scotch. "Not to worry," he told himself, a phrase he used when he was very worried. Columnists need material. To keep their readers and their television ratings they often had to take strong positions. The hearings started the next day so drugs and drug prices were of interest to the general public. It could be as simple as that. Next week Grant could play God for another cause. That was the media business. But with all his rationalizations, Joseph remained uneasy. A crusading Grant MacDonald was a formidable adversary, a real threat to the industry. But greater than his practical concern was Joseph's worry that if they remained on opposite sides in this struggle, it could damage and perhaps destroy their life-long friendship.

As a young boy, his father's known drunkenness, the fact that his mother was a char, and poverty, with the resulting clean but shabby clothes, had made Joseph feel painfully inferior, then stand-offish, and finally defiantly abrasive. He had become friends with Grant by accident, the incident itself as clear to him now as if it had happened yesterday. He remembered running through the park toward the Canadian National Museum after delivering ten dollars, the month's rent, to the landlady, fingering the nickel she always gave him. "Rat-tat-tat," — a new kid swooped down on him. "I'm Tailspin Tommy, ace fighter

6

pilot, you wanna play dog-fight?" Joseph ached to play the famous hero of the comic book series but the new kid owned the Tailspin Tommy helmet and ring. Twenty box-tops and ten cents. Arms outstretched, Bristol and Fokker, plane, pilot, and machine guns, they flew about the park. Then the new kid let him wear the helmet and ring. Let him take a turn at being Tailspin Tommy. "My name's Grant, Grant MacDonald. What's yours?" They had become friends for life.

Grant was his first friend, his only friend; Joseph had never made another as close. Never wanted to. Very much a loner, he preferred the company of women to men. Even though he had moved to New York years before, he and Grant still managed to see each other for several days at least once a year. Either Grant would come to New York for a round of theatre and talk, or Joseph would go to Ottawa and after spending a day with his mother, he and Grant would drive to Algonquin Park to camp and canoe for a week. During those times they would talk of philosphy, books, ideas — never of the present or what they were doing to earn their living, as if that were beneath them, not important because it was not essential. Work was something one had to do to eat. Apart from those few days they had little contact, never writing and rarely exchanging telephone calls. Grant had wanted to be a novelist, and instead had become a political reporter. Joseph had wanted to be a university professor and perhaps paint, and instead he had become a management consultant. They were both forty-two years old, had known each other for more than thirty years. A lot of water under the bridge.

Joseph sipped his scotch. Strange to find himself on assignment in Ottawa, his home town, the capital of Canada. When he accepted the assignment, and it was true he had no choice, he did not think that returning to Ottawa would be different from working in any other city. Although he had been born here, home for many years now had been a two bedroom apartment at Eighty-third and First in New York. Not overly fashionable, it was reasonably priced and, more important, was in the middle of a neighbourhood that retained its ethnic character — a melange of Baltic peoples with their foods and shops. The area had a heartbeat that he found provided him with reality, a sense of place. It was relief from the sterile Fifth Avenue offices of Daniels and Company, one of the nation's largest firms of management consultants — refuge from the arrogance of the technocratic minds, minds that not only found solutions for every problem, but believed every problem was solvable.

He never tired of his apartment or the area — one of the reasons undoubtedly being that he was away so much. As a management consultant, travel was a way of life. In the last year he had supervised an administrative reorganization of the railways in Korea, completed a quick study of agricultural distribution problems in Tanzania (a little awkward as he kept running into experts from Communist China), and carried out an executive compensation review for a chain of banks in southern Texas. And now, the assignment of directing the International Pharmaceutical Association's lobby in Ottawa to prevent any change in the status quo.

Joseph glanced around the hotel room. With his books lying piled in different spots on the floor, his papers all over the sofa, his portable typewriter set up on the desk, documents on either side, and his chess set on the coffee table, his room looked as though he had lived in it for years. When he checked into a hotel, no matter where it was in the world, his first act was to make it untidy. He always brought stacks of books — books on art, philosophy, psychology, politics, more than he could possibly read — and, deliberately, placed them haphazardly around the room. His pattern was to read at least six books at a time, dipping into one and then another. Books gave him a sense of peace. Books, his apartment in New York and, when he was alone, not wearing any clothes, were some of the many hedges he used to keep his sense of self.

It would have been good to spend the night with Grant talking and drinking like they used to, but the hearings started tomorrow and he would have to be fresh. He smiled. Worrying about how one would feel the next day was a sure sign of middle age.

8

Besides, he would see him at the party on Saturday and, in as careful a way as possible, would probe to find out if Heister were right about there being more behind Grant MacDonald's attacks than just the newspaperman's ordinary opposition to big business. He must also try to discover the source of Grant's obviously one-sided material and, if Grant continued, have the Association reply with contra evidence either in the form of scientific extracts or monographs. One thing for certain, Grant would respond to reason.

Joseph finished his drink and went to bed. Deciding to read for relaxation, he started a book he'd just bought at the airport — Truman Capote's *In Cold Blood* — until his eyes closed and the book fell out of his hands. Tomorrow it would begin. . . .

"Gentlemen, I see a quorum."

The chairman, who was both a medical doctor and a Member of Parliament, struck his gavel firmly on the green felt-covered table, signifying the start of the Special Committee on Drug Costs and Prices. He called the roll, and when all twenty-four members of the committee responded, expressed the wish somewhat sardonically that their work, so important to Canadians, would always be favoured with a full turnout.

The site for the Special Committee on Drug Costs and Prices was the Railway Committee Room, one of the largest in the Houses of Parliament, about one hundred by seventy-five feet, the ceiling a good fifty feet high. On the east wall hung a twenty-foot-wide painting of the Fathers of Confederation — a copy, the original being burned in the Great Fire of 1916. To add to the thoroughly dismal setting, the mustard walls were decorated with poorly drawn, faded murals depicting the various modes of transportation used in Canada during its history — birch bark canoes, Red River carts, steam engines, and jet planes.

The committee was composed of elected Members of Parliament representing the numerical strength of their respective parties in the House. The power of the people, Joseph thought with as much wonder as cynicism. Small town doctors, a half-dozen lawyers, several druggists, the token woman, and the rest, businessmen. As individuals they failed to impress. Some wore suits rumpled and out of style, shirt collars and cuffs were frayed, and the only woman had somehow made herself look very mannish. Although several undoubtedly had the guile to succeed in New York, only Frank Flanagan, the pharmaceutical industry's captive politician, looked as though he could. While separately they seemed shabby, almost rag-tag, their togetherness in committee, the mystique of being elected, gave them a power which in contrast to their individual ordinariness made them the more threatening. Seated on their chairs in a long line they appeared to be awaiting the order to charge, like a nineteenth century cavalry troop.

Dean Sorenson and Joseph arrived ten minutes early and were soon joined by Ron Kendall, information officer with the Canadian Drug Association. Sorenson suggested that they take seats in the third row, close enough to observe the committee members but still be inconspicuous themselves. Joseph thought it foolish, but said nothing. There was no way the three of them would be inconspicuous once the hearings actually started, so why bother now? Within minutes the room began to fill until several hundred people were milling about. Kendall pointed out those who were members of various governments; politicians who were not on the committee but who had a special interest; reporters (surprisingly, Grant MacDonald was not there — was that an indication he would turn his attention to other matters?); public relations men holding a watching brief for various drug manufacturers; representatives of several consumer groups; and committee members. The informality surprised Joseph. It was obvious that most of the Ottawa people knew each other. They joked softly together and there was much handshaking and waving. At ten o'clock sharp, the guard closed the door and everyone quickly found seats.

Joseph had been prepared for war, but the vast drabness of the setting made all the plans so carefully worked out in New York with Heister and Sorenson seem absurdly inflated, like a scenario for a melodrama. He had the feeling of being at an old-fashioned town hall meeting.

"Take a good look at them, Mr. Mann," Sorenson said. "They're the enemy."

But was that automatically true? A special committee such as

11

this, set up to deal with a specific subject, was different from standing committees, such as those on banking or external affairs, whose work went on day after day as matters were referred to them. It was different, too, from a Royal Commission, for it could not force people to testify. From what he remembered of his Political Science II at university, "in committee" everyone was an individual, interested men and women concerned about what was best for Canada, irrespective of party loyalties. They were not rubber stamps. He hoped he was right because part of his tactics would be to meet them all, learn about their backgrounds, financial status, who could be persuaded by reason, who by gifts of one kind or another, and who were philosophically or emotionally opposed to the industry. He planned to work on them methodically, doggedly, to convince them of the rightness of the industry's opposition to a change in the patent laws. It was not until he had read the background documents that the patent problem was actually brought into focus.

Historically, Canadian patent law followed American law, which had itself initially developed from the old British usage in that the discoverer of a new drug or process had exclusive right to his discovery for seventeen years, after which it was in the public domain. By ending patent protection, the Canadian government hoped that many firms would manufacture all drugs as soon as they were approved by the Food and Drug Directorate, the resulting competition forcing prices down in accord with the market thesis of supply and demand. It had been a surprise to Joseph that a country the size of Canada could present any threat to the international industry until it had been explained that if Canada ended patent protection and drug prices did fall, then other countries would follow Canada's lead — the domino effect. Obviously, it wouldn't take very long for a member of Congress, or the British Parliament, or the German *Reichstag*, or the French Assembly to realize the vote-getting appeal of lower-priced drugs. If other countries removed patent protection the industry would no longer have any control over manufacturing, marketing, and pricing. Profits would drop. Dividends diminish. The stock market would react and the in-

12

dustry would be as good as dead. It had happened to other apparently sound enterprises — railways, coal, even the auto industry looked shaky as cars lost their status symbol and people turned from them as evil inventions poisoning the air.

From the little Joseph knew, the industry had reason to fear. Excess and irresponsibilities had been proven. Profits were too high. Some drugs had been marketed too soon. But he was convinced that, on balance, the system was better than anything else that could be devised. Certainly better than state-controlled drug manufacturing. If Dean Sorenson was an example, the industry's main problem was its arrogance. Like doctors they considered themselves, by definition, to be above reproach.

The chairman moved briskly through the first items on the agenda. It was settled that the Minister of National Health and Welfare should appear; that in addition to the agreed upon list of government departments, consumer bodies, and paramedical and scientific associations, the six largest drug manufacturers be invited (subpoenaed would be more accurate, Joseph thought— the effect was the same) to present their arguments as to why the Patent Act should not be changed; and that the committee hold its meetings on Tuesdays and Thursdays at 10:00 A.M. As well, it was agreed to hire a lawyer and accountant, and to publish the transcript of the hearings.

When the chairman completed the routine items, he asked the committee members if they had any items to raise before he proceeded.

Without warning the mood altered dramatically as Dr. Henry Lewison, a sixty-year-old member of the Liberal party, rose and spoke. "Mr. Chairman, before we begin the investigation, I think it would be of interest to this committee to determine if any of its members have a financial interest either directly or indirectly with any of the drug companies in order that this may be investigated in a thorough manner, as we intend to do, so that no member may be prejudiced in this investigation."

"Christ," Kendall hissed, "no committee has ever raised the conflict of interest question."

Joseph froze with the sickening realization that the unex-

13

pected had happened. In the opening gambit Frank Flanagan was under attack.

A rising Liberal Member of the House of Commons, a parliamentary secretary in line to being appointed a full-fledged cabinet minister, and an articulate member of the parliamentary committee, Flanagan was the key to the industry's entire strategy. During committee hearings he was to question aggressively anyone who attacked the industry and to highlight the positive statements of those in favour. As well, he was to lobby among his own party members. At the completion of the special committee he was to include himself on the smaller subcommittee that actually wrote the recommendations based on the hearings. During this phase he was to bring drafts to Joseph and Sorenson who would suggest alternate wording, rewriting sentences that were clearly harmful to the industry, thus rendering them innocuous or capable of double meanings. Hence, even if the will of the committee were detrimental to the industry, with Flanagan it was hoped they could control the final detail of the report. They couldn't afford to lose him.

Flanagan had been beholden to Heister for over five years now and would be for the rest of his political life. When he had been elected to Parliament for his second term, his printing business, a storefront family concern that printed wedding invitations and letterhead, was on the brink of bankruptcy. Brian Allen, Heister's Toronto public relations consultant, had learned of Flanagan's problem, contacted Robert Heister directly, and soon large printing orders not only from the Heister firm, but from other drug manufacturers as well, had saved Flanagan from going under. Heister even loaned the money needed to buy new equipment so that Flanagan could print glossy brochures and package inserts in four colours. Within a very few years Flanagan was prospering to the extent that he was earning fifty thousand dollars a year from his printing business alone.

The chairman replied to Dr. Lewison, "I do not think the chairman should ask each member of the committee here and now. I think it would be obvious that anyone who has a conflict of

14

interest should declare that. As chairman, I am quite willing to say I have no conflict of interest in any of these areas."

"Mr. Chairman," Dr. Lewison continued, "that's not what I mean. I think that this session should be adjourned so that committee members can examine themselves and study their assets and if they find a conflict should resign from this committee. It is very important to the people of Canada that we approach the subject with an unbiased point of view. I purposely said directly or indirectly because an indirect interest could be just as great as a direct interest."

Discussion, some of it heated, took place among the committee members.

"That blows Flanagan," Kendall said. "They're not going to embarrass him by asking him directly. Nobody wants blood. They're giving him a chance to resign from the committee quietly."

As if to underline Kendall's view, the committee adjourned with the understanding that anyone with a conflict would resign and not attend further sessions.

"But he doesn't own one share of any drug company," Sorenson said. "We've always been scrupulous about that."

"Directly or indirectly, Dean," Joseph corrected. "What would you call the president of a printing firm that derives more than sixty per cent of its business from drug companies — a disinterested bystander?" Joseph wasted no time in useless wondering. As things stood, Flanagan would have to resign. What to do? What to do? There had to be an answer, a way of changing the set.

In other investigations the industry did not have to rely on one man. They had controlled two cabinet ministers as well as the then prime minister's personal doctor (advising him when to buy stock in various drug companies) and the ministers of health in three provinces. But with the change in government two years before, other than Flanagan they no longer controlled anyone of importance.

"Kendall," Joseph said sharply, "get Flanagan. I want a meeting right away."

15

"He's got to go back to his riding for the weekend. Tomorrow is July the first, Dominion Day. He has several speaking engagements."

It flashed through Joseph's mind that that was the reason for Grant's party.

"You can't be too heavy-handed, Joe."

"All right, then get him back for a meeting in my hotel suite on Sunday. In the meantime you get word to him that he is not, repeat *not,* to resign from that committee."

"What have you got in mind?" Sorenson asked.

"I'm not sure yet, but until I am, he hangs in there."

"Joe, you can't lean on him. That's not the way we do things here," Kendall warned.

"Both of you may be satisfied to accept this without fighting. I'm not. You tell Flanagan what I told you."

The belligerence in his voice shocked both Kendall and Sorenson, and Kendall knew that whatever else Flanagan might have planned for Sunday, he'd better cancel it and meet Joseph.

"I think we ought to call Bob Heister right away. When something like this happens he wants to know about it," Sorenson said, trying to hide his agitation.

"You do what you want, but I am not running to New York with the very first problem. I'm telling you there is no way Flanagan is going to resign from that committee. The only way he'll get off it is to be carried out feet first."

Sorenson didn't reply. He didn't know how to deal with Mann yet. Certainly he couldn't control him as he had thought he could. Mann had an intensity, perhaps even a suggestion of violence, that kept Sorenson on edge. As president of Heister Pharmaceutical International, the holding company for all Heister subsidiaries in the world and the joint-ownership companies in Mexico and Japan, Sorenson had been the chief lobbyist for the international companies for years, leading the fight during the Heath Commission in England, the Kefauver hearings in the United States, as well as previous ones in Canada. This was the first time he was not in command and the necessary adjustment confused him. Robert Heister had overriden his opposition to

16

Mann's appointment. "Dean, listen to me," Heister had said, not unkindly. "You go into those meetings wearing a halo as if the world owes us something for giving them antibiotics. It's all changed, Dean, all changed. I want Mann there for the very reason that he's not one of us. He has the appearance of being independent, a professional. I also want him there because he's a Canadian and I don't want the industry to be a scapegoat for anti-Americanism. There's enough of that up there now. And Dean, you're sixty-five and this is going to be a long, hard one, the toughest yet. God knows what we'll have to get into to win. I want you there as an advisor, not dead of a heart attack. Besides, Grant MacDonald is his friend, not yours."

As Sorenson and Joseph walked across the Rotunda, after leaving the committee room, they had to manoeuvre through hundreds of tourists, cameras dangling from their shoulders. "Confederation Hall," the uniformed tour guide intoned, "sometimes known as the Rotunda, is the inside entrance to the Parliament buildings. Here, soaring pillars and arches form a noble architecture of enduring beauty. Around the arches the carvings represent many aspects of federal and provincial life. The great central tower of the Parliament is called the Peace Tower. It contains war memorials, the memorial chamber with the Book of Remembrance and the carillon of bells. The Tower stands two hundred and ninety-one feet high. The flag flies on a thirty-five foot bronze pole during the day when the House of Commons is in session. At night a red light at the top of the pole burns until the House rises."

When they walked out of the Parliament Centre Block into the strong June sunlight Joseph blinked, adjusting to the brightness. The sky was a cloudless, piercing blue. The cannon boomed, followed immediately by the giant clock — a replica of Big Ben — atop the Peace Tower signalling 12:00 noon.

To Ottawans the complex of Parliament was known as Parliament Hill, or simply the Hill. The members and politicians called it "the House." When in session, the phrase used was, "the House is sitting." The three buildings of Parliament — East, West, and Centre Blocks — were of Gothic design, built of a warm Nepean sandstone found in the Ottawa area. The roofs were copper, now oxidized green. With the Mounties patrolling in their red coats the picture was of another age, and Joseph was reminded of the difference between Ottawa and Washington, the latter heavy with slabs of granite and monuments to the military, reflecting a warlike nation. By contrast, Ottawa was peaceful, a city without tension, a leafy city where only a year or so before a by-law had been changed to permit buildings higher than ten storeys. In Ottawa it was still possible for a man not to feel dwarfed and inconsequential.

In front stretched the expanse of lawn, perfectly groomed, bordered by beds of petunias, roses, and rhododendrons, and divided in the middle by a wide cement broadwalk. Mini-skirted office girls had already begun to lunch sitting on benches or perched on parapets, their knees drawn up suggestively. Old people sunned themselves and listened to the Carillonneur begin the first selection of his daily noon summer concerts, "It's A Long Way To Tipperary." And Mounties in their useless redcoats, relic of a glamorous past, posed for photos with tourists, mainly Americans, outwardly smiling while inwardly gritting their teeth and wishing for duty other than patrolling Parliament Hill as a tourist attraction.

But Joseph blanked out the scene and set his mind in intense concentration trying to find loopholes in the solution that had just occurred to him. If Flanagan would agree, it would be ridiculously simple to keep him on the committee. What bothered him was that, as he didn't believe in chance happenings, it meant Dr. Lewison and perhaps others knew Flanagan supported the industry, and they wanted him removed. But then why hadn't they considered the simple countermove that he had? In the meantime, until he thought through every angle, all the ramifications, he decided against debating the merits of his plan with either Sorenson or Kendall.

As they walked in silence down the broad path, Sorenson took out his pocket watch and checked it against the clock on the Peace Tower. "Minute fast," he said, annoyed.

Facing Parliament was the American embassy and Sorenson

18

remarked to Joseph, forgetting that he was a Canadian citizen, that no matter what country he was in he always felt a thrill and a security when he saw Old Glory waving in the breeze. Sharp-featured, lean and tanned, with wispy gray hair and blue eyes only slightly faded, Joseph had put Sorenson at fifty-five and was amazed to discover that he was ten years older.

Although Sorenson tried to mask his feelings, Joseph was aware of his hostility.

"You realize, Mr. Mann, I was against your appointment only because of the crucial nature to the industry of these hearings. There was nothing personal. Your references and experience are superb. I felt that it was an error to choose an outsider, one who knows nothing of our industry. But I want to assure you of my every support. We are working together in a common cause."

"Thank you," Joseph said, smiling inwardly at the old-fashioned quality of Sorenson's way of speaking. Even though they had spent hours together in meetings, and would presumably be working together for months, he continued to call him Mr. Mann.

"About this Flanagan problem. Do you have something in mind?" Sorenson asked.

Joseph hedged. "I'm not sure yet," he said. A management consultant often alone on assignment, mostly in hostile environments that resist change, soon learns to keep his own counsel, to trust no one.

3

"God's teeth Joey, glad you could make it." They walked toward his violently contemporary house, Grant's arm around his shoulder. "Glad, that's the understatement of the year. You being here makes the party."

As always Joseph was overwhelmed by Grant's energy. A health enthusiast, he jogged two miles daily, worked out in a gym four times a week, and didn't smoke. Grant was lean and muscular. Joseph believed in fitness, but exercising bored him. He preferred the competitive exhilaration of racquet sports: squash, tennis, and even paddleball.

A red-flowered Hawaiian sarong was wrapped around Grant's waist and hung down to his ankles. A lei garlanded his neck and a flower was pinned to his hair. His high cheekbones and slightly slanted eyes had long ago convinced Joseph that there was an Indian lurking back among his ancestors, along with the United Empire Loyalists of whom Grant was so proud. Joseph saw Grant as the stereotyped Canadian — healthy, outdoorsy, good, and earnest. Oh, Grant has a full measure of Canadian earnestness, he thought.

"What's with the suit and tie? Didn't I tell you we're having a luau? You'll get lobster all over you. Hell's bells, man, you are my old buddy, Joseph Adam Mann. Aha!" he said, pretending to be struck by a revelation. "You're in disguise. I should have guessed it. Smart." And he tapped his forefinger against his temple. "You're just dressed like a New York superexecutive. But Joey, you're here with your people. You don't need your costume."

20

"Don't let the uniform fool you," Joseph said, taken aback at the caustic quality in Grant's voice.

They pushed their way through the clamour of two hundred voices and the crush of two hundred bodies, some dancing to heavy rock amplified to the point of pain, toward the bar. Although it was only ten o'clock, the party seemed to have taken off. In New York people would just be arriving.

The bartender filled their glasses and they held them up and touched. Grant smiled. "Good to see you, old cock."

"And you." The ambience was still there. Of course. He always felt a peace in Grant's presence, a sense of body and mind being in balance, unjangled, an absence of hostility. The friendship provided Joseph with a security he had discovered in no other human being. Others wanted to take or compete. But Grant's youth was mine he thought, and mine, his. And right at this moment Joseph was certain that part of Grant's mind was remembering, as he was, the pictures always in his head, like a continuous movie of days lived.

"Joseph, how maaarvellous you could come. We're ecstatic to see you," Grant's wife, Thelma, gushed, possessively putting her arm through Grant's. "Grant has been talking about nothing else but you since you've been back — not all of it flattering. But concerned, my dear, all of it concerned." She lowered her voice, "How are Genevieve and the boys? Do you see your boys often? She's remarried, I heard, and in Montreal."

Grant's mood changed. Earlier he had looked youthful, a good five years younger than his forty-two, but with Thelma's arm through his, he seemed suddenly old and powerless. Passive. Once petite with black eyes and jet black hair, five feet and one hundred pounds, Thelma was now full-hipped and busty, twice her previous size and with no waist at all. Cylindrical from top to bottom like a beer barrel. But thick as she was, she still retained a bustling, nervous energy, a high-pitched, effusive manner of speaking, a gushiness that could drown anyone.

"Don't you think a Hawaiian luau is a maaarvellous way to honour Dominion Day? We have a different theme-party every year and charge twenty dollars a person, the proceeds going to

21

charity. This year we are buying books for an Eskimo school. Next year we'll celebrate Expo '67 with a fantastic affair. It will be our Centennial project."

"I think it's fucking awful," Joseph said, as usual making a point to offend her phony sensibilities with four letter words. Once he had accused her of being too polite to fart even when she was alone. This time she had started it with that reference to his ex-wife. She knew how he felt about not seeing his children. Bitch.

"I might have expected you to be facetious about our national birthday now that you've sold out to the Americans. Are you still a Canadian citizen?"

Still alive, the old hostility between them. He was her everlasting enemy. Always remembered and never forgiven that he tried to talk Grant out of marrying her.

"The Prime Minister's aide arrived a few minutes ago," she said to Grant. "The P.M. will be here momentarily. We must be at the door to greet him."

As Grant meekly followed her, a guest whose idea of a good time was to take everyone's photo, hailed, "Hold it." Instant hilarity appeared on her face.

Although surrounded by a dozen men and women, Joseph alone stood by the bar — his mind one moment on the party, the next trying to look at his solution to the Flanagan problem from every possible side. Other than those he presumed to be young reporters and their feline women, almost everyone else was middle-aged or older. Here was middle class Ottawa — doctors, lawyers, political chiefs, architects, a sprinkling from the Diplomatic Corps, Members of the House, two deputy ministers, and of course the social coup — the Prime Minister.

A few people he had known and hadn't seen in years, said hello. He hadn't recognized any of them which was depressing in a way, but not more so than the impossibility of communication. After the first hopeful, "What are you doing now?" there was little to say, everyone too caught up in his own world to crack through any barriers. And so until he could speak to Grant again, he preferred to be alone, hunched over his scotch, eavesdropping as if he were a visitor from another universe. And that was the way he felt.

"It's high time we did something about American militarism. Bombing Hanoi will be next, dammit."

"For Christ's sake, what do the French-Canadians want? *Maître chez nous*. What does it mean? I mean what does it mean?"

"I dig Jewish girls the best. They like to take it in their mouths."

"America is the only nation in history that has gone from barbarism to decadence without an intervening period of civilization."

"Somebody said that."

"Israel is too intransigent, and that doesn't make me an anti-Semite."

"What do the French-Canadians want?"

"The world is breaking down. The problem is there are no standards."

"What do the blacks want?"

"The church is the answer to our permissive society. I mean here is the rock. We know where the rock is, and you go from there."

"The flower children aren't that wrong. Our society *has* lost its humanity. If only they weren't so dirty."

"Canada's existence proves to the world that Americans do not want world domination."

"Don't be naïve. They own Canada now. Seventy-five per cent of our industry and resources belong to them. They're even buying our cottage land."

"Tim Buck said that years ago when he was the leader of the Canadian Communist party. Are you a Communist?"

"If Quebec separates, there'll be no Canada."

"Bay Street is like Wall Street. The only difference is that Bay Street would sell us out tomorrow and Wall Street would buy us."

"There's precious little left to sell. They own it all now."

"Wrong. As we look toward Centennial year, there's new hope. Our land is strong."

23

Listening to them Joseph was amazed at how important they thought Canada was — and even more, they spoke as if Ottawa were the centre of the universe, as if what Ottawa politicians did mattered outside their own country. And yet he supposed that because they lived in the capital city of Canada, Ottawa people — especially reporters and television commentators — believed that what they thought was important; because they lived where the seat of government was, by some curious osmosis they had power. The squabbling of the politicians on Parliament Hill was a serious matter to them, and they scored off debating points as passionately as other Canadians followed the leading scorers in the National Hockey League. All these people really believed that they were free to decide policies in their own country. Even Grant. And like other Ottawans' Grant carried with him a sense of responsibility, dour and heavy. But like Alice at the tea party, nothing these people did mattered; nothing they said mattered a damn. Joseph wondered, with some sadness, how these people would react if they had an inkling of what went on in the executive suites in New York—and how their lives were affected by corporate decisions made there. Undoubtedly the senior politicians and mandarins knew, but kept it a dark secret from the Canadian people.

Weaving from too much to drink, and sucking a lobster claw, Grant led a woman up to him. "This is Louise," he said, and to Joseph's total amazement added, "the woman I love. Sounds cornball I know, but how else do you say it?"

Like others of Grant's choice, Louise, at first glance, was strictly Parkay — at least six feet tall, round face with hair in braids wrapped tight around her head. She looked like a big healthy Swedish farm girl.

"So you're the great Mann . . . pun intended . . . . I feel intimidated. If I don't join the worshipful throng, Grant will discard me."

"Never." He put his arms around both and led them to a relatively quiet corner. "The two people I love most in the world . . . if only Joey hadn't got himself mixed up in this drug thing. Let's talk."

24

But they were barely settled, oblivious to the swirl of people around them when Thelma bore down. "Grant, I've been looking all over for you. It's time to put a fresh batch of lobsters on to boil. Oh! Louise, I didn't see you. You've met Joseph. Now Joseph, Louise is one of our favourite people, so don't be a monster to her." And as quickly as she had appeared, she was gone with Grant in tow.

"Bitch," Louise hissed. "Poor man doesn't have a moment of his own. The cunt will kill him."

"Probably saw him having a good time without her and couldn't stand it."

"I think I like you."

"She doesn't know about you and Grant?"

Louise shrugged. "Or pretends not to. Formidable opponent. She'll never bring anything to a head." She was quiet, alone with her thoughts for a moment. "What about you and this pharmaceutical thing?"

"Have brain will travel."

"But Grant is serious. I've never seen him so dedicated to a cause, and he has some idea in his mind that you're letting him down by representing them."

"And I feel that he's not looking at both sides."

"I sense tragedy coming," she said, holding out her empty glass. "You must know that he looks up to you, admires how you have become a success on your own — he tells everyone about your accomplishments. He is identified with you, and now you've come back, in effect to humiliate him." As Joseph took her glass, she said, "Better make it a double."

By the time he elbowed his way back with the drinks, a tall blond young woman was standing talking to Louise. Louise turned to Joseph. "This is my good friend, Dr. Violetta Norgela. Violetta, Joseph Adam Mann."

"Oh, you're Grant's friend," she said smiling, showing strong white teeth. She lifted her head and regarded him with wide-set blue eyes.

He felt he was being appraised in much the same way he looked at women. "What are you drinking?" he asked, the party suddenly becoming interesting.

"No more for me, thanks, I was just offering Louise a lift home."

"You came alone?" Louise asked, surprised. "No Douglas?"

"Service to the nation comes before a party."

"I have no nation to serve, so stay," Joseph said. "You can't leave now. We've just met." He wanted to move in on her fast, New York style, knowing, sophisticated. But that was only possible if everyone played the same game; otherwise, you looked ludicrous and awkward, like a prize stud who had to be helped on in order not to injure an equally prized mare.

"Ask me to dance then." There was a mischievous look in her eyes.

Joseph had the feeling that she knew exactly how she had affected him and was amused, and had decided to play the coquette with him. And he wasn't so far wrong.

The music was made for young people and, while he had been graceful on the basketball floor, was still a hot squash player, and had been considered a terrific jitterbug dancer twenty years ago, he could not quite accommodate his body to the multi-rhythms that she, magnificent animal, absorbed so sensually. It was her generation's music. But finally the group played a slow piece. He held her close, and for the first time in a long time — or was it the first time ever? — he felt his body fit with another. Like a teenager, he shut his eyes. Eventually feeling self-conscious, knowing that conversation was expected but being unable to think of anything intellectually provocative, Joseph asked, "Norgela, what nationality is that?"

"Lithuanian."

"Louise said you were a doctor. Philosophy? Social work?"

"Do all women have to be in social work?" she shot back. "Sorry. Private fight. I'm a doctor of medicine. I graduated two years ago."

The fact that she was a doctor, with all those psychological ramifications, and yet so young and beautiful, confused him. And she felt so good — tall and solid, with natural blond hair that fell in soft waves to her shoulders. The music stopped and he

26

held her.

"I must go now, Joseph."

Too moved to be either flippant or aggressive, Joseph led her back to Louise.

"How did you two natural enemies get along?" Louise asked. "I watched you on the floor, and before you wind up in the sack with him, Violetta," she said facetiously, "remember that he represents the international pharmaceutical industry. He's one of *them*.

"I know who he is. I saw him at the hearings the other day," she said playfully.

Joseph was at a loss, and looked it.

"Violetta is with Food and Drug," Louise explained. "She keeps watch to see that your *them* don't poison *us* masses."

"You were at the hearings? How could I miss you?"

"You seemed involved. Some kind of trouble," she said mockingly. "Conflict of interest or something like that. Well, I must go."

"I'll walk you to your car." Though disturbed by her remark, he decided not to respond.

"It's at the bottom of the hill."

"The farther the better," he said taking her by the arm.

"Don't get lost in the woods," Louise called after them.

Orange lanterns bobbed in the breeze among the trees, and burning torches outlined the lawn and the steps, two hundred of which had been hewn down the side of the hill. Halfway down, a swimming pool had been carved out of a natural formation in the rocks. Some of the guests, one of whom looked remarkably like a cabinet minister, were cavorting naked in it.

"These steps are treacherous. Be careful, Violetta," Joseph said. "I'll walk in front. That way if you fall, I'll catch you."

"*Ah-tchu,*" she said and then exclaimed, "That's the first time I've ever spoken in Lithuanian to an anglo-saxon. How curious."

"But what did it mean?"

"Thank you, that's all."

"Before the new road was built, Grant had to keep these stairs free of ice and snow in the winter, a back-breaking job. It's a long

27

way down if you slip and fall."

"I don't intend to fall."

Nor I, he thought as they reached her car, a racy Firebird. "Will I see you again?" he asked, taking her hand.

"At the hearings, of course."

"You know what I mean."

She looked up at him with frank curiosity. He was good looking. Towering. Black hair and black eyes. For a moment her eyes were wide, defenseless; almost as if she were speaking to herself, she said, "Yes, I think so," aware now that the game had its dangers.

Without thinking he lowered his head and gently placed his lips on the fullness of her mouth. Large, wide mouth. A sweetness not to be believed.

And for her the giving — even though for a moment of time only — was replaced by anger. By what right did this arrogant bastard presume he could touch her, crash through her space. But it hadn't been that way and she knew it. She had invited his lips. And it had been gentle, a tentativeness. "Good night, Mr. Joseph Adam Mann," she said hoping that her voice was not so breathless to him as it was to her own ears. And then she got into the car, closed the door, and without looking at him again, drove off.

Not only did Joseph watch the car disappear, but he remained staring into the night for several minutes, as if willing her to return. Then he shook his head, not quite believing the intensity of the past few minutes. And it passed. He threw back his head and laughed. The whole thing wasn't real. Violetta Norgela. "You're not real," he shouted to the stars. "I must be stoned out of my mind." Then he started to laugh at himself as he remembered how carefully he regulated his life in New York; how he applied management consulting techniques to the budgeting of his time: time for work, time for culture, theatre, music and books, time for exercise, and time for women. And even there he had worked out a way of life suited to him. He had many women — he thought of them as his disciples. Some were intellectuals, accomplished in various fields and were only to talk with. Some

28

were fine gourmet cooks. Some were beautiful and pleasant to drink with and be seen with. And some were to have sex with. But none were to be emotionally involving.

Joseph walked slowly back up the stairs, enjoying the magic of being alone at night among the trees. He looked up at the star-filled sky, and for some reason tears came to his eyes. Why? he wondered. Ottawa? Grant? Violetta's kiss? He permitted the self-indulgence for a moment only and then made his way back to the bar just as the Prime Minister was leaving, a crush of bodies following him to his car. Wishing to avoid the noise of the band and further human contact, he went to Grant's study and shut the door. Good Christ, there over the fireplace was the painting he had done of Grant when they were both twenty-one. He averted Grant's eyes, suddenly so emotional that he was unable to face it immediately. Carefully avoiding the painting, he began absorbing the details of the room — Grant's study was small, with books on every subject lining the walls. His desk was solid oak, cluttered, with a typewriter in the centre. Joseph remembered the fireplace Grant had built himself, laboriously gathering stones from the fields, pink and silver and gray. And then, and only then, did he look at the portrait.

He felt nothing. Seeing it now, detached by the distance of time, he was unable even to feel he had painted it, could not remember the Joseph who had thought himself a painter, or wanted to be a painter — long before Genevieve's surprised pregnancy, his self-enforced marriage, and the need to earn money. He shook his head. The painting was bad. Facile, but unoriginal.

That was my curse, he thought. My goddamned facility. If I saw someone's work I liked, I just automatically painted like he did. But as he looked closer, he saw the eyes were good, catching the hope that had been there, the sense of wonder. He had caught that. And there it hung, a reminder of lives never lived.

But Grant had done well — as well as he had. Starting as a reporter for one of the Ottawa newspapers, he had been as-signed to the press gallery to cover news on Parliament Hill. Eventually he had been given a column in which he was able to

29

syndicate to many papers in Canada and several in the United States as American interest in Canada increased. He then landed a nightly five minute commentary show on television and became a minor national celebrity. Several times a year he produced hour long specials on various aspects of national interest.

Joseph stretched out on the sofa to study it from a more comfortable position and was soon fast asleep.

"Three o'clock, buddy." He woke to Grant shaking him gently by the shoulders, and sat up.

"I was looking at the painting."

"Long time."

"Hard to believe."

"Nightcap, Joey? Play some of the old seventy-eight jazz records?"

"Another time. I've had a pailful. It was a good party."

Grant walked him to his car. "Careful driving."

"I drink so much I wouldn't know how to drive if I were sober."

They laughed.

"Joey, are you going to stick with it — even after the conflict of interest question. You know who that was directed to." He did not mention Flanagan's name.

"I have no choice."

"I'm sorry."

"Maybe we can talk it out?"

"Maybe."

As he drove off Joseph was certain they had a unity that could not be smashed by this drug thing. It would pass as all their differences through the years had — all except Thelma. They had always been able to discuss their viewpoints openly, without malice. And it would be the same again. He did not doubt for a moment, with the facts he had been studying, that he would fail to convince Grant to change his view. Grant could always be counted on to listen to reason.

He drove on, different thoughts flashing through his head— Grant's warning, Violetta's comment, Grant's success. Two cars. A large house on acres of ground. A lover! And a thought struck

30

him that left a residue of shock, almost terror. *Do I really know Grant anymore?*

Then he laughed at himself. He was letting Grant get to him. Grant warning him. Hell, he was the one who didn't really understand the resources of multinational industry. Flanagan would certainly know tomorrow.

Anyway, that was enough for one day. Much better to think of Violetta. . . .

4

The hair of the dog, Joseph thought, pouring himself a drink while he waited in his hotel suite for Flanagan, Sorenson, and Kendall to arrive. As far as he could reckon the scheme he had devised to keep Flanagan on the committee was sound. It was unfortunate to put Flanagan through the ordeal, but it had been his choice to become involved with Heister originally. So it was his problem.

In the eight days since coming to Ottawa, Joseph had spent a total of twenty-four hours with Frank Flanagan — long enough to get to know and like him. Flanagan's knowledge of the political scene was as important to Joseph as knowledge of the pharmaceutical industry, and so in the first days he had tried to divide his time, making an intensive study of each.

A rough, outgoing man who pounded you on the knee or punched your arm when he spoke, he was the image of the fighting Irishman and never let you forget he had been a star football player. Round-faced now, pattern baldness, eyes either prematurely rheumy or the whisky had backed up in his system, he was past fifty and reminded Joseph of some of his mother's relatives — hard-drinking, warm-hearted, and with an eye for a fast buck — though unlike Flanagan they had never made it. He was also crafty and calculating.

"Look at that sky," he had said one night walking Joseph back to his hotel after a long session.

"Agreed. You don't see sky in New York. You just don't look up. It must be the low buildings here."

"You're of Irish descent?"

"My mother came from Douro. It's a farm settlement about a mile from Peterborough."

"I know it well; dirty Douro the Protestants called it. Begun in the early 1800s."

Joseph was aware of Douro's history, an Irish farm settlement visited by D'Arcy McGee, one of the Fathers of Confederation. Appalled by the way the Irish were living and being mistreated in New York City, he had travelled the country looking for farm communities in which to resettle them. "I'm only part Irish. In fact, I'm nothing really. My father was a mixed bag — English, German, some Scottish, even a little French-Canadian." He wasn't buying that Irish togetherness crap.

Flanagan looked up again for a moment and then said, "Joseph, understand one thing. I do what I do because I believe in it. I believe in the drug industry. Some years ago my wife took sick," he lowered his voice, "mental breakdown. A drug saved her, brought her around. It had only been on the market a year. Without it, she'd be useless today, in some institution probably. As long as she keeps taking it, she's all right, like her old self. It's a miracle." The tone of his voice changed again, becoming what Joseph imagined to be his political platform manner. "So notwithstanding anything else, I feel we cannot take a chance of upsetting the industry, cannot risk a change in the system."

Joseph said nothing.

"It's important I explain myself to you because we're working closely together. For one thing, I believe in free enterprise. I am what I am today because of our free enterprise system. I'm not trying to pull the wool over your eyes, Joseph. I'm a practical politician, never forget it. As you well know there are three major drug manufacturers in my riding employing several thousand workers. I've been accused of being on the side of the drug industry because so many of my voters work for them. The point I want to make, Joseph, is that I'm an honest man. I belong to no one other than myself. Heister has never asked me to do something I don't believe in."

"I know that Frank," Joseph said, feeling badly that Flanagan

33

was so compromised.

It was a good thing Flanagan believed in what he was doing, Joseph thought, otherwise life would be intolerable for him. But now came the crunch, when he would have to risk exposure or be put through the financial wringer again. Too bad.

He sat on the sofa, the unopened file folders on his lap, sipped his scotch, and reflected on last night's party and the meeting soon to start. Until now he had thought the assignment would be a piece of cake, a logical series of moves, like a chess game. He had even prepared a critical path program much as if he were managing the construction of a large project. But now he realized several factors he hadn't taken into consideration. First, there was obviously an organized faction operating against Flanagan, most likely an intra-party rivalry headed by Dr. Lewison. Second, he could not expect much creative help from his colleagues. Third, Grant was going to be a problem, although why he held his views so strongly Joseph couldn't understand. And fourth, being back in Ottawa was going to take an emotional toll that he hadn't counted on. He thought of Thomas Wolfe's, *You Can't Go Home Again,* and smiled. You *shouldn't* go home again was closer to the truth.

The telephone interrupted his thinking. Flanagan and Kendall were in the hotel lobby. He told them to come up, then called Sorenson in his room. A few minutes later the four were settled in Joseph's sitting room, each with a drink.

Joseph orchestrated the conference slowly and carefully.

"Someone or some faction is out to get you, Frank. I guess they're afraid of you. You can take that as a compliment I suppose. Certainly points up how important you are to us."

"Oh, I don't know Joey," Flanagan said nervously. "Shouldn't make too much of it. This sort of thing happens from time to time. Conflict of interest has been on people's minds lately."

Surely Flanagan didn't expect him to buy that. "I don't believe in supposedly innocuous coincidences when our heavyweight gets knocked out."

"A conspiracy?" Kendall said with derision. "This is Canada."

Joseph had discovered in his first two days that Kendall was

34

weak and dumb, too involved in role-playing to be of much use. He was a swinger, Ottawa-style, and Joseph disliked and distrusted him. Short and paunchy. Bald with a bushy beard. Forty-five. Obscene. Probably still reads *Playboy*. From his manner, the way he drank, and his constant references to the novel he was writing, it was clear he considered himself another Hemingway.

"Either way, it appears to me as though Frank has no choice but to resign," Sorenson said.

It struck Joseph as funny that he would have to sell Sorenson and Flanagan. Joseph admired Sorenson's success, but was wary of him.

"He does, you know," Joseph said softly, casually sipping his martini.

The three waited expectantly, their emotions and faces masked. Sorenson understood Joseph well enough by now to know he had an idea, one that probably had merit. But he faulted him for not discussing it with him in advance. The others may be outsiders, he was not; he and Joseph represented New York and the world. Kendall, angered by Joseph's contemptuous attitude toward him would be overjoyed to see him fall flat on his face. And Flanagan was tense, in the centre, knowing that this might be the moment he always dreaded, the time when a Heister man would ask him to do something he shouldn't, something that would trip him over the fine line he walked.

"Frank can't stay on and deny he has a conflict of interest," Kendall rushed in heatedly. "Too many members know of his connection. He has a chance to be a cabinet minister. He's not going to jeopardize that for a few printing orders. Remember Joseph, when Frank becomes a minister, maybe prime minister one day, he'll be more important to us in the next ten years. We can't chance blowing his career."

Joseph didn't even bother responding to Kendall. He was thinking of what Heister had told him. "We own the mortgage on Flanagan's equipment. We own Flanagan. Play it cool. Don't rub his nose in the dirt. He may resist from time to time, but in the end he'll do anything we want. He likes being successful, likes

35

the things money buys, and we can put him out of business overnight."

"Frank, you have a conflict of interest because your printing firm derives over half its business from the drug industry," Joseph said.

"We know that. That's the point," Kendall said.

"What are you getting at?" Flanagan asked warily.

"Well, if your firm stopped getting orders, like right now, you wouldn't have a conflict of interest and wouldn't have to resign." Joseph was secretly amused by the look of dismay that crossed Flanagan's face. And he was also well aware that if the firm stopped getting orders, the industry would stop getting Flanagan's help. "That's right, isn't it?"

"I suppose so," Flanagan said, laughing weakly. "I'd also be out of business in no time at all. You can't find new customers to feed those machines overnight."

"Then why not look at it another way? Supposing you didn't own the business. There'd be no conflict of interest either, would there?"

"You mean sell my business?"

"Yes . . . and no. All you have to do is sell your shares to your brother. Before you get apoplexy, hear me out," Joseph smiled. "You can have a separate and secret trust deed with him signing the shares back to you for one dollar or something like that, and you can put that document, there'd only be one copy, in your safety deposit box. Then your brother owns the company, not you. Presto! No conflict of interest."

For a moment no one spoke, overwhelmed at the simple expediency of the plan.

Kendall got up to leave. "I don't want to know about this," he said.

"Sit down," Joseph ordered. "You leave this table and you're out of a job, and I'm not kidding." Kendall hesitated, then returned to his place, flushed red but speechless. "There's nothing improper in my suggestion. We're breaking no law." He paused. "You do believe in the moral rightness of our cause, don't you Ron? If you don't believe that we're right. . .

36

"Of course I believe we're right."

"Then why should we play by anyone else's rules?" He turned to Flanagan. "What do you say, Frank? Your brother can handle the business. He runs the day-to-day operation anyway now, doesn't he?"

"Only since I've been active in politics. I promised my constituents to be a full-time member and I've kept my promise. But I built the business. It was nothing when I took over from my father. I can do any job in the plant — set type, make plates, match colour, run any of the presses. Many's the time, even of late, I've rolled up my sleeves when there's been a rush. I make all the big decisions and have all the contacts for the big jobs, the big runs — where we can make a buck."

"Like the work for drug firms," Joseph reminded him. "But your brother has been in the business ten years. He can handle all that. And even though you wouldn't own the firm you could still help, if you wanted to."

Flanagan nodded. He didn't like the idea, but he couldn't argue it.

"That's it then. Your brother will become sole owner and you remain on the committee. When it ends, you buy back the business for one dollar."

"I hope my lawyer will agree," Flanagan said half-heartedly, not sure of what he was concerned about — the obvious deceit or whether his brother might find a way to keep the business. "Your suggestion goes against the intent of the committee. Would I be committing a perjury or fraud?"

"Not if the legal documents are back-dated to a year ago."

"If your lawyer won't handle it, ours will," Sorenson said. He was annoyed that he hadn't thought of the scheme.

Grateful for Sorenson's support, Joseph realized he had worried needlessly about him balking at the ethics involved.

"If this ever becomes public knowledge, my usefulness to the industry is finished. Is it wise to take that chance?" Flanagan asked. "You understand what I'm getting at, Ron?" Flanagan looked to him for support.

"You have no choice," Sorenson said, interrupting Kendall as he was about to speak. "Refuse and you will be out of business. We'll break you."

Flanagan's face went white. He hadn't expected that kind of treatment from Sorenson, who had always been most gentlemanly. "I don't like being pushed around. I'm with you because I believe in you. What kind of shit is this? I didn't say I wouldn't go along. I'm just not sure in the long run it's wise. I can think, you know. I'm not a puppet. That's the trouble with you Americans."

"Dean didn't mean it that way, Frank," Joseph said in an effort to placate him. Sorenson had been too tough. If Flanagan dug in his heels and refused, what then? Most likely they would do nothing to him because the industry might still need him in the future, as Kendall had rightly suggested. "Frank, we're all edgy. Our backs are to the wall. We need you. The point is, if the essence of politics is compromise, where is the logic in removing one side totally? How do you arrive at consensus that way? What about the socialist Member? Should he be removed because he has a bias? Doesn't his very philosophy also give him a conflict of interest? Who's not attached to one position? Everyone on the committee starts from his own special point. Again, I ask, where is the fairness in removing one side?" It wasn't necessary, Joseph knew, to provide a rationale for Flanagan to agree with, but it was important if Flanagan were to keep his self-esteem.

"You're right, Joey," Flanagan said, leaping at the justification — forced and cynical as it was. It would have been just as easy for Joseph to argue the other way. "It's time I turned the business over to my brother. I'm too involved in politics to give it the attention it needs. I'll even give him a raise in pay."

Joseph relaxed. This had been a test of Flanagan on another level, because it had occurred to Joseph that Flanagan's sharp mind might have engineered the whole play. If he sought a cabinet appointment, his close identification with the drug group against the stated interests of the majority of his own party would certainly hinder his chances. This way he would be out of danger and still in favour with Robert Heister. It was traditional to have an Irish cabinet minister from Toronto, and at the moment there was a vacancy. True or not, Joseph would never again accept Flanagan without reservation.

In their leave-taking it was obvious by the way the three made a point of shaking Joseph's hand that he had now taken psychological charge of the project. Before today, it was clear that Sorenson, Kendall, and Flanagan had each wanted — and planned to gain — control. But Joseph was now the leader. Trial by ordeal, he thought cynically. Such a simple expedient.

Well, so they would be able to keep Flanagan, Joseph thought. But that wasn't all the industry had going. It was Joseph's judgment that their first strength lay in the fact that the subject was too complicated for the general public to follow. Thus, they would soon lose interest. As well, however, a careful set of strategies and tactics had been worked out during a series of meetings in Heister's office before Joseph had arrived in Ottawa. In the months to come the pharmaceutical lobby would hammer away at four points. By mail, in speeches, through medical journals, and in personal meetings, key political figures, business and labour leaders, and doctors and other influentials would be told first, that drugs were not higher priced in Canada than in any other country when related to the earning power of the Canadian worker; second, that lowering patent protection would not lower prices but in fact increase them, as firms would have a shorter time to realize on their investment in research; third, that ending patent protection would end research in Canada, throwing thousands of university-trained and other skilled workers out of jobs; and fourth, that granting of licences to anyone to manufacture and import drugs from any source would result in a flood of uncontrolled, uninspected, poor quality, literally unsafe and dangerous drugs from China, Poland, and other communist countries, and from fly-by-night companies, some even controlled by the mafia. It would mean that the public could never be sure that the medicine they bought would be safe or therapeutic, as was now the case.

After they left, Joseph napped for two hours; then, as there was still time before he was due at his mother's for Sunday dinner, he opened a background file prepared for him by the Pharmaceutical Association. At times like these the costly speed-reading course he had subjected himself to proved worth the time, money, and effort.

"Experts put the total number of diseases that afflict man at somewhere between 1,500 and 2,000." The advances made were summarized, and it was evident that until the penicillins, the tetracyclines and other antibiotics, and the psychoactive drugs that enabled the mentally ill to be treated without the horror of electric shock — all developed in the discovery explosion of the last twenty years and all related in some way to the pharmaceutical industry — doctors had had little of actual help. And the next twenty years looked even more exciting. The digest contained a forecast:

"**1975:** Compounds to speed learning processes, to improve co-ordination and dexterity, to counter stress and fatigue; vaccines for mumps and influenza; medicine to decrease the body's synthesis of lipoproteins and to dissolve fibrin of blood clots; chemicals to prevent death in the first critical hour of heart attack; diuretics less liable to cause a loss of potassium; drugs to aid arthritis; and powerful anti-depressants.

"**1980:** Progress in controlling chronic recurring infections; control of atherosclerosis; control of blood pressure; control of dementia; drugs to control secretions and aid muscle tone during operations; fewer people requiring kidney transplants; control of allergic conditions and psychosis arising from genetic or biochemical abnormalities.

"**1985:** Replacement chemotherapy to correct inborn disorders; ways of stimulating the body's production of interferon; control of basic mechanics of cell membranes and cell enzymes; the aging process delayed or even reversed — a further increase in life span until 125 years; epilepsy and migraine eliminated; 70 per cent of cancers controllable.

"**1990:** Medicines to give a youthful appearance to the aged; ability to predict impending coronary thrombosis attack and drugs to minimize chances of dying; artificial hearts."

And none of it possible without the drug industry, Joseph assured himself. He looked at his watch. It was time to go to his mother's. He looked forward to seeing her pleasure at the bouquet of red and white carnations he had sent.

As he drove his Thunderbird toward his mother's house, through the remembered streets of his youth, his preoccupation with the drug industry, with Grant, and with his colleagues began to fade. He found himself hoping someone would recognize him in his expensive car, and was instantly contemptuous of the emotion. Soon he was in his neighbourhood. He had walked these streets a thousand times on the way to Lisgar Collegiate, past Rhoda's house with her Lana Turner mammaries displayed to their fullest by a selection of a dozen tight sweaters. Once she had been sent home from a Saturday job at a department store and told to change into a dress. He closed the windows, turned on the air-conditioning, and pushed in a tape deck. Bartok filled the car. Lost in the luxury he almost drove past his mother's house.

After parking he was aware that the newness of his car — fire engine red — reinforced the near slum quality of the street because of the contrast with the rusted, almost vintage cars, and the crumbly gray brick of the row of houses, paint peeling on verandas. He didn't get out of his car immediately, realizing with a surge of guilt that he didn't really want to see either his mother, or his married sister and her family.

Often on welfare, the family had lived — still lived — on the shabby edge of Sandy Hill, a mainly middle-class area of Ottawa. For thirty years, until only a few years ago, his mother had been a charwoman, cleaning offices in the Parliament buildings. His father was a handyman drunk who had finally died from a combination of diabetes and alcoholism after having a leg amputated.

Joseph still carried the resentment toward his mother, sister, and dead father that he, one of the top students in school, had to quit after grade ten. A teacher had helped him get a job at a bank where he became a teller. Grant remained his friend although it was unusual at that time for boys who remained at school to mix with boys who didn't. Hateful, boring job, but better than training to be a welder, as his sister had wanted.

"If there had been no war I might still be at the bank counting

41

other people's money. The war saved my life," he used to say cynically. Joseph had joined the navy, becoming a pharmacist's mate. At sea aboard a corvette, he performed an emergency appendectomy, having read how to do it from a manual only an hour before the operation. The seaman survived and Joseph was decorated, but that experience, plus his constant seasickness, made him want out. Fortunately, because of manpower needs, the Air Force had lowered their initially high scholastic requirement for air crew and he transferred, easily winning his wings and becoming a fighter pilot, an officer, and gentleman (to Joseph's amazement this was the way they considered themselves — a cut above the other services). But more important, he knew he had projected himself out of his class for all time.

Taking advantage of the veterans' grants after the war, he returned to school, completing grades eleven, twelve, and thirteen in less than two years of furious cramming. At university, to add to the meagre veterans' allowance of sixty dollars a month and to send some money now and then to his mother, he took whatever part-time jobs he could find — tutoring, marking papers, driving taxis. He even joined the reserve army as an officer. His decision to move in with Genevieve, a perky, black-haired secretary with an amusing French-Canadian accent, was taken to save money.

Then, within one month after completing his final year, all his plans changed. He missed a major scholarship by half a percentage point, effectively ending his chance of staying on at university and earning the graduate degrees he would need to become a professor; Grant MacDonald married Thelma and a trip to Europe they had been planning was cancelled; and Genevieve conceived and they were compelled to marry. Joseph felt his whole life was ruined, felt he would never paint, that he would be trapped like his father, as he had always feared. The world simply could not be overcome, and he had walked around carrying a gun for a week, contemplating suicide. Grant would not leave his side, day or night, and finally it passed, and Joseph accepted what had to be accepted. It had been a bad time, but out of it had come the firm belief that a man has a right to take his life, that his ultimate freedom is the freedom to choose his time to die.

After working with the Ontario Hydro Electric system for three years, he landed a job with a major electrical firm in New York. Two years later he inveigled a leave of absence at full pay while he obtained his degree in Business Administration from Harvard. Six years more and he was administrative vice-president. It was during this period of intense effort that Genevieve left him and returned to Quebec. He was not sorry. She was not the brightest girl in the world and was no asset to his career in New York. Shortly after she left he joined Daniels and Company, a leading firm of management consultants, as a senior consultant; within two years he became a principal of the firm. To him, a management consultant had the same status as a university professor, but earned considerably more money. He was where he wanted to be.

Joseph got out of his car. He knew what he dreaded. He was an outsider to the family. They didn't value him as a person, weren't interested in his work. Yet they considered him a "man of means" and as such it was his duty to give and their right to take. With a down feeling he walked up the slate gray stairs, through the front door to the dark hall that seemed to trap years of cooking odours.

"Why here's Joseph, mom," his sister Mary said, with a little less animation than the lead in an afternoon TV soap opera. Her nasal Ottawa Valley twang always surprised him. They hadn't spoken that way when they were kids. She must have picked it up from her husband, Tom, who had been born on a farm in Kemptville, the heart of the Valley.

"Hi, mom," he said putting his arms around her, an old lady strangely vacuous, he sensed uneasily. Although to Joseph, there was always the black emptiness of feeling nothing, she at least would have a sweet smile for him. "Hi, mom," he repeated, the word conjuring up nothing for him. He recoiled inside at the feel of this old woman and the expected reek of the bar soap she had used for so many years scrubbing floors. Brown, harsh smelling bar soap. For the past twelve years, he had seen her

43

once a year at most; during the war not at all, and when he was a boy, because his father was sick, she had spent all of her time, when she wasn't working, with her husband. Mary had looked after him, with all the love of an elder sister saddled with a chore.

The magic word "mom" evoked nothing for him other than resentment and bitterness. He hated coming home. Wondered how his sister could stand staying here after she married Tom, a streetcar conductor, even though the rent was cheap ("someone has to stay with the old lady"). He wondered what she felt like. All he could think of was, "I got out. I got out."

Tom and the two boys, Tom Jr. and Joseph, named after him, were watching television and drinking beer. Without turning their eyes and attention from the set they were able to greet him in a friendly fashion. When the city had finally changed from streetcars to buses, Tom was not retired early at reduced pension, like so many of the others, but had been given a bus to drive; Tom Jr. drove a truck "for a very good company"; and Joseph had left school and was working in a factory that made clocks — if he stuck at it for ten years or so he had a chance to make set-up man or even foreman. Not one of them would break out as he had done, Joseph thought. All were tied, owned by the world they worked in. Not one was free as he was, although young Joseph had the brains and should have cracked through. When Genevieve had left and taken the children he had even considered bringing young Joseph to New York to live with him, but the realization of the expense helped him decide to let the boy make it on his own. I did it; if he wants to, he can, too.

Joseph was proud of what he had accomplished. Once he had accepted the fact that his first career choice was closed, he turned himself inside out. His view now was that organization and production were the dynamics of the contemporary world, and to be a management consultant in New York was to be at the centre of that world. In the jargon of the management consulting profession he was termed a "generalist" — one who could tackle any assignment, a problem solver. As such he had worked on a score of projects, from lobbying in Washington to helping Iceland find new ways to market fish so that the little country wouldn't have to be so totally dependent on bulk sales to the Soviet Union; from preparing an administrative manual for one of the country's largest banking organizations to supervising the instalation of robot computers. He had put a South American airline in the black, and conceived a manner to speed up the selection of the right kind of lumber in a forest operation. And during this period with Daniels and Company, as part of his continuing education, he attended dozens of business seminars, often as guest lecturer; mastered two computer languages, Fortran and Simscript; completed a course in industrial engineering (Methods-Time-Measurement and Critical Path); and taken part in T-Group sessions. He was a success. And he lived fully — sometimes thinking himself the modern counterpart of the Renaissance man — scientist, philosopher, poet, businessman. Sober, he thought of himself as "the complete technocrat." Drunk, or experimenting with various drugs as he occasionally did, he thought of himself as being as macho as any Mexican — total sex, and he expended himself violently.

As expected, his sister served Boston butt, a roast of pork they had every Sunday and on special occasions. Boston butt, mashed potatoes, and peas. Every Sunday all their lives, so ingrained that when he was married it didn't feel like Sunday unless Genevieve served it, until one day while carving he became enraged, and using the carving knife like a machete he hacked at the roast, screaming obscenities, hunks flying all over the floor. And even then not satisfied, he had gotten down on his hands and knees and continued to hack the bits laughing hysterically until there were shreds of pork meat and fat all over the floor. And Genevieve, crying, had locked herself in the bathroom.

"Is she still alive, Mrs. Polovsky, the old lady who owns the house?" he asked.

"Gone now. Last year," his sister said. "She was good to mom. One of her daughters looks after things now. It's not the same. Those girls all have their noses in the air. Mom went to the funeral. I didn't want her going into the synagogue... you know ... but there were lots of Christians there and she said it was the same as our funerals. They've raised the rent."

His father had been Mrs. Polovsky's handyman, when he felt well enough, right up to the day he died. That was why she kept the rent at ten dollars, when everyone else's was creeping up to thirty and forty dollars. God knows what it was now, maybe a hundred. He wasn't going to ask. The jewlady he used to call her, but never to her face. Every time he took the ten dollars rent money he would be summoned into what she called the "green-room," with green flocked paisley wallpaper he liked to touch and a green marble fireplace, ordered all the way from Italy. The brass and iron set was an antique from New York. There were portraits of her mother and father on the wall, taken shortly after they were married. A magical house, it was his idea at the time of a mansion — spacious, quiet, and clean with a winding staircase that he would have loved to climb and explore the floors above.

The old lady would sit at her oak desk, her blue eyes crinkling while she reached into her purse. After much searching she would find a nickel, his heart having stopped in fear that perhaps this time there wouldn't be one there. She would pat him on the head, ask about his mother, and then if he were hungry. But he always said no, not knowing whether he was ashamed to admit his hunger, or afraid to eat Jewish food.

A funeral home was across the street from Mrs. Polovsky's and one day, the first time Grant had come with him because he had wanted to see the inside of her "mansion," they noticed a line of black limousines on one side of the street and a crowd of people on the other, right in front of Mrs. Polovsky's house. They ran down to see what was happening. As they got closer Joseph saw that the people were standing on her lawn, looking down at a man lying on the ground, his feet up in the air. His father! The old lady was trying to explain to a man dressed in a long, black jacket and striped trousers, that she was sorry, that Mr. Mann had gotten into the homemade Passover wine. The man spoke harshly to her saying she should lock up the wine if she were going to have drunken bums working for her. He warned her to get him inside her house and off the street because this was a funeral of a very important person, a former cabinet minister, and it was against the law to make wine and if she didn't get that drunk out of sight, he would report her and call the police to cart the man away.

Joseph stood rooted, while with the help of two of her daughters Mrs. Polovsky managed to get his father to his feet and into the backyard, where they laid him down on the grass to sleep it off. Joseph remembered running down the street, his face burning, hoping Grant wasn't following him. But when he arrived at the park and sat on the bench, Grant was there and sat beside him. They sat for a long time without saying anything. "I've got to take the rent money to her," Joseph said.

"I'll come with you. Then what do you say you and me go to a movie. I've got some money."

Joseph brought Grant in and introduced him to Mrs. Polovsky. He said nothing of what he had seen to the old lady, but she insisted on taking him into the kitchen and showing him a brand new kitchen cabinet. Then she took him into the dining room and showed him a portion of the hardwood floor that had been perfectly repaired. "Your father is a very good workman," she said. She had seen him, and as he realized only years later, he was grateful not so much for what she was trying to tell him, but for the picture of Mrs. Polovsky and her daughters gently helping his father. For the first and only time she gave him a quarter. "Be a good boy, be a good boy," she said in her strange accent. "Do not judge another's burdens."

Outside Joseph said, "I'll treat for the movie," and he and Grant ran up the street laughing at their good fortune.

After the movie, a western, Grant insisted they become blood brothers. He took out his pocket knife, made a quick slit in his thumb and handed the knife to Joseph who did likewise. Then they pressed their thumbs together and let the blood flow into each other. It was a solemn, always to be remembered experience.

After dinner Tom helped his mother into the living room and turned on the television. The two boys went upstairs to their

47

rooms to get ready to go out. Joseph and Mary were left alone, facing each other across the table.

"Tom has a lot of headaches since he took his new job," Mary said.

"Lucky to have it from what I understand."

"Gives him fierce headaches. We don't know how long he'll be able to keep it. The doctor gives him these here pills. They cost a lot but don't seem to help much. I don't know what we'll do if he's pensioned off early."

She seemed so old. So down. Her hair entirely gray. How had he turned out to be so good looking and she so plain, he wondered. Did she ever smile? Then it hit him. She had mentioned the rent might be raised, that Tom might have to quit. She was leading up to a demand for money. With everyone working they must have more than enough. And his mother got the old age pension. What else did they need? And he sent money, from time to time, certainly often enough.

Tom walked through the dining room on the way to the kitchen for another beer. Overhearing what Mary said, he explained, "Well, with a streetcar you're on the rails. You know what I mean? You follow the tracks. No problems, so long as you don't bump into the fellow in front." He laughed. "But with the bus, now you have to stop and start and pull into traffic and get over to the curb and there are a lot of dumb car drivers you wouldn't believe, guys that don't give you any chance at all. And the smell of exhaust all day long just makes you sick to your stomach. I'll never figure out why they took streetcars off." And he went down into the basement.

"Did you notice mom, Joseph?"

"What do you mean?

"Didn't you notice how strange she is? Blank? Hardly talks? Cries a lot? Says she doesn't want to live."

"Have you taken her to the doctor?" he asked, alarmed. Then he remembered she hadn't mentioned receiving the flowers although they were in plain sight.

"It's just old age."

"How do you know? How dumb can you be. An old lady

48

doesn't change her whole personality without someone taking her to the doctor. She's strong as an ox, that woman, and if she's changed, then she's sick. How can you watch her deteriorate without doing something?" He felt terrified. Why?

"Where do you get off, coming in here and ticking me off for not looking after mom? Seems to me I've had either you, or her, or my kids, or Tom — my whole life, I've looked after someone. When are you going to help? Give a little money for mom's keep?"

There it was. Finally. The bitch got it out. "I've sent money. Lots of it."

"Bullshit." Her language and ferocity surprised him. "You don't send it regular. A bit one month and then nothing for six. I'm talking about regular. Money we can count on."

He felt like he was going to explode. Didn't she understand anything? "I have two kids to support. Remember?" But it was weak and he knew it. Despite all the money he earned, he was always short, and often missed payments to his wife. Where did it go? Liquor? Women? Clothes? His car? The good life? He got up angrily and went into the living room and sat down. They still had doilies on the arms of the sofa and chairs. Didn't they know anything? He looked at his mother. She was watching television but her face was a blank. Jesus. He was too nervous to sit beside her and went down into the basement where he heard Tom hammering, finding him in the workroom. "Hi, what are you doing?"

'Straightening nails."

"What?" Joseph asked, not believing what he had heard or, indeed, what he was witnessing. Tom had baskets of bent nails and was methodically hammering them straight and putting them into jars according to size.

"Straightening nails." And then he stopped and said kindly, "Joseph, brothers and sisters shouldn't fight. Like we say at the bus barn, 'don't sweat the small shit!' If you get my meaning. Mary works hard and she worries about me and the boys and your mother and you, too. I swear she feels as close to you as she does to her own children. You were her child too, remember? In

49

a way, her first. And you know she has your mother with her every minute. Now that you're back, you should come by and take your mother out for a drive now and then. Give your sister a little time off." He tilted his beer bottle to his lips, a heavy set man with red hair and light freckled skin. "You should know someone we can take your mother to see in this new job of yours. She just won't go and see her old doctor, says he reminds her of a death's head."

"I'll find someone," Joseph said, making a mental note to ask Kendall.

"You know, Joseph," Tom said apologetically, "I'm not a big earner. I grew up on a farm and I figure I'm lucky to have the job I have. Your sister, well, she can't go to work because she always had to be at home to look after things. The boys work but they don't earn much. They give us room and board, but they need spending money for themselves. They're good boys, thank God, no trouble with drugs, they just drink a little beer now and again. All in all I'd say we're lucky. But if you could help us a little with support for your mother, it would be appreciated."

The dignity of the man came through to Joseph, and he said, "You're right Tom. You're absolutely right. I'll do that." Tom was a good soul and in an expansive gesture Joseph took out his chequebook and wrote a cheque for five hundred dollars and handed it to him.

Tom rushed upstairs with the cheque. "Look Mary, look what Joseph has given us."

And suddenly Joseph felt like a damned fool. What did he owe his mother? That she got up at four in the morning when he was a child and went to work and he never saw her? Did she work for him or because his father was a drunk? And should he pay for that? She hadn't been interested enough in him to make him feel she cared. Should he now have to feel guilty, have to deprive himself of one bottle of scotch or one girl to take to bed? Not bloody likely. That would be the last money they would get from him in a long time. But he knew he was lying to himself. He would do what had to be done.

Funny. As one got older the burdens got heavier. And unless

he was either a fool or insensitive and uncaring, the older a man got the more he hurt inside, every day. The wisest thing his mother had ever said to him was last year when he asked what she felt about life. "Joey, I couldn't understand it when I was a little girl, I couldn't understand it all the years with your father, and I still don't — why people hurt each other so."

Why did you hurt me, Mom? he found himself thinking. But that was Freudian crap too and he knew it. That was just using a situation as an excuse.

5

"Are you covering today's session?" Joseph asked, surprised to find Grant in the corridor outside the committee room.

"I thought I might look in," Grant said casually.

Dr. Violetta Norgela, accompanied by a short, thick-set man, walked toward them.

"Violetta, you're even more beautiful by daylight," Joseph said.

"Ah, the enemy," she teased, a devilment in her eyes. She introduced Douglas Clark. He nodded to Joseph and then, putting his hand on her elbow, said, "We'd best take our place, Violetta."

"Does he own her?" Joseph asked.

"Not yet, but the word is he'd like to."

"She really gets to me."

"Forget it, Joey. From what I hear, they're almost engaged. A bright guy, war hero. Shot down. Captured. Five attempted escapes."

"Big deal. I wasn't shot down."

"Joseph, you're the enemy. This is Ottawa. The battle lines are drawn."

"I'm not her enemy. And I wasn't aware I was yours."

"I didn't mean it that way."

Joseph smiled and patted his shoulder. "See you." On his way to join Sorenson and Kendall he stopped beside Violetta who was sitting by the aisle — intentionally? — leaned down, and whispered in her ear, "Will you have a drink with me later?"

"Why?" she asked, as if challenging him.

A grin crossed his face. These kind of games he understood. "Because you're you and I'm me," and he left before she could reply.

"How do you know him?" Douglas asked.

"I met him at Grant's party."

"You know of course that he is one of the New York lobbyists for the drug industry?" She nodded. "What did he want?"

"To kiss me again," she said teasingly.

"Gentlemen, I see a quorum," the chairman struck his gavel. As the chairman called the roll, Frank Flanagan slipped into his seat.

Dr. Lewison immediately jumped up. "If the chairman will permit a question of privilege based on the last session?"

"Here it comes," Joseph whispered.

"Doesn't the honourable member, Mr. Flanagan, from Toronto, agree that owning a printing company that does extensive printing for the pharmaceutical industry constitutes a conflict of interest?"

Flanagan rose, rather than speak from his seat. He sounded truly shocked by the inference. "If that were the case it certainly would be a conflict of interest and I would be the first to admit it and disqualify myself; everyone here knows my record on many committees. In the past I was connected with the family firm, as you all know. Many of you here were kind enough to honour my firm with your printing needs," Flanagan said with extravagant sarcasm, the inference being that he hadn't always been paid. "For the record, and Dr. Lewison's suspicious mind, the firm was started by my late father, may he rest in peace, and has been in the family for more than twenty years. But I have no shares in it, no interest at all, and haven't had for some time. My brother is the sole owner. I don't have time to be involved in business anymore. Some of you may recall the promise I made to my constituents, that if elected I would work full time on their behalf. And I'm proud to say I've kept that promise."

"Bastard," Douglas Clark whispered through clenched teeth. "Getting rid of him would have made our job so much easier."

When the session adjourned, Joseph, Sorenson, Kendall, and Flanagan met for a victory drink. Kendall raised his glass, "Down the hatch and up the snatch."

Sorenson, who had allowed himself a martini, said, "To success, gentlemen." And without thinking he might be offending the Canadians added, "It's a good day to win our first skirmish. It's the fourth of July, Independence Day."

And Flanagan, not wanting to think about what had just happened, held up his glass. "May the balloon never burst."

But Joseph wasn't thinking about toasts, or congratulating himself. He was remembering the way Grant had looked at him after the failure to unseat Flanagan — with unconcealed contempt.

"Say, who was the bird I saw you speak to?" Kendall asked.

Kendall just had to open his mouth to be annoying. Joseph turned on him viciously. "The bird happens to be Dr. Norgela. She is with Food and Drug. I would have thought it was your job to know that."

Taken aback, Kendall mumbled, "Must be new." And then, recovering, added, "Curious that she was sitting with the key deputy assistants from the departments of industry, finance, and consumer affairs. Those departments are usually so jealous of each other's territories they never associate."

Later that day, at four o'clock, a meeting of INTEGRAL, the top secret Interdepartmental Planning Group for the Control of the Pharmaceutical Industry, took place. It was a sombre and dispirited group that gathered in the private office of J.O. McKinnon, one of Canada's senior and most powerful deputy ministers.

"I was against the flamboyance of that kind of move; there was always the danger of tipping our hand," Douglas Clark reminded everyone. "Now here is a sample of the hard facts we must tell the committee and, through them and MacDonald's columns, reach the Canadian people." He held up a chart prepared by his research staff showing the costs of drugs and their selling prices. "Here are a thousand tablets of a drug that costs three dollars and eighty-eight cents to bring to Canada. Cost of packaging is ten cents, labour seven cents, factory overhead another seven cents, bringing a total factory cost of four dollars and twelve cents. Price to retailers is seventy dollars and fifty cents, and the suggested price to the public brings the price of an item that costs four dollars and twelve cents to produce to one hundred seventeen dollars and fifty cents."

There was a spontaneous outcry of indignation as Clark presented other examples, equally as outrageous.

Wilfred Noel, French-Canadian and on an equal level to Clark in the government hierarchy, but with a different department, and whose idea it had been to sponsor a quick thrust to get rid of Flanagan, rose to engage in heated debate, speaking in French as was his right. "That is all very well, Douglas. But the public does not relate to figures. We all know the industry has sent two hotshot lobbyists here. You can be sure they are not going to deal in dry facts. They are going to hit at the belly — crying that people will lose jobs, that brand names are safe and sound."

"Yes, yes, but what is your point?" Clark countered in French.

"We must find a way to concentrate on emotional issues."

J.O. McKinnon wondered whether Noel was right and, furthermore, whether Grant MacDonald could develop one of his hour long specials on the subject. If McLuhan was to be believed — that is, when he could be understood — then there was nothing more immediate or powerful than television. He made a note on his pad. He would talk it over with Grant.

Although he rarely took an active part in the cross-floor discussion of INTEGRAL, he had single-handedly started the battle five years ago, slowly winning adherents in other departments — departments that rarely co-operated with each other, jealously guarding their areas of responsibility. Step by step he created INTEGRAL, dedicated to the objective of smashing the hold that the international drug interests held over the people of Canada. Each department had its own reason for joining. One wished to create a Canadian industry in order to provide more jobs, one wanted greater taxation and to stop the flow of dividends out of the country, one wanted to encourage more original research in Canada, and several were concerned with the problem of sovereignty — the Americans were already challenging Canadian possessions in the Arctic.

Each department which had a representative on INTEGRAL had its own vested interests, but Grant's purpose in joining was basically humanitarian. J.O. had taken Grant into his confidence, explaining in detail the cost and safety factors involved. "But Grant, it goes beyond the curing of the sick, it's the high pressure marketing of dangerous drugs for the most base of all human motives, profit. Grant, it's worse than bread and circuses. When we become a little upset at the way things are going, they give us mood altering drugs, happy pills to take our minds off the realities of life."

"What do you want me to do?"

"You could be of enormous help to our cause, to our country, to your fellow Canadians, if you become our leading spokesman in the media. Only two other people in our group know that I'm speaking to you. If you refuse, you will not be embarrassed." He hurried on. "We'll supply you with the facts and figures. Besides anything else, the material is good, strong reading."

Grant did not answer immediately. To be taken into the confidence of the Ottawa mandarins was a compliment, a knowledge base that would assure him of continued access to other material, as the years went by, in all areas. A columnist needed reliable sources. So there was an accrual, a benefit to him if he agreed. "Have you got some material I can read before I give you an answer?"

"I would expect that."

The information in the documents shocked Grant. As a humanist and an ardent Canadian nationalist, he was truly horrified at what he read. He telephoned McKinnon later that night and agreed to be part of the group.

As the weeks had gone by and he became more and more committed to attacking the drug industry, he continued to convince himself of the righteousness of his cause. He never admitted that one of the underlying motives behind taking such a hard moral line was that somehow he was assuaging the guilt he felt because of his continued affair with Louise.

J.O. closed his eyes, and his mind went for a moment to other projects he was motivating — all long term, all designed to help his countrymen. At one time he had been an active Marxist, almost rounded up in one of the rings revealed by the sensational Igor Gouzenko case, which had first shown to the Western world the very active espionage the Soviet Union was conducting. But the R.C.M.P. had only uncovered one of the three rings, and J.O., watching the development of Stalinism, had finally seen that Russian Communism was not applicable to Canada. He resigned from the party and began to address himself to practical problems. Reformist and revisionist they called him; so be it. He was still a Marxist. Still opposed to the profit principle. Knew that the twin pressures of population and technology would one day make the present form of profit system seem barbaric. But one had to live. And he had dedicated the rest of his life to do whatever good he could for his country.

And in this project there was more involved. The American government, wanting to break the high price structure of drugs in the United States, was providing INTEGRAL with facts and cost statistics. If Canada won, the people in the United States would benefit as well, perhaps people everywhere in the world.

Douglas Clark was speaking again. "My view is that we must be so conscious of protecting the secrecy of INTEGRAL that we must not even sit together during the hearings. If the industry finds out about us, their publicity people would stir up the country with accusations that Canada was being run by the so-called mandarins and not by their elected representatives. The pressure could even force the government to clamp down on us, and all our work be wasted."

With that remark, Violetta realized for the first time why Douglas had left his university post and well-paying consulting jobs to join government service. He was indeed what the press called a mandarin and did want to run the country. In many ways these mandarins were more powerful than the politicians. She looked at and listened to Douglas as if he were a stranger, not the man she had been to bed with the night before, the man who was pressing her to marry him. According to Louise, he was considered to be the best catch in Ottawa. The one thing Violetta didn't need was a catch.

Although she could not relate to the childishness of the civil service mind with its delight in acronyms (INTEGRAL was laughable), and bored by the constant vying for supremacy within INTEGRAL, especially between Noel and Clark, Violetta was fascinated at being involved. It had all happened by accident. Midway through completing her second year of interning and wondering whether to enter practice or to specialize further, she had become interested in the relatively new field of clinical pharmacology, the study of what happens inside the body when a patient is given medication. Thus, when a position became available at the Food and Drug Directorate, it sounded as though it would help her decide whether that was the specialty she wanted. She applied and was accepted. But six months later she was assigned to INTEGRAL, her responsibility to provide technical answers to medical questions asked by committee members, stemming from briefs that were presented. Naturally, INTEGRAL wanted the answers to be relevant to its aims, and so Violetta had been included and there met Douglas Clark. To maintain her medical proficiency, she still worked four nights a week at the hospital.

"It's all so cloak and daggery," she commented later at dinner.

Clark explained as if to a child, and she listened, too tired to complain about having heard it before. "Violetta, some of us have been working for five years on this project, slowly building statistics, planning tactics, persuading politicians — who, as you know, are the world's most stupid, self-serving humans — bringing in other departments as needed. We were sure we had the drug industry beaten during other hearings, only to find they'd outsmarted us. But this time, no matter how the committee report turns out, some of us have already drafted the Bill that the Prime Minister has agreed to put before Parliament."

"You mean this whole committee is a charade?" she asked, honestly surprised.

"Not entirely. Although we have his solemn promise, the P.M.

58

is a politician and can change his mind. So we must strive to get a strong report, one with clear recommendations. And even more important, we must arouse the people of Canada. And we will." Clark continued, hypnotized by his own concepts. "What American business wants, it usually gets. In a way this is one battle in a war and unless we realize that, Canada doesn't stand a chance as a nation. We'll become totally dependent, or a collection of states in the union, in our lifetime. In my view there is little difference between the imperialism of America and that of Hitler Germany or Stalinist Russia. What they did with troops and tanks, the Americans do with briefcases full of dollars."

At this Violetta, who had lived through part of the war in Europe, reacted. "That's the most stupid thing I've ever heard you say. You just don't know what you're talking about. No American has fired a gun at us."

"Not since the war of 1812, but wait until they want our water . . . need our water, our oil, our forests . . . and we won't sell to them. They'll take what we have, rationalizing that it is in their own national interest. Now is the time to make ourselves independent in everything, in every way, before we are nothing. Fill ourselves with another five or ten million people, preach anti-Americanism, nationalize our resource industries. If we do that, perhaps they'll hesitate to send troops across our borders."

She couldn't help looking at him as if he were insane. Nationality, or at least Canadian nationality, meant nothing to her. Even though legally she was a Canadian citizen, she felt herself to be a Lithuanian. In her view, neither Canadians nor Americans were a people nor would they be for a thousand years, if ever. And though Lithuanians were a subject people, with as many scattered over the world as in Lithuania, they remained a people.

He held up his glass. "To us, and to victory. We'll win unless your friend, Joseph Mann" — he emphasized the word 'friend' — "is a lot smarter than I think he is."

"He is not my friend," she said coldly.

[6]

"You could have killed my father," Violetta said, the words no sooner out of her mouth than she wished she could take them back.

Although he only smiled or nodded to her during the committee hearings, with bits of conversation if they happened to meet face to face, Joseph's interest in and attraction to Violetta increased during the next two weeks. Finally one day he caught up with her as she left the building during the luncheon break, without her keeper for once. Joseph asked her to walk around to the back of the Parliamentary Library, look at the flowers and the river and the Gatineau Hills in the distance, and then have lunch. She agreed and they were chatting amiably when he asked her when she had come to Canada. "In 1948. We escaped from the Russians in 1945 to seek safety in the American sector."

"Strange, I was flying over those areas about the same time."

"You could have killed my father."

Why did she say that? To be arch? To create a barrier between them? If so, why did she feel the need? Then, seeing the disturbed look on his face, she told him the whole story of how her father had been killed. There were about twenty men, women, and children in the escaping group and, while some of them, including her father, rested in a farmer's field, her mother took her into a thicket to relieve herself. Violetta remembered hearing airplanes, a soft coughing sound, and terrified screaming. And she remembered her mother picking her up and running back to the field where he father was and finding him crumpled

60

and bloody, face down on the ground, dead. And then more planes came and the survivors scattered and they never did bury her father. And they never knew whether the planes were German, Russian, American, French or British.

"I didn't strafe D.P.'s" he said.

D.P.s. Strange to hear the term again after so many years. After living in a displaced persons' camp for what seemed forever, she and her mother emigrated to Canada, first to an uncle's farm in Alberta and then to Toronto where her mother got a job in a dress factory.

"D.P., lousy D.P." the children would call, chasing after her. Violetta remembered running home. It was Saturday and her mother was home and she hugged her and stroked her. "Don't cry Violetta, don't cry *pupa*. All those children are the same as you. They are all D.P.s. Maybe they came to this country sooner than you, maybe not. Everyone on this street is a D.P." But still Violetta was inconsolable. And her mother said, "Listen to momma. In English D.P. means displaced person, but in Lithuanian it means God's bird. Don't be frightened. God loves his little birds."

"The guidebooks will tell you that the Parliamentary Library is one of the finest Gothic structures in the world," Joseph said, trying to change her mood. "Styled after the reading room in the British Museum."

They stopped and looked over the iron grate fence across the rapids-filled Ottawa River to the city of Hull and in the distance, the Gatineau Hills. Silent for a time, sharing the moment of being overwhelmed by the northern blue sky, the trees, and rocks, all only a few seconds from the automobile infested city.

"When Grant and I were kids we used to explore on our bikes. Ottawa was only a third of the size then. We'd try to get lost and then see if we could find our way home. Sometimes we'd cycle here and climb down the cliff, clutching at the trees to keep from falling."

"It's steep," she said looking down. "Oh look Joseph, there's a logger."

In the river below several loggers with pikes and spiked boots were jumping nimbly over the slippery logs, poking them to keep them moving down the river.

"Ottawa used to be a hard driving lumber town. I guess those are the remnants. And ironically the Russian embassy is the former home of one of the Ottawa River lumber barons." He glanced at her sideways. She was so beautiful, her blond hair long and ruffling softly in the breeze, her blue eyes the colour of the sky. It took all his self-control to keep from putting his arms around her, from kissing her. "Time for lunch and a martini," he said. They walked back, glancing at the statues. Sometimes their shoulders touched and he wondered if it were possible that he could feel the force of her without her feeling it as well.

At lunch over martinis she said, "You're really involved with this town whether you like to admit it or not."

"I hate it. Or I did. I used to hate coming back even for a visit. Maybe it's beginning to get to me. Somehow I feel something crucial to my life is going to happen. Don't people usually come home to die?"

"That's morbid."

"Now that I've met you, maybe I'll be reborn." He raised his glass. "To us."

"*Iss vay kata*," she said. "It means 'to your health', in Lithuanian. A safer toast."

"Do you feel caught between cultures? Do you still think in Lithuanian and translate into English in your head?"

"When I speak Lithuanian, I think in Lithuanian, and when I speak English, I think in English, and when I speak German . . . "

The waiter brought the Dover Sole Amandine and a bottle of Pouilly-Fuissé. Joseph had decided to live on his expense account and save his salary, and taking a member of the Food and Drug Directorate to lunch was definitely business, even though they talked only of themselves.

At first Violetta was reserved, wondering if Joseph, knowing from Grant or Louise that she was divorced, was thinking like most men—that she needed servicing and considered himself the prize stud, an executive stallion she should be grateful for.

62

But soon, perhaps because of the martini and the wine, she had a feeling of potentiality. They were able to communicate and she told him about herself, something she never did, abhorring the ritual of meeting a new man. Each person seeking not to reveal, but to hide in pigeon holes that already existed in the mind. Every man asked the standard questions, from "do you ski?" to "where have you travelled?"—but every question meant, "will you fuck me?" It was so tedious. No one ever seemed to be able to get across to people, able to offer anything other than the packages they created. But she didn't feel that way with Joseph and talked easily, telling him about her life, an important beginning if they wanted to know each other.

Shortly after moving to Toronto, her mother married again. There had always been a man in her mother's life. At the displaced persons' camp, her mother's man friend made sure Violetta was well fed; in Toronto, there was a man who bought presents; and finally, there was the man her mother married. "When I was older," she said, "I was almost certain that my mother would not have chosen the men she did except for me. It was a bad thing to think about. You know, did my mother choose those men only because she needed help to look after me?"

And then she stopped talking, remembering something too intimate to say. Her mother was only nineteen years older than she was, they looked more like sisters than mother and daughter. "Do you love him?" she had asked her mother once, referring to her stepfather. "Do you love him like you loved my father? Is it the same? Can a woman love twice?" And unasked but there, understood, the question that if it was the same, is love real? Or if one has the capacity to love, then why do people make so much of the possessive quality? Why the ego? Why the sorrow when it ends?

Her mother had sighed. Violetta would always remember the heaviness of that sigh. "It is a different time, a different place, and ... we are alive, and he is dead." But was that true? Because sometimes, even now, she caught her mother staring at her. And once her mother had said, "You are a very beautiful child. You look like him, your father. The same broad forehead. The same blue eyes, wide like an angel." And she had caught a sob halfway in flood and rocked slightly. "Oh, oh, oh, the same smile behind them, the full mouth that kissing my lips made my heart stop. And the love, you have the same feel for love and I am afraid for you. God forgive me Violetta, sometimes I look at you and I crave him. I forget where I am and what has happened and then when I see where I am, I hurt. Yes *pupa*, sometimes I look at you and I hurt, like a knife in my heart. Because he's gone." And then Violetta had known that for her mother and for her, for the kind of women they were, a woman loves once. Once only.

She wondered again why her mother had pushed her into a loveless marriage, and then fought fiercely to stop her divorce. The Lithuanian thing? The pride thing? The fear for her security? All it had led to was an abortion and lonely years of study at medical school.

She felt Joseph's eyes seeking her's, and was afraid. She had a feeling for him. Long before she met him, she had heard about him from Louise, who had been told all the details of his boyhood and young manhood by Grant. The moment she had seen him at the first session she felt his energy, knew that unless she was careful she would want to be with him.

And despite herself, everything seemed to lead—by accident, by a slow escalation—to an excitement. The truth was, she was afraid she could love him. Afraid for Joseph to be her one love. She knew that now. Too many conflicts separated them. Different cultures for one thing. Nonsense. That didn't matter a damn. As Douglas had said, they were in a war, and Joseph was the enemy. She must not see him again. It was foolish and could be hurtful to both of them. It was not their moment. Perhaps after the committee and INTEGRAL had completed their work. But for now, best to end it before it began. She looked at her watch. "Time to go. Thank you for the lovely lunch."

"Will I see you again?"

She was about to put him off with one of the various methods with which she was expert, but said, instead, "No Joseph, that would not be wise."

And while he resented being rejected, he was also relieved.

They walked back to the committee session in silence, each step that brought them closer to the Hill taking them further apart.

Walking down the corridor toward the committee room for the afternoon session, they met Douglas Clark who nodded to Joseph and, without saying a word to Violetta, went inside the room and took his seat. Later, at dinner, he asked, "Violetta, what the hell is going on between this Joseph Mann and you?" Then seeing the shock on her face, he added quickly, "Look, I'm not prying, your life is your own, but in this case, I don't think it makes sense for you to see him again, for lunch, cocktails, or any other time."

Her astonishment could not have been more complete. Thick-necked and stolid, Douglas had the same stubborn possessive male set that had been engraved on her first husband's face.

"He's got bed written all over him, I know the type."

Go slow Douglas, she thought. You don't own me. Not yet. Not ever. I am Doctor Violetta Norgela. I am somebody. Myself. At great cost. "Douglas, don't you ever talk to me again with that tone in your voice."

Her fierce intensity shocked him, challenged his maleness. This was a Violetta he had not been aware of before; nor was it the kind of woman he was sure he wanted to marry.

7

Joseph stepped out of the elevator directly into a spacious foyer dominated by a map of the world, the outlines of the countries etched on a free-standing walnut slab, easily fifteen feet in length. Across the top, gold block letters spelled out:

THE HEISTER WORLD
Heister Pharmaceutical Laboratories Inc.
Medicines for Millions — In Sixty-Four Countries

Blinking green lights indicated the location of the world-wide network of Heister plants, subsidiaries, warehouses, research facilities, and sales offices. Down one side of the map, also in gold lettering, was a list of the trade names of all Heister ethical medicines. On the other side was a much smaller list of Heister proprietary drugs, chiefly various types of vitamins, laxatives, and antacids.

"My name is Mann," he said handing the receptionist his business card. She wasn't the same girl who had been here during the first meeting with Heister, when he had been given the assignment.

"Joseph Adam Mann, Principal, Daniels and Company, Management Consultants." She read it aloud, as if his card were the needed absolute proof of his being, and then began to search for his name in an ornately hand-tooled leather appointment book. A pretty blond thing, her slow preciseness both amusing and appealing. Her horoscope predicted that an attractive new personage, male, would enter her life today and that she should

66

be aggressive, make her essential life force felt. And there he was, Joseph Mann. It was almost too much to believe. She picked up the phone and punched two numbers. "Mrs. Billington, Mr. Mann is here," she said, all the while bathing him in sexual radiance. But it was wasted. Joseph was not aware of her, his mind fixed tensely on the upcoming meeting with Robert Heister. He wondered what the crisis was, why he and Sorenson had been summoned to New York for this meeting. As far as he could tell everything was going well.

Mrs. Billington, a formidable looking woman somewhere in her fifties, appeared instantly. Typically haughty as befitted the secretary to the top man on a very high totem pole, her hair was a natural no-nonsense steel gray and she wore an expensive black couturier suit with a diamond clip at the collar. "Mr. Heister has asked me to apologize. He will be delayed for several minutes. He suggested you might enjoy seeing our Little Museum." Somehow, she managed to sound the L and M as capitals.

The museum was a room approximately fifty feet square and decorated in the same manner as the foyer—grasscloth walls, cork panels, and black leather chairs. It had the feeling of the dozens of men's clubs across the country which Joseph had lunched in during various consulting engagements.

Mrs. Billington explained that the exhibits were from the Heister Medical Museum—"The Big Museum we call it [capital B, capital M] in our main plant, which as you know is outside Detroit. On this side," she said, indicating with her left hand, "are extracts of remedies and cures dating back thousands of years. The other side contains the most famous advertisements of Heister products—slogans that have become part of the American heritage, part of our very language."

Three suspended glass cases dominated the centre of the room. One held a collection of ancient medical instruments, the second contained one sample of every product ever produced in the one hundred years that the Heister firm had been in business, and the third showed the development of their newest product, an anti-cancer drug. Mrs. Billington asked if he wanted coffee; when Joseph nodded and said, "Black, no sugar please," she marched off, admonishing him never to drink it that way. "Puts too much stress on the stomach and kidneys."

Joseph looked at the displays. The development of the anti-cancer drug was eye-opening. Behind a three dimensional model showing the molecular make-up of the drug, which more than anything resembled a three-year-old's tinker toy creation, was a chart depicting all the stages in its discovery and manufacture. These included basic research, testing in vitro (test tube), testing in animals, testing in vivo (the human body), clinical trials, pilot manufacturing, engineering for mass production, quality control, and marketing. An impressive endeavour which had taken seventy-three months and cost ten million dollars. He wondered if it worked.

Wandering about the museum with no fixed plan, he read the extracts hanging on the wall in random fashion.

On being brought her son Horus, close to death with swamp fever, Isis says, "I know how to quench this fire—with the healing flood waters I have between my thighs. If I pour this over his body, his vessels will recover and the fire will leave him." With care she places the boy between her legs which she has set wide apart. "Water is in my mouth and the nile between my legs." Her urine washed the burning boy and he is cured.

Joseph couldn't help but be impressed. A museum as part of a corporation's executive offices on the fortieth floor of one of the newest buildings in New York had all the hokiness of the old travelling medicine men—but updated, with style. But then even during their first meeting, Joseph knew the kind of man Heister was.

After bleeding the patient, take a young black cock and pluck all the feathers from its posterior; holding the bird by the beak, apply the bare posterior to the pustule. If the cock dies from the poison it has extracted, repeat the process until eventually one survives. It is after all the simplest method of extracting poison from the patient. (From *Measures to be Applied During an Outbreak of the Plague: Council of the Free City of Nuremberg, 1533.*)

"Imagine trying to fill a prescription for a black"—Mrs. Billington, back with the coffee, searched for a word other than cock—"rooster, a black rooster at your local drug store. Barbaric isn't it, Mr. Mann?" Startled, Joseph turned quickly.

"Surprised you," she clucked, as she set the rococo silver service on an antique marble pedestal. "Happens all the time. Visitors become utterly fascinated by our Little Museum [she did it again, capital L, capital M]. I've brought you biscuits as well. And your vitamins," she said handing him a bottle. "Heister vitamins with added minerals, your day's molecule of health."

The Heister TV commercial! She spoke in slogans. Did everyone in the industry? "An apple a day may have been good enough for your grandfather, but on-the-go America needs Heister vitamins with added minerals — your day's molecule of health."

"We've come a long way in curing sickness and relieving pain," Mrs. Billington continued as she poured his coffee. "I say we're lucky to be living in this day and age." And she left again.

At the fools' feast at Savatthi, revellers smeared their bodies with ashes and cow's dung and danced through the towns. Hindus offered a fist of ox dung and cow's urine to kin who smeared these on his face and chest. The Dalai Lama receives a gift of the faeces of the reincarnated Buddha. A dung car stood outside the cathedral of Dijob at Christmas and dung was thrown onto the faces of the crowd. Dung was a healing substance— God's miracles are to be found in the smallest piece of dirt.

Five minutes later, Robert Heister entered the museum through a double oak panelled sliding door, so finely crafted that it appeared to be part of the wall of his office. "How's it going Joseph?" he said warmly, shaking hands. "I'm sorry to interfere with your schedule but something has come up that I think could have a considerable bearing on the eventual course of action the Canadian government takes."

As before, Joseph was impressed by the grace and courtesy of the man, totally unlike what one would expect from a man with such power. Robert Heister headed one of the largest firms in the world, solely in the ethical drug field. It sold more than two hundred million dollars worth of product and employed over ten thousand people in sixty-four countries. He pointed to one of the plaques. "That one is my favourite—it represents the cry of the multitudes for help. The eternal cry." And to Joseph's surprise he read it aloud:

O Takman, thy arrows bring horror:
Over the sick thou pourest fire:
Whilst the frost stiffens their limbs:
Spare us from thy brother, the cough:
Spare us from thy sister Phthisis:
Spare us from leprosy, thy cousin:
Look up Takman, see our neighbour:
He does not pay thee homage.

Joseph noted again, as he had at their first meeting, that while Heister was power and looked it — indeed, like a feudal lord, had been born to it — the unfailing courtesy of his manner belied it. He was a tall, good looking man with intelligent eyes, only a few years older than Joseph. Except for the suggestion that there were a lot of martinis accumulated in his body, he radiated the health and vigour that one would expect from a man in the medicine business. "I'm sorry to keep you waiting, Joseph. It was unavoidable."

When he entered Heister's office, Joseph was struck again by the paintings on the walls—a Picasso, a Mondrian, a Toulouse-Lautrec, a Chagall—his favourite painter—and a Wyeth—a million dollars' worth of art. It hardly seemed possible that anyone could be that wealthy. The room itself was the size of the Little Museum, with the same general decor—grasscloth walls and beige carpet, but with oriental rugs scattered on top.

Dr. Flaschner, a thin, nervous looking man who kept chewing at his bottom lip, was introduced as Director of the Heister prison testing facility. They were immediately joined by Sorenson, limping noticeably. Heister sat behind his desk as if he were about to lecture the three men grouped on the other side. "I called this meeting because Dr. Flaschner has uncovered a conspiracy by two of the inmate volunteers at our prison testing facility that could conceivably be a factor in helping us convince the Canadians not to change the patent law."

Heister explained, for Joseph's benefit, that the hospital was designed for clinical testing of drugs in humans and was within prison walls, but there the similarity to prison life ended. It was a

70

separate building with sixteen beds in eight rooms, a common area with sofas and soft chairs, and television and games. There were clean sheets on real beds, all bars were hidden by curtains (in case constant awareness of being in prison would in some way affect reactions), and inmates could move about at will.

"I thought it important enough, Dean, Joseph, to ask you to come here at short notice to listen to a tape Dr. Flaschner has made of a conversation." He turned to the doctor and nodded.

Dr. Flaschner switched on the machine placed on Heister's desk.

"Well what do you say . . . look I always been successful counterfeiting pills. I been in that business for twenty years . . . never had a bummer."

"What are you doing here?" an educated voice responded.

There was a pause as the man obviously hesitated.

"All right, I'll tell you. I had to make a run for the 'people', you know what I mean. Most of the big companies, and I mean big, manufacture millions of 'bennies' . . . speed . . . you know, and they fake shipments to Mexico, but really at the border, the stuff is put into trucks and driven right back to New York and then distributed across the country. A stoolie tipped the Feds. You can bet he ain't in the land of the living anymore."

"I'm not going to be involved in that sort of activity."

"That's not my business. My business isn't dangerous like that. Look, I got my own pill machine under my garage floor and with it I can make anything that will sell. You name it. Vitamins, tranquillizers by the thousands. All brands . . . you name them . . . Heister, Parke-Davis, Smith Kline, you name it. It's so easy to copy stuff by the big firms. I sold through a network in the midwest to doctors, druggists, wholesalers . . . they're all so greedy. What do you say? Throw in with us. You'll be a partner."

Flaschner stopped the machine for a moment. He identified the voices as Tony Ferrilio and Fred Smith, a disbarred lawyer.

Heister added that Ferrilio was known to the industry as a mafia soldier who had been involved in many counterfeit drug operations. Pharmpress, the industry's investigative arm, had a complete dossier on him.

71

"Fred Smith is basically a decent human being," Flaschner said.

"Lawyers who get caught with their hands in the till usually are," Heister added sarcastically.

Flaschner started the tape again and they heard Fred Smith's voice ask, "Why me?"

Joseph listened spellbound.

"I told you, this time I'm going to work in Canada. I've got big connections there. And there's no one doing it up there, like we can have the whole country to ourselves. And from what I hear, they got so few inspectors——"

"But you haven't answered my question. Why me?"

"Because you're a lawyer. What I need is someone to study all the laws, to make sure we don't do anything, nothing, that can get us in trouble, to set up the dummy companies——"

"For the hundredth time, Tony, I've been disbarred and I don't know the laws of Canada."

Up until the day that Flaschner recorded this conversation, Ferrilio approached Fred Smith only during exercise period. Each time he resisted. But this time Ferrilio caught him at an extremely low ebb. All day he had been reliving the awful experience and sickening feeling when three years ago the auditors for the Bar Society had walked into his office unannounced. A two hour spot check of his books easily revealed that he had used half a million dollars of a client's money from his trust account for his personal use. Conversion. Fraud. Disbarred. Jail. Divorced. Never to see his children again. Was that possible? Bankrupt. Unbelievable. Not him, Fred Smith. Silver medal winner class of '45. So many lawyers use trust funds. But he had been caught.

"I know all that," Tony said. "I know you can't do the law swindle here no more. So what are you going to do? A lawyer's a lawyer. You think like a lawyer. You'll study the laws. You'll know what to do."

Yes, he'd know what to do. Fred Smith, common name from a common family, who grew up in a common clapboard street in a common small town but who had propelled himself into an uncommon man, would know what to do. He had boosted himself through university with a combination of hard work, self-deprivation, and scholarship, and then went on to become a successful lawyer. And the money started to roll in and he became Fred Smith swinger, dancer, lover, man-about-town recognized by all the maître d's. He'd always known what to do.

"The way you talk you could even handle sales to druggists and doctors."

"I'm not coming back to prison again. Ever."

Actually, he had been one of the lucky ones. Prison had not been as difficult as it could have been. Placed in charge of the prison library for the first two years, he was able to forget who he was. The books helped him, gave him a perspective, made him realize that he was no worse than any other man, just a victim of the private property society in which he still believed. He had not been smart enough to be a winner; his sin was to get caught. Then he lost his library job to a newly arrived syndicate member and was transferred to the machine shop. After only two days of noise, metal on metal, the crush and smell of human bodies, he knew he would not last, would crack. So on the third day, when a call for volunteers for pharmaceutical testing came, he applied immediately.

The hospital had been a godsend.

Once he overcame the shyness at the invasion of his bodily privacy, he actually began to enjoy talking about his reactions and became absorbed in the functions of his body, diligently assisting in the collection of his urine and faeces to check absorption rate and length of time chemicals remained in the body. He didn't mind having his saliva and mucous from his nose gathered. "Harvested" he had remarked once to the amusement of the researchers. His heart and blood pressure were checked daily and sometimes he was wired when he was asleep. Even the ends of his fingers were studied and parings taken from his fingers and toenails. But for Fred Smith the most important difference was that he was in contact with educated people — doctors, nurses, chemists, pharmacologists — people of his own academic attainments. They treated him warmly, appreciat-

73

ing that he had volunteered, permitting him to observe them at work in various laboratories.

Another prisoner apparently entered their room. "Tony, I think I got a rash on my back. I should never have tried out for this. A guinea pig. You could get sick. Poisoned to death." Then there was the sound of him wandering off.

"Dumb Mex," Tony said. "The drug they're testing is not new. It's a combination of two other drugs. Don't you remember Dr. Flaschner telling us that because some people build up a resistance to antibiotics, they believe that putting two together have a syn . . . ."

"Synergistic effect," Fred helped.

"You picked up a lot since you been here," Tony said. "Well, what do you say?"

"Leave me alone. I don't want anything to do with counterfeit drugs. Tony, how do you even know what to make?"

"How do I know what to make? How do I know?" He swung his feet off the bed and started to walk up and down. "How does anyone in business know? You make what you can sell. Whatever is in demand, that's what you make. We're no different from the big companies. Like right now, from what I hear Tolbutamide is hot."

"What?" Fred laughed at the words coming out of Tony's mouth.

"Tolbutamide, an oral anti-diabetic. But we could make any of the tranquillizers, like valium."

"Where do you get the ingredients?" Fred sounded interested.

"Anywhere and everywhere. Italy. Chemical manufacturers here. Anyone will sell anything for cash. Sometimes we don't put anything in the pill. It just looks real. What's wrong with you? It ain't going to hurt anyone."

"It won't help either. No, it's not for me."

"Ah, shit, half these pills are no good anyway. But we don't have to do that if you don't want to. It costs nothing to make the real thing. Costs more to print the label."

"I still don't understand where you get the know-how. The recipes. How do you know what to mix together?"

74

"That you got to take on trust. I know. I got a couple of chemists who work for the big companies. You can always get a chemist to work at night. And there's this book, the red book they call it because it's got a red cover and it tells what's in every drug to meet standards. It's put out by the government and you can't get closer to God than that. There's no danger."

"And if you get caught?"

"The worst they can do is fine you. It's too hard to prove anything. I got friends who are millionaires today from making copies of Miltowns in their basements. Some have even gone half-legit if you can believe. But they'll still handle my shipments, slipped in with regular stuff."

"But is it safe, can someone die?"

"Is it safe? Is it safe? I never had a death yet as far as I know. But you know yourself from being here. Everyone is different. God made us all different. We all get different reactions. Don't we all get the same doses here? The same injections? The same everything? And you get a rash and I get diarrhea and someone else gets pains. Listen to me, Fred," the tone was hushed, personal, "you got to look out for yourself. You got to make a living. Unless you want to be a nobody for the rest of your life for one little mistake you got to throw in with us. You won't be sorry. I promise you. And you don't know, make a bunch of money and in a year or two you may have enough to put in a fix in some state and be able to be a lawyer again. I mean you don't know these things."

There was no doubt that Tony made sense. He was soon to be paroled. Out on the street. How could he earn a living? How could he eat? What was he going to do? Drive a hack like his father? Live in a crummy room, an outsider with no way to make the money that would buy back respectability. No more made-to-measure suits, no dining in the "best" restaurants, no cocktail parties unless one of his old associates or friends invited him as an oddity — "someone who had been to jail" party conversation. And there'd be no wheeling and dealing, no fun. And though as a result of exercising and volunteering for this prison testing hospital he was in the best physical shape of his life, he looked

75

old, hair thinning and gray, the sparkle of self-confidence vanished. He sighed. It was worth the gamble. He really had no other choice. He could stay in the background, put his name to nothing, and if it began to look chancy, he could always walk away. And this time until he saw how it was going he would save every dollar.

"Equal partners, you said?"

"All the way."

"All right, I'm in. But hear me now. I'm going to be careful."

"You won't be sorry, I promise you."

But that night as Dr. Flaschner listened to their entire conversation, he knew they would be very sorry. There was nothing he could do to help them.

Every room in the prison testing hospital had been electronically equipped at his insistence following the death of a patient who failed to report side effects from a new drug until it was too late. Some volunteers were shy and withheld symptoms, or were frightened, but they often checked with each other. And unknown to them, all these conversations were recorded. Sometimes a patient's life was saved this way and sometimes other matters were uncovered.

Heister clicked off the tape. "The rest is more of the same."

"Have you reported this to the police?" Joseph asked.

"Where's your head this morning? What have they done? And they're already in prison. Besides, it could be embarrassing to reveal we use listening devices inside a state authority."

Heister looked around at the other faces. "You still aren't with me? Look, I'm not sure we want them caught so soon. Think a moment. Relate this tape to the hearings in Canada. One of our key points is that if the patent law is changed, Canada will be inundated with unsafe drugs. Drugs from many sources, including counterfeit and black market drugs. These fellows, Ferrilio and Smith, plan to operate in Canada. They could be the first." He paused, tapped his fingers on the desk, leaned forward and said in a confidential tone, "Now do you get my meaning?"

"Go on," Sorenson said coldly. "Let's hear it all to be sure."

"Supposing we let Ferrilio and Smith go into business, maybe

76

even help them, make it easy for them and then at the right time, and only if we can't convince the committee of the correctness of our point of view by normal lobbying techniques, we call the police and the press, and reveal the whole operation. What do you suppose the effect will be on the Canadian people and the politicians?"

A setup! Sorenson understood all the ramifications before Joseph did and for a moment was too appalled to say anything. Flashing through his mind was the question, Why? Why was he always in opposition to Heister? Even after all these years he didn't understand him. Heister was typical of the new breed in the business. Not a medical doctor like his grandfather, nor a pharmacist like his father, nor a production engineer like himself. Heister was a marketing man. To his credit he had tripled the business in five years after becoming president; but at what human cost? He eliminated obsolete products and the people with them, preferring to duplicate others' discoveries by molecular manipulation rather than do basic research. And it was over Sorenson's objection that these executive offices had been moved to New York — two entire floors housing the senior vice-presidents, financial, marketing, and legal for their world operations. "New York is the financial capital of the world. We've got to be there," Heister had argued. It was getting more and more difficult to know what was right. Everything was changing so rapidly. Things Sorenson had always taken as absolute now seemed worthless. He had even seen the American flag stomped on during the musical *Hair*. His stomach had knotted and it was all he could do to keep himself from making a scene. But to coldly allow a counterfeit drug operation to be organized, to allow counterfeit drugs — perhaps ones that would kill people because of contamination — to be widely distributed, to encourage the operation, help it, was beyond some line of behaviour he was certain had once existed.

"You can't do that, Bob," Sorenson finally exclaimed.

"Dean," Heister said, "I'm not some kind of monster."

Strange, his own grandson had accused him just a short while ago of being a monster. He had spoken of the people of the

77

Third World, and wouldn't listen when Sorenson told him that it was the drug industry that had removed the awful suffering caused by amoebic dysentery, yaws, filariasis, sleeping sickness. "Technology is the answer, not politics" he had said to deaf ears.

"I don't like this any more than you do, Dean," Heister assured him. "But what would you have me do? Hundreds of thousands of people who work in our industry depend on us for their livelihood. Hundreds of thousands of shareholders look to us for those dividend cheques every quarter. And what of all the people who will not get well if our industry is destroyed? So, if I have to entice, even sacrifice, a disbarred lawyer and a cheap hood to keep our industry going, then you can be sure that's what I'll do and not lose any sleep over it either."

"Bob, it's dangerous and . . . immoral."

"Don't talk to me about morality," Heister said in a voice that fought to contain its hostility. "I know about the deal you made with that Nazi Kurt Manheim and my father years ago. Where was your high and mighty moralizing then? I'm not saying we'll do it, Dean, just let's be ready. We have to do what we have to do to survive, no matter who gets nailed. Right?"

Shocked by Heister's revelation that he knew of his deeply buried secret, Sorenson didn't respond immediately, the whole of the incident taking possession of his mind.

When the first American tanks had broken through to Northern Germany, Sorenson was Colonel in charge of occupying the Manheim Works. His orders had been made crystal clear: Dismantle. The philosophy behind the orders, equally clear: Destroy Germany's economic power and you destroy her ability to make war in the future. He remembered so clearly the soft day in July when, with a team of experts, he summoned the managers and directors of Kurt's great enterprise and there in the boardroom read to them the law of the Occupying Powers, requisitioning their industry. It was much like a Hollywood scene; he remembered feeling even at the time like a soldier of old, capturing and dividing booty — except instead of gold from

78

the dead it was whole industries.

Later, he helped write the document that would destroy the enterprise entirely, detailing how it was to be dismembered into dozens of separate, individual, and hopefully competing, smaller firms.

One night, a week before the break-up order was to be put into effect, Kurt invited him to his home for dinner. "To the future," Kurt toasted, "peace and prosperity." And then he came right to the point, unusual for a European businessman, and made his offer. He would turn over to Sorenson all the secret techniques, procedures, formulae, and patents for all their pharmaceuticals. Sorenson could do what he wanted with them. Start his own company in America, take them to Heister or any other plant. In return, Sorenson was merely to go slow on the break-up of the enterprise. "Colonel Sorenson, the time is quickly coming when there will be tension, perhaps war between Russia and the West. The efficient functioning of our enterprise will be important to you. Germany and the United States will be allies, as they always should have been, even in this war against Russia." He raised his hand to stop Sorenson from speaking. "I know at this moment it seems difficult for you to accept and your superiors from Washington are pushing for quick destruction of the works." Kurt always referred to the giant enterprise that sprawled for miles and employed over fifty thousand people as "the works." "But within six months, a year at the most, everything will have changed. You must give us that time. Merely go slow. Your job will be difficult anyway. You are the expert and you know how complicated and interrelated our organization is. No one will know. Colonel Sorenson, a strong West Germany is vital to your interests." He paused and while Sorenson was thinking rose and started opening his briefcase. "Here, I've brought all the papers." They stayed up the whole night while Sorenson studied them. Incredible how advanced the Germans were in so many areas.

"But Herr Manheim, some of these new drugs, these ideas, how could you test them?" It bothered Sorenson that Kurt's firm had been accused of approving inhuman testing on humans, all

79

kinds of bizarre injections of Jews and Poles, among others.

"Our scientists, remember, were always in advance."

That was true. Koch, Erlich, Dogmack and many others. Nevertheless, Sorenson was later relieved when the Allied War Crimes Commission could find no solid evidence that Kurt's firm had engaged in the vilest research imaginable. But in his heart he always wondered.

Sorenson stuffed his briefcase with the chemical formulae and testing results, robbing Kurt's firm of their advantage in the pharmaceutical world for years. It was easy to stall. The detail of such a complex firm, with two hundred separate factories, really didn't bend easily anyway to an order emanating from Washington. Nothing short of an atom bomb could have stopped Kurt's enterprise from surviving intact, except for what was in the Russian zone, which was simply removed.

And when, in fact, the orders were changed and Kurt's firm allowed to continue as he had predicted, because of worsening relations with the Russians, Sorenson had his meeting with Mr. Heister, Robert's father. He traded the secrets for a chunk of stock and an assured place in the Heister hierarchy.

Sorenson kept the briefcase, at first as a hair shirt. Now he regarded it as a sentimental item, rationalizing long ago that if he hadn't taken those formulae other firms would have. Had he profited out of man's inhumanity to man? The question was too complex and, in fact, didn't everyone? The point was that the politicians had been wrong and Kurt had been right.

How few years had gone by before the Americans financed the build-up of a new Germany. That was why he had so little guilt about having disobeyed orders. And yet, why was he so shocked that Bob Heister had known all these years? That the father had told his son? He suspected why. Knowing that his son was a different type, the old man must have extracted a promise that Dean Sorenson's position at Heister Pharmaceutical was inviolate, for as long as he lived. But was Heister finally nudging him out? Was that the real reason why Joseph Mann had been put in charge? He couldn't let it alone. It festered.

Was this a clue to what drove Robert Heister? It wasn't money, certainly. Nor was it power for its own sake. He hadn't forgiven his father for almost ruining the business the grandfather had built. He knew that Sorenson had brought patents from Kurt Manheim that saved the business, in return for giving a sizable portion to Sorenson. That was why he worked so hard. To build a business on his own. To prove to everyone that he could succeed not simply because of inheritance or stolen patents, but because of his own merit. In fairness, Sorenson realized that there was more to him than that. Curiously, he was an amalgam of the old-fashioned business leader who did feel a direct responsibility to the employees in his plants, and the cold new marketing type who would do anything to increase sales. Heister had pride; perhaps more than anything else he wanted approval from his peers.

"We do what we have to. Right Dean?" Heister repeated forcefully.

"You tell me why the car industry or anyone else can charge what the traffic will bear and competition allow and we can't? High prices for drugs — that's a politician's demagoguery. If you're sick or in pain or dying, what difference does the price make? And if you take a drug that gets you back to work in one day instead of being off for weeks the way it used to be, then that cost and saving has to be considered. Is there a moral difference between making a profit from people's sickness and misery and from their pleasures? If we shouldn't profit from sickness, should someone profit from hunger, from the food we eat? What is wrong with profit? That's what makes the whole thing go."

"Yes, of course," Sorenson heard himself saying. There was no other way. The industry was all he had. It was his life. His son dead in Korea. His wife dead. His grandson some stranger.

And then Heister revealed his plan. "Kurt Manheim has just bought a plant in Italy which we had licensed to manufacture one of our tranquilizers. When Ferrilio gets his operation going, we arrange for him to buy these drugs from Kurt — the real product, but without our marking. The only thing counterfeit about the drug will be the marking. And, as you know no one can

81

stamp identical markings to ours; it must be done during the manufacturing process, not after. Inspectors will automatically assume the drug was counterfeited."

No patient would get hurt from that drug, Dr. Flaschner realized. But what of the other drugs that the counterfeit group distributed before they were caught? What dangers were they exposing people to? He said nothing. Both Heister and Sorenson knew that risk existed.

"When we notify the police and the Food and Drug pick up the drugs, they will assume they are counterfeit drugs because of the labels. And they will also find other drugs which will be counterfeit. The press will trumpet the story. By the time the pills are analyzed and shown to be therapeutically sound, all Canada will be aware of the counterfeit drug problem, of what will happen if patent laws are changed and they are exposed not only to fly-by-night companies, but to counterfeiters by the score."

"But when they analyze the pill as you say, Bob," Joseph asked, "won't they know the drug is okay? Doesn't that defeat your purpose?"

"Joseph, forgive me, but you still have a lot to learn. That pill is a combination of chemicals and molecular structures so complex it will take them two months just to discover its chemical make-up, and by that time we'll have succeeded in what we wanted."

Dr. Flaschner sat in silence. Tony Ferrilio was a drug counterfeiter and because of men like him not only did drug manufacturers lose millions of dollars yearly, but people often died either from taking contaminated drugs, or drugs that didn't help. Still, he wished Heister would permit him to reveal to the men that their plans were known, play the tape, talk to them, explain what would happen if they persisted, explain the dangers to people who took counterfeit drugs. That would have been the human and honest thing to do. But he did not ask. Nor had he even considered not bringing the tape to Heister. He couldn't take the chance. All tapes were numbered.

He still remembered with bitterness and frustration the time Heister had flown to the prison hospital unannounced, arriving unexpectedly. A new drug being tested had a 5 per cent incidence of liver damage, too high to pass Food and Drug. Alone in the laboratory Heister had asked him to destroy the evidence showing the side effects, his points being that the drug was beneficial and worth the risk, which only showed up in massive doses anyway. Shocked, Flaschner pleaded for more time to determine whether his findings were right. "Perhaps the incidence is 10 percent, perhaps not as high as we think."

"Dr. Flaschner, this country has been good to you. Sometimes in a free enterprise a man has to take chances. We are being hurt by a competitor and this is the closest we have come so far to copying his product. Surely you realize there is no point, no point at all in maintaining this prison testing facility if we cannot get results fast enough to get competitive products on the market."

Flaschner had been dumbfounded; it had never before occurred to him that this elaborate facility could quite simply be closed. But not every firm maintained volunteer prison testing facilities. There were other ways to test. And the old fear of being on borrowed time took hold of him again.

He had been a doctor in Hungary. After fleeing to Canada during the 1956 uprising, he discovered that he could not practise medicine in that country. Only luck produced this job. Or so he thought, until he realized why he had been hired. The pressure to produce results and suppress contra-indications and side effects was a factor he had not counted on. But he had a wife and two children, and he had done as asked and thanked God no one had died. The whole exercise had been pointless because eventually the drug was supplanted by a better one.

Heister owned the whole thing, the hospital and everything in it—every test tube, ampule, syringe, bedpan, sheet. And him. Yet, if one had to be owned, better to sell one's soul here than one's life in Hungary. No, he had no choice. There was no place in the world he could escape to. He had risked his life to live in this country. And while it lacked much, he had his books, his family, a small circle of friends, his music and sometimes, even though he could not practise his beloved surgery, he did manage to perform some important testing.

And what difference did it make anyway? Even medicine had changed. Doctors were nothing but pill prescribers. They gave pills to people because some drug detail man told them what illnesses certain drugs were for. They rarely realized what happened inside the body, why a drug worked or why it didn't, or what side effects might result in one or five or ten years. Doctors today were little different than those who thousands of years ago used remedies they observed might work — like the remedies in the Heister museum. The doctor as a medicine man. This time Smith and Ferrilio were the devils to be exorcised. The thought amused Flaschner.

Everyone was given his assignment. "Dean, when the time comes, you will fly to Germany and explain the situation to Kurt and arrange for him to manufacture a batch without our insignia," Heister said. "We'll need his co-operation. Flaschner, your job is to keep me informed. I want detailed reports of these men, the tape sent to me each day by courier. And I want you to be friendly with them. Give them all the chemical information they want. Make it easy." Heister slid open a panel behind his desk that opened onto a smaller office, his "working" office. Inside was another desk covered with files and note paper. He picked up the phone.

Joseph was surprised at how vague, almost disoriented Sorenson seemed. In the background he heard Heister call an influential senator. Within minutes he arranged for Smith's and Ferrilio's parole to be months sooner than normal.

When Heister returned, Joseph wondered tensely what his part in this scheme was to be. To avoid Heister's eyes, which at that moment seemed to want a statement of commitment, he stared at a point over Heister's left shoulder, only to be confronted by Heister again. On the wall behind were photos of Heister at college playing football, Heister playing tennis, sailing, schussing down a slope. Heister in control.

A setup. Like in the movies, only this was real. A plan. A game plan. Help the counterfeiters get into business and then destroy them. Sorenson had his job. Flaschner his. And when the time came what would Joseph's be? The hatchet man? To blow the whistle? If not him, who? And Ferrilio was the mafia.

Suddenly the memory of Cynthia flashed through his head. A former prostitute who had operated one of the largest call-girl rings in New York, Cynthia was the wife of a leading mafioso, retired and living in Miami. Periodically he let his young wife come to New York to shop. Joseph had met her in a bar by chance two years ago and it had been wild. She taught him the joys of kinky sex, especially sex with speed and LSD. And she also told him about the mafia, that whatever he had read was all true and more — criminal groupings were everywhere, interwoven into the illusion of the free enterprise system. The one did not seem to be able to exist without the other.

Flaschner was dismissed. Heister rose from behind his desk and moved to a grouping of upholstered chairs where Sorenson and Joseph joined him. He must have buzzed Mrs. Billington because she appeared with tea and a bottle containing multivitamins. Heister said he would prefer a martini. Sorenson had vermouth and Joseph had scotch. Mrs. Billington didn't approve but served the drinks and then left. Heister began to question them in detail about events in Ottawa, as if the incident with Dr. Flaschner had never occurred.

Prior to today the American- or foreign-owned multinational corporation had been an abstract concept for Joseph. As a management consultant he had served them on a variety of assignments, and like most consultants, took pride in doing a good job. It was exciting to use his mind to solve problems, to make things work better — people happier at their jobs, or more product produced, or new operations totally organized. Consultants kidded each other that the only reason a man entered that profession was because he wanted to be loved and admired; being a consultant was better than going to a shrink. But Heister and Sorenson were the flesh and blood behind the billion dollar corporations. They even looked the parts they played, looked like they deserved to be where they were in life (where he wanted to be) — a new kind of super-élite. And clever as he knew himself

85

to be, and as much as he too looked the part, tall and handsome, Joseph recognized that he wasn't their equal, at least not yet. It wasn't even an academic hypothesis. Heister and Sorenson controlled. These were the men who created the new system, who were the embodiment of the new idea of industry as a supranational entity — a nation within nations, above and beyond the individual laws of each separate country.

As much as he thought he understood the dynamics of American industry, the unstudied arrogance of these two men, calmly sipping their drinks high above New York while they plotted to confound an entire sovereign nation, especially after having just decided on a course of action that might destroy two human beings, unnerved him.

How different he felt now from the first meeting in this office. Then it was as if he had been given the key to the dynamics of American business. The "chance of a lifetime." The project had promised to be the most exciting of his career — involving medicine, politics, and a major world industry. And watched by these giants, there was no telling what he might be offered next. As he believed that proper use of technology assured the greatest happiness for the greatest number, the moral stance of an industry had never concerned him. He was a professional — a technocrat. Now he would be on the periphery of dealing with the elements of organized crime. Other than a little fear there was no real hesitation in his mind. He knew he would do whatever was necessary to make himself healthy, wealthy, and wise. But what he could not hide from himself was that he felt dirty, like one of the fools at the Feast of Savatthi rubbing shit on himself.

"When do you expect to be in New York again, Mr. Mann?" the receptionist asked as Joseph waited for the elevator after the meeting was concluded. The invitation in her voice was obvious. She was perfectly groomed, white, even teeth — capped no doubt at Heister's expense. Plastic New York woman communicating instant availability. He knew the type. About twenty-five, a superb sexual partner, without brains and craving love. A sure score. Tedious but diverting. And for a moment

86

Joseph considered staying over, losing himself in sex and scotch as was his pattern when the reality of life got through to him. But the smell of her perfume was overpowering and he had to get away from the kind of shit women poured over themselves and he had to get away from New York, the city of shit. He was being unfair and he knew it, but sometimes when he got depressed he couldn't control the blackness of his thoughts.

At Kennedy airport, on a sudden impulse he didn't understand, he called Violetta. Even as he gave instructions to the long distance operator he kept asking himself what he was doing and why. It would be peace to see her, have a drink with her. He remembered that incredible lunch. He had felt her as a totality, not body only, face only, eyes, lips, voice, brain, movement only, but a totality in which he could not distinguish the parts; he was aware of a force so strong that when his eyes met hers he had to turn away. He hesitated before he dialled. But it would only be ten o'clock, perhaps she would come out for a drink.

Deep in study, the phone startled Violetta. She was angry at the intrusion, but when she heard Joseph's voice she felt the same pull toward him that she had from the first.

"Violetta, I know we agreed not to see each other but . . ."

Her heart sank. Here it comes, she thought. He was going to pitch her. She was so fed up with men calling her any time they felt like it. At three o'clock in the morning some idiot would call and say, "Violetta, I'm sorry, I couldn't sleep, do you mind if we talk for a while." Douglas was like that. And sometime she would be so tired she would cradle the phone on her shoulder, close her eyes, and wake up several hours later in the same position, not even remembering who had called. Recently she had been plagued by three men. There was the disc jockey who, because he earned seventy-five thousand dollars a year, felt he was a lady's man of some renown. They had met at a party in Toronto and he was forever calling long distance, at all hours, wanting to take her for weekends to exotic places. Last week it was to Acapulco. Incredible that this fat man of fifty felt that because idle women listened to him chatter and play records during the day, he had some kind of appeal. Then there was the senior chemist where she worked. He still got his kicks making whisky in the lab the way he used to do at university twenty years before. And the Lithuanian contractor her stepfather had wished on her. She couldn't make up her mind who was the worst.

"Violetta, look, I'm sorry I called. I had a tough meeting in New York today and I thought we could have a drink when I arrive back, but I realize it's nuts. And you know, now that I'm talking to you, I realize I didn't want a drink."

She waited silently, refusing to join the word games by asking archly as in the worst kind of TV dialogue, "and what did you want?", hoping he wouldn't say what she thought he was going to suggest.

"Violetta, please don't laugh at me. It's going to come across kind of silly, but I guess I called because I wanted to make contact. And now I feel better. How do you figure that?" he asked in honest wonder.

She felt flustered — and touched.

"Violetta . . ."

"Yes?" she said, almost saying, "yes love."

"D.P. also means dazzling people. And I think you're dazzling. Good night, Violetta," he said quickly. "Violetta," repeating her name again because he liked the sound and feel of it. "Sleep tight."

"Good night Joseph. And thank you for calling."

Later, as she drifted off Violetta made two decisions. First, the fact that she and Joseph were on opposite sides in their daily work world was not sufficient reason to keep themselves apart as human beings. And second, she would stop going to bed with Douglas Clark. It wasn't satisfying . . . she didn't love him. At best Douglas was a typical, unfeeling, anglo-saxon animal type. Sex was something you did when enough sperm built up in you to make you "horny." You "took" a woman and then you despised her a little. She had never been able to relate to two men at the same time and Douglas was an accidental convenience. She thought of lying in bed with Joseph, naked, and wondered what kind of people they would be together. And as sleep overtook her she hoped she would find out soon.

8

"Gentlemen, I see a quorum," and the chairman struck his gavel signifying the start of the ninth session of the Special Committee on Drug Costs and Prices.

A month had passed in which the Tuesday and Thursday sessions created the rhythm of Joseph's life, sometimes rudely broken by the sound of the division bell summoning members who were not paired with other absentees and had to scurry to the House for a vote.

Under Joseph's prodding the well-equipped publicity operation of the Pharmaceutical Association, administered by Ron Kendall, had sent out forty thousand pieces of mail — to every doctor, dentist, and druggist in Canada — explaining the position of the industry and asking the recipient to contact his Member of Parliament and stress the danger to the health of the nation if the patent act were changed. And every Member of both federal and provincial Parliaments was contacted not once but half a dozen times, by different influential groups. But it was only when the powerful professional and business associations — the Canadian Medical Association, the Quebec College of Physicians and Surgeons, the Canadian Manufacturer's Association, the Canadian Chamber of Commerce, the Canadian Chemical Producers' Association, and the Canadian Electrical Manufacturers Association — agreed to present briefs in favour of the pharmaceutical industry that Joseph himself began to realize the clout wielded by the industry. It made little difference to Joseph or to anyone else that Grant MacDonald, in one of his columns, identified the Pharmaceutical Association of Canada as being controlled by American firms.

More accurately it was controlled by the thirteen chemical and pharmaceutical organizations that accounted for more than 75 per cent of the world's output of chemicals, dyes, and drugs. There were several German firms including Kurt Manheim's, one Swiss, one French, two English, and the rest American. There were thousands of pharmaceutical and chemical firms in the world, some quite large, but the thirteen were in control. Although they competed for markets and breakthroughs, they closed ranks when governments anywhere in the world tried to interfere with their "free" enterprise. While they participated in all associations, they also had their own tight grouping, and it was this group, through Heister, that was directing the strategy of the Canadian lobbying activities. Unknown to Joseph, Heister had been selected because he controlled Frank Flanagan.

Founded in 1914, the Canadian association contained close to seventy firms, including the Canadian subsidiaries of the international group of thirteen, and accounted for 90 per cent of all Canadian prescription drug sales and much of the over-the-counter sales as well. In more than fifty years it had become part of the structure of the society, interconnected with every institution — educational, medical, scientific, and governmental. When Sorenson recounted the millions of dollars given by the industry both as grants to universities for research and as donations to political election funds, his comment, "It's dues-paying time," was more matter-of-fact than cynical.

Even locals of Canadian unions, which Joseph thought would oppose the industry, refrained, as they too were controlled by American unions which certainly had little to gain if prices of drugs were lowered. They understood all too well that their wages would be jeopardized.

Everything was proceeding according to plan, except for one unsettling incident from an unexpected source. As part of his tactics, Joseph had written a letter to the editors of all the medical journals and other trade publications representing related fields. It was a stock letter: "Dear [personalized salutation]: As you know, we are engaged in one of the most desperate struggles ever mounted against the industry by the government and the forces of socialism. We need your help. I know the last thing the busy editor of a fine journal dedicated to the fostering of better medical care needs is another task, but we implore you to help us, to prepare a brief in defence of the patent act, as it stands. If we lose there is little point in spending a lot of money to advertise and, without advertising, journals like yours — so necessary to bring information to doctors — will be unable to continue to provide such service . . . ."

Hamish Jarvis, editor of one magazine, telephoned Joseph at his apartment. He introduced himself and then said, "Let me give it to you straight, Mr. Mann. I've just been fired. Without cause. And if you don't do something about it, I'll write a brief to the committee that will blow the whole thing wide open. I'll sit down with Grant MacDonald and tell him things about this industry that even he doesn't know." There was a harsh, almost insane sound to his voice, and Joseph intuitively knew that this wasn't an empty threat.

Hamish Jarvis had just been given a month's notice and a letter of reference from his publisher praising him in glowing terms. All he could think of was what would he tell his wife. He was fifty and had also been fired from his last job. He was terrified. So much so he felt like going out and getting drunk, but that terrified him too. He had been around that bend. If he couldn't fight it, he would call an AA brother.

And he was angry, not sorry for himself. He had done a good job. In one year, a bad year economically, who could have done it better? But not enough for those high-powered Americans who owned the magazine. He put his head on his hands and the tears fell from his eyes. He didn't bother to brush them away. Damn mush alcoholic brain. He had served the industry all his life and now they were throwing him out. No way.

"Hello . . . hello," Joseph said. "Are you all right?"

"I'm just fine. Now what are you going to do about it?"

"I'm still not clear what you mean."

"Look, mister. I've been fired. Without cause. I know everything about drug manufacturing. I've been there. I've been a detail man. I've worked in hospitals. I've called on doctors. I know about drug safety, about marketing. I know all the tricks that are used to push drugs."

"What can I do to help?"

"I told you. Get me a job. In the industry. I know the business better than anyone. You can check me out. Sure I was a drunk. But I haven't touched the stuff in five years. Member of AA. So help me God."

"Let me see what I can do."

"You better. I've got one month."

Joseph called Kendall and asked him about Hamish Jarvis.

"No one will hire him any more, Joseph. He was a bad drunk and the industry has given up on him."

"But he says he's with AA."

"He's been given chances before and slipped back. I'll ask around, but I think our best hope is that the hearings end before he's actually on the street."

With that in mind, Joseph immediately called Heister and had him force the American owner of the Canadian trade journal to give him a longer notice, at least until the hearings were over. He then called Jarvis, explained what he had done. "That gives us more time to find something at the right level for you." It seemed to suffice.

Everything was in order, Joseph reflected as he listened to the debate, except for Grant MacDonald and Dr. Lewison. He had not found a way to soften the attacks by Dr. Lewison. During each session Lewison led a well-organized attack on the industry with research provided by Douglas Clark and INTEGRAL. Twice now Joseph had lunched with him, only to run into a stone wall of an old-fashioned sixty-year-old M.D., from the small Ontario Town of Cornwall, who was almost pathologically opposed to the "big interests."

"Hey, how are you making out with that bird?" Kendall asked.

Despite Kendall being a hard worker who had helped him personally — he had leased and furnished Joseph's office having

92

it ready for him the day he arrived in Ottawa, had hired a woman who turned out to be an excellent secretary (although he was surprised that Joseph stipulated an older woman), and had even found Joseph a satisfactory, furnished one-bedroom apartment — still Joseph couldn't like him: He found him obnoxious.

But from Kendall's remark, Joseph wondered how obvious was his fascination for Violetta. Often he would catch himself gazing at the back of her blond head knowing she felt him looking at her; sometimes she would turn and they would smile. And often he would wait outside the committee room in the corridor until she came so he could say, "good morning," or simply meet her eyes. It was adolescent he knew. But as much as he wanted to ask Violetta out again, he hadn't. The only time he had seen her outside the committee room was when she had agreed to examine his mother. Joseph had asked her because his mother refused to see any more male doctors, possibly equating all males with her husband and his ruination of her life.

He had driven them all to the hospital, his mother, his sister, and Tom. He signed his mother in, told the admitting nurse that she had an appointment to see Dr. Norgela, and felt a curious pride when he heard Violetta being summoned on the floor speaker. At first he didn't recognize her as she walked down the hospital corridor. Her hair was pulled severely back and fastened with a clip, and she wore horn-rimmed glasses, a white coat, and solid brogues. A stethoscope hung partially out of her pocket. So different from the girl, the young lady, at the hearings. And notwithstanding the lovely smile on her face as she stretched out her hand to shake his, he was aware of her professionalism.

He stood slightly apart from his mother, sister, and brother-in-law, unused to the family grouping, uncomfortable with it, almost ashamed at being associated with their commonness, their inferiority, and then ashamed of that. Yet he was obviously different. No one looking at the trio would take them as a family, Joseph towering six-feet-four, dressed in the latest fashion, everything perfect — hair, shoes shined, the way he carried himself, so at odds with the two dumpy women and the lumpy man awry in their working-class attempt to emulate in style and dress what was decreed but impossible to achieve with the cheaper clothes and shoes they were forced to buy.

His mother was ill and vague, but Mary seemed overwhelmed in a different way, like many of the poor confronted by the institutions of society — frightened and yet prepared to trust herself to them. Joseph knew that this organization existed for him, had a picture in his head of the logic behind it, was at home in its systems and routines. Knew how to use it for his benefit.

"Mother always took so much care about what she wore, and always kept her hair combed until just a little while ago," his sister reported to the doctor, her nasal twang embarrassing Joseph.

"Please come into the examination room with her, "Violetta said.

"You two men can wait here," she said indicating the chairs lined against the wall along the corridor.

Joseph watched her walk off between his mother and sister and shook his head as if to clear it from the feelings he felt. He and Tom sat and waited.

Concerned that Joseph's mother might not take to her — old people often resented having a young doctor examine them — Violetta was especially sensitive to the old woman, taking her time, not rushing, smiling constantly.

"She don' clean house no more, don' want to meet anyone, don' even wan' to go out of bed in the morning," Joseph's sister said. Violetta was aware of how the moment she was out of Joseph's presence, her language became sloppier and she dropped her *t*'s and *g*'s. And she remembered how embarrassed she used to be when her mother spoke English in a store or to her teachers, her voice guttural, heavily accented, thick and coarse. But in Lithuanian her voice was soft, young, and lilting.

"And complainin' all the time that she don' get no sleep, that the cramps in her legs give her no peace, none at all, poor old thing."

"Is she on medication of any kind?"

Mary took a bottle of pills out of her purse and handed them to

94

the doctor. "For the pressure."

Looking at the pills, it was clear to Violetta that the doctor had prescribed 50 milligrams of hydrochorthiazide every morning. Checking the old lady's blood pressure, Violetta found that it was remarkably high. "Do you remember what your pressure was when you were given these pills?" There was no answer.

"I have it written down," Mary said searching her handbag. "Here," she said pulling out a scrap of paper. "Two hundred twenty and one ten."

Violetta felt the old woman's arm and leg muscles. "There does appear to be muscle tenderness." When she tapped the old lady's knees, they were inactive. But there was a flicker in the muscles themselves as though the muscles were jumping in an asynchronous way.

"She complains that her heart beats extra fast sometimes," Mary said as if not believing it, regarding it as the peevishness of an old lady.

Violetta checked the old lady's pulse again and discovered the extra beats that hadn't shown the first time. "She's right."

"I just didn't listen. I should have listened," Mary said, allowing herself a few tears. "She always talkin' about dying and how everyone she ever knew is dead. Says she has more friends underground than above. I dunno. She used to be jokin' and laughin', always doin' something for the boys, my boys, and always in the garden. She had a real green thumb, she did, yes."

Suspecting that the depression might be related in part to the reduction in the serum potassium level, a result of potassium loss from the kidneys due to the diuretic she was taking to lower her blood pressure, Violetta took a sample of blood and sent it to the biochemistry lab. "I marked it rush, but even so there'll be a wait of an hour or so. Do you mind waiting outside while I see other patients?"

Two hours later Violetta came along with his mother and Mary. "Joseph, you'll be relieved to know that I think it should be easy enough to get your mother back to her old self." To his embarrassment, Mary started to sniff into her handkerchief. "I believe your mother's depression is due to her low serum potassium. The reading is only 2.5 milli-equivalents per litre." Then she explained the treatment she planned. "First, we'll reduce the diuretic, the blood pressure pill, to half a tablet every second day. I'll call your doctor to tell him you've been in and what I——"

"Don't want to see that man," his mother spoke for the third time that night.

"We've got to watch your blood pressure, then we'll replace the potassium loss." She directed her remarks to Mary. "Now Mary, you'll have to make sure your mother drinks a lot of orange juice every day, and she must eat several bananas and apricots as well... everyday. I mean it," she said, suddenly severe. "Keep her salt low. Then I've prescribed potassium chloride tablets," she said writing out a prescription. "A 250 milligram dose. Your mother should take eight a day at first. If they make her sick, let me know immediately and I'll put her on something else." She smiled and indicated they could leave.

"That's all?" Joseph asked. "And she'll be all right?"

"I think so."

He felt a rush of warmth and like a fool the tears almost came to his eyes. Why? He didn't even like his mother. "Thank you, Violetta."

On the way back to his mother's house, his sister said, "Young to be a doctor, isn't she? I wonder if she knows what she's doing. I've never been to a woman doctor before. I wouldn't go to one myself, you know."

"She's a nice girl," his mother suddenly said. And Joseph felt pleased. Ridiculous. He was snapped out of his reverie by the tough Dr. Lewison who had risen to speak.

"Some years ago my wife had to take largactil. Here's a drug selling in France for three cents a tablet and in Canada for twenty cents a tablet. In his excellent book, *Therapeutic Nightmare*, Morton Mintz quotes many such examples. I refer you to page three fifty-two, where three companies were selling a drug for one hundred and seventy dollars a thousand tablets, while another was selling the same drug under the generic name for only twenty dollars and ninety-five cents a thousand."

"You'll get what you want," Flanagan interrupted. "Headlines

96

across Canada tomorrow screaming that drug companies make one thousand per cent mark-up."

That Flanagan was worth his weight in gold, Joseph thought.

During the committee hearings he would aggressively question anyone who attacked the industry, exposing the fallacies of their arguments time and time again. And he managed to highlight the positive statements of those in favour.

"If the shoe fits wear it," Lewison countered Flanagan's outburst. "But I assure you headlines were not my intention," Lewison continued. "Part of the reason is the cost of promotion. I note in the brief by the last pharmaceutical firm that a drug costs eleven and a half cents to manufacture, only two and a half cents for research, one and a half cent for labour, and eleven cents to market. I would like to show you what goes into that eleven cents to promote." He lifted a grocery store carton from the floor and dumped the contents on the table in front of him. Joseph could see the reporters craning to see what was there, alert and ready to take notes.

"Here are some of the items sent to my office by drug companies" — and he held each item up as he named them — a shoe cleaner, dozens of prescription pads, a measuring tape, half a dozen letter openers, kleenex — "presumably to blow my nose until the infection gets better, matches" — kits to repair ladies' stockings, tourniquets, a practice golf ball and tees, hundreds of calendars, plus hundreds of actual samples of drugs." He sipped a glass of water. "I can cite an example of a detail man who came to my office and as he detailed the product, I said, 'Is not that the same as so and so?' 'Yes Doctor,' he said, 'except for the dietary factor.' 'What do you mean by the dietary factor?' I asked. 'If you don't buy my brand, I don't eat,' he said." Lewison looked along the line of fellow committee members. "Gentlemen, to me there is an excessive amount of junk that is advertised to an intelligent profession. One way to cut the costs of drugs is to stop companies from engaging in wasteful and insulting promotion."

Dean Sorenson asked if he could speak as a representative of the industry. It was one of the rare occasions he would do so, and when he rose his manner was so distinguished that he automatically engaged everyone's attention. "Gentlemen, I admit there are excesses in promotion of our products, as there are of all products in our society. And if this hearing does nothing else, it will have served to make us aware of this waste, and I can assure you, our Association will itself force a cutback. Yet, I ask you to consider this: The most miraculous life-saving drug is useless to the sick until physicians know it exists, how it should be used, its success and failures and what precautions are connected with it. Communicating this vital data is the function of pharmaceutical promotion, through the detail man, through advertising of one kind or another. May I quote from the United States Food and Drug commissioner. 'We believe that good medical advertising is essential to good health in America today.' The educational value of journal advertising and all forms of labelling is greater than the dollar outlay for it.

"Sir Derrick Dunlop, chairman of the British Committee on Safety for Drugs, said — and I quote, 'It is probable that without mass-marketing techniques, which are so often bitterly assailed, few of the drugs on which modern medical practice depends would be affordable at all.' Everyone my age," Sorenson continued, "remembers that all a doctor used to have was a good bedside manner, and that was how he was judged by the patient. With the drug armentarium he has today, not only does the doctor rarely have to visit, but the patient rarely has to take to his bed.

"Finally, let me read from an article in *Pravda*, 'The few new drugs on the market are not widely used because either the workers in the medical field and the doctors do not even know of their existence or have only a faint knowledge of their possible uses.' Again, if I might add a personal note. I opened up Russia for my company and was able to sell products made in the United States, in fact, arranged a licencing agreement for them to produce one of our products, so I have first-hand knowledge of what I say. And promotion relates to the whole question of patents. For those who question the role of private research and the patents which make it possible, two undeniable facts stand out. The USSR, which has made great advances in physical medicine, has produced no new products in all the years of its existence. Italy, another major manufacturing country, has produced no new products since Mussolini abolished patents in 1937. Yet in the plastics field, where Italy does have patent protection, it has become a leader. Our industry is a world. A world of its own. In it there are scientists, medical doctors, druggists, marketing men, production workers, engineers, botanists combing the primitive jungles of South America searching for rare herbs, pharmacologists, biochemists — right now there are experiments of all sorts taking place all over the world. All these people are joined in one goal — to cure the sick, to relieve pain. All those people are interdependent and all are depending upon those of us in the position of leadership to keep their world from falling apart, and it *can* fall apart if Canada changes the patent laws."

Working beside Sorenson, Joseph had come to admire him, but also to realize that his thinking was too rigid for this struggle. It became increasingly clear why Heister had not wanted Sorenson to lead the industry lobby on his own. Both the supreme engineer and the "ugly American," he had started with the Heister firm as a production technician, had risen to plant manager, supervisor of construction of plants in foreign countries, and president of the entire international operation. Joseph regarded him as the perfect example of the self-made man. Sorenson personified the American dream. And Joseph was aware too of his feeling that if Sorenson could make it, he could too — especially now.

Joseph found himself studying Sorenson. He spoke many languages fluently, was travelled and sophisticated, and yet it seemed as if he lived in another century. He upheld all the middle-class puritan ethic ideas, believing that a girl should be a virgin when she married; that the anglo-saxon (he was of Dutch descent) was the highest form of man, no other people could be trusted; that engineering was the only profession that provided a truth you could depend on; that the British parliamentary system was the best, but the American "way of life" was without doubt the finest in the world and anyone who disagreed was either a hippie or a commie.

At the second meeting with Heister in New York, Sorenson had been waxing idealistically about the industry when Heister had snapped, in a way that seemed out of character to Joseph, "Let's stick to realities. Dean gets all romantic about our industry. But I'll tell you what we're about. Joseph, were you ever so constipated, so bound you'd give anything to have one healthy crap? Well, one hundred years ago, my grandfather started the family fortune with a recipe that would loosen you up. Started this business with an old Ojibway remedy. Later he stole a process for making it into a pill you could depend on to dissolve in your body every time. Believe me, that was a step forward. Half those old pills came out the same way they went in, intact. And that's how Heister Pharmaceutical began, from a pile of shit. The other firms? The same way. Laxatives, stomach powder, and dyes. Snake oil and horse liniment, and it's not much different today."

"For God's sake, Bob, there's more to it than that," Sorenson said.

"Right, add sex and syphilis. The desire of some European ladies of the nobility to outdo each other in their pretty-coloured dresses led to the search for new dyes, which in turn enabled Koch and Erlich to stain tissue and in the process found modern chemotherapy. But shitting and fucking, overeating and pride is what it was all about, and if you throw in today's mood-altering drugs, it's still the whole story. And profit. Don't forget profit."

Yet, despite the fact that Sorenson took himself and the industry so seriously, or perhaps because of it, or because he was obviously so knowledgeable, there was a hush among the committee members and the audience when he sat down. He had cleanly and effectively demolished the argument against what Lewison had called "wasteful promotion."

The next day Joseph searched Grant's column in vain for a reference to Sorenson's remarks. Instead, he read with mounting anger, "A recent survey has shown that prices for five identical prescriptions for five common drugs varied by as much as 164 per cent in five pharmacies polled in Toronto. Similar sur-

100

veys in Montreal, New York City, Chicago, and Los Angeles revealed the same variances. These differences do not mean the public can buy inexpensive drugs by shopping around. The price differential is created because some pharmacies have marked up drugs so that they make excessively high profits, while for the rest, the markup is designed to yield moderately high profits." The column contained a box comparing the prices of a number of generic as against brand name drugs. "The drug industry and the retail pharmacist make exorbitant profits. The doctor who is usually in a different wage bracket than his patients rarely thinks of the price of the drug. The drug industry also wastes a fortune each year in promotion and everyone is involved in this disgusting profiteering, governments and medical professions included."

Joseph put the paper down angrily and dialled Grant's number at the press gallery. "Grant, I read today's column. You're way off base. I'd like to come up and see you."

"Okay, but I'm busy until after nine. Come up then."

It had been a bad day for Grant. He had lunched with Louise at her apartment, made love, and was now suffering from acute guilt. Guilt toward Thelma as well as toward Louise. He had never actually told Louise he would leave Thelma; perhaps he might have voiced a wish it could be so in moments of passion. He had never consciously misled her. But today she had pressed him to leave Thelma, told him that he would never write books as long as he continued to play the role of husband, father, and political guru. The last was said contemptuously. She well-knew how to stick it to him, knew that in his heart of hearts he still wanted to write novels, that he had taken a job years ago saying to himself that it was only until he saved enough money so that he could quit and write what he wanted to write. Of course, it had never happened. Nor would it, she claimed. His work was not creative nor did he have any real influence for good as he supposed. When he put the phone down after inviting Joseph to come up, he thought, she's wrong about that as she'll see. The one thing Grant prided himself on was his power — the power of the media — to shape events for the better. He was an old-fashioned do-gooder.

McLuhan's views on television and the global village not only provided Grant with an understanding of his role in life by elevating the status of communicator, but Grant interpreted "the medium is the message" quite literally, and used his television shows to confront and engage his audience.

Some time before the hearings began, J.O. McKinnon asked him whether he could create a TV special that would communicate the complexities of the pharmaceutical industry in a way ordinary people could understand. Grant had spoken to the producers in Toronto who controlled public affairs programming for the Canadian Broadcasting Corporation, and they had agreed. It only remained to entice the drug industry executives to expose themselves before the television cameras. And now his friend had taken the bait. Grant supposed he should feel more like a bastard, but he didn't. He was going to use Joseph's trust, but Joseph had been sent to use him, Grant was sure of that. Besides, he had warned Joseph to drop the assignment and he had not.

To be posted to the press gallery was one of the senior reporting jobs in the country. Here were the correspondents of the world's largest and most influential newspapers, The *New York Times, Pravda,* the London *Times,* all the wire services, and most of the large Canadian dailies. On the third floor of the Centre Block, the press gallery, or "hot room" as the correspondents called it, was located at the south end of the House of Commons, and reserved exclusively for reporters. Here on the rim they made notes of debates and speeches and judged with trained eyes the performances of politicians. It was only a sixty second dash to their working room if a hot story broke. Anything but prepossessing, the working room itself was nothing more than a large room filled from one end to the other with row on row of steel-gray desks, each with its own typewriter, a bank of teletype machines, radio lines, and other equipment for the instant transmission of news.

There were other parliamentary galleries, two at either end for the general public who often had to stand in line to get in when an important issue was being discussed, and galleries for members of the House of Commons to bring their constituents to when they visited Ottawa, and for senators and other dignitaries, all of which were reached through various doors guarded by officers in uniform. But a member of the press gallery had complete freedom of the Houses of Parliament. He could make long distance telephone calls free, could eat in the parliamentary dining room, could come and go at any hour of the day or night. And after a parliamentary reporter had been in the building for several years he developed a camaraderie with others of the parliamentary staff — lawyers and experts on parliamentary procedure, secretaries, pages, the various police forces (there were three; guarding the outside of the buildings and the grounds were the Royal Canadian Mounted Police, and the Commons and Senate each had its separate forces), M.P.'s and senators. One never knew where a leak or lead for an important story might come from.

As Joseph walked the few blocks from his office to the press gallery, he realized that this meeting would be the confrontation with Grant he had put off for too long. And yet he had been heartened by the friendly tone in Grant's voice. Perhaps it was clearly a question of Grant's bias stemming from being misinformed. That could be corrected.

Walking up the central path he was struck immediately by the cleanness of the air compared with the smell of New York. And a quietness, almost a feeling of being in a vacuum. And then he realized that what was missing was the constant roar of New York traffic. For a moment if felt good to be in Ottawa. Ottawa was home. But then he looked at the Parliament buildings and gasped. The imposing silence of the gothic structures, church-like in the soft, silver glow of the moon, seemed to have a meaning, a durability that transcended the stone and mortar. This was the institution he was assulting. He shivered despite the warm summer's night.

As he entered, an officer approached him to ask what he wanted. Unless Parliament was sitting it wasn't usual for anyone to enter after hours. Joseph expalined that he had an appointment with Grant MacDonald in the press gallery and then he recognized the man, or thought he did. "Luther? Is that you Luther?" Luther Schneider, one of their gang in grade seven, but so fat. He had been lean and tough then. From a poor family, always hungry. "I'm Joseph Mann. Remember? At school? York Street school?" A quick, embarrassed smile flitted across his broad face. "Yes sir. Hello. I thought I seen you here for the hearings."

Joseph stuck out his hand and they shook hands and he felt that Luther was uncomfortable at his expression of equality. And was he being patronizing? There were ribbons on Luther's uniform, medals from the war. Wild that Luther, who had always been in trouble with the police, was a policeman. "Mr. MacDonald's in the gallery, sir, I seen him there myself." And he escorted Joseph up in the elevator.

Demoralized by the "sir", Joseph stopped himself from saying, "we must get together for a beer and reminisce." Impossible to bridge the gap. "Thank you," he said. Who would have thought Luther would be doing what he was doing? Or me doing what I'm doing? Or Grant?

As Joseph walked down the corridor and turned into the "hot room" he felt very strongly that he was on Grant's turf.

"Cock of the south," Grant shouted, and an object that turned out to be a wrapped sandwich came lofting through the air.

"Cock of the north," Joseph yelled and leaped high in the air, managing to grab it. It had been their signal that a pass was coming when they had played on the basketball team at high school.

Grant picked up a wastepaper basket from the floor, jumped on top of a desk and held it out as if it were a basket. "Take a shot. Shoot."

Executing a graceful manoeuvre, Joseph faked his imaginary opponent out of position and looped the sandwich sideways over his head. His aim, as it had always been, was dead on; the sandwich soared in an unerring arc and would have landed in the centre of the basket, when to his dismay, Grant moved it, and it fell with a dull thud.

"Lost your touch buddy. Getting long in the tooth."

"Hey Jean, *un verre de scotch avec de l'eau pour mon ami,*" Grant called to a man at the far end of the room. "*Et pour moi, la même chose.*" Then seeing the bewilderment on Joseph's face, he laughed. "Jean is our parliamentary bootlegger, but he only serves if the order is in French. His contribution to bilingualism. Without him we'd all be very dry."

As they walked toward the reporters' sitting room through a door at the far end of the room, Grant explained that in the original House there had been three bars for members, but it had burned down. As the new one had been designed and built during prohibition, to avoid controversy, the architects left out any provision for a bar. As members were not noted for their sobriety, from Canada's first prime minister on down, Jean's father, who had been a senior parliamentary page when the new Parliament opened, had organized a shuttle service, sending young pages by streetcar to Hull on the Quebec side to buy liquor for the members. In time, even though half the pages were involved in the shuttle service, the demand for liquor could not be satisfied, so a small area back of the "hot room" was quietly stocked with liquor, an inventory as large as that carried by many a small hotel.

Jean brought their drinks. Relaxing on one of the large, soft leather chairs, Joseph said, "Can we get to the point now, Grant. We might as well have it out as best we can."

"What's troubling you, Joseph?"

"Grant, I think your columns are dangerous in that they frighten people who are sick, people who might not take the medicine they need. I don't like to say this, but some of your stuff reads like what used to be called yellow journalism."

Grand stiffened. "Easy Joseph. Never say that to me. All my material is well-researched."

"Is it really? What about today's column? You mentioned nothing of what Sorenson had to say yesterday in defence of disseminating medical information."

"What did he say . . . that, yes, some firms waste money on promotion, that they're bad boys? Listen Joseph," Grant's voice rose, "this isn't some ordinary management consulting job where you reorganize the production line to turn out more shoe polish. This is an industry that sells drugs to people who don't need them, often drugs that aren't safe, often with side effects hidden, and always at unconscionable prices. Don't tell me about research. Have you read the Kefauver reports?"

"Old hat Grant. That was years ago. Doctors and public alike know that a drug potent enough to cure is also strong enough to have potentially dangerous side effects. You sound as you did when you belonged to the Communist party. We happen to live in a capitalist, free-enterprise system. Profit isn't either a sin or illegal."

"Joseph, I get a crawly feeling when you talk like that. What the hell has happened to you down there in New York? You seem to have become a caricature. Doesn't matter what the machine does so long as it works. All hail the new human. I need another drink . . . you?"

"Might as well," Joseph said somberly.

While Grant was going to collect them Joseph realized that this was turning into an argument. That was stupid of him. "Listen, Grant," he said when he returned with two more scotches, "turn off your bias for a moment. Let's try to talk facts. Today, when a doctor writes a prescription, in seven out of ten cases it's for a drug not developed before 1950. With the modern broad spectrum antibiotics and other miracle drugs, the ten biggest disease killers of the past, including pneumonia, tuberculosis, and diphtheria, now account for less than two per cent of all deaths. Grant, the industry has been a godsend to people living in tropical countries. And think of the childhood diseases that no longer terrify us. Infantile paralysis — remember one year there was an epidemic and we couldn't go to the Annual Ottawa Exhibition — whooping cough, measles, smallpox, scarlet fever, and meningitis. Did you know that the industry has had a hand in developing cures for all of these, either by industry scientists,

106

or by grants to university researchers, or by developing the engineering necessary for mass production? I've studied this situation. If you would only talk to our people, visit several plants, see the research, see the quality control processes for yourself, I'm certain your view would change. I know the industry isn't perfect, but it's not as bad as you make out either."

Appearing to reflect on what Joseph had said, Grant toyed with his glass, got up, and walked up and down the room. Then he turned as if he had just made a major decision. "Tell you what. I'll do all that. I'll meet your people. Research the thing. The whole bit. On one condition. If it looks like there's enough material there I want to do a television show, live, providing your people will come and be interviewed on camera. And I mean real, deep probing. I'm not interested in a puff piece."

"Are you serious?" This was far more than Joseph had hoped. But then Grant had always been fair, could always see two sides.

"Before you get too turned on, you better check with your employers. They might disagree, might not want to come on." For a moment Grant almost hoped they would refuse, but that was childish. One had to have the courage to act according to one's beliefs.

"We'll come on gladly. We have nothing to hide," Joseph said confidently.

[9]

The people of Babylon do not suffer leprosy because they eat beets, drink beer and clean themselves by bathing in the waters of the Euphrates.

(Rabbi Chanina, *The Talmud*)

Robert Heister opened the door of his office and said to Joseph and Sorenson, who had been waiting in the Little Museum, "Come on in fellows." He noticed Sorenson limping. "Leg bothering you today?"

"A little." It angered Sorenson that at moments when he needed his strength most his body let him down. His opposition to the idea of a television show produced by Grant MacDonald had forced this top level meeting with Heister. He and Joseph had flown in on the 8:00 A.M. plane and were booked back later in the day. Limping over to the sofa he sat down with relief. He had broken his leg skiing several years ago and it had never healed properly; although he liked to play two sets of tennis every day, he did so with pain. He knew he would soon have to stop playing for good. It irritated him that his body was decaying so rapidly. At the same rate as the country, he thought grimly.

To bolster his argument that Grant could not be trusted, he had brought a sheaf of Grant's columns, two written after the suggestion for the TV documentary. "Listen, I'll read at random." Slipping on his reading glasses, Sorenson was suddenly

108

aware of how old, how anachronistic they made him look, so like a character out of Dickens. And it occurred to him that perhaps he was being personal about Mann and not objective at all, perhaps still resentful that Mann had been hired — in effect to replace him at this and future government-industry confronta-tations. It had been a great, personal shock when Heister had told him earlier, "Dean, we want you in Ottawa, need you there in the role of advisor, but we have decided to retain Joseph Mann to manage, perhaps co-ordinate is a better word, the industry's lobbying activity in Canada."

And although with stock options and bonuses over the years he was not without power — as a director of the Heister firm he held a position second only to Robert Heister himself — he nevertheless had allowed himself to acquiesce to Heister's de-mands. The only alternative was to call a Directors' meeting, at which he would have lost face as well.

He had known many men of his age, men at the top of the hill, kings of their castles, who had been tumbled by the dirty rascals. He'd done some fair pushing himself, and had never under-stood until now why everyone fought so bitterly to keep his perch, making such fools of themselves in the process, going with such lack of grace. There was usually nothing personal in the struggle, almost always it was a function of time. But now it was happening to him. Not only was he still in his prime — although almost sixty-five — and not ready, but the industry needed him, could not do without his accumulated knowledge in what might be its crucial struggle for survival.

When he had finished reading the columns, he asked, "How can we continue to trust this man?"

"We have to educate him," Joseph replied. "Besides, those columns could have been written before Grant agreed to study our side."

"I don't trust him," Sorenson said. "You're aware we have no control. The way it works up there with the Canadian Broadcast-ing Corporation, which is one of their national networks, is that you can't even see any public affairs show before it's televised. And you certainly have no rights at all to control the material or the slant of the show. It's too damned dangerous."

"There's nothing unusual about that. It works the same with the networks here. And if *Time* magazine or any other publication wants to do a major story, do you think you have any control? It's not an advertisement you're buying. Either we believe that we have enough rightness on our side that if we get the message across to the majority of people it will help our cause, or we're engaged in the worst kind of hypocrisy possible. It seems to me it's time the industry grew up. We're not completely without sin. So what? No one is, and the public understands that. Our objective in the program should be to show just how difficult the whole problem of discovery and manufacture of medicines are. Besides, the show is live — or most of it will be. Surely with you being interviewed, Dean, and industry scientists, and if the screen shows the kind of machines and technology the industry uses, it can't fail to impress the public."

"Normally I don't like to take these kind of chances," Heister said. "Joseph, are you sure Grant will be fair, will present both sides?"

"If we can get him the right material, he'll read it. If we can get him to visit one of the plants and see for himself the research and the quality control, he will report it. Grant is first and foremost a reporter. He's not out to get anyone. Now he is reporting what he knows. When he gets a correct set of facts, he'll report those."

"If the program is fair it will be good for us. If it isn't, it will hurt. You were right in your idea of how to prevent Flanagan being thrown off the committee" — Joseph was startled that Sorenson had reported the incident — "so I'll go with you this time, but it's your responsibility."

Elated as he was at winning his point, Joseph began to have doubts. He wondered if he were kidding himself. If the program turned out to be unfair, harmful to the industry, he knew his associates would be delighted. Obviously, Sorenson would be number one, followed by Kendall and Flanagan. He had forced them all to do what he wanted; humiliated them in a way and he had the feeling they were all waiting for him to make one mistake. He must explain to Grant how exposed he was.

Sitting alone at the bar at Kennedy airport waiting for his plane — Sorenson having elected to stay in New York to see friends and clear up some problems connected with Heister International — Joseph felt worried and depressed. Why the hell had he stuck his neck out? It hadn't been necessary. A television program, even if it extolled the virtues of the industry, wasn't crucial to the outcome of the hearings. Blunting Grant's attacks, or turning their negative impact into a positive one, was valuable; but he didn't believe it was as important as Heister did. Then why had he gone along with Grant's suggestion? And then he answered the question himself. It was the old problem. He wanted, needed, Grant's friendship. Had to prove to Grant that he was right and good and worthy. He was still the poor Irish kid with the drunk father grateful to have Grant MacDonald as a buddy. Shit. Would he never get over his beginnings? Not very professional, he thought wryly.

He was lonely and filled with angst, and he wanted to call Violetta. He resisted the mood for another drink, and then called.

"Where are you calling from?" Violetta asked, the sound of her voice bringing its own kind of instant peace to him. "New York, I'm just catching a plane out. Will you have dinner with me tonight?"

She laughed. "What happens to you in New York that makes you call me?" she asked remembering the tenderness of the last phone call.

"I'll tell you some day. But will you? I know we agreed not to see each other, but say yes. Please."

"Yes," there was a happiness in her voice. "But here at my place. You must be exhausted."

"I'll bring scotch."

"Make it vodka."

"Of course, my lovely Lithuanian."

"And I'll get two huge steaks."

"I'll bring them."

"You haven't time," she laughed. "You bring the wine."

"Any preference?"

111

"Surprise me."

All said excitedly like children planning their first picnic. He put the phone down in wonderment when he heard the boarding call for his plane.

When she opened the door, he kissed her gently, taking her by surprise, closed his eyes, and felt absolved. When their lips touched the ugliness of New York vanished. It was possible once again to feel like a human being.

"Hi," she said shakily at the unexpected intensity of his need revealed in the touch of mouths. Wanting reassurance that she hadn't misinterpreted, she searched his eyes as they opened, surprising a reality of being, exposed for an instant only before it rushed back to the safety of its darkness.

He made martinis and they sat in the living room, a shyness settling on them after the audaciousness of the kiss. He met Mylita, Violetta's eight-year-old daughter, flaxen-haired and blue-eyed, the magic of the mother in the daughter's face. When it was time for her to go to bed, she insisted that Joseph come and kiss her goodnight. For a moment, as he sat on the bed and leaned over her and held her, his careful structure cracked and he had to leave her room hurriedly or make a fool of himself, feeling the loneliness and sense of time lost with his own children, never to be recovered.

He sipped his martini and listened to Violetta talk to her daughter in Lithuanian, wishing he could be within that warmth, felt from the texture of the sounds. Something he had never experienced with his mother. Was it only the difference of the sound of the language, or something deeper, some coldness, some inability bred into the anglo-saxon mother?

Returning to the living room, Violetta took out a cigarette, Joseph realizing slowly that she was waiting for him to light it for her.

"You believe in the feminine mystique?"

"I'm liberated. A living example. But I still like little attentions. Why not?"

"Light your cigarette, hold open the door of the car for you, all that. You want it both ways."

"If I can get it," she smiled mischieviously.

"I like your place."

She lived in a neat two-bedroom apartment on the fifth floor of a new apartment building. "It's got a sauna, gym, and a day care centre for children. Who could ask for anything more?" And then they lapsed into silence again, withdrawing from the first closeness. "What's troubling you, Joseph?"

"Nothing," he said, her directness taking him by surprise. "I'm sorry I was so into myself."

But she knew men, had always known men — their needs, their fears — and she knew he needed to open up, to talk. To make it easier for him, and also because she wanted him to know her, she spoke of herself.

Some of the story Grant had told him: "Married to a steel-worker at eighteen, you know the type. Works hard, drinks beer, watches TV every night until it's time to go to bed, wants to fuck, gets off fast then turns over on his side with his back to her, sleeping heavily with all the appropriate sound effects — belches, farts, and snores."

Discovering herself to be pregnant with her second child, she left her husband and with ten dollars in her pocket got a room at the Y.W.C.A. The next day she met Louise who was checking a government employment office. They hit it off and Violetta moved to Ottawa where she lived with Louise who loaned her the money for her abortion. And when Violetta confessed that she had always wanted to be a doctor, Louise encouraged her and somehow, with various part-time jobs, she had put herself through. She got a divorce, and after two years her husband agreed to let her have the child back.

Strong woman, Joseph thought. Incredible human.

The phone rang, her mother calling long distance. Strange that Violetta seemed even more animated when speaking in her own language. "My mother worries about me," she explained. "Calls twice a week. Always asks, 'when are you going to get married?' Can't understand what it means for me to be a doctor. Like most women my mother has been tricked into believing that

113

they can fulfil themselves only through marriage and children. And my stepfather is worse. For him a woman is a possession, a receptacle, a container for childbearing, although he refused to have a child in Canada. Didn't want a Canadian child. Didn't like them."

"It's really beautiful to see someone so close to their mother."

How to explain to Joseph that as Mylita was hers, she was her mother's. That when she was at home, her mother still wanted to soap and scrub her back, and while she sat on the edge of the tub and rubbed her shoulders, white and young, they would speak of life and her mother would try to understand, but wanting to feel the body that had come out of her through love, and that man lying dead forever in a far-off field. How to explain that though Violetta had left the Lithuanian community, how proud her mother was that she still spoke and wrote Lithuanian so well, and that she was bringing up Mylita the same. Violetta attended a Lithuanian school, learned their ancient history, took part in dancing and singing groups and travelled to other cities for Lithuanian celebrations. How to explain how proud her mother was when at Christmas Mass, she walked down the aisle of the Catholic church beside her for all the Lithuanian community to see this daughter.

And as Joseph listened to her different world he thought of his own crabbed childhood, except for Grant. Thought of the hardness of his father and of his mother's people, opening up only when they got drunk and then either to vomit or vent their rage in senseless violence against a hostile world. And he the same.

She told him that she was certain the only reason her mother married her stepfather was to have someone to look after her. "There were rats where we lived and my mother had to go to work earlier than school started, and she would leave me in our room sitting on the kitchen table with instructions not to get down until the hands of the clock pointed to the numbers when I could run to school."

Her mother and stepfather had worked in a factory, and saved, and like so many thousands of ethnic people, had bought

114

a house, and all three of them lived in the attic and rented out rooms until the house was paid for, and even then they stayed in the attic because her stepfather bought another house until now he owned fifteen houses. And he had a variety store. And, though he was worth over half a million dollars, he still kept the store and fixed his houses himself.

And Joseph thought of the difference between the small businessman and Heister, or himself.

She told him about how she struggled to get through medical school, about her schemes to get men to take her out for dinner so she could eat. She told him of taking whatever a man wanted to give, and in return in most cases giving her company only. She hadn't been like a lot of girls going to bed for her supper, but she had indicated she might, which in some ways she now thought was more dishonest. Some of the furniture in this room had been presents from hopefuls, who rarely succeeded. It was cheap and she was over it now. But she had done it. Or rather, as she looked back, a woman with her name had done it; the woman she was then had done it. "What's troubling you, Joseph?" she asked again. "Did something happen in New York today?"

"Yes ... no ... I don't know. This time, last time, the detail is unimportant. But Violetta, I sometimes feel I'm no longer in control of myself, that I've no choice. I've always been in control or thought I was, thought of myself as being free. My own man. I don't know. I think I'm kidding myself. When I came back to Ottawa I felt a new power, I really felt as if I controlled my world, that it didn't control me. Maybe that's too egotistical. Maybe pivotal is a better word. Yes, pivotal. As if what I did was important. Mattered."

"And now?"

"I don't know. I just don't know. I used to love the tension of New York. Of business, of life lived real; and yet today I rushed back here. Ordinarily I would have stayed and, frankly, got a woman. But I didn't. I feel I'm caught and it frightens me." He stopped talking suddenly. He had said too much about his feelings and it embarrassed him.

"Maybe you wanted to come back to your home town, couldn't

115

stay away," she teased.

"Come on," he laughed. "You know that's not why. Ottawa is a lie of a city. A put-on. You may be right about one thing, though. I'm getting sucked into my past. Every street is meaningful to me. There was a happening in my boyhood on each street I walk or drive. I remember it all and it's troublesome to me in a way I don't understand and can't always block out. I suppose I'm in conflict with the essence of what the city was to me. Not that I relate to the people now, not even my own family. I'm not as lucky as you. It's to the people who were me and them then, if you know what I mean. I don't know," he stretched his long legs and threw his head back in surrender. "Sometimes the whole thing seems too much for me." He thought again of Heister's setup plan to use Ferrilio and Smith and about Grant's TV program. "I need another drink."

"Well, you're not alone. Since you've been back all your old friends are in the process of re-examining their lives. The addition of you has changed all the relationships. They've been role-playing like crazy, pretending they are involved . . . in art and music . . . in an independent Canada, but all I can see is that they have affairs with each other's wives and husbands. Your arrival on the scene reminds them that their lives are passing."

"You're not too sympathetic to us middle-aged," he said sarcastically.

"It's such nonsense," she said shrugging her shoulders. "And I don't like your friend Grant. I don't like what he's doing to Louise."

"What's he doing?" Joseph said angrily. "He's in love with her."

"She's in love with him. But he's using her. He's the type that would screw anything that walks. Bad news. Just another middle-aged man having a sex affair. And this ultra-Canadianism of his? It's good for readership."

"You're a cynic."

"I don't trust him."

For a moment Joseph thought of the discussion about the TV show. Sorenson used the same words. There was still time to

116

back out. He had the strangest feeling she was trying to warn him. But what the hell did she know about Grant?

"Perhaps if your industry would discover a pill that would make men treat women as human beings, with dignity, as equals, I'd switch to your side."

He laughed, but thinking again of the scene in New York and the setup planned by Heister, he asked, with more intensity than he had meant to, "Violetta, can we leave the industry and the committee and Grant and that whole damned world outside this apartment?"

"I can, if you can," she said. "And gladly."

Eventually they had had enough martinis and it was time for dinner. Without realizing it they walked into the kitchen hand in hand. He felt good there, at peace. He cut the onions and put them on to fry, and she made a salad and put the potatoes in to bake. She set the table and lit the candles and he opened the wine to let it breathe. And at the last moment, when everything was ready, he put on the steaks and timed them exactly, his eye never leaving his watch, exactly three minutes to a side.

"I didn't realize one cooked with a watch and not a stove," she teased.

They sat down, and as delicious as the meal was, they were unaware, caught in each other's eyes. This was the way he had always dreamed of being with a woman, and never had. There had never been this simplicity. He didn't have to be Joseph Adam Mann, superintellectual, or Joseph Adam Mann, super-cock. They talked of simple things, of things he hadn't thought of in years. Nothing things really . . . about a poem he had liked, an exhibition that had been meaningful to him and he had never told anyone, about the colour of the sea off Barbados, about a cousin who had been a friend and was dead, about how he used to look at people on a streetcar and realize that they were all as important to themselves as he was to himself. He had been ten at the time and he had never gotten over that insight, all those people, each one a world. And finally the food was eaten and the wine drunk.

"You go into the living room and put on some music. You

cooked. I'll clean. Let me play house, old-style."

He did as she asked and put on some music, stretched into a chair, and listened to the sounds of her washing dishes. But he couldn't stay away from her. "I'll help."

"You must be exhausted."

"I have my trusty supply of pep pills."

"Be careful Joseph," she said concerned. "They're more dangerous than you think."

"We made an agreement. The industry and its products stay outside the door."

She sighed and started to put the dishes away, reaching up the cupboard, her back to him. He put his arms around her and felt her body blend into his as if they were one body. For that moment she surrendered her separateness. Her head tilted exposing her throat; he kissed the curve of her neck where she offered the pulse of her life. Was the scene real or fake, he wondered. How did he feel? Did he feel anything or was it role-playing again? Too many movies, too many women, too many novels, so one never knew whether it was real or some pastiche of the world in you. And then she turned and their lips touched. A softness, a fragrance, and he stopped thinking.

"Violetta. Let's go to bed."

She opened her eyes and looked into his black eyes and had the same feeling as when she kissed him, as if she was inside his head and body and he was inside hers and for whatever reason God made a man attractive to a woman, she wanted him, wanted to make love with him, to him, finally she wanted to know him. But she was afraid because she had seen the faces of too many men. And would Joseph be the same? Another Douglas Clark, or worse, someone like her husband? Desire was always confused with love until the desire was satisfied. Would he too have the hard edges men were cursed with so they could not be real with a woman, one to one . . . but must possess? And especially his generation, so afraid to be open, always in conflict with hers. She wanted love but was wary of being cheated, humiliated, debased, used. And because she knew she was open to Joseph and knew she could be bruised, she hesitated and asked, foolishly, "Why?"

118

"Because I want to. Because I need you. Because we would be good. Beautiful. It would be beautiful. Because . . . because . . . ."

"How do you know?"

"I know."

And they kissed again, and in the opening of this kiss, so different from the others, he knew she had said yes. Now he was terrified, tempted to remain under the bright kitchen light, so hard and hurtful in his head even though his eyes were closed; tempted to hold her and let the moment pass, afraid of what might be revealed, but knowing that if he did that, it would never come again. And then he had contempt for himself and thought, a girl is to fuck, what's wrong with me? And again he became Joseph Adam Mann, New York superjock. And led her into the bedroom and helped her undress down to her bra and pants, and then she became shy and went into the bathroom and took a quick shower to wash the cooking smells off her body, even though she had had a bath before he arrived. She touched her body with perfume, her neck, her arms, her navel, the pubic hair, and behind her knees. Wanton bitch, she thought to herself, but suspected the totality sex would be with Joseph.

Waiting in bed, part of him said, I know this kind of chick, doctor or not. She's a honky and loves to fuck and will I give it to her. And he knew too that he was role-playing, lying to himself. Somehow he felt an unprecedented tenderness toward her, so new he could not define it, only sensed that if he were able to give himself to it, a different world would open.

Naked, she came into bed, with drops of water still on her. "Hey, don't look."

"I'd be a fool if I didn't."

Later, in their togetherness, he was able to see the parts of her. She had a way of holding her head, and he didn't realize her waist was so small, or her ass so large. "Beautiful hunky chunky behind," he would say and for some reason she would blush at that, but at so little else. But now he was not aware of parts, not even of body as separately defined physical body, aware only of colour, and feel, and smell and more, of reaching out.

The quality of her body was such that his chest felt tight. She

119

got into bed beside him, in a way, childlike — trusting, hopeful; and in a way, wanton. Her skin was silk, alive. Their bodies knew each other before they touched. And whatever hard shadows of cynicism Joseph felt, disappeared . . . .

Forgotten was the learned sexual athlete, the accomplished slick performer, the cocksman supreme. And in time, when she helped him delicately place himself into her body, he knew he would remember that first entry for all time. He was still for a moment while he looked at her face and saw there a dozen historic peoples . . . the Lithuanians, Letts, Tartars, Visigoths, Huns, a passing of eternity. She opened her eyes and let him see, because he looked, and didn't turn his eyes away like so many men ashamed, or close them out of guilt, disgust, or to focus on his own physical senses. And the passion caught him by surprise because of its totality, of mind and body as a oneness, and then he was unaware. Lost. Together lost, knowing his own mortality and not being afraid, reaching for death in surrender, transcending it for the moment, being one with all life . . . all the fragrance and all the colours and all the sounds, and they shared life and death and life again.

It seemed forever to focus, and when he was aware of her looking at him he felt naked again and it was painful, too painful, and he wanted to hide in words.

"Don't. Don't say anything. Don't speak for a bit, Joseph, just hold me."

And then the terror took hold of him. He had experienced his own death, solitude, balance, togetherness all at once. What did it mean? He had thought she would be a pleasurable lay, an addition to his collection, a notch in his gun, but not different from any of the hundreds of women he had slept with. Lies. Lies. That was a lie. He knew it would be different the moment he danced with her at Grant's party.

"Violetta . . . don't love me. I . . . ."

She smiled, knowing what he had been thinking and more. And for her part she wanted nothing of love either. Sex-love, maybe. But not "in love" because for her she knew it would be a once thing and she wasn't ready and maybe would never be

120

ready, never want to give what had to be given. And besides, whether they had agreed to keep the drug thing outside the door or not, it was there, inside. "Don't worry. I don't want it either. You and I will be sex mates. How does that sound?" Mischievous. Laughter in her eyes again. Violetta again.

And coming out of wherever he had been, it sounded perfect, safe, each having escaped the other.

Joseph dozed only to be awakened by the telephone. "Aren't you going to answer it." She shook her head. "And what will I think when I call and there is no answer? Will I picture you with some other guy?"

She put her finger to his lips. "Don't spoil it."

Within a moment the phone rang again. Twice. Stopped and rang again.

"Code?"

She knew then it was either Douglas or Louise. But most likely Douglas because she had broken a date with him tonight to be with Joseph on the pretext that Mylita was ill. She didn't answer. She'd make up some excuse — she was in the washroom, or sleeping, or something. "Do you want the code?"

"I want my own code. Different. Special for me alone. Mine will be with three rings. The magic number three."

"Joseph Adam Mann," she said teasingly. "The magic three."

He wanted to stay the night but accepted when she said it would be difficult to explain to Mylita in the morning.

In time, after he left, she lay in bed smoking, still shaken, thinking about him. She didn't know whether she had drifted off to sleep or whether a second passed when she heard a knocking on her door. She leaped out of bed, frightened, wondering who it was. Went to the door. Listened. Was it Joseph? Then she heard Douglas Clark's voice, "Violetta, Violetta, open up, I know you're there," he said harshly.

She felt trapped. She would have to open the door. He knew her pattern. Either she would be at home or there would be a babysitter. His knock, his presence, was the same as her husband forcing her legs apart with his powerful knees when he wanted her. She unlatched the door and he pushed his way in, like her

121

husband ramming it into her without grace or love.

"I saw him leave, I saw him leave your apartment. Don't deny it." He was shouting. "Tramp. Cheap D.P. tramp. I don't care who you fuck. But let me tell you this, whatever I said about marriage, forget it."

She started to laugh, as if she would ever have married him. Stupid man. "You can't go on being single forever," he said once before to her amazement. "Why not?" she had asked simply. "You have a child. You'll want more. It's a woman's destiny. Who will look after you?" She remembered becoming haughty and saying, "I would think a woman with a medical degree can look after herself very well." But Douglas was so like her stepfather and ex-husband that all he could say was, "a woman needs a man to look after her." And that was that.

"You and I are through. I want you to know that," he said as if denying her her part in some sanctification. "But I hope you didn't tell him about INTEGRAL. I hope he didn't get to you. I warned you about him. You didn't reveal anything, surely?"

"You bastard," she screamed, and then poured curses on him shrieking in Lithuanian, taking him off guard until he found himself pushed out the door and it slammed in his face.

Inside Violetta was shaking. Why, why did men have the power to make her feel guilty, unworthy, inferior? Because she was a woman and couldn't be trusted, because she was a D.P. still. It was a good lesson. She had almost lost herself with Joseph. It would turn out the same. And she wanted to be free and to be free you could not allow yourself to be possessed. Love is not eternal. Society is so evil in its regard for women that it is impossible for a man to love and impossible for a woman to be loved and to love herself. Always remembered how when she was an intern she had heard a grandmother telling a son's wife, who had just had a difficult birth of a baby girl, almost bleeding to death in the process, "She's a pretty little thing, but isn't it too bad with all that trouble, it wasn't a boy."

She went into the bathroom and took a sleeping pill, and even so had trouble falling to sleep. When she did, she dreamed of the rooster. On her uncle's farm, when she had first come to Canada,

122

she had come too close to a rooster. It lunged at her and nipped her lip, and when she saw the blood pouring down, she ran into the kitchen screaming. Her mother tried to comfort her, but she would have none of it. Crazy with anger, she took an axe and went back into the barnyard. She chased that rooster round and round for two hours, swinging at it when she got close enough, until eventually it tired and she hacked it to death. Then the rooster's head changed into Joseph's and she woke in terror.

She lit a cigarette and thought of the night, of Joseph, of his arms and his mouth. What a beautiful man, she thought, and butted the cigarette and slept.

In the morning, the ringing of the phone woke her. Three rings. Silence. And then ringing again. She felt beautiful. Happy. "How is the loveliest woman in the world . . . my wild Indian?"

"I feel," and then she lowered her voice, "I wish you were here right now, I'd eat you up for breakfast. "And then she blushed. "Got to hurry, 'bye."

She got out of bed. *"Labas pupa,"* she called to her daughter. "Good morning Mylita, my love."

10

"Gentlemen, I see a quorum," the chairman said striking his gavel to signify the start of the fifteenth session of the Special Parliamentary Committee on Drug Costs and Prices.

"Mr. Chairman, I would like to read the following into the transcript," Frank Flanagan said, jumping to his feet, as instructed by Joseph.

"Is it very long?" the chairman asked in his sardonic way.

"It is very important."

"Providing the other member whose turn it was to question, Dr. Lewison, if I remember correctly, has no objection, you may proceed."

"Who could object to Mr. Flanagan," Dr. Lewison said. "One learns to live with him."

"Thank you," Flanagan said, undeterred, and read, "The American Congress finds and declares that there is substantial traffic in counterfeit drugs simulating the brand or other identifying mark or device of the manufacturer of the genuine article: that such traffic poses a serious hazard to the health of innocent consumers of such drugs because of the lack of proper qualifications, facilities, and manufacturing controls on the part of the counterfeiter whose operations are clandestine: that while such drugs are deemed misbranded within the meaning of the section of the Federal Food, Drug and Cosmetic Act, the controls for the suppression of the traffic in such drugs are inadequate because of the difficulty of determining the place of interstate origin of such drugs, and, if that place is discovered, the fact that the implements for counterfeiting are not subject to seizure, and that these factors require enactment of additional controls with respect to such drugs without regard to their interstate origins." Flanagan paused to drink some water, and then continued. "The term 'counterfeit drug' means a drug, or the container, trade name or other identifying mark, imprint or device, or any likeness thereof, that simulates that of a drug manufacturer, processor or packer or distributors." Flanagan paused again and continued. "Counterfeit drugs are produced under disgusting conditions. Pills that you take by mouth made on machinery minutes after that same tablet machine was used to make poisonous pellets without being cleaned in between. Often sewer pipes drip into machines used for drug mixing. Often none of the active ingredient is even used in a counterfeit drug, and some have been found stored in containers that had been used before to hold rat poison."

Flanagan placed the document he had been reading from on the table in front of him. "Gentlemen," he thundered, "if the Americans can't keep track of counterfeit drugs right in their own bailiwick, if they get flooded with the stuff, what, I ask you, what are we going to do if we remove patent protection? I see the Director of the Food and Drug Directorate sitting in the audience. I would like to ask him a question as part of this period. Sir, have you got the staff to protect us?"

"Mr. Flanagan," the chairman interrupted angrily, "that is quite out of order."

"However, I see the press scribbling away," Dr. Lewison said.

The stage was being carefully set to make the country aware of the dangers of counterfeit drugs. Fred Smith and Tony Ferrilio were soon to be parolled and Heister had instructed Joseph to increase the references on the dangers of counterfeit drugs. He noted with satisfaction that all the reporters present had written copious notes when Flanagan was speaking. It was frightening even for Joseph to realize that when he took a pep pill, as he was doing more often, it could be fake. Or the pills his mother took.

Because of the bitter debating between Flanagan and Dr. Lewison, the session lasted longer than usual. Not only was there not enough time to have a drink with Violetta before she went to

125

the hospital, but there was a message at his office from Grant cancelling a dinner appointment.

Joseph was uneasy about the way Grant's television show on the pharmaceutical industry was shaping up. Uneasy because he didn't know how it was developing. Originally he thought that he and Grant would work together on it. But his role so far had been to arrange interviews for Grant, and plant tours in various part of Canada and the United States. When he asked Grant if he could see an outline of the script, Grant put him off by saying that that wasn't the way he worked. He preferred to leave himself "open" to discover and then, when all his research was completed, write the outline. He claimed that if he worked from a preconceived outline, it narrowed his research.

Joseph couldn't disagree. It was a plausible method of working. But still he felt uneasy. The fact was that Grant was shooting film on his investigation trips, had already taped an interview with Sorenson and others. When Joseph asked why, since the program was live, Grant responded that as the show was an hour, he liked to intersperse the live dialogue with film and stills. "Otherwise, the show is dull. Remember, Joseph, television has to be entertaining. That's the first requirement."

Perhaps. But he would feel better if he could go over what Grant had put together so far — in detail.

Joseph couldn't decide what to do. He could drink with Flanagan or rehash the day with Sorenson. Instead he returned to his apartment, poured himself a scotch, and tried to work on the brief the Association was going to present to the committee. But the picture of Violetta kept getting in the way. Almost as much as going to bed with her, he enjoyed relaxing over a few drinks and chatting. Once he had told her, "Your whole personality changes when you drink. A lovely warm flush starts at your neck and works its way up to your face. Your eyes become shiny blue and every time you sip your martini it's like Popeye eating spinach, or like the change in Captain Marvel when he cries, 'Shazam.' "

"Captain Marvel? Shazam?" She had laughed. "What on earth is that?"

"You make me feel so old. All my remembrances come from before you knew which end was which. I've never felt old before."

"You're not old" she said laughing. "Not my sex mate. How could that be?"

She was really something, that girl, he thought. How incredibly complicated his life had become. When he had been assigned to Ottawa he had thought the whole thing would be a piece of cake. But he had become involved — and on so many levels. With the drug industry. With Grant. With his mother. With Violetta. With himself.

He had long ago accepted himself for what he was. Made peace with himself. Found a way to live for and with himself. His view of man was that he was base, imperfect, and imperfectable. Yet he wished he wasn't. He was an atheist, yet he wished there was a God in heaven. He couldn't understand how people could identify passionately with anything: Grant and his love of country, Violetta and her love of family, Louise and her belief in love, Sorenson and his belief in the "industry" and American values. And yet he wished he could.

He knew that with his views, he should opt out. But he didn't want to be a fool. If he was smart enough to win the rewards of the society, then why not? If he was going to sell himself, he might as well get as much as he could. For a time he had taken sustenance from the status of a car and other trappings. And he still relied, or tried to rely, on the principle that *now* was the key. That each moment is all eternity and, therefore, pleasure is paramount. He had had it all — the alcohol, pills, and sex. And it worked most of the time to keep away the blackness, the fear of death. Or really not so much that as to keep away an awareness of loss of self, loss of ego. He didn't want to lose that, was terrified to lose sense of self.

Intellectually he could accept the fact that there was no tomorrow, that nothing had intrinsic worth, aware of dust unto dust. Partly because of that he had long ago turned his back on his true nature and made himself fit into the world of things and ideas, rather than senses. For a long time he had been of the quantita-

127

tive world, a world that could be measured, added, weighed, rather than felt, sensed, experienced. He had spent the last fifteen years of his life involved in the day-to-day in order to escape confronting himself, yet always keeping himself detached from the essence of the day-to-day in order to prevent himself from being lost. He used to study his colleagues wondering how they could survive, how they could be so involved, or believe that what they did was important. He had never understood how their lives were enough for them. He had seen those bright young men who, because of family and business pressures and perhaps lack of human sensitivity, become their very jobs — engineers, corporation men, lawyers, and so on. Like changelings, at some point they had stopped role-playing and become the part. And he had seen others who had turned their backs on the whole of society and fled into drugs; or into strange, unrewarding pursuits — unless one was lucky enough to be in the creative fields, and even there the commercial nature of the society eventually won. Joseph had never been able to rationalize, accept the relationship of either middle- or working-class man to his job. Job was what man did when he stopped being a boy. Pushed into it. To reject it was adolescent. So Grant had wanted to be a novelist but had been mature and gotten a job. He, Joseph had wanted to paint. Obviously neither had wanted what he said he wanted very strongly. Or they would not have escaped into job. And once you accept job you run the risk of becoming job — Grant had; it's like an identification card, a way of being known and a way of knowing. While in the past he had contempt for people who lost themselves in a business or profession, he also envied their outward peace. The possibility that something might engage him totally seemed inviting. At first he had not known enough about the industry to judge one way or the other. Normally it didn't matter. He was a management consultant — a professional. And yet, now he felt that perhaps it was a worthwhile cause, something he could commit himself to. Prior to this he had been detached, both inside and out. His choice to carry the burden of the schizoid life. Yet it wasn't easy to play the part of being and not being involved, and

128

yet function.

You're born, you eat, you work, you fuck, you die.

Now he found himself wondering if, in reality, he had spent his life running away from himself. He remembered that as a gift to himself on his twenty-first birthday he had planned to spend the whole day alone, as he had read John Steinbeck had done, and to try to look into himself and know himself and know what he wanted. Somehow he had never gotten around to doing it. Perhaps he had considered killing himself that time because, without knowing it, that was really what he had wanted all his life. Certainly the purposelessness of life and the nothingness of death always conspired to poison the joy of the present.

Until now.

Joseph realized with surprise that because of Violetta he was happy. She made him feel happy. With her his body became unjangled. He had never felt that way in his life before.

He shook his head. Forced himself to concentrate on the Association brief.

While Joseph struggled to write the brief, drank scotch, and thought longingly of Violetta, Violetta was fighting to save a girl's life from a botched abortion.

A twenty-three-year-old girl had been rushed into emergency, blood pouring out of her like water from a drain pipe rusted through and there was nothing she or the emergency team could do. The girl finished her life bleeding to death before their eyes.

Violetta had seen death many times, but it had never affected her like this. When her duty shift ended she went home and like her stepfather, poured herself a scotch, straight. Drank it down and poured another. Then she walked through the dark hallway into her daughter's bedroom and sat on a chair beside her bed, filling her eyes and soul with her daughter's sleeping form, trying to keep the memory of that other time out of her head. And she thought of Joseph's mother, and her mother, and of herself, mother to Mylita, and of the time she had ripped out of herself that other child. She sat in Mylita's room, head down, shoulders slumped, silent tears dripping like blood for the girl who had died tonight and for that other, and gave herself up to the memory, lacerating herself with it again.

Louise, who admitted to having the incredible number of three abortions, had taken her to a nurse, a lumpy, shapeless woman with flat, dull eyes.

"So you got knocked up, eh? Too bad. I always tell you girls. Okay, go fuck yourself crazy, but don't be stupid. Look after yourself. I tell you, no man will. My husband, now he's a bastard from the word go. No good drunken fart. Threw him out years ago. What's the matter, dear? You look worried. Pale. Nothing to worry about. I never lost a patient yet." She gave a hearty laugh that ended in a cough she had difficulty stopping. "Too much smoking," she said, lighting another. "Listen hon, I been doing this for twenty years. I'm a nurse you know, or was, until I got sent to jail for six months." She shrugged her shoulders. "It was a phony. This guy, no good bastard, got caught breaking and entering and made a deal with the police to let him go if he turned in an abortionist. He did. Me. Came to me with a girl and I was in the middle of trying to help her and the police bust in. So what good did it do. The girl never got the job done and had the kid and is she happy? Is that kid happy?" She shrugged again. "I went to jail, and all for what? So some house-break idiot could go free to only get caught the next time and get sent up? Go figure that. All right, that's enough bedside manner, honey. You get yourself into the bathroom."

"Do I have to get undressed?" Violetta asked.

"You have to take your pants off. You took them off fast enough to get laid." And she laughed coarsely until Louise told her that Violetta was married, had left her husband, and didn't want another child. "Oh shit," the woman sneered, "I've heard that one before. Now who crosses my hand with silver? Money first." Louise opened her purse and counted out four hundred dollars. "Here."

"Thank you, Louise. You should get a commission. Tell you what, next time you're in trouble, it's on the house." She laughed again, put the money in a desk drawer, and locked it. "Money first, that's life," and laughed again. "There's a bathroom

130

around the corner, first door on your left. Go on in there and take a piss or whatever you have to do."

Violetta went in, closed the door, took her pants down and sat on the toilet. The woman followed her. "Don't be embarrassed honey. I'm a nurse. I've seen a thousand girls and men, too, pass water. What the hell is that? That's the trouble with people today, too squeamish. Violetta closed her eyes, did it, and flushed the toilet.

Mrs. Cawardine — "Call me Bonnie," she said — picked up a Pyrex coffee pot from the floor (Violetta hoped it was clean), filled it with warm water, Sunlight soap flakes, and a carefully measured amount of Lysol. She stirred the mixture with a wooden spoon. "This technique never fails. And I didn't learn it at no nursing school either. My mother taught it to me. She did abortions for years. It's an old recipe." She took a long tube with a squeeze bulb in the middle and knelt down on the tile floor. "Spread your legs, honey." Violetta closed her eyes again out of shame and did what she was told. Bonnie inserted her finger up her vagina, probing carefully. "You're close to two months. Don't worry. I've given my eldest daughter two abortions, one when she was past three months gone, dumb bitch." She raised herself off the floor. "Now you will have to help me do some of the work. I'm going to put this end up your cunt. You hold the other end in the water, in the Pyrex." She knelt down again and inserted the tube, pushing it up as far as she could. "You keep that tube in the water. Don't let go. If any air gets up inside you, you could die."

Violetta held the tube in the water with rigid concentration. Frightened as she was, she realized later that the thought never occurred to her to say "stop." To have the baby.

"I'm going to start squirting this mixture up. You tell me when you feel dizzy and then I'll know when you've had enough."

After only a few minutes, Violetta began to feel lightheaded.

"It's knowing the right amount that counts. Too much Lysol, too much soap, too much of the other acid, my secret formula that I put in when you weren't looking, and you could be in trouble. You could die."

131

Now a sickening dizziness swept over her and it was all she could do to concentrate on holding her end of the tube in the water. "Stop. Stop, I'm going to throw up," she lowered her head. Couldn't hold it straight. She groaned, "Is the tube in the water? I don't want to die." But Mrs. Cawardine had ceased squirting the liquid the moment Violetta cried out.

"You tell that man of yours that if he wants to fuck you once more before you lose that thing inside you, he better fuck you right away. As soon as you get home because if he fucks you later on tonight, his prick will be eaten away. Serve the bastard right if it fell off", she cackled away, obviously not believing the truth that Violetta was married and had left her husband.

Violetta stood and started to pull her pants up, nearly fainting in the process.

"Here now, just a moment. Put on a napkin." The woman rummaged in a closet and got her one. "Don't worry about the dizziness, it will pass soon." She helped Violetta to the plastic covered sofa, told her to lie down, then got her a hot water bottle and put it on her belly. All this time Louise was sitting in a corner of the room, tense, saying nothing, doing nothing, reading nothing, just being there. Violetta would be forever grateful because she didn't know what she would have done if Louise hadn't stayed with her.

"You take these." Mrs. Cawardine handed her four tablets. "Penicillin. I'm putting twenty-four more in your purse. Are you listening? You take two every two hours. You won't have any infection for sure."

After half an hour Violetta started to feel better, and sat up. The woman told her to do a lot of walking. "As soon as you get home, you get out of that car and walk. It should come in about seven hours."

"What will happen?" Violetta asked nervously.

"Nothing more than the curse and a few blood clots. Maybe a little more painful."

Louise took her back to her apartment. On the way Violetta said, "I don't feel good. I'm still dizzy." And she broke into a sweat. When they reached the apartment she wanted to lie down

132

but Louise forced her to walk. They went out and walked slowly block after block toward the downtown section. A couple of times cars with men stopped and tried to pick them up. It all seemed so unreal. People hurrying by, cars streaming, the light from taverns and stores, and none of it related to her. "How far do you think we've gone?"

"About a mile. We'll walk another mile and then turn back."

Four miles, she thought. "I haven't walked that far since I was a kid." She remembered for the first time in a long time running away from the D.P. camp at Dorpheim. Four times she had run away, miles across the fields, and each time was found in the same farmer's patch. "Oh." A cry escaped her mouth.

"Bad?"

Violetta clenched her teeth and shook her head.

"It's the walking. I remember."

Violetta gasped and fought to suppress a scream and a terror that made her want to take a taxi to a hospital and confess what she had done. "I can't walk anymore. I can't move my legs." Sweat poured off her face, her makeup ran in dark streaks.

"I'm scared."

"Stop being a baby," Louise said harshly.

Somehow she got back to the apartment and threw herself on the bed. "I'm dying. I'm going to die. The pain is killing me." She was terrified of death and of the pain, and humiliated at herself writhing in fear and pain and panic. Then she gave herself over to the pain and the fear, and knew in her blood that if she survived she would never be afraid again.

But her fear became infectious like some dreaded primeval disease. Louise called Mrs. Cawardine, explaining Violetta's symptoms. "She seems worse than I ever was."

"Tell the stupid bitch to wash floors, anything. Just keep her moving."

Violetta did as she was told with eyes closed, aware of her body as a separate thing with its own being, its own life. She had considered her body an object of beauty to be desired, pampered, enjoyed, to be controlled and commanded. She had not considered it as something that made its own demands. She

133

remembered her own swollen belly with her first child, and the swollen bellies of the women waiting in doctors' offices. Animals, she thought. We're just like animals. Primitive. Primordial. We are no different from cats who have litters, or dogs, or cows. I have no separate life from my body, no freedom in the sense that I am the master of my body. My life is predetermined by my body. Is that true? "Oh God, I don't want it to be true," she wept, washing the floor, doubled-over with pain, waiting for the gushing forth. Surely being a woman doesn't have to mean this.

When the floor was finished she walked doubled-over to the sink, filled the pail again, got down on her knees, and washed the floor again, and then again, every so often stopping to put her head on the floor and cry out with the pain and the frustation and the humility and the hate. And by six in the morning, exhausted, she went to bed. At eight she was wakened by a pain she understood. The beginning of labour. She lay there and waited hopefully, timing her contractions as she had done with her first child. Within an hour the contractions had speeded up from one every ten minutes to one a minute. Then she went into the bathroom, closed the door, and sat down on the toilet.

Standing outside the door, Louise, who had been wakened by Violetta's scream, asked, "You okay? Is it coming?" She thought Violetta should unlock the door in case anything went wrong, in case she fainted and hemorrhaged, but she didn't know how to say that for fear of frightening her. "You okay?" she asked, talking to ease her own anxiety.

"I think so."

Finally, one immense stab and she felt like something was tearing her in two. She was sure her insides were being ripped out. It hadn't felt like that when she had given birth to Mylita. Stuff was coming out. She could feel it drip down from inside her. The pains stopped for a moment. Like a silence. She got off the toilet, went down on her knees, and looked at the mass of bloody, spongy material. A form there! Oh God she hadn't thought that. With an insane curiosity she took her steel comb, reached down into the toilet, and fished out a piece of the stuff. Could it be an arm? Another part like a face. "Oh my God."

134

"You okay Violetta? Violetta!" Louise shouted.

"Yes," she said weakly. Another tear forced her to sit on the toilet again. This time a great grunt wrenched her whole body, made her feel totally out of control, made her feel that she was nothing, in the power of a gigantic hand that squeezed her middle as if it were a toothpaste tube and she was empty. And it was over. She flushed the toilet. The tears started to cascade. Not guilt yet. Just a sorrow for those bloody pieces, a life not to be lived. She cleaned herself, wiped the bathroom floor, scrubbed the inside of the bowl, washed herself again, removing all stains of death. And only then did she open the door. Louise put her arms around her and led her into her bed. She lay down, Louise's arms around her, and they cried, the unique cry of women. And they slept.

Remembering now, the sense of loss still within her, and the loss of the child who had died tonight, a rage at the unnecessary and irrevocable destruction welled up inside her. Her view now was that abortion was wrong, it was killing. A society that killed was evil, a society that condoned killing rather than permit a girl to have a so-called illegitimate child was sick to the point of dying itself. The act of birth was glorious. A woman should be able to have her child, keep it or give it to others to love, all without stigma. Abortion was just another man-made method of debasing life and women, the will of the collective once again forcing, moulding people into unreal forms. She shuddered. By not admitting to reality, to anything authentic, society in effect was saying that killing was better than life, unless life could be lived only within some kind of approved set of beliefs and organization. Incredible. At the time she had been desperate to have an abortion. She knew now that it had been wrong. But she was mature enough now, even at twenty-nine, to live with it, carry the burden, understand.

Joseph woke slowly to the siren of a fire engine trying to run him down in the dream in his head. It was the phone. He had fallen asleep head-down at the desk. He looked at his watch. Two in the morning. "Hello."

"Joseph?"

"Violetta," he said surprised. "What?"

"Did I wake you? I'm sorry."

"It's nothing. Just dozed at my desk. Violetta, what is it?"

"Can we talk? A young girl died tonight."

"Do you want me to come over and sit with you for a while?"

"Would you?"

"Be there in a few minutes." He put the phone down, went into the bathroom, and washed his face with cold water. He took a dexedrine out of the bottle, caught some water from the tap in his cupped hand, and swallowed the pill. Poor kid, he thought. She sure worked hard. Food and Drug, the hearings, the hospital, looking after Mylita. And he realized that he had never questioned her strength, never thought that she might get tired sometimes, might feel down, might find life overwhelming as he sometimes did. He had never thought about Violetta as Violetta from within Violetta.

11

"My hands are heavy," Grant said. "I can't lift my hands off the table." There was a note of terror in his voice. "I'll never to able to write again. I can't move my hands."

They had finished dinner and were smoking up in the living room. "Try. Try. You can't give in. You've got to try." Louise left her chair and walked around to where Grant was sitting, looking at his hands pressed flat against the table. She started to lick and kiss his hands, lick them like a dog, and they came unstuck.

She took his hand and led him to the sofa, while he mumbled, "Man alone — the quality of endurance; man the transient — ever-searching; man the destroyer..."

"That's poetry," Louise said.

"I'm going to phone," Grant said moodily.

"Who?" Louise asked. "Who are you going to phone?"

"Who is Sylvia, where is she?" Joseph became hysterical, laughing at the memory of Mrs. Saunders, black-haired with the fierce mouth, the choir director in public school. She formed her lips in a perfect oval and hooted like an owl. "Hoo, Hoo," she sang as she walked around the semicircle formed by the boys and girls in the choir, bearing down on those who didn't make a perfect "hoo," then shoving her finger in their gut forcing them to exhale "hoo" and not understanding when one of the boys, looking at the shape of her mouth said, "I bet she sucks."

"Call Twiggy, she's significant," Joseph said cynically.

"I'll call all the people in the world with my message. Whatever it is, I can't remember. Grant started to laugh. Louise, beside him, nestled into his shoulder and stroked him between his legs.

137

She pressed her lips against his neck and eyes, moaned and writhed as if in some epileptic fit, and he would give an answering moan and contortion, and then she would shudder and say, "Do you feel it? Do you feel it?"

It seemed a travesty of love to Joseph who was angry anyway. He had invited Grant over so that they could have a serious discussion about the TV show scheduled in three days. If he had known that this was going to be a party, he would have invited Violetta or cancelled and spent the time alone with her. But when he opened the door there was Louise with Grant, bringing with them a quantity of marijuana. (Grant used to grow it on his property until Thelma had forbidden it; what she didn't know was that Grant had buried a considerable amount in a plastic bag.) Clearly Grant had used the meeting with Joseph as an excuse to get out of the house, a cover to be with Louise.

"Enough moaning," Joseph said, certain that while Louise was probably real, Grant was surely faking it. He was too inhibited to behave that way, moaning like an animal. He knew Grant.

"I'm communicating with Grant's soul. Don't be so up-tight," she said, continuing to stroke him between the legs. "I want to get fucked. Won't someone fuck me?" She stood and pulled Grant up, who was really out of it.

"Use my bedroom," Joseph said. "Follow me." He led them dizzily through the apartment to his bedroom, strewn with sheets, underwear, socks, and books all over the floor and bed — books on pharmaceutical subjects, on psychology, on philosophy, novels. He always read half a dozen different books at a time, often with the aid of pep pills, until four in the morning.

"What the hell is that thing?" Grant asked, pointing to a large aquarium.

"My fish's private swimming pool."

"But there's only one fish in it."

"I ate the rest."

"Poor, lonely fish, " Louise said. "No one to fuck."

Joseph became very serious. He had been walking by a pet store one day, saw the aquarium, and bought it. Made a thorough study of the subject — a twenty-nine-gallon tank, thirty inches long, eighteen inches deep, and twelve inches wide. "It cost forty dollars. Soon I'll have thirty fish in there. But I want to do it one by one. I want to get to know my fish. To relate to them." Then he proceeded to lecture about water temperature and the type of heater, and he interrupted himself as Grant echoed, "Poor, lonely fish." Angrily, Joseph said, "You don't understand fish just like you don't understand anything else. This fish is not lonely. He is not frustrated. He is master of all he surveys. There is no other fish to get in his way." Joseph scattered a little marijuana in the fish tank. "Highly recommended."

"Not too much."

Joseph made an incantation over the fish. "I'm fishing for fish souls."

"I'd like to fuck Grant now," Louise said, taking her clothes off. She had surprisingly full breasts. "Can I fuck Grant on your bed?"

"If I fuck, Joseph fucks," Grant said. "We are blood brothers. Show Louise your thumb."

"I'd rather see something else."

They held out their thumbs. The scar was so faint that Louise said, "You can hardly see anything at all. And anyway, he doesn't want to stick it into me, he wants to stick it into Violetta. I know."

"Hop to it gang," Joseph said walking out of the bedroom, back into the living room. He poured himself a cognac and smiled as he listened to Grant heaving and, forcing himself to keep silent, laughed noiselessly until he thought he would burst rolling around on the floor. And then he lay quietly on the floor as pictures of Grant exploded in his head.

One day when Grant's parents were out, Joseph helped him ransack his father's study, searching for a photo taken when he was six. His father forced him to pose in the nude with an Indian feather stuck in his hair, aiming a bow and arrow at his equally naked cousin while she mugged for the camera. Finding it tucked in an envelope, Grant ripped it to shreds and flushed the pieces down the toilet.

Once a week, the gang, — Joseph, Leo Lafortune, Davy Gordon, whose father was a cantor, Grant, and Michael O'Rourke, would drop into Finsness' Drug Store to buy a comic book. Finsness allowed them to take their time deciding until he discovered that while grouped around the comic book rack, Joseph was stuffing comics under his shirt; *Captain Marvel, Superman, Batman, Torch, Submariner* — all his favourites. For every one the gang bought, they read five while in the store and stole another five. Finsness grabbed Joseph. All the others ran and escaped except Grant, who stayed until the police came and drove them home. Grant's father slapped him so hard on the face he spun around smashing his nose against the corner of a wall. And the blood gushed forth.

Joseph remembered university, and the two Polish sisters they found, blondes, who loved screwing. The four of them spent several nights a week in the girls' bed. In her puritan belief that no one had sex before going to bed for the night and that there was safety in numbers, the landlady permitted the girls to have male visitors, providing it was a foursome, and that they left by eleven. Staying past curfew one night Joseph had to piss or bust. It was too late to go down the hall to the bathroom so he pissed out the bedroom window. The wind blew his golden steam through the open living window directly below onto the landlady, still crocheting on the sofa.

And then he thought of Violetta, isolated thoughts that came all at once, all together and all separate, not one after another in rational order, but all levels at once, so that it was more a remembered feeling than a thinking. Once he had touched her and asked playfully how you say vagina in Lithuanian. *"Putyte,"* she told him. "I like that word better." He thought for a moment. "I'll be able to call you my little *putyte* when we're out and no one will know."

"But why is it a better word than vagina?" she persisted.

Because it doesn't say what it is, he thought, ashamed of himself, resentful of the ugly remains of his upbringing.

At twelve midnight, Grant rose from beside the sleeping

140

Louise — he never permitted himself to fall asleep, afraid he might not wake in time — and not wanting to share that intimacy, he dressed silently, hoping she wouldn't awaken. He did not want to face her mute eyes, silently asking him, Why? Why did he have to leave, why go home, from one bed to another? Why not stay with her? That's what he really wanted, wasn't it? He did not want to see her sadness and sometimes her tears; it was too bitter to bear. He was resentful, too, because they had both enjoyed. And now that the semen was out of him, it was a time to return to the world as it was; and in truth, now that it was out of him, he felt nothing toward her. Only the certain knowledge that he would want her again, mainly because she had taught him to be sexually free. So wasteful to have to wait until one was past forty to be able to enjoy bodies.

On his way out he saw Joseph sleeping on the floor, his face soft, just as when they had been kids. And he was filled with remorse at what he was doing. Awful, the way life turned out. But that was ridiculous. Joseph was the Fifth Column, and he must never forget it. Evil product of New York and big business. Tainted. This Joseph was not the Joseph of their years before, and it was foolish of him to pretend that because of the past he had some claim on Grant. Joseph was not the same and neither was Grant, although he had remained truer to whatever had been pure in his younger years than Joseph had. And thinking of the TV show he jotted a note on a napkin and pinned it on Joseph's shirt. "Good-bye Tailspin Tommy."

Downstairs in his car he realized he was dizzy and tired, and would have to drive carefully. He opened the window letting the air rush in, hoping it would clear his head. He couldn't come home drunk or spaced or with the smell of Louise on him. But he had been afraid to wash, afraid the sound of running water would awaken her. Thelma would be destroyed if she knew his secret life — the marijuana buried in the garden outside the house, and his penis buried in Louise. And yet always after he slept with her he was filled with guilt and guiltier if it was at night rather than in the day. It was easier on him if he could go to her place during lunch; at night meant he was taking time away from

141

his family. If only he could go to Thelma and tell her, "I am sleeping with Louise, I have this sex thing with her. I need her but I'm not going to leave you. I just want to be able to go to bed with her once or twice a week and maybe it will only be for a few years and then it will be over." And she should agree.

There was no question that he would ever leave Thelma. He believed in marriage; it was necessary to provide a framework for children. Why can't I have a wife and a mistress all in the open? Why is it that sex in marriage gets so lousy? Louise maintained that marriage not only destroyed love, but also the individuals. But she wasn't a Christian. And Grant was.

Surprised to find himself home so soon, he parked in front of his house. Had he been conscious the whole way? The house was dark. He closed the door silently and then tested his walking. His head seemed clear. No point waking anyone. He opened the front door carefully. He should have phoned. If he had phoned there'd be no problem. Thelma told him "If you're going to be working late, just call me." But it was hard for him to call and lie when he knew he was going to be with Louise.

There was a note on the fridge door. She knew he would get himself a glass of milk — that was the feeling of wifeness that Louise didn't understand. A comfortable knowing of each other's habits. That wasn't destructive, damn it. It was good. He read the note. "Next door. Come on over for a nightcap."

Relief surged through him. He went into the bathroom. God, his eyes were red. Maybe she wouldn't notice. He washed his face twice with soap and water and still he could smell Louise on him. He loved to have his face between her legs, his lips and tongue into her. Once, before he had washed, Thelma had kissed him on the mouth when he walked in the door. She hadn't noticed, but that guilt would never leave him.

He had an urge to see his children, and tiptoed silently into each bedroom. Then he left to go next door, vowing to himself that he would get into the swing of the party, and for sure get it up for Thelma tonight. It had been weeks.

Her head spinning beautifully, Louise smiled, rolled over, and put her arm out; but Grant was gone. And the undertow pulled her into a deep blackness. She dreamed her dream of blood. Her father shaving in the bathroom. She was nine and lying on her parents' bed looking through the open bathroom door (he mustn't have known she was watching, couldn't have known) as she sometimes did, and suddenly blood started to pour out of his throat, and she heard herself screaming for her mother and was unable to close her father's throat, another mouth larger than the one she knew, ear to ear, and there was blood over her hands and face and she thought she was bleeding to death and her father slumped over the sink and her mother now trying to hold it in with a towel. And worried about the mess. And then the funeral and down into the earth. Blackness. Covered over. She had never forgiven her father for being so weak that he had let her mother force him to destroy himself.

"Grant, Grant," she called.

Joseph woke and, still dizzy from the drinking and the grass, stumbled into the bedroom. He looked at his watch. It was four.

"Where's Grant?" she asked. And then saw the note pinned on Joseph's shirt. "He's gone. Left me. Bastard. Wouldn't drive me home. Wouldn't even wake me to kiss me good night." She sat up and the covers fell away, not realizing she was naked.

"You've got a fantastic pair of tits," Joseph said reaching down, unable to keep his hands off them. "Mmmmm, good. With your clothes on, no one would know."

She laughed pleased, but took his hand away. "Forget it. Two men are not going to get into me the same night. Come, sit down beside me," she said patting the bed unmindful of her nakedness. "Talk to me." He got them both cigarettes.

"What's going to happen between you and Grant?"

"Nothing will happen. I try to talk him into leaving his wife. Oh yes, I'm the other woman with a vengeance. But he won't. Too many commitments, too many loyalties. To his wife and children, to his mother and father, to his church . . . he's an elder, of all things. To his university alumni . . . you knew he was president this year? And even to his relatives . . . uncles, cousins, and on and on. He's sort of the boy in the family who made good you know, and must be at every wedding, anniversary, and funeral. He's still got hundreds of relatives in the Cornwall area. Glengary school days, United Empire Loyalists, and all that shit. And of course, his commitment to his readers and viewers—his public. He has more contacts than any other reporter in Parliament. You may not realize just how influential he is." She dragged nervously on her cigarette.

"Oh, I know."

"The fuck of it is, there is precious little left for me. Sometimes I feel if you stripped away all the things he's loyal to, that have a claim on him, I wonder if there would be a Grant MacDonald left. I sometimes wonder if there *is* a Grant MacDonald, or just all these images merged into one that walks and talks, like one of those dolls you wind up. He can't understand, or won't understand that if he moves to my place the earth will not shift on its axis. He will still be able to see his children, perhaps have a more meaningful relationship with them, and God will still be in His heaven. Damn it Joseph, he should be apart now, writing something more lasting — a book. If he were with me he would have more freedom. The only time we have together for sure is Wednesday lunch."

Joseph laughed and shook his head. "Freedom. That's what Thelma promised him. Ah, Louise, why not just enjoy what you have and let it go at that. Why build a superstructure?"

"You don't believe in love?"

"Tell me what it is. Show me where it is. Let me feel it. No."

"Even if you were right, I'd at least like to sleep with him more often than I get a chance to."

She was definitely Grant's type, a thinking girl, someone he could talk with, analyze political events or discuss social abstractions, but who really wanted to strip down and go at it. It had always been hard for Grant to come at it straight like that. He had to seduce a girl by talking about the political shake-up in some country or the price of wheat. He couldn't ever say to himself, as Joseph did, "A woman and a man are to fuck."

She threw herself backwards on the bed. "Well, I'm staying the

144

night. I'm not going home now." She looked up at him. "Come keep me company. Sleep beside me, but no funny stuff."

Joseph undressed and nuzzled in beside her. He couldn't help himself, couldn't keep his hand from her full breasts, and whether it was the grass or that he wanted to experiment, discover how he would feel having sex with a girl other than Violetta, test whether the curious, inexplicable and unique merging he felt was more imagined than real. He started to stroke her until the marijuana in her responded and she said, "Oh all right, what the hell," and she started to work his penis and his balls and it was great because, like him, she was a sex machine. But that's all it was, good sex, friendly sex, but it left him with an emptiness, a solitude, and he lay in bed a long time awake, giving himself into the aloneness, even with her woman's softness touching him. Violetta, Violetta. He thought the name over and over. What have you done to me?

She woke first in the morning and, parading around in the nude, washed the dishes. "What do you want for breakfast, you seducer of women?" she yelled.

Joseph buried his head under the pillow, but there was no escaping her. She jumped on top of the bed, her great breasts swinging freely and pulled the pillow away from him. "Come on, breakfast time. What do you eat? I'm starving."

"My usual. An orange, two tablespoons of strawberry jam, a couple of slugs of milk out of the bottle, and an amphetamine. No dishes."

But she made bacon, eggs and coffee, and brought it into the bedroom. They sat in their nakedness, eating and talking. He liked her. She was tough, direct, cynical, yet bitter too, a sorriness for herself lurking somewhere. Strange mixture. When she spoke of soft things, sentimental things, her lips often curled in derision contorting her face. Was it a quick curl of the lip or a tear to hide, he wondered. She wasn't feminine in the plastic terms of actresses and performers; there was a real sexual power to her. She looked ageless, was probably around thirty-five and would look the same when she was fifty. Like most people in Ottawa she worked for the civil service.

145

"I'm a high-class gestapo. I analyze jobs to determine if pay increases are warranted. You can imagine how popular I feel when I enter a department to do my two-step."

"Higher level clerical work measurement — my firm has considerable expertise in that field." They looked at each other naked and were aware of what they were talking about and laughed.

"You're more hooked by the society than I'll ever be," she said.

"I never would have believed that I could be sitting close to a girl with the nicest pair of tits I've seen in a long life of looking at tits, hundreds and hundreds of tits . . ."

"In one's and two's and three's," she laughed.

"And talking about clerical work measurement, I'm going to have a scotch."

"This doesn't become a habit, you know, that you can have your way with me when Violetta isn't around," she said using the Victorian form for emphasis. "Just because I don't get enough from my lover."

"I know," he shouted to her from the dining room, but wondered if what she said was to plant a suggestion in his mind. Of the possibility.

"You're a nice male animal," she shouted. "But you're not Grant."

"I know what you mean," he said, and he thought, you're not Violetta.

But they became friends that morning. Separate and independent from Grant and yet because of Grant; separate and independent from Violetta and yet because of Violetta. But mostly because of themselves.

"Louise," he called, trying to be casual, "do you know anything about the TV show Grant's doing on the industry?"

"Nothing. We never have time to talk anymore. He comes to my place, we make love and he leaves. But haven't you seen the tape?"

"What do you mean tape? It's going to be live."

"Oh is it?" she said, suddenly realizing what Grant was doing. Jesus, oh Jesus, he *was* a bastard. He was using Joseph just as he

146

was using her. For an instant she contemplated warning him, perhaps she would have, except she still believed that one day Grant would leave Thelma and come to her, and she didn't want to do anything to jeopardize that.

12

Joseph and Sorenson, in agonized anticipation, watched as Grant's television documentary began. The whole program had been taped. That morning Grant had told Joseph over the telephone that this had been a last-minute decision by the producer on the grounds that the show worked out better that way.

"Better for whom?" Joseph wondered. When he asked if at least he could see the tape in advance, he was told it was against policy.

"It's scary you know," the woman's face on the TV screen said, "especially when I've never had any trouble with my eyes, and then suddenly a doctor tells you you may be going blind and all because of a new drug I was given for another condition."

Watching the program on Joseph's colour TV set, Sorenson exclaimed, "That's a hell of a note to start on."

Grant MacDonald stood in the middle of an aisle of one of the largest drug stores in Toronto, one listed on the stock exchange. As the camera panned showing hundreds of medicines both over the counter and prescriptions, Grant's voice was heard. "There are twelve thousand drugs licensed for sale in Canada, and every year, Canadian doctors write over fifty million prescriptions."

The camera zoomed to a close-up of Grant's face looking directly out of the screen at the audience, as if he were talking to each viewer separately and intensely. "You spend hundreds of millions of dollars a year on drugs. Do you need them? Do they help you? Are they dangerous? Do you pay more than you should?Who owns the companies that make them?"

There was a crash of heavy music as the titles and credits rolled on the screen:

TO KILL OR CURE —
MEDICINE FOR PROFIT
An Eyewitness Report by Grant MacDonald

On screen, four men and Grant sat around a table on comfortable leather chairs, the camera cutting to close-ups of their faces as Grant introduced them. "To consider these and other questions about the pharmaceutical industry, we have with us tonight Mr. Dean Sorenson, President of Heister International, a network of sixty-four manufacturing companies in as many countries and typical of the small group of large companies in the world that control the drug industry; Dr. Ian Sherway, Chief of Medicine at University Hospital; Dr. Lawrence Greenaway, Director of the Food and Drug Directorate; and Dr. Henry Lewison, Member of Parliament and a member of the select committee appointed and meeting right now to probe the high cost of drugs."

This was followed by a quick succession of close-ups of people in home situations as Grant's voice-over described their problems. "Meet Ralph Sebastian. He earns one hundred seven dollars and fifty cents a week and spends forty-one dollars every two weeks on prescription drugs. This is Mrs. Dorothy Klebnikoff. She and her husband, a superintendent , have a monthly income of two hundred and sixty-eight dollars, slightly more when she babysits. Drugs for her epileptic sister cost one hundred dollars a month. Here is Mrs. David Daniels, seventy-eight years old last week. She needs to take medication every day to stay alive at a cost of ten dollars a day."

The camera zoomed into a close-up of Grant's face. "These are not isolated instances, but merely three examples picked from hundreds our researchers turned up. Figures indicate that the average price of a prescription in sixteen years has increased one hundred and forty per cent, while the comparative rise in the overall cost of living index has been forty per cent. The large

149

companies assure us that the high cost of drugs is . . ."

"Goddam it, Joseph, I knew this would happen." Sorenson leaped up. "That's the second time he's mentioned the high cost of drugs as if it were an established fact."

" . . . due to the costs of quality control and the cost of research. They keep assuring us that this is a research-based industry. Let's look at quality control. Certainly, you would want to be sure if you were sick that the medication that was prescribed was the same all the time, that the bottle of pills you bought today was the same as the one you bought last month."

On camera an air view of the sprawling Heister main factory appeared. Through the sound of the helicopter engine Grant explained, "Below us is the Heister plant, the largest building in terms of ground square footage in the world."

The camera cut to a worker inside, dressed in white, a surgical mask over her face. "Hi," she said, then explained the twenty-eight different tests she had to do on one capsule before it was approved for packaging and sale.

"Thank God for her," Sorenson said. "I guess he couldn't edit her out of the film."

The camera closed in on many of the delicate instruments and machines used in quality control while Sorenson's voice explained, "That is a Tablet Dissolution Rate Apparatus to indicate the solubility of a drug; cost, nineteen thousand dollars. The next machine is an Automatic Dispensing Analyzer; its job is to analyze the potency of tablets; cost, twenty-eight thousand dollars. The next machine costs sixty-five thousand dollars and is called a Combination Mass Spectrophotometer and Gas Chromotographer; it identifies the structure of compounds and analyzes for foreign materials."

"That stuff has to impress people, no matter what," Joseph said. "Maybe he will present both sides."

A hand-held camera then moved to another building identified as the Think Tank. Grant's voice-over explained, "The drug industry claims that it spends massive amounts of money on research." On screen appeared dogs, thousands of which had been bred for uniformity over the years, each one exactly the same — a computer's living litter — so that when tested, one could be certain that reactions were caused by the drug and not by some inborn and unknown genetic defect in the dog. The camera moved on showing mice bred for obesity, cats and monkeys in cages, and white-coated chemists in their little cubicles; then it passed signs marked "Dangerous—Radiation—Keep out." And again it passed fascinating machines, now described by Sorenson's voice. "Mass Spectroscopy which identifies chemicals on the basis of their unit weight and how they break apart when hit by electron beams; Electron Microscopy, the study of how drugs act on cell structures; Nuclear Resonance Spectroscopy, which helps determine the molecular structure of unknown compounds; Liquid Scintillation Counters, enabling the biologist to learn how a labelled compound is metabolized."

The camera cut back to Sorenson in the television studio. "Modern drugs are usually a combination of many chemical substances. The scientist who designs a drug must have complete knowledge of all the properties of each substance, whether they will react with each other and what the effect of such interaction will be. Some questions that have to be answered are, What should be the dosage form? Should it be a tablet? A liquid? Injectable? And once inside the patient, how long will it take to be active? If an oral drug, how will it taste? Will it be small enough to swallow?

"As we will see," Grant interrupted, "some critics contend that much of the money spent on research is not spent wisely but on duplicating products of other companies, or on molecular manipulation to get around patent laws."

"Minor changes in molecular structure of chemical compounds have sometimes provided completely new and better and safer therapeutic products," Sorenson continued. "The new penicillins come to mind, as does the whole field of tetracyclines. The antibiotics are much stronger and produce fewer side effects than the older miracle drugs. Another is the conversion of a chemical known as Compound A into cortisone."

"You look good, Dean," Joseph said, feeling a little better. Sorenson looked at least as honest as Grant.

151

And then the character of the program changed. The camera closed in on Dr. Sherway, and Grant's voice took on a hardened quality. "Well doctor, we've seen all the marvellous machines and listened to how much they cost, although the fact that they cost a few thousand , last for years, and that the earned profits of these companies run into the millions of dollars really is not that impressive. In fact, figures revealed at the special inquiry show that out of every dollar earned by the pharmaceutical companies only one and a half cents is spent on research."

"The real problem," Dr. Sherway contended, "is that most of the research is directed either to clinical testing or molecular manipulation in a frantic struggle to have the latest model, not on what causes sickness, not on the basic nature of man. There is very little money for pure research. And as far as Canada goes, there is hardly any research done here at all, except for clinical testing required by the Food and Drug before a new drug is qualified for sale. And I don't class that as research at all."

The camera cut to a close-up of Dr. Lewison. "It is said that eight thousand drugs are readily available across Canada. In the United States there may be twenty thousand; in the U.K. from five to seven thousand. In the Netherlands, an expert committee has reduced the list to four thousand. At the Kefauver hearings one of the witnesses offered to run a New York hospital with three hundred and fifty-nine drugs. The complex relationship between the producer of a substance who advertises it (usually accentuating the positive, like the old song), the pharmacist who dispenses it, the physician who chooses and orders it, and the patient who pays for it"—"and swallows it," Dr. Sherway cut in—"is one which should be controlled by the doctor."

The camera cut to Dr. Sherway. "It is utterly impossible for the practising physician to keep up with the new drugs. He depends on the drug detail man for his continuing education. The drug detail man — a salesman."

Camera cut to a close-up of Grant. "What percentage of hospital beds are now thought to be filled by patients with reactions to drugs, some so serious as to be irreversible, some causing death horribly?"

152

Camera cut back to Dr. Sherway. "I don't want to frighten the audience, but though doctors do a good job, I would say anywhere from ten to thirty per cent of hospital beds are filled with the people you describe; ill from adverse drug reactions."

"Are you in this program, Dean? He interviewed you for three hours?" Joseph asked angrily. "Three hours of taping and you've hardly been on."

Camera cut to close-up of Grant. "Morton Mintz in his book, *Therapeutic Nightmare*,"—"I knew he'd drag that book in," Sorenson said — "tells of a harrowing case, typical of thousands. 'In January Mrs. K died in California. The last eight years of her life were a tale of horror. Eight years ago, Mrs. K was given an antibiotic for a minor gum infection. She contracted aplastic anemia, a painful blood disease that kills half its victims. To counteract the anemia she was given massive injections of hormones. A beard grew on her face which became disfigured by acne. She sued the company who made the drug and was awarded a two hundred thousand dollar settlement out of court. This company still manufactures and sells this drug all over the world.' "

Cut to Dr. Lewison. "I was astonished to learn that two or three years ago, a drug I was ready to nominate for oblivion was enjoying a sale of a million tablets a month in Germany."

"And we haven't even discussed the mind- and mood-altering drugs, tranquillizers and such," Dr. Sherway said. "Other than patients who actually cannot function outside an institution without them, no one should take them. And yet they account for half the drug sales in the United States and Canada."

The camera zoomed in to a closeup of Grant showing just his eyes and mouth. "Well then, why does this happen? Surely those fine young scientists we saw are not out to kill us? They are not doing the research they want to. They do what they are told to do. And that nice lady who was so proud of her job in production — you can be sure no pill that leaks ever gets past her. Does she want to hurt us? Certainly not. Well then, who decides on the research? What kind of man decides to market a drug he knows is dangerous? Why are adverse reactions hidden?" When Sorenson denied that they were, Grant picked up the transcript from the Kefauver hearings that proved they were. Even Heister's company had been caught out on a minor item.

Grant continued. "Why are the names for drugs so long? Why has a system never been devised so that the person who pays for a drug has a clear idea of what he is buying and what the side effects might be? Why do drugs cost so much? And why do they vary? One price to a hospital, then different prices to almost every different drug store. Grant displayed a chart showing the differences in the prices of the same drugs in cities across Canada.

The camera cut to Dr. Greenaway. "Perhaps all I need to say is that this industry is a large international industry, comprising mainly very large international firms whose economic and commercial policies tend to be determined, quite properly from their point of view, on the basis of maximizing profitability of world-wide operations of the international firm. These policies do not necessarily coincide with the best interests of the Canadian economy and the Canadian branch of the firm. The selling price of an unpatented drug, which is subject to free competition in the market, is directly related to the cost of production. The pricing of patented drugs, where there is no competition, is priced at what the traffic will bear. Penicillin G, which was not patented, was two thousand three hundred dollars for one billion I.T.U.'s in 1947, and dropped to thirty-three dollars for the same amount in 1959, and is less today. Another, which is patented, has a cost of a dollar thirty-two for one thousand tablets and is priced to the consumer at one hundred twenty-five dollars."

"Son-of-a-bitch, that's not the whole story," Sorenson said, as Dr. Greenaway quoted further examples.

Camera cut to Grant. "I would like to quote from one doctor's remarks to the United States Subcommittee on Monopoly. 'The pharmaceutical industry is unique in that it can make exploitation seem a noble purpose. It is the organized, carefully-planned and skilful execution of this exploitation that is the problem, and constitutes one of the costs of drugs that must be measured not only in terms of dollars, but in terms of inroads the industry has made into the entire structure of medicine and medical care.'"

The camera cut to the five men sitting around the table in calm discussion. Grant asked, "But should the price of a drug that might save your life be a consideration at all?"

"Obviously not," Dr. Sherway admitted. "But most drugs don't fall into that category. Those are drugs for the chronically ill, the aged with some type of deficiency."

"Or as a society because we cannot endure pain," Dr. Lewison said. "For some reason, and I accuse the drug industry's advertising for this, we feel as human beings that we have a right to live a pain-free life. So each little pain becomes magnified; each headache, backache, and so on."

"But gentlemen," Sorenson managed to cut in, "drugs which get you back to work faster, even from such things as influenza, drugs that reduce the risk of you developing pneumonia and other serious illnesses from the common cold, save a great deal of money for the community, to say nothing of their impact on the individual. And how can we judge the costs of drugs in a society that spends billions on cigarettes and alcohol?"

The camera at that point cut to a film clip of the late President Kennedy whose voice was heard. "Over twenty per cent of the new drugs listed since nineteen fifty-five were found on being tested to be incapable of sustaining their sponsors' claims regarding their therapeutic effect. There is no way of measuring the needless suffering, the money innocently squandered and the protraction of illnesses resulting from the use of such ineffective drugs."

The camera dissolved to Grant, standing in the drug store. In front of him and around him was a pile—as high as he was—of pills, boxes, vials. "All these are made by members of the Pharmaceutical Association, not one member of which is a Canadian company. The profits from all these drugs leave the country. Of more than three hundred patents held on antibiotics, less than one-half of one per cent are held by Canadian residents."

The camera zoomed to a close-up of Grant's face, his voice soft and insistent. "Who is to blame for high prices, for drugs that kill

155

rather than cure, for drugs you don't need? Right now a special committee of Parliament is in session probing these questions. One way to bring down prices is to stop protecting American and other foreign companies. To change patent laws. I advise every one of you to find out about this committee, and in the interest of your health, of your children, and of your country, to write your Member of Parliament. It need not take long. Write a letter tonight. Just say, 'I'm in favour of lowering prices for drugs. End patent protection now.' "

Joseph and Sorenson remained wordless as they watched the closing credits and the following commercials, almost hypnotized by their disbelief. "Feel like another scotch?" Sorenson asked.

"I'll get it, Dean," Joseph said, strangely mechanical as he poured the drinks and brought them back.

Grant had turned on him. Had deliberately lied to him. Had led him to believe that the show would be live and it was taped. That it would be unbiased and it had been a hatchet job, a magnificently clever hatchet job, the way only television people could do — rearrange film, put words into someone's mouth when they looked particularly sinister. Sorenson had been taped supposedly for background for an exhaustive three hours, and yet had been edited down to a few minutes. And the questions and answers had been put in an order that suited Grant, not the way they occurred.

As much as he had trusted Grant, he never would have agreed to a taped show. TV editors could make Jesus Christ appear like Hitler. His mind was spinning. Humiliation at being made a fool. A sense of frustration that the clock could not be turned back. An emptiness at the loss of Grant. A sense of failure. And rage.

He picked up the phone and called Heister in New York. He wasn't about to duck any responsibility. "It was a disaster, Bob. I'm sorry. It was my fault, I gave you bad advice."

"I know, Pharmpress told me. They had the show monitored. They're studying it for possible law suit."

"You can have my resignation if you want."

"Is that what you want?"

156

"No, I want that son-of-a-bitch MacDonald," Joseph screamed. "I could kill him. I want to stay on the job."

"Fair enough. I don't blame you, Joseph. It was calculated risk. But you were chosen because of your relationship to Mac-Donald. There were four management consultants, each of equal ability. The deciding factor was that you knew MacDonald and we hoped you could influence him."

Joseph had suspected that, known it, but stated so baldly it was cruel to his self-esteem, especially this time.

"Now Joseph, I want the gloves off." And in a tone that shocked Joseph, he said, "I want MacDonald's balls on a platter. No more talk. I don't care what you have to do, figure a way. See his publisher, tell him we'll pull ads out; tell his wife about that girl he's fucking; hire some hoods and get him beaten up. I want him stopped."

When Joseph put the phone down he sank in the chair, his head in his hands, the realization of what Grant had done to him sinking ever more deeply into him.

The phone rang.

Sorenson picked it up and handed it to Joseph. "It's for you—a lady."

"Joseph."

"Violetta." It was all he could do to speak her name without breaking down.

"You okay?"

"Uh-huh."

"Why not come over here?"

"In a little while." And he put the phone down. "I'm going to get that bastard," he said slamming out of the room, pushing Sorenson aside.

Speeding across the bridge suspended over the wide, rapids-filled Ottawa River to Hull, on the way to Grant's house, Joseph was aware of the sprawling lumberyards and mill of the E.B. Eddy Company on the other side. He remembered when the whole pile of logs, as high as a forty-storey building, had burned to the ground (black humour because the firm manufactured matches), the flames soaring in the air, lighting up the sky. Uncharacteristically, thousands of Ottawans stayed up the whole night to watch the firemen and their futility; no water could put out that flame until all was gone and the flames flickered across this very bridge.

Ottawa and Hull were twin cities except Hull was in Quebec. A shabby collection of frame houses, mostly unpainted to keep taxes low (but some lovely inside), roads narrow and filled with potholes, Hull was a French-Canadian, working-class ghetto, peopled by blue-collar workers wearing windbreakers.

Joseph was driving at speeds in excess of ninety miles per hour, over twisting, back-country roads on land that stretched along one of the highest ridges in the Gatineau hills — reputedly one of the oldest mountain ranges in North America. It was a half hour's drive from Ottawa to Grant's house. Ten couples had bought land there (the "hillbillies," they called themselves) at a time when for many reasons no English-Canadian would live on the Quebec side; the Quebec government was corrupt, the schooling inferior, the Catholic hierarchy kept the province backward, the taxes higher, the services nil. And of course now, another danger for those English who considered themselves like bwana in a black land — the potential violence of French-Canadian separatism.

Joseph's head was a mass of pain and rage, and if Grant had appeared before the car he would have run him over. Consciously, purposely, gleefully run him over.

And finally at his house, roaring at him. "I trusted you, you dishonest bastard. The one person in my life I trusted, would have given my life for. And look what you've done."

"Joseph, listen, I was doing my job and you were doing yours. I warned you right in the beginning that you were up against more than you knew, that you couldn't win. I was being your friend when I told you to get out of it. And I still say it. You can't win. And you shouldn't. What you represent is wrong. The drug industry is basically destructive."

But in Joseph's mind was a picture of his mother who had

changed from a defective old lady who would never go out of the house to a bouncing, active woman who now ate well and took part in a senior citizens' bowling league. And Flanagan's wife had been cured by modern drugs.

"Joseph, the group you work for is the most venal ever developed by man. And whether you know or care, prescription drugs are like the tip of the iceberg. Below are the oil and gas from where the petro-chemicals, plastics, dyes, and animal feed come from. The oil and gas that plays the nations' game, sending thousands upon thousands of young men to kill other young men. The oil and gas that poisons us all. And you're part of it. A killer."

"I was your friend. I trusted you. And you betrayed me. You could have cost me my future, my life."

"Cut the dramatic shit. You knew where I stood, Joey. You thought you could use me. That you could come to Canada and use me. Well, it didn't work."

And the dialogue got locked in set speeches, communicating nothing. Joseph's head was spinning dizzily. The phone rang for Grant and it was someone obviously calling to say what a great thing he'd done, because he heard Grant say, "Thank you, yes J.O., I thought it came off well, but I better call you back."

"Grant, I'll get you. You warned me, now I'm warning you. Be careful what you write. We'll sue unless every fact is right. There'll be a detective following your every move so I wouldn't see Louise if I were you, because that evidence will be given to Thelma. And by the way, I fucked her. Do you hear," he shouted, hoping Thelma was listening, "I fucked your lover Louise. Can't win. You just watch me. I will win. Goddam it, I've never failed at anything."

At that revelation Grant almost lost control, almost told Joseph about Violetta's role in INTEGRAL. But he stopped himself. For all he knew, she, too was using poor, dumb Joseph for the purposes of the general good and therefore, no matter how violated he felt himself to be, he said only, "I'm fighting for my country — and yours. And you, Joseph, what are you fighting for?"

159

Those words stayed in Joseph's head as he drove ever so slowly and carefully back through Hull and Ottawa toward Violetta's. What was he fighting for? Was Grant's sense of rightness so strong that sacrificing Joseph and their past was a small cost, of little matter. Did the industry, because it was based on sickness (if everyone were healthy there would be no industry) create its own sickness at the top? Were all its leaders struck by some soul-wasting disease? Joseph thought about the only other time when he and Grant could not resolve their differences, and it had changed both their lives. "Don't be a meathead," he had said when Grant told him he had asked Thelma to marry him. "You've just finished university, just got out of a war. Why be trapped? Why the rush for the white picket fence? For children? I bet you can't even get into her pants until you're married and even then she won't stop talking long enough." When he saw Grant's averted eyes, he shouted, "I knew it. What do you do, talk about Kant instead of cunt? Women are to fuck, not to marry." But Grant had married and then Joseph had moved in with Genevieve ... and married too.

"You don't look so good," Violetta said when she opened the door.

"I don't feel so good."

"Why don't you just get into bed and I'll give you something to make you go to sleep."

"What about Mylita?"

"What she knows, she knows."

"Can we sit up a while?" he asked, almost like a little boy. And her heart went out to him. He had some fear about going to sleep, afraid, like old people are, to lay his head down, some intuition about blotting out life, about never waking up.

"I saw Grant's TV show. I'm sorry." Difficult to understand how two men, friends since childhood, could let themselves get so caught up in the externals of life that they sacrifice their friendship. "You trusted him. I know how you must feel. I knew he wouldn't be unbiased." And then with horror realized that she was doing the same to Joseph as Grant had.

"I guess everyone did but me," he said, missing the invitation in her voice to ask how she knew. Not sharp because he was not expecting he would have to be alert, on guard, animal-aware with her.

And then she felt torn. She had almost told him, would have told him about INTEGRAL and Grant and herself if he had asked. And not understanding why she didn't tell him now. But that wasn't true. She didn't tell him because she didn't want their relationship to end, as it surely would. What was real? Was it no longer real to have a friend? No longer possible to love? To love? Did she love Joseph?

Too edgy to sit, she had to get up. She brought him a scotch without asking and sat beside him, again wordless, almost wringing her hands in anxiety. And he sipped the scotch and was into himself and was aware, slowly and deeply, of his and Grant's life as children and that it was gone. Suddenly he felt his age, forty-two. He undoubtedly had more years of living behind him than ahead, years of playing snakes and ladders at different jobs. The truth was that he hadn't achieved much. Thirty thousand dollars a year plus wasn't up to the expectations he had had for himself. And then he was out of himself, because Violetta was there beside him and he felt a new wholeness start within him; despite everything he felt his body open itself out and he couldn't understand it, fought to stay in the blackness of himself. And they were silent together and he had a sense of oneness, the same as when he had made love with her, a sense of not being separate, not being repelled by the other body, not feeling a field force of separation — as always before with others — but a flowing. Until now everybody he had encountered in his life had been an enemy, a threat.

He was perilously close to letting down all the carefully structured defenses that kept the outside blackness out and the inside blackness in. He thought of New York and his method of seeking peace in excess, doing anything to keep active. At these moments he could escape the nothingness inside him, afraid to discover and make friends with his human solitude. But now, with her beside him, he was free. And the tears came out of his eyes. His eyes wide open and staring and the tears slipping down

161

his cheeks. And he was not humiliated.

She leaned over and kissed his eyes and the tears on his cheeks and his mouth and she covered his hand with hers. He touched his face to hers, breathing in the sweetness of her life. And he looked into her eyes and was open and unafraid. Sank into them, into the blueness that was the eternity of sky and sea. And whatever that was, it was more than rational, more than animal, and more than human; whatever was life was in the totality of that feeling, like looking into the sun, into the sky until your head becomes one with it; like looking into the eyes of the mother of a newborn baby; like seeing death creep through the fragile parchment face of a still breathing, beloved grandmother.

The mystery of all for naught and all for everything, of all the people in a togetherness they know and can't know and can't accept and must. Alone and unafraid. Open and unafraid. Exposed totally. "Violetta," he said. But it was hard to form the words he wanted to say. Not hard to think or to feel or to know, but hard to make them come out. Finally, out of necessity, with a wrench he said, "Violetta, I love you." And then surprise and wonder at the sense of new life and peace. "In love. I am in love with you."

"And I you," she said simply. *"Us mylu tave.* I love you."

And side by side they sat, the night long, hands held, awake and not awake, a duality, an intensity, a oneness, non-existence that was total existence, a magnified awareness of solitude because of being together, and Joseph felt himself to be alive. And for that night they transcended their individual deceits; he knowing the ugliness and hate he would be capable of to win; she knowing she was deceiving Joseph in the same way Grant had, knowing he would find out and then there would be an emptiness and aloneness that would be unendurable. But for now the other world was outside her door, and Violetta was in love and loved.

Side by side they sat until the sun rose and the vitality of Mylita exploded on them.

162

[13]

Following a desperate round of working around the clock, the brief to be submitted by the pharmaceutical industry had been completed. Joseph breakfasted with Dean Sorenson who maintained a suite at the Château Laurier, and then they walked along the Rideau Street bridge toward the Parliament buildings. That morning he felt close to the pinnacle of success and happiness. The people they passed on the street might not know, but this gracefully aging man with the slight limp and battered briefcase was one of the most influential men in the commercial world, and, despite the conflicts that often erupted between them, Joseph was proud to be with him.

He had always been curious about Sorenson's briefcase, the only facet of his appearance that was not fastidious. When asked, Sorenson explained that he had had it since the war, it had travelled everywhere in the world with him, and he had developed a fondness for it—the way some men do for an old hat, or their favourite chair or pipe. Conversely, Joseph's case was a soft brown alligator, a new one for which he had paid one hundred and fifty dollars. Not for him the production line models carried by every junior executive in downtown New York.

"Take a cruise down the canal and the Ottawa River, see the fall colours," a hawker dressed in sea captain's cap and blazer hustled, waving tickets at them.

Joseph stopped and looked over the side of the bridge at the Step Locks of the Rideau Canal. "You know, Dean, this canal was

163

first proposed during the War of 1812 as a means of transporting supplies from Montreal to Fort Henry at Kingston through an inland waterway. That way they could avoid the American guns dominating the St. Lawrence at Ogdensburg. See that old stone building down there," he said pointing over the railing. "That was Colonel By's house, the engineer who built the locks and the canal. Ottawa was originally called Bytown."

To the left as they walked along was the War Memorial, in the middle of Confederation Square, renamed Confusion Square by the thousands of irritated Ottawa motorists who were forced to negotiate the system of one-way streets, blind turns, and diagonal crossings.

Looking back, Sorenson said, "The Château Laurier looks like a castle on the Loire with the morning sun glistening on the green spires. I remember the first time I visited here. My wife was alive then. We couldn't find a restaurant open after eleven to get a cup of coffee."

Typically American, Joseph thought, surprised to find himself nettled by Sorenson's patronizing tone. He was being idiotic. Philomen Wright, the first settler in the area, was an American from Boston. Bytown was named after a Scotsman. Greber had been brought from France to design the new Capital City Plan. There had always been so much foreign input into Canada — English, French, European, Jewish, American, Italian; so much movement back and forth across the border — American TV, magazines, and movies overpowering feeble Canadian attempts. Where was the vaunted Canadian culture Grant had accused him of selling out? There never had been a Canadian culture. Nor would there be because there wasn't a Canadian people. A French-Canadian culture, yes, but not a Canadian one. Then why did Sorenson's remark anger him?

The centre doors of Parliament and the Rideau Club faced each other, the line between them perfectly straight, intersecting the lawn and crossing Wellington Street, named after the conqueror of Napoleon. Beside it was the American embassy. Of the dozens in Ottawa it was the only embassy that faced the Canadian Parliament buildings. From a certain angle, Joseph realized that many of the elements of political power in Canada were in view. Parliament itself, the Rideau Club, the Bank of Canada, and the Supreme Court building all appeared to be balanced on the fulcrum of the American embassy.

Before turning into the gate to Parliament Hill, Joseph had a cartoon vision of a little man with binoculars at the window of the American embassy watching Canadian Members of Parliament to be sure they voted the right way on all things important to the United States. It would be possible, he realized, for Americans to bug Canadian cabinet meetings, or, like a coach in a football game, have the Canadian prime minister wired for instant orders that would fit into an overall American "game-plan" — whatever it happened to be that week. Facetious perhaps, but that foreign building on this street, in front of Parliament, symbolized American domination over Canada. He shrugged. So what?

As he waited for the committee to begin he looked for Violetta, but she hadn't arrived as yet. His eyes swept the room and rested on the painting on the wall of the Fathers of Confederation. Sometimes he wondered what they would think of all this. He had sat in this room so many days, he was certain that he could tell how each individual's mind worked. And what amused him more and seemed to provide added incongruity to the situation was the fact that after the original painting was burned in the Great Fire, the artist who was commissioned to paint a copy had added several of the Fathers who had missed the original sitting, and had changed the actual position of another, crossing his legs in a different way in order to create a more pleasing composition. Joseph thought of the hundreds of thousands of school children who trooped into this room when it wasn't being used and listened while their teachers described the painting and the men in it, or saw it reproduced in school books across Canada believing they were looking at an actual historical happening.

"Gentlemen, I see a quorum." The chairman struck his gavel.

Flanagan and Dr. Lewison immediately engaged in procedural wrangling.

165

Colin Moore, the Parliamentary lawyer (whose office Joseph's mother had kept clean), an expert in procedure, was called. While this went on, Joseph reviewed his position. Of the twenty-four members of the committee, fourteen were Liberals, eight Conservatives, one from the Socialist party, and one from Social Credit. If it came to a vote he could now count on all the Conservatives, the Social Credit member — which made nine — and three Liberals, including Flanagan. Half the committee were committed to retaining the Patent Law as it existed. He knew, of course, that until the hearings were over there could still be much shifting. One of the keys would be to figure a way to stop Dr. Lewison, by far the most articulate Liberal and deeply opposed to the industry. Fortunately Grant's TV program had not had the effect on the general public that he had anticipated. Neither the committee nor Members of Parliament had been flooded with letters. Part of the reason was the lucky fluke that the special had appeared opposite a heavily advertised American movie with major Hollywood stars.

The debate on intricacies of procedure seemed to be taking up most of the morning. When such idiocies occurred, Joseph would look at Violetta — who had arrived late taking the only empty chair — beside Douglas Clark. She felt his eyes burning into her, turned and smiled.

"You're making a spectacle of yourself," Douglas muttered. "Don't you get enough of him at night? You and your lover."

Violetta looked at Douglas triumphantly and said, "Never. Never enough, Douglas, never ever."

So mad were Joseph and Violetta, so much did their bodies need each other, that often they sped to her home during lunch or evening recess (INTEGRAL devised the idea of lengthening the sessions to include evening sittings in order to put terrific physical pressure on those in the industry lobby), even though it was only an hour and a half or at the most two, to be alone, together, to kiss, hold hands, to drink martinis while standing at the kitchen counter eating sardines out of an open tin, sharing a fork. And sometimes so mad were they that they rushed home hardly able to wait until they stripped down and threw them-

166

selves lustfully on the bed, he laughing afterwards while she tried to adjust her hair and make-up with shaky hands.

"How do I look? Do I look okay?"

"You look beautiful, eyes shining, cheeks flushed, like a girl who's just made love."

He had an awareness of her body that was almost metaphysical, as if his body and her body had their own separate knowing, their own separate being. Her body was imprinted inside him, inside his head and wherever one is aware of a totality of feel and smell and being. And he delighted in lying naked beside her and in feeling her, all the parts, layered in foam under skin that was satin; small breasts, large thighs like the peasants in the fields in Lithuania. And impossible not to touch her, stroke her, caress her; sometimes he placed his hand on her flesh and could feel all the essence of her body flow through his hand, so close did he feel to her. And he could run his hand an inch above her body, not touching her and yet feel her body flow into his hand and she feel his hand as if he were touching her, so close were they. And he was possessed by the wonder of the force that emanated from one to the other. So hard to believe, to permit oneself to believe, especially for him, that what he was feeling he was actually feeling, so difficult to give oneself up to it.

"Do you feel my hand, even when I'm not touching you?"

"Sometimes bether."

"Witch, damned Lithuanian witch."

"Anyway, you like witches bether."

"And you can't speak the language." Sometimes her tongue slipped on certain words and she said "bether" instead of "better" and often started a sentence "anyway" when a conjunction was what she was looking for. Joseph had never made love before without feeling soiled and disgusted — except with Cynthia, but that was different, too, because she was a whore and they shared an animal lust that itself was a contempt for humanness. He had always felt something ugly about the vagina and the womb, some physical fear that he fought and blotted from his mind, a disgust he could not fathom and did not admit totally, that led him always to leave the bed quickly and take a shower. A

167

worry always that he had no feeling, was unable to feel (and this he blotted out as well), and yet it never affected his performance. But inside he had always felt a part of him bruised. Part of his soul violated. But not with Violetta. When she placed her mouth on his mouth, her lips on his lips, his body, his very being arranged itself without tension and he experienced peace. Once he felt her looking at him naked, as she liked to do. He would lie on the bed and she would sit on her haunches and look at him and touch him and play with him and study his reactions, ever-fascinated with his testicles. "They move you know, when I come close. They know. They have a life of their own."

He felt totally naked before her eyes. At first it was uncomfortable for him. He had been naked in front of many women before without being naked. But she saw him. "You have a beautiful body. Aside from everything else, you really are a good-looking bastard." She touched the flat scar on his left cheek, barely below his eye, from a beserk barroom fight during the war; and she felt the thickness on his nose and traced the ridges with her tongue where it had been broken, twice — once while playing hockey in high school and once during a basketball game at university. And then on top of him, which she loved, to be in control of her own climax, or of his if she chose, her face close to his. "Black eyes, like the earth, like death," she said once, and shivered and got under the covers and cried.

She owned him and he wanted to be owned. She had a way of owning his penis, of making him feel the power of her ownership with the total control of it in her hands and inside her body and inside her mouth. Sometimes he felt all these things together, felt his whole body deep inside her, held by her, cradled by her, while she was on her knees naked in bed over him and he naked on his back and she held him with both hands.

"Witch," he yelled. "Lithuanian witch.

"You think my penis is the Great Oak that your people worshipped in the forests. Yes, I know where you come from." He had read about the tenth-century Waidelots who brought their offerings and placed them at the foot of the Great Oak. He knew and it was part of his love for her that her people went back further than recorded history, their language one of the two thought to be closest to the original Sanskrit. But Christianity, as it had destroyed everything else, had destroyed their forest religion — although in remote villages traces of their original practices still remained. Their people had always been a tribe of barely over a few million, rarely with their own kingdom, usually part of some larger grouping owned by Poland or Russia, and perhaps this had led to a sense of *people* in the same way that it had for the Jews.

And this was what he felt, insane as it might seem, that when he penetrated her, merged with her, that he was part of the origins of everything, of all that was the mystery of life.

And she smiled that deepest of all smiles in her blue, bluest of all blue eyes, that went back centuries. "*Us mylu tave*," she said. "I love you."

But though they had agreed never to allow the other world in, and it became difficult at times to know which was the real world, she asked him one day, "Is it true that you warned Grant that a private detective was watching him all the time and that if he saw Louise the evidence would be given to Thelma? Would you do that?"

"Yes, it's true, I did that," he said, remembering the distaste he felt when Louise called and pleaded with him.

"Louise is torn apart."

"I know. But it's Grant's doing not mine."

The first casualty, Violetta thought with a shudder. God, what was going to happen to them all?

"This morning we have the brief of the Pharmaceutical Association," the chairman said as he stopped the wrangling between Lewison and Flanagan. "Copies have all been placed before you. As you can see it is quite thick. It is an excellent and well-organized brief, but will take considerable reading and study."

One of Joseph's ideas had been to make the brief so thorough and so formidable that it would overwhelm the simpler members

169

of the committee by its sheer size. Flanagan had been coached on the key parts that proved that doctors, drug stores, sales tax, corporation and other taxes, the cost of new drug applications and quality control—which was necessary to protect the health of the nation—were the real reasons for the price of drugs being what they were. Not patents. In fact, Joseph was counting on the twin factors — the size of the brief and Flanagan's intimate knowledge of it—to enable them to control all discussion and the resultant press reaction.

"Congratulations, Joseph," Sorenson said. "It can't do anything but help that the chairman praises our brief."

"Let me remind you that I worked hard on that brief as well, and my staff gathered the facts," Ron Kendall said with evident bitterness. Joseph's ability was galling.

"You won't get any argument from me on that score, Ron," Joseph agreed.

But he had taken the original draft and, using the section in CAMP referring to the proper style of writing reports, had rewritten it. CAMP was the acronym for the Daniels and Company's *Catalogue and Manual of Practices*. It detailed every aspect of consultant-client relationship, even to the manner of carriage, style, and colour of suit (various shades of dark blue or charcoal gray, plain or pin-striped), and length to have one's hair barbered. Further pages were added to encompass new situations until now three gold-embossed ring binders were needed to accommodate CAMP's two hundred and eighty-five pages. Every consultant received a copy of his own the day he joined the firm, his first assignment to take a week to study it thoroughly.

It hadn't taken Joseph long to discover that he was the only member of the firm who regarded CAMP as absurd, and that he could not openly display his view; yet needing at least the illusion that he was still partly his own man, he hit upon the amusing idea, or it started out as an amusing idea, of following its strictures to the letter, like the "Good Soldier Schweik." And so he wore the dark blue and charcoal gray suits, of the finest cloth and tailoring, and had his initials sewn on his made-to-measure white shirts, wrote detailed conference reports, submitted his weekly

170

time and expense sheets by ten o'clock every Monday morning and, if he was out of town on assignment, made sure they were on the accountant's desk with the first mail. He refrained from calling his secretary by her first name. He kept his daily log which was broken down into fifteen-minute time segments, completely up-to-date, both for billing purposes and so that he knew what he had accomplished every quarter hour of every day of the six years he had been with the firm. He took no more than two drinks at a client cocktail party and did not smoke cigars (no hardship). But his greatest success was not only in never being late for a meeting — that was easy enough — but in always being ten minutes early; unfailingly, reliably, ten minutes early for any client meeting. The approach to report writing was contained on a plastic card that every consultant carried in his wallet, a card as important to him as his American Express card. It stated:

· Talk to your reader — use 'we' and 'you'
· Use simple words: the language of talk
· Use active verbs: 'Man bites dog'
· Keep sentences short (under two lines)
· Start paragraphs with strong topic sentences
· Keep Fog Index below 12 (ASL=%P) 0.4

Joseph's knowledge of CAMP and his observance had made him a legend at the firm. His colleagues were in awe of his apparent fundamentalist approach to CAMP (and indeed it was often referred to as the "Bible"). Unknown to them, however, Joseph drew the line at perfection and permitted himself two exceptions from his otherwise total obeisance. He cheated on his expense account (not to put the money in the bank; he liked to live well), and he slept with clients' secretaries, wives, daughters, and even mistresses when chance permitted.

"We would have had the brief sooner if we hadn't had to worry so much about getting a proper translation into French," Sorenson said. "Costly time-wasting foolishness."

"Canada is a bilingual country," Kendall reminded him somewhat testily.

"When it comes right down to it," Sorenson admitted, "I know

171

so little about Canada. We've always treated it as a branch just as if it were another state like Michigan or California. I know more about Europe and the Far East."

It was said in an off-hand way, without malice, but Joseph felt Kendall stiffening with resentment, and he also had the curious insight that if the United States took Canada over entirely, as he was sure would happen, the French language would not continue too long in Quebec, as it hadn't in Louisiana. In one way Sorenson was right. Judged by efficiency standards, bilingualism didn't make sense.

And then he heard Dr. Lewison say, "The brief is no doubt excellent, and I am sure when we come to study it, and discuss it page by page, we will become so enmeshed in the intricacies that our desire to reduce the high price of drugs will seem impossible —and perhaps for the rich areas of Canada, parts of the big cities like Toronto and Montreal, where there is full employment, the price of drugs is not a factor of life. But most Canadians still live in small urban or rural areas. My constituency for example is one of constant unemployment, as are many in Canada. Let us not be bamboozled by the size of this tome. We must reduce the price of drugs."

Suddenly a way to stop Lewison's articulate and forceful opposition occurred to Joseph and the idea had been suggested right out of Lewison's own mouth. He had become the leader of the Liberals on the committee who wanted to change the patent laws and always seemed armed with probing questions and facts hurtful to the industry. But now Joseph was sure he could shut him up.

Lewison represented the area around Cornwall, Ontario. Only some fifty miles from Ottawa it was the heart of a pocket of unemployment so serious that it had been declared a depressed area by the provincial government. As such, manufacturers who built new plants there were entitled to substantial government loans at low interest. Several weeks ago a Swiss pharmaceutical firm had decided to take advantage of the financial situation and the low pay scale and had announced plans to build a plant that would employ two hundred people. That many new jobs would

172

make a sizable dent in the unemployment.

Well, unless the powers in the area stopped Lewison, Joseph thought, that plant would be built. It would be a simple matter for Heister to get the Swiss to co-operate. And Joseph was certain that if it came to a choice between something abstract in Ottawa pitted against the loss of a plant employing two hundred people and the thousands of voters those two hundred could influence, Lewison would be stopped. As soon as the session ended, Joseph called Heister. Within an hour Heister had called back. The Swiss were in agreement. Joseph had a free hand.

14

Fred Smith looked nervously at the men sitting around the polished mahogany boardroom table; an ostentatiously furnished room for such an old, block-long building in a run-down section of east side New York that contained a forest of such buildings. Tony Ferrilio, wiping his head, was talking, talking, trying to convince the other men: Victor Romano from Toronto who coughed a lot held a handkerchief in front of his mouth and had trouble breathing; whenever he wheezed or fought for air, all conversation stopped and sometimes it was difficult to pick up the threads; a man with him, he hadn't caught his name, who said nothing, but whose sole job seemed to be to look after Romano; another man, well-dressed with lacquered fingernails, also an Italian from New York, who was the go-between. As Fred Smith understood it, if they were to do business in Canada it must be approved by Romano, but if they were to meet here in New York to make the arrangements, it must be approved by Polished Fingernails. Completing the group were Harry Romasky, the owner of the plant they were in, and his friend Jack Greenstein, a stock promoter from Montreal.

It was a strange world, but two facts could not be denied. First, he and Tony Ferrilio had been parolled a week ago, six months sooner than expected; and second, he was as close to being in business—to having money again—as it was possible to be. And this meeting should take care of that.

Ferrilio explained his idea to open up Canada. The FDA would be watching him in the States so that starting a jobbing operation with a little manufacturing in Montreal would be a cinch. "Romasky here can help."

"What would you handle?" Romasky asked.

Victor Romano started to cough and fight for air and all conversation stopped.

"I'm not sure yet, Harry," Tony answered when Romano's spasm ceased. "I would study the situation and see what prices are, but I would plan to operate like you. A little of everything."

They had been taken on a tour of Romasky's plant, and to Fred Smith it looked all right. Approximately one hundred women were processing a number of salves and ointments. At the moment Romasky had gotten hold of a freight car of spoiled cough syrup and a chemist he had hired was trying to figure a way to make it palatable and safe. "It won't cure anyone's cough," Romasky said, "but no cough medicine is worth anything anyway."

"You're not pushing dope in Canada?" Romano wheezed, wanting to be assured, and started coughing again.

"No problems that way. This is a faster way of making money than hustling junk. Tranquillizers is where the big money is. Stuff that's easy to copy."

"You might look at Orinase or Diuril," Romasky advised. "I'm using over eight thousand Orinase a week."

"I don't want no heat," Romano wheezed.

"You still got my Stokes machine?" Tony asked Romasky. He nodded. "We take that machine to Canada and we can turn out five thousand tablets an hour. That machine can run twenty-four hours a day." He turned and explained to Romano, "The beauty of Romasky's operation is that it's partly legitimate. Sometimes the large manufacturers can't keep up with their orders and they come to someone like Romasky. Now to make the stuff they have to loan him the dies. They all have special shapes — hearts, blue heavens, red dots, and so on. And they have to loan him the marking machines, to put their trade names on. Out west there's a die-maker who'll make copies of these machines. He charges like a bastard, a thousand dollars for a machine that should cost fifty dollars. But he knows what it's

175

going to be used for. So Romasky is sort of in the machine business as well."

And then Tony Ferrilio decided it was time to close with Romano. Sometimes you could talk too long. "I don't know how well you know this business, but for twenty-five dollars I can get all the chemicals I need to make thousands of dollars. Take speed," and he explained how, with the dry materials in a bathtub or a garage, a small drum, some colouring, and a potato ricer, the mixture could be poured into a tablet compressor and he could counterfeit a drug.

Fred Smith watched and listened and said nothing. Tony had told him the truth. To get the money to operate in Canada, he needed two things: permission from the mafia in Canada—and that was Romano — and a loan of at least fifty thousand dollars to get set up. That money would either come from the mafia, or from the Jew Jackie Greenstein, a big operator in the mining stock promotion business, who was apparently looking for other businesses to turn into stock promotions. From his own experience Smith knew that no stockie would put up money in front. And the company would not be ready to go public as a junior industrial for at least a year. Perhaps Romasky would put up money and come in as a partner. But Ferrilio seemed to want to be on his own, except that Romasky had a lot of contacts in the business. Somehow all of it had to come together. Approval, money, and contacts, and then a stock offering.

"You could buy a building up there easy for fifty thousand down or rent one suitable for fifteen hundred a month. Equipment costs. But with a thousand dollars of machinery you can make a hundred grand a month."

"You have to think of a good name right now," Jack Greenstein said. "You have to look ahead to where the big money comes from when you start to sell stock. The name has to have something that sounds pure in it, like if you could call it the Pure Chemical Company. Pureco, something like that."

"That's good, I like that," Romano coughed.

"You're going to need salesmen," Romasky advised. "To call on druggists and doctors. There'll be no problem selling the stuff because you'll be cheaper than anyone else for what looks like the same thing, but you'll need someone who knows his way around."

Greenstein started to get excited. He was a tall man with balding hair and blue eyes. He rubbed his hand across his forehead and through his hair, "You know, maybe we could go public sooner than we think. I mean, what the fuck, if we had a building and products and some contracts and customers, maybe we could get a mining company with some cash in the treasury, one that is listed on the stock exchange, and turn it into an industrial, maybe in six months."

Romano nodded. "I have to get out of this air. I can't breathe. How much do you need?"

"Fifty thousand dollars for starters. Remember, I ran the bennies for the group. It wasn't my fault a stoolie tipped the feds. I wound up in the can. I'm owed a favour," Ferrilio said.

Romano nodded at his silent associate who opened a briefcase and counted out the money. Then Tony counted it. Then Romasky. And everyone agreed that indeed Romano had loaned fifty thousand and given the okay for them to operate in Canada.

"We're in business, kid," Ferrilio said in their hotel room after the meeting. "I knew they'd go for it."

Within days, Pharmpress had provided a run-down on everyone who had been at the meeting: Victor Romano, based in Toronto, representing the Buffalo mafia family that dominated that area; an unidentified New York man thought to be high in a New York family; Harry Romasky, on the fringes of counterfeit and substandard medicines for years — no convictions; Jack Greenstein, Montreal stock promoter reputedly worth millions since switching from mining promotion to promoting stock in land companies based in Freeport, Bahamas — always operates with mob approval.

The first item of business for Tony Ferrilio and Fred Smith was to buy clothes, three made-to-measure suits each plus shirts, shoes, ties; total cost, two thousand dollars. Next was to buy two of the most beautiful call girls in New York. And the next thing

177

was to do nothing but eat, drink, and screw for one week. And all that week Fred Smith couldn't believe that only a week ago he had been in jail, and now he was out in New York swinging with a pretty girl with big boobs who would do anything he asked. It was too much. In his darkest days he never believed he would ever live this way again.

Only at night, after the girl had exhausted herself on him and gone to sleep, did the worry come. He would have to be careful. Not get centred. But he already was, because at the meeting something was said that he was equally responsible for paying back the loan, that he was a partner with Ferrilio. That frightened him although it seemed easy, if Canadian laws were anything like American; you could piss in a batch of stuff in front of an FDA inspector and, because the Act was not well-defined, there would be nothing he could do. In a way it might be possible to run semi-legitimately. And then the real sadness came; he wanted to call his wife — ex-wife — to talk to his children. It had been so long. But he didn't know where they were, although it would be easy to find out. No, he would wait until he got set up and things were going well and then drop in on them, bring them presents. And if his wife made trouble, why there was Polished Fingers who could help him.

He turned and put his arm around the naked, sleeping girl, but it only reminded him of those close times with his wife, when things had been good for them. And he craved to be walking with his little daughters (he must remember that they were older now), holding their hands, swinging them to his shoulders, hugging them. What a mess he had made of his life. Unless he could really make a lot of money with Ferrilio, it would be better to be dead.

Every day all Ferrilio's and Smith's conversations with others, business and personal, were recorded by Pharmpress operatives, and the tapes sent to Heister, Joseph and Dean Sorenson.

One day Heister called and asked Joseph if he'd listened to the latest tapes. "It looks like they're ready to start. They've rented a building in Montreal."

Joseph felt his throat tighten.

178

"I want you to keep your eyes open for people who can work for them as detail men. If we go ahead with this I want Pureco to be as big an operation as possible with many drug stores carrying their products. And the only way we can do that is to make sure they have salesmen."

"I don't know that side of the business, Bob. Why not bring Kendall into the picture now, or some of the top people in the Canadian companies?"

"We can't trust anyone but ourselves. Maybe we'll bring Kendall in on this later, maybe not. But right now, make it your business to find out about detail men, how they work, who is being fired, who is available. And think of a way to recommend them to Ferrilio's company without any of us being involved." He paused. "Say, what about that fellow, Hamish Jarvis? The editor. He'd be an ideal candidate."

Feeling a physical sickness in his stomach, Joseph now knew the reason for Heister's call. Nothing he did was idle chatter. He remembered clearly the day Hamish Jarvis, the editor of a medical trade magazine, had called and threatened to tell all to Grant MacDonald.

"He's cooled out, Bob; he won't give us any more trouble," Joseph said, with as much casualness as he could muster.

"That's not my point, Joseph. Working for Ferrilio and Smith is a better use of Jarvis for our purposes. They belong together. They're all losers."

When Joseph put the phone down he was shaking. What was he, a management consultant, getting involved in? Perhaps he would take part in the exposure of Pureco and perhaps not. He wasn't too keen on being the object of mafia vengeance. It seemed odd sitting here in Ottawa, about to go to a committee meeting in the Parliament buildings of Canada, that he should be concerned about the mafia. And for a moment the complexity of the world and its weird interrelationships made him feel his powerlessness as an individual human being. He shrugged the thought away. Anyway, one thing for sure, he wasn't going to contact Jarvis, wasn't going to lead someone into certain trouble, big picture or not.

179

Some things he could do easily. Tomorrow he was driving to the Cornwall area, Dr. Lewison's riding, to meet with the Industrial Commission in a move he hoped would stop Lewison's opposition. That was fair game. What Heister wanted him now to do seemed a step over some ethical line, albeit imaginary. He recalled Heister saying in his soft manner, during their very first meeting, "There is nothing the industry won't do to stop Canada."

15

Using the two finger method, he typed on the ancient machine: 'The Reverend Marcel S. Larivière,' paused, and then added, 'Ph.D., S.T.D., MSW.' Definitely not a sign of pride, he assured himself. It was proper to affix one's credentials. Perhaps a little proud but excusable, for at age fifty-two he had combined the two disciplines he loved most — that of parish priest and sociologist — and he had just completed a five-year sociological study of his parish. He continued typing, his eyes turning from the pencilled draft to the keyboard. "A View of Suburbia, Our Lady of Fatima Parish, Riverview, Cornwall, Ontario." Soon it would be ready to send to the bishop.

"Although most parish priests usually state that they know their parish without the need of any scientific survey, many have been surprised, after a survey has been made, at their lack of knowledge of many of the important facets of their parish. The ideal pastor is not necessarily a great builder, an expert financier, a community organizer. Without disparaging these qualities which are useful, indeed necessary, the pastor above all should be what Christ was, the true shepherd of the flock. I know mine and mine know me."

He stopped typing and ran his hand over his bald head. That was the key, he thought. Many of his fellow scholars from Columbia and Laval Universities had not understood when he chose a parish over a teaching post at one of the great universities. "I'm certain there isn't one man with a degree in your whole parish," his friend Maurice had said, trying to dissuade him many years ago. "Who will you talk to? But Maurice had been wrong. There

181

were four, five now counting the new doctor, in addition to himself: the dentist, the lawyer, a Presbyterian minister, and his old friend Dr. Lewison, though unfortunately, now that he was a Member of Parliament, he wasn't able to see him as often as before.

No matter. He believed in his mission; the people of his church were his flock — in the old sense. And still he was able to be a modern priest, taking part in wider community affairs. That was why he had joined the Industrial Commission several years ago. And he reminded himself of the luncheon appointment with the commission and a very important person, a Mr. Joseph Mann, come to discuss the new pharmaceutical plant that one of the large drug companies was planning to build here. It would give employment to over two hundred persons. He looked at his watch. Eleven. Still time to work on his manuscript. He continued his typing.

"The territory within the limits of the parish of Our Lady of Fatima" — he wondered whether he should repeat that so often, deciding to wait until he had typed the entire manuscript and then count the number of mentions; it would be gauche to have too many — "is one of the most historic and beautiful sections of Canada. The parish extends along the banks of the majestic St. Lawrence River for nine miles. Within the confines of the parish are some of the most historic sites of Ontario. One mile east of the church, at Stone House Point, stands the ruins of Glengarry House, one of the oldest rcorded houses of Upper Canada. This was the home of Colonel John MacDonnell." He typed on, detailing all the old houses and the names of the people who owned them. ". . . .to east and still known as Fraser's Point, where at one time stood the temporary home of Sir John Johnston (1742-1830), leader of the United Empire Loyalists and Superintendent of Indian Affairs for Canada."

Father Larivière again stopped for a moment and dreamed of the early settlers of the area, of the men and women who came here from New York, driven out because they wished to remain loyal to the King — were they the arch reactionaries of the time, he wondered; why so honoured? It seemed this area, because of

182

the waterway, was destined to remain a haven for transients. No one who was born stayed, or if they did remain on their farms they seemed to be an example of reverse evolution. So many people: the loyalists, German mercenaries, a long period without change, then the new Canadians — hard-working Dutch and Polish who bought the farms from the descendants of the loyalists who no longer wanted to work hard, and turned them once again into good producers. And then the construction of the St. Lawrence Seaway and with it thousands of hard, sinewy skilled workers — electricians, plumbers, diggers, welders. Most moved on when it was done, but some had made the mistake of staying; too many from the farms, and too many labourers; and, he would have to admit it, too many children. And then in the thousands were his own people, French-Canadians from the poverty areas of Quebec, coming the few miles into what they thought was rich Ontario, only to be fooled. At present, 25 per cent of all males and 50 per cent of all women in the area were unemployed. And now the government had stepped in offering large loans to industry, mostly American, but some moving from Quebec to establish firms here because it was cheaper to loan money to industry than to have people on welfare. He started to type again from his notes.

"The knowledge of who his parishioners are, how they live, their occupation, their educational achievements, their ethnic background, the language they speak, their spiritual life, their social life, their attitudes, are all pertinent data of which a true pastor should be aware if he wishes to truly shepherd the flock consigned to his care. What is true of the parish and its relationship to the pastor is equally true of the diocese and its relationship to the bishop. To be a true pastor of the diocesan flock the bishop should know his people."

"I hope that's not too strong," he said aloud.

"What did you say, Father?" Yvette, his housekeeper, had entered without knocking, as was her custom.

He looked around, startled. Poor Yvette, she was getting so wide she would soon have to enter the door sideways. Amazing that these women of the country, so dainty in their teens, grew

183

into such huge proportions by middle-age, while their menfolk became slighter and slighter.

"Mr. Archibald is here to see you, Father," she said, not hiding her dislike of the Industrial Commissioner. It was well known that because of him the English got the best jobs and the French the worst in the new plants that started up in the area.

"No wonder it has taken so long for me to complete my thesis," he sighed. So many interruptions. What could he want? It was still an hour until the luncheon meeting. He started toward the door.

"Your jacket and collar," she admonished.

"Yes, yes." He looked around. Curious, he could not work on his sociology with his priest's collar on. But where had he put it?

She collected the collar from the cluttered bookshelf, the jacket from the crank handle of the manually-operated duplicating machine. "What will I do with you," she muttered. "The ladies from the auxiliary will be here tomorrow to run off the parish letter. You must give me time to dust and place everything neatly. What will they think of me if they see your study like this?"

"Yes, Yvette," he agreed sheepishly, realizing he was becoming more and more preoccupied like a professor and Yvette, since her husband died and her children gone off to Montreal, had only him to look after. (And them, a cloud on his mind. One of her sons, a separatist, had come back recently to stir up trouble among the young who were unemployed.) She went down the long dark hall, past the dining room into the foyer and returned with the Industrial Commissioner.

"*Bonjour, Monsieur Archibald, ça va?*"

"*Ça va mal,*" Geoffrey Archibald said. Although he had lived in this area of Cornwall all his life, among French-Canadians, it was one of only ten idioms he could speak.

"Sit there, in the leather chair, it is more comfortable," Father Larivière said, used to speaking English to English people; in fact, never questioning the necessity until recently. But now the thought did cross his mind — if he wishes to speak to me he should speak in my language; or bring an interpreter. Why must

184

I cater to him and speak in his?

The leather chair was torn, a gift from the doctor's wife, not so nice but perfectly serviceable. He sat on the hard oak desk, chair beside the typewriter, his fingers craving to type his manuscript. But he was used to Archibald coming without an appointment. Typical anglo-saxon arrogance. "*Bien* Geoffrey, you have not come for confession," he said to show he could make jokes and get along with Protestants. "What is the problem?"

"This Joseph Mann, the big management consultant from New York, and the plan to build a factory here employing two hundred people . . . you know, we are having lunch about it today?" It was hard for him to talk in this room. He felt as if he were in the presence of an evil force. The room was a pigsty. It just showed you that even educated French-Canadians were dirty. We should let them separate, he thought, see what happens to them then. "You know I've done a lot of work on this."

"Yes, yes." What was the man coming to, Father Larivière wondered. And he was irritated. Archibald had done a lot of work. *Incroyable!* He, Le Curé, was the crucial person on the Industrial Commission. No manufacturer would set up a new industry even with the loans provided by the Ontario government unless they were certain there would be ample workers. And workers who would not immediately join a union. Workers who would work for low pay. When a new plant was being considered, Father Larivière would call a meeting in the parish hall of all the people in the area. The father would introduce the owner and manager of the factory and would explain the kind of work and the pay, and the training that would be provided by the factory (although in a way that was a lie, because the government reimbursed the manufacturer for training costs). If the father didn't say, "work for this factory," the people wouldn't work. And he always said, "work," no matter how low the pay; always said that it was God's blessing that a plant would be built here.

He didn't like his role, but people needed work and a low paying job was better than no job at all.

"The situation is this," Archibald said. "There is at this moment a government hearing about the pharmaceutical industry

185

and Dr. Lewison, our Member of Parliament, is opposing the industry; he wants to make changes in the law. It is very complicated. But to put the matter crudely, I was called to Ottawa last week by Mr. Mann and he told me that unless we can convince Dr. Lewison to stop opposing the industry, which after all makes lifesaving drugs, antibiotics and such (Archibald still wasn't sure what the problem was, even after three hours with Joseph), the factory will not be built."

"Not be built! But we have already had the meeting, promised the people two hundred jobs." Strange things were happening. Two of his parishioners had asked if he had heard the rumour that the company in Montreal was soon going to stop buying pregnant mares' piss. That could be very serious. Many families depended on the money and kept ten or more mares pregnant all the time so they could sell the piss. He forgot what kind of pills they made.

"Father , this is politics. Cold, hard politics. I am head of the Liberal association. I headed the group that raised the money to finance candidates. I will say to Lewison, you are ruining a chance of two hundred jobs. But, I need the Industrial Commission behind me."

Father Larivière didn't believe all that Archibald said. He knew that Archibald often bought land for next to nothing and then sold it at huge profits to industries for whom he had already arranged government loans. It would be a good joke on him if he got stuck with the land. What if he had paid a lot? Come to think of it, he was no fool that Dutchman who sold him the land. Supposing the drug company backed away and Archibald lost his tavern that took so much money from his people Friday and Saturday nights. That would be a good joke. "Unfortunately, it would have provided many jobs. Nice clean work. But it is God's will," he shrugged.

"Father, I know you don't like taking part in politics and Dr. Lewison is a special friend, but we must have a united front. That plant will employ more than two hundred people. A thousand and more people can eat. Think of the children, of fathers counting on work."

186

Archibald was right of course. The church must get itself involved in day-to-day affairs, and be on the side of the people. It wasn't enough to provide spiritual welfare; the church must make sure the system enabled people to eat. It was a time of ferment, and even he, here, was touched by it. One friend had left the church and married, another was working with the Bolivian tin miners, another in Africa. Sometimes he worried he was not involved. But that was romantic. What was more important than caring for a parish? He would take a stand. But what stand? Was it important to work on behalf of a drug company in order to provide jobs? Or, in the larger sense, was it more important to fight the industry? But that was too complex. No, in his small way he would do whatever was necessary for the people in his parish, men and women and children he saw and talked to every week. Those souls were in his care. Once you got into abstractions beyond direct cause and effect, then you were lost. No matter how he tried to puzzle through the mysteries of man's organization of temporal life, he always came back to one message which he clung to: "Love thy neighbour." More than that he couldn't understand.

"You are right," Father Larivière said. "We must speak to Dr. Lewison and make him stop opposing the drug industry so we can provide jobs."

After the luncheon meeting Joseph headed his Thunderbird through Cornwall and down the twisty, bumpy Prescott highway toward Ottawa. The last time he had been in this area was when he and Grant had visited the MacDonald homestead. It was ironic. One side of Grant's family had remained in the United States during the American Revolution. Their descendants belonged to the Daughters of the American Revolution. The other side had migrated across the line to the Cornwall area. Their descendents belonged to the Independent Order of the Daughters of the Empire. To this day many families, both French and English, lived on both sides of the line. So much for history. He turned on the radio and over the Canadian government broad-

187

casting system heard a commercial sponsored by the State of New York, urging companies to relocate there. He laughed to himself. In effect, Canadian taxpayers were subsidizing New York State, subsidizing the removal of wealth from their country.

What would Grant say of that? And Ontario raided industry in Quebec, promising them loans to relocate in Ontario and thereby creating more unemployment in that province — adding to the bitterness of the French-Canadians. Ridiculous. Continentalism was the only answer. Anyway, exit Dr. Lewison.

Joseph's plan succeeded. Dr. Henry Lewison, age sixty, idealist, descendant of a United Empire Loyalist, was the next casualty. His view of life, his long friendships, his concept of service was so shaken when the Industrial Commission headed by Geoffrey Archibald and Father Marcel Larivière visited him in Ottawa and told him to stop opposing the industry or they would not support him in the next election, that he himself decided he would never run for office again. Deeply disillusioned, he doubled his efforts against the industry, determined to make his last service a substantial contribution. But he had not counted on his age, nor the psychological blow when the people from his area, formed into an organization by Kendall under Joseph's direction, turned on him, petitioning for his resignation, French-Canadians contemptuously referring to him as the *Anglo* who was taking jobs away. One night stones were thrown smashing the windows in his home, and he suffered a heart attack — fortunately mild, but serious enough so that he was invalided, could no longer attend committee meetings, and therefore resigned.

Still humiliated because he had trusted Grant, Joseph felt nothing other than a sense of achievement when he reported to Heister that Lewison had been removed.

"But Grant MacDonald, what have you done about him?" Heister asked. "And have you taken steps to get that chap Jarvis a job with Pureco? We're getting down to the short strokes Joseph. The hearings will soon be over. Time is of the essence."

188

[16]

"Gentlemen, I see a quorum." The chairman struck his gavel and the one hundred and fifth session of the Special Committee on Drug Costs and Prices began.

It was bitter cold outside, the city almost brought to a halt by a raging blizzard. Fifteen inches of snow had fallen in the last twenty hours, forcing the schools to be closed. Joseph had forgotten just how bad an Ottawa winter could be. Once, when he was still in junior high school, the city had been paralyzed for five days. First, it had snowed for three days and they had skied to school. Then the snow changed to rain followed by a cold snap, with the temperature plunging to thirty below. The streets, sidewalks, and roads were turned to ice. Streetcars were frozen in their tracks where they had last stopped. The overhead wires were sheathed in ice and the branches of the bare trees glistened and cracked. Neither trucks nor cars could manoeuvre the streets. All engines stopped and the city quieted like farm country in winter. And rather than being annoyed everyone turned out to see and hear the unknown. The streets filled with skaters, young and old, everyone laughing and gay. Joseph and others had even skated to school.

And suddenly, it seemed that this committee was in a cul-de-sac, no longer front and centre. Beginning with the new year, 1967, a catalytic change occurred in the country as everyone was buoyed by the realization that it was Canada's Centennial year. Further, by all preliminary reports, Expo '67 in Montreal promised to be Canada's greatest collective achievement. Canadians began to feel they were at last taking their place on the world

189

stage. There were practical political expressions of this that concerned Sorenson; Canada refused to permit the entry of an American bank, and a cabinet committee was created to study foreign ownership of Canadian industry.

"Not to worry." Joseph assured him. "It's like pissing in the wind."

"I thought the hearings would be over by now, but it looks like another month and then we'll have to work on the report. I always spend winter in Nassau. I'm not sure my old bones can take a whole winter here," Sorenson said. "But it looks like we're stuck in."

"I guess the leg bothers you in this cold," Joseph said.

Sorenson nodded.

But everyone seemed to be a little tired, worn down — the members of the committee, the press forever present taking notes, and Joseph, too, felt drained. For weeks now he had worked twelve hours a day, seven days a week. Days were devoted to meetings, planning; nights to study. He devoured digests of medicine and pharmacology prepared by the Association staff, read through the transcripts of all previous investigations into the industry in all countries, made notes of influential people he had met, studied the *Hansard* verbatim reports of the hearings, read clippings from all newspapers in Canada, and kept a box score of the industry image. And days and weeks and points seemed to merge. It was almost like a basketball game with one side scoring a basket, then one being scored by the other side. But the game was never-ending.

Some days they received severe setbacks, as when the director of Food and Drug stated that there was no observable proof in the difference in therapeutic value between a generic and brand name drug. A murmur swept the audience and some reporters dashed for the "hot room" to write a story.

"I can see the headlines in tomorrow's papers," Frank Flanagan said. " 'Head of Food and Drug says generic drug equal to brand names.' Do you realize what harm your statement can do? Most people have a high regard for Food and Drug. When a statement like that comes from on high, so to speak. I am

190

not a doctor, but aren't we talking about therapeutic equivalence? And you can only know this by testing in humans? Do you test in humans or in vitro in the test tube?"

The head of Food and Drug answered testily, "Of course we don't have the facilities to test humans, but . . ." and he explained the tests they employed.

With the removal of Dr. Lewison much of the sting had gone out of the committee; however, several of the committee members then started to use Grant's columns as a basis of attack against the industry.

"Mr. Chairman, may I read into the transcript a section of Grant MacDonald's column which seems to be pertinent?" the single female member of the committee asked. "What is unusual about research by pharmaceutical houses is that they sanctify it. They nurture this sanctity by association of their drugs with the betterment of health and the lower death rate among humans. But the fact is that improved nutrition has contributed much more to human health than drugs. It seems significant that the drugs that have been the least successful are those for cancer or for the heart, which may be caused by nutritional factors. Some have even said that modern drugs obstruct advancement in public health because they are not designed for the avoidance of sickness. Instead of designing preventative drugs, manufacturers concentrate on the more profitable curative drugs of yesterday and today."

Ron Kendall countered by reading into the record a list of drugs that had been developed for rare conditions and were often made available free or at factory cost to physicians. "Food for infants suffering from phenylketonuria, an inborn error of metabolism which can result in retardation; drugs for indigent patients to control cerebral palsy; antitoxin for botulism, a rare but often fatal type of food poisoning; specifics are made available against leprosy, malaria, sleeping sickness; sera against snake and black widow spider bites; and recently a drug for schistosomiasis; an agent to diagnose toxoplasmosis, an unusual condition that results in the birth of a blind baby. Products required in unusual surgical procedures are also provided," and Kendall

191

described an essential one used to protect the cornea during a particularly intricate type of eye surgery.

As the hearings progressed, Kendall had changed, taking on the role of head of the Association in Ottawa. Joseph permitted it. The irony was that Kendall was expendable. It had been decided in New York by Heister that the president of the Drug Association would keep a low profile and stay out of Ottawa during the hearings, concentrating on internal industry matters. This would keep him untarnished in case events became dirty as they surely would. When it was over he could come back, not having lost any friends, and pick up the pieces. Kendall was to front, be sacrificed, and probably never be of use as a public relations man in Ottawa again. Instead of realizing he was in the middle, he interpreted the president's absence as indicating a new power for himself within the Association, another reason he resented taking orders from Joseph.

In those last days of the hearings Grant was the remaining clear and effective opposition. Heister was on the phone every second day to Joseph urging him to think of some way to stop his columns. Against his better judgment, Joseph had actually made the mistake of seeing Grant's publisher only to be told that in Canada there was a free press, and that if the drug industry wished to pull out its advertising, it was free to do so. He also reminded Joseph that most drug advertising appeared on television or through specialized drug magazines that went to doctors. As Grant no longer saw Louise, or if he did Pharmpress' private detective didn't know of it, they couldn't compromise him that way. They had considered bugging Grant's house and office telephone, but then decided that the adverse publicity would be too damaging if the devices were discovered. Grant and Joseph had even stopped talking when they passed each other in the corridors of Parliament.

It turned out that Sorenson had been right about the hearings carrying through the winter. It wasn't until the last week in February that the chairman struck his gavel with resounding force on the cedar block and, while flourishing it over his head for a second crack, said, "Gentlemen, I now declare these hearings completed."

Suddenly the aura of officialdom disappeared. Men on the committee who had been bitter enemies seemed to doff their masks and become friends again, as indeed they were, among them even Flanagan and the socialist member. Some stretched and yawned, some made jokes. The committee ceased to exist and the twenty-four members became separate human beings again.

It had been a long, hard hearing, apparently one of the most difficult ever, Joseph was to discover. Forty-six representations had been received, some involving as many as a dozen witnesses. These included the Minister of National Health and Welfare, the Director General of the Food and Drug Directorate, the Minister of National Revenue, the Assistant Deputy Minister of Customs, the Canadian Pharmaceutical Association, the Canadian Drug Manufacturers, a consulting biologist, all the largest pharmaceutical manufacturers (each submitting individual briefs), the Consumers' Association of Canada, the Alcoholism and Drug Addiction Research Foundation of Ontario, the Medical Post, a large drug store, the Patent and Trademark Institute of Canada, the Canadian Society of Hospital Pharmacists, the Department of Defence Production, the Department of Industry, the Department of National Defence, the Department of National Health and Welfare, the Department of Veterans' Affairs, the Canadian Wholesale Drug Association, the Canadian Cystic Fibrosis Association, an individual maverick manufacturer, various departments of the Food and Drug Directorate, the head of a large hospital, the Department of the Registrar General, including the Combines branch, and the government of the Province of Alberta.

Without realizing it, Joseph and the industry had won a partial victory because, despite Grant MacDonald and INTEGRAL, the hearings failed to awaken public interest to the extent they had hoped. And now began the period of drafting the final report. As Heister and Sorenson originally planned, Flanagan had included himself on the smaller subcommittee that was responsible for writing the report, based on the submissions received at

193

the hearings, and the resulting questioning of the witnesses. As the actual wording of sentences was often significant in the way a Bill was drafted and presented to Parliament, Flanagan would bring copies of the pages the committee had worked on each day to Joseph and Sorenson. The three would then stay up late into the night and together rewrite sentences that were clearly harmful to the industry, rendering them either innocuous or capable of double meaning. The following day Flanagan would take the reworked passages back to the subcommittee and fight tooth and nail for his wording to be accepted. In most cases, as he came with well-prepared arguments, and as there was no one of the calibre of Dr. Lewison to counter his views, he won. In this way, even though the will of the majority of the committee was detrimental to the industry, with Flanagan the industry controlled the important segments of the final report.

During this period, Violetta returned to her job with Food and Drug, and Joseph had free time during the days. An unspoken tension that had been between them dissolved and their relationship became softer, more fun. They went skiing and sleigh-riding, they scuffed through the snow arm in arm, their breath making crazy patterns in the air, and they laughed a lot. It was good to laugh. In serious moments they considered what their future together should be. Both were afraid of marriage. They talked of other solutions, of living in apartments side by side, so they could be both alone and together. They were afraid to lose the love they had, certain it would surely happen if they lived together every day. And part of it was what Joseph should do. Return to New York or stay in Ottawa and build the Canadian subsidiary of Daniels and Company? He had already picked up a few accounts and had hired a consultant to look after the new business. It would not be difficult. If he went back to New York he would have to leave Violetta. She wanted to start her specialized medical studies and wasn't sure herself yet where that would take her. Could he leave her? Did he want to live in New York?

Finally, by the third week in March, the report was completed. Three weeks later it was printed by the Queen's Printer and submitted to the Minister of Health and the cabinet. While recommending many ways in which drug prices could be reduced, it did not recommend abolition of patent protection. Joseph and Sorenson had won a victory greater than they had hoped for. The committee did not advocate the end of the patent laws. It did not recommend the establishment of a government formulary for hospitals and clinics to obtain cheaper drugs. It did not insist that brand names be abolished and generic names only be used. It did not roll back prices on a number of leading drugs on which the mark-up had been shown to be a thousand per cent. It did not insist that a stated percentage of original research be done in Canada in order to build up a community of research expertise. It did not even stipulate a top percentage that companies could spend on promotion. It talked vaguely about encouraging a Canadian drug industry, and making funds available to generic houses, and publishing booklets that would indicate to doctors the relative value of brand name drugs as against generic drugs. And very little else.

Grant MacDonald wrote a slashing attack on the committee's report. "Wishy-washy on drugs . . . the committee's conclusions are more watered-down versions of earlier and tougher reports, apparently in an attempt to reconcile sharp divisions of opinion between members of the committee on how to lower drug prices. It is a great victory for the American drug companies."

"Sour grapes," Joseph said. Grant had said he couldn't win. Well, he had.

Heister called. Jubilant. "Good work fellows" — Joseph and Sorenson were on extensions — "we stopped them cold."

Lionel Coles, head of Daniels and Company, called. "I guess you'll be winding up there soon. We've got a big project at Bayovar, Peru——"

"Where?"

"Peru. To design an entire fish port with manufacturing facilities and so on. The Peruvians have been reading how much fish the Cubans are catching and want to modernize their facilities."

"Hey, let me get my feet on the ground." He wondered if the

195

job could be done from his Canadian operation in case he decided to stay in Canada.

"I'll send you all the material. Let me know as soon as you can. We've got the assignment. I think you're the man to handle it."

Putting the phone down he thought of his aquarium. Well, I suppose I'm an expert on fish.

Joseph, Sorenson, Flanagan, and Kendall treated themselves to an elegant dinner, everyone becoming very maudlin and assuring each other they were the best of people. "What happens now?" Joseph asked.

"If they bring in a Bill to change a few laws you can be sure it won't affect us," Flanagan said.

"But on the basis of that report I don't see how they can change anything. Remember what I told you right in the beginning. Governments like to follow, not lead."

Joseph had reason to feel his part of the assignment was completed. He would have to decide what to do. Usually at the end of a project he returned to New York, there to begin another assignment. But, there had never been a Violetta.

Later, at Violetta's, when he told her about Peru, she said it sounded like a worth-while assignment. She asked how long he would be gone if he took it and when the project started, thinking that if he left soon enough, perhaps he would never find out about INTEGRAL and her part in it. She knew that in two or three weeks the Bill that would be presented to Parliament would have no relationship at all to the recommendations of the committee. The Prime Minister had decided, even without the support of a strong committee report, to act on the advice of INTEGRAL.

Lying in Joseph's arms that night, Violetta wondered which time would be the last time. She felt his body after he had gone to sleep, got the whole of it into her mind, into her being, because she was cold with fear and wanted to keep him with her forever, this Joseph, this man, her man, who had trusted her with his being.

196

When Frank Flanagan left the weekly caucus of the party, his face was ashen. The Prime Minister had revealed the details of the Bill relating to patents and the drug industry that would be presented to Parliament. It contained all the elements that the drug industry and Flanagan had fought against for the last ten years; chiefly, it abolished patent protection. Flanagan was doubly shaken because a veiled reference by the P.M. made it clear that unless Flanagan stopped supporting the drug industry, he would never be appointed a cabinet minister.

The moment he got to his private office he arranged a meeting with Joseph and Sorenson.

"I don't believe it. I can't believe it," Joseph said, striding up and down Flanagan's office in the Parliament buildings. "How can they draft a Bill that is exactly the opposite of what the special committee recommended? Go ahead as if we hadn't spent almost a year on hearings?"

"I don't understand either," Sorenson said, looking very old and very bewildered.

"There's nothing to understand, those are the facts." Flanagan explained, harassed, worried that he might be held responsible by Heister. "There was a secret group called IN-TEGRAL composed of high-level civil servants. They drafted this Bill, and it has the Prime Minister's approval." He explained that the Bill consisted of five points: removal of sales tax, modification of anti-dumping duties, programs of information regarding the use of generic drugs, government support for the production and marketing of generic drugs, and amendments to the Patents and Trademarks Act removing the automatic seventeen-year protection — the main item the industry had fought so hard to retain.

"Jesus, Jesus, Jesus! What the hell is INTEGRAL?" Joseph shouted.

"A secret civil service committee of the highest level." Flanagan raised his arms in frustration. "A man named J.O. McKinnon" — Joseph remembered Grant talking to a J.O. — "very powerful, Douglas Clark, and many others. And that girl I've seen you with, Joseph, Dr. Violetta Norgela. And *you* didn't know." Flanagan continued to explain what departments had been involved, but at that moment Joseph's hearing stopped, his mind went blank, he couldn't breathe and felt he would faint, that he was falling . . . falling.

"Well, it starts all over," Sorenson said with a sigh. "Now we have to fight the Bill in Parliament. We better call Heister, Joseph. Joseph . . . ."

Joseph looked at him, knowing his name was being called.

"I say we'll have to call Heister. We'd better get a plane to New York right away."

And Joseph felt the anger and the hate well up in him until he thought he would go beserk; felt the minutes drag while he forced himself to function; wondered if he could contain himself until he called her; and then, finally alone, at home in his apartment, packing to go to New York, putting off the call; and then all packed and waiting for the taxi to pick him up, sitting with a scotch, looking at the telephone. And finally he dialled her number.

"Hello." Her voice. Confusion between the joy he always felt at hearing her and the intensity of his hate. "Hello, Hello."

"Violetta." Finally he could say her name.

"Joseph, hello my love. How has your day been?" Always before said in a way that brought comfort.

"Violetta . . . Violetta." His voice now the cool voice of the technocrat seeking information.

"Yes." And she knew and knew and knew and waited for her

198

life to end.

"You were part of a secret civil service interdepartmental group, INTEGRAL?" It was so absurd, part of him didn't care; it was too insane.

"Yes, Joseph."

"All the time, right from the beginning?"

"Yes, Joseph."

"And Grant too, then?"

"Yes . . . yes . . . yes," she screamed. "Please, Joseph. Listen, my love . . . ." But there was no one there for her to speak to. The line was dead.

Joseph realized it was April first. April Fools' day, and he was the biggest fool of all.

When there was no answer, when the line went dead, she called Joseph's office only to be told that he was not there. She called his apartment and heard the phone ring and ring. She felt a rushing in her body, as if her body were demanding that she run to all the places he might be, everywhere at once, amuck. And then she started to ache, a physical ache she had never known, an ache in her chest that she knew would never leave her and she felt like her mother, felt like a D.P. again, who walked, head down, walked, walked, to anywhere, trying not only to endure, but to find a reason to endure.

She left her office and went home, driving mechanically through the traffic. There, she took two tranquillizers and a slug of scotch, and then another, and she sat by the phone, hoping he would call again. Many times in the next hour she picked up the phone to call his office, but didn't, afraid, afraid to talk to him, to expose herself to the words of hate that she knew were there waiting to be unleashed against her. She ached for herself, but mostly for him, for knowing better than Joseph the thin line he walked. And finally after several hours by the phone she called Grant at the press gallery, hysterical.

"I'll come right over," Grant said. And somehow she felt easier. He would find a way to speak to Joseph.

Within twenty minutes there was a knock on the door and for a crazy moment she hoped it was Joseph. She rushed to the door and opened it.

"I left as soon as I got your call," Grant said.

"Thank you." She threw herself at him, sobbing.

Grant led her to the sofa and sat her down and then went into the kitchen, found the scotch, and poured them both large portions.

"Will you call him for me, Grant?" she asked. "Please call him."

"Violetta, you know he won't talk to me, about me, let alone you. Joseph and I are through, just like you and Joseph are through. And honestly, Violetta, you knew right from the beginning. This is the way it has to be."

"But why can't you call?"

"Violetta, if you think it was rough during the committee hearings, wait till you see what's going to happen when the Bill is presented in Parliament. I expect all kinds of real dirt and dishonesty from Joseph and his owners."

"You don't understand. He's not like that. You don't know Joseph." And then she stopped, shocked. He didn't know Joseph, didn't know the Joseph who had depended on him as a friend; that childlike, idealistic Joseph so well hidden; the Joseph she had helped to destroy once and for all.

"Violetta, you're better off without him. He's changed. He's a bad guy."

Yes, she realized. He had changed. Through love. And now what kind of Joseph would there be?

Grant poured them two more scotches and the effect of the tranquillizers and the scotch was making Violetta lightheaded. He looked at her and suddenly felt he'd like to go to bed with her. Would she, he wondered. He sat closer to her on the sofa and put his arm around her as if in a brotherly fashion, stroking the back of her neck and her shoulders. "I know you were pretty hung up on him, but Violetta, this is all for the best."

They were silent for a time and he wondered how he could manoeuvre her into bed. Her daughter came home from school and Violetta told her to make her own supper and then go to her room. Meanwhile she and Grant continued to drink. And all he could think of was, what the hell, she slept with Douglas and

200

switched to Joseph. "You know I've always been attracted to you, Violetta." He bent down and tried to kiss her.

She pulled back in horror at his touch. "Grant. Grant. What are you thinking?"

"Don't worry. Louise and I don't see each other, not since Joseph put a detective on me, and anyway, we always agreed that we could go to bed with other people, that it would be foolish to limit ourselves, and the truth is, I don't love her. I like going to bed with her, but ——"

Violetta was so disgusted she felt she was going to vomit. She held her stomach. "Get out. Please get out." Why did she think she was going to cry?

"Don't be like that, Violetta," he said softly, putting his arms around her. "I know how you feel, but listen, I'll be good for you, we'll be good for each other."

She tried to push him away, but felt so weak, afraid of this man so strong, so muscular. She pushed at his arms as they encircled her and they were like steel and she felt that he was within seconds of raping her and with her last strength she screamed an oath in Lithuanian, the sound of which was more animal than human to Grant's ears and he loosened his hold.

"You made out with Joseph, why not me? And Joseph and Louise went to bed. Did you know that?" Joseph *had* told her and about the revelation he had had about his love for her; poor Grant would never understand that.

"Oh Grant, I beg of you," she sobbed, "leave now. Remember Mylita is in her room."

He studied her face, trying to decide how far he could get if he pushed, what would happen if he forced her. Some girls said no, wanted to be forced so they didn't have to take the responsibility of admitting they wanted it as much as a man. He couldn't take that chance. A scene would be disastrous. He had forgotten for the moment that her daughter was in the next room, and that she sometimes played with his youngest daughter.

It was no go. If she had said yes, everything would have been fine. But this was too messy.

He stood up and drained his glass. "You're very attractive,

201

Violetta, remember that. So don't blame me for wanting you. That's the way I am, very human. I'm sorry about you and Joseph," he paused for a moment, "and believe it or not, I'm sorry about Joseph and me. We all seem to be playing our roles. You, Louise, Joseph, me, Douglas Clark—and J.O. McKinnon too"; he wondered . . . no, he was his own man. "I've been a fool Violetta. If you can, blame it on the scotch or" — he suddenly remembered — "April Fools' day. Please do." And as he left he made a mental note to think of some April Fools' trick to play on his children at supper that night.

Violetta sat for the longest time, holding herself in, summoning all her resources and training as a doctor to psychologically overcome what was building up in her, threatening to burst into hysteria. She was alone. No one she could turn to. Joseph was lost to her now. And she could never again look Louise in the face, not after today with Grant. Douglas? She shuddered. She walked into her daughter's room and watched her colouring. And when it came time for Mylita to go to bed Violetta got in beside her, remembering that when she had been a young girl she would sleep in the same bed, when troubled, as her mother, her father moving to her bed.

She put her arm around Mylita, kissed her, and after a while fell asleep.

[18]

Take the urine of a boy who still enjoys his innocent youth, allow the urine to stand a while until it goes bad, preserve it well and do not allow anything to evaporate from it. Then dry the residual matter and extract the salt from it. Take half a pound of this salt and mix it with five pounds of clay. Take care to blend it well and form it into small pellets. When they are dry, the pellets are distilled over an open flame in the retort. This distillate is a wonderful secret remedy for ailments of the chest and lungs and useful in the treatment of pthisis, six grains to be taken in wine of a palatable syrup. (Christian Franze Paulini, 1643)

This time Heister didn't keep Joseph and Sorenson waiting more than five minutes. And the change from the reflective atmosphere of the Little Museum to the intensity of Heister's office was more abrupt than usual. Heister had never been one to discuss the niceties, the trivial chitchat that usually preceded a business meeting — that talk about the weather, a sports event, one's children, the latest locker-room joke, one's favourite TV program, and always one's golf score — a twenty minute ritual to become comfortable, establish rapport, that agreement was there, that the basics of life were understood, shared, before settling down to business.

"The only mistake we made was in not realizing the power of the civil service in Canada. Men like Douglas Clark. We saw them at the hearings every day and still we didn't tumble to what was going on," Joseph said. It was his fault and he knew it. He had been warned, the hints had been there, veiled warnings from

Grant. The very first move to get rid of Flanagan; he had read it wrong. He tried to remember whether Violetta had said anything. Yes, when he first met her at Grant's party. If only he'd been alert then. Stupid. "What I can't understand is why our Association didn't know. They're in Ottawa all the time. Dean and I come in like two idiots. We should have been briefed." More openly aggressive than usual, hopped up on dexedrine, Joseph raged. "And Kendall. What good is he? He's supposed to know. (There was no such thing as love. He had known it before. Had always known it. A sickness. A sick need. A woman is to fuck. Period. Bitch Lithuanian. I loved you. Why? Why did you do this to me?)

"But we're into Food and Drug," Sorenson said. "That's what I can't understand. It's not as if we're enemies. We always considered them a captive agency, same as HEW is here!"

Heister paced up and down. "Postmortems won't get us anywhere now," he said softly. "Unless we can influence the members of Parliament, they're going to present that Bill and it will pass because the government has a majority."

"It doesn't work that way, Bob," Joseph said irritably. (Did the man never lose control?) "It's not the same there as in the United States where each congressman and senator can vote pretty much the way he wants. In Canada the members of the party vote the way the prime minister says. It is a complete waste of time to lobby individual members. They have no power. What we must do is get to the cabinet, to the key men in the cabinet. Three or four cabinet ministers, three or four individual men at most can decide."

"Okay, okay, take it easy," Heister said. Walking across the room he slid open a panel, revealing a small but complete kitchen, with refrigerator, stove, counter space, cupboards. "What will it be? I'll pour the first and then you're on your own." They all took scotch and soda. Heister brought the drinks on a tray and suggested they sit on the upholstered chairs. "Let's stretch out and be comfortable. It's going to be a long session. We've got to keep our heads," he said, clearly referring to Joseph.

When Joseph shut off Violetta, his first thought had been to run, to take the job in Bayovar, to leave the battle. Basically his work was done. He'd been hired to lobby the committee. That was over. He felt choked, wanted to get as far away as possible from Ottawa, his family, Grant, and Violetta. But when he telephoned Heister and told him, Heister had guaranteed him a seventy-five thousand dollar a year job as president of one of his companies. Win or lose, he had it. And he thought, fuck it, why should he run away? He wanted to win, goddam it, or to make things difficult up there with as much anguish for everyone as he could. He'd get even with them all.

That night they stayed in Heister's office until five in the morning devising a four-point plan. First, Operation 100, in which the presidents of the pharmaceutical companies in Canada would contact the hundred largest international firms in Canada — the auto-makers, gas companies, and so on, pointing out that the Canadian government had decided to abolish unilaterally protection of industrial property rights owned by foreign companies. Each company president would be asked to write to a member of cabinet stating that their companies would reciprocate by pressuring their governments to refuse to recognize the rights of Canadian companies abroad. Second, as Canada did not have her own scientific capability to reproduce any of the new drugs — antibiotics, steroids, tetracyclines — without the international group of drug companies, it was decided to meet with the Canadian cabinet directly and tell them simply that if they went ahead with the Bill, the international group would pull the whole industry out of Canada, close up every factory; no medication would be available in Canada. Third, Pharmpress was to exaggerate reports of epidemics around the world to make Canadians aware of how safe they were because of the arsenal of drugs that was available to them, and conversely to make them aware of what would happen if there were no drugs.

"And we should be prepared to do what some companies have always done when they get stuck with too much stock, because of a warm winter and not enough people getting sick."

205

"What's that? Joseph asked.

"We'll start an epidemic."

"Bob, we at Heister have always been opposed to that."

"A flu epidemic is easiest to start and control, and less risk of death," Heister continued, ignoring Sorenson.

"Except for older people," Sorenson said.

Fourth, it was decided to go ahead with the setup plan.

"It's the only move that will work in my opinion," Heister said. "These men, Ferrilio and Smith, are now in business in a small way. They'll get caught sooner or later anyway."

They all took specific assignments. Sorenson was to fly to Germany the next day to explain the situation to Kurt Manheim. "He can then arrange for the Italian companies on their own to contact Ferrilio and make the sale," Heister said. Joseph was to return to Ottawa, start Kendall on Operation 100, and then go to Montreal to determine whether Hamish Jarvis was the man to put to work for Pureco, and if it could be done anonymously. He accepted the assignment without hesitation. Heister would start Pharmpress working and using his connections, attempt to make contact, secretly, with either the Prime Minister or his deputy. "I may need you for that meeting, Joseph."

Much later Joseph went to Roma Davidson's house, Heister's ever-available receptionist. She had told him to come up anytime, no matter what time he was through. He'd fuck the ass off the bitch. He didn't need Violetta. Walking through the Museum on his way out of Heister's office one of the framed extracts caught his eye: *There can be no doubt whatsoever that pestilence and fever and other serious illnesses are nothing but the work of the devil.* (Martin Luther)

The next day Sorenson left for Germany. As always the power of the giant 707 thrilled him as it lifted off and thundered across the Atlantic. A marvel of engineering. How many trips had he taken for the industry, how many countries, how many times across the "pond" and the Pacific and the Mediterranean. And he remembered that long, incredible journey, for two years right through South America, opening up the whole continent for Heister. And now he was on the road again. After Germany, he would swing through Switzerland, France, England, and Japan, to meet with the heads of the major pharmaceutical firms in the world, present the facts on the situation in Canada, and convince these men it was the time to use their influence with their governments to bring pressure upon the Canadian government — even to the extent of threatening retaliatory economic action if the patent laws were changed. They had the power and Sorenson was sure the move would be at least partially effective. At this point, what it really came down to was time. They were fighting for years. If the Patent Act must be changed, surely there was a bargaining position between the seventeen years protection they had now and the zero protection of the new Bill.

But chiefly, the reason for the trip was to see Kurt and get his co-operation in the setup. There was no doubt in Sorenson's mind that Kurt would agree. He ordered a scotch and relaxed in his wide-seated, first-class passenger section. Fortunately there was no one sitting beside him so he wouldn't have to talk, or be rude and not talk. He wanted to sip his scotch and be alone with his thoughts. Setting his battered briefcase on the floor, he accepted the pillow that the stewardess brought and thought of Kurt and Joseph. It had been wrong to have had doubts about Joseph. He was one of them. Sorenson reflected that he had been about the same age as Joseph when he first met Kurt, the time of life for a man when his career either ended or took off. Joseph's would succeed as his had, and for the same basic reason — he compromised with morality. Sorenson sighed. As far as he knew that deal with Kurt Manheim years before had been his only immoral act in his whole business life — until now.

When he stepped off the plane, Kurt was there to meet him, as he knew he would be. He looked surprisingly old. "Kurt, you look marvellous."

"Ah, you know we are both slipping away, my old friend. Come. My man will collect your baggage." What problems was Sorenson bringing? Every time the American came, it meant something would have to be done. He noticed Sorenson's brief-case and remembered other times. A wave of bitterness quickly passed over him. He sighed.

What difference did it make? Look how well they had done. His company was one of the three largest drug firms in the world. But in Sorenson's briefcase had been the pride of his middle years.

As they walked toward Kurt's Mercedes, Sorenson said, "The new firm you took over in Italy—it has a licence to produce one of our tranquillizers."

"I didn't know," Kurt said, surprised. "The business gets too complex even for us. But first a little schnapps. You'll stay at my house, of course."

These Europeans, Sorenson thought, a charm, a politeness that was fast disappearing from business. And there was time. One phone call from Kurt would set in motion what was neces-sary for someone in the the Italian plant to also make a phone call, this one to a jobber who would sell unmarked tablets, ship-ped in from South America, to Tony Ferrilio's new company, Pureco.

Less than ten days following Flanagan's report on the contents of the new Bill, one of Canada's most influential industrialists, a director of many of the country's largest firms, including a bank, arranged a dinner at the Rideau Club for Robert Heister to meet with the Deputy Prime Minister of Canada. He had been able to accomplish this because he was one of the largest suppliers of election funds to the party in power. It was to be an unofficial dinner, with only the minister, Heister, and Joseph present. Sorenson was still in Europe.

The Rideau Club was Ottawa's oldest and most exclusive club — perhaps the most exclusive in all Canada. It was mainly for politicians—Members of Parliament and Senators, regardless of party—and for senior civil servants (the mandarins who, accord-ing to some claims, actually governed the country), newspaper publishers, and lawyers whose function as fund-raisers for the Liberal and Conservative parties enabled them to make personal fortunes as lobbyists. As such the club reeked with the self-indulgence of élitism. For the last hundred years, club members liked to think that most of the laws of Canada had been devised, agreed to, or compromises arrived at, over a friendly dinner or comradely scotch. Club members thought of themselves as being both custodians and creators of Canadian history.

The waiter brought the drinks and quietly left, experienced enough in serving men like these to know they wished unobtrusive service.

The minister was a small man, nondescript, a man with a tight smile and a prominent lower jaw which gave him the suggestion of tenacity. He spoke in the clipped, flat fashion of the civil servant which, in fact, he had been for many years before entering politics.

In a way he seemed no match for Heister, a large physical man, tanned and healthy. The dinner passed in pleasantness until coffee was served. Then Heister began. "Let me be direct, sir. I asked for this meeting and I am grateful to you for seeing me because of the urgency of the situation. You are about to introduce a new Bill into the Canadian Parliament relating to drugs and drug patents. We feel if the Bill is presented as it is constituted, with the clauses removing patent protection, it will endanger our industry in Canada. We would prefer if that aspect were changed; you would then have our co-operation on all other parts of the Bill."

"Mr. Heister," the minister said, "the patent legislation under which the pharmaceutical manufacturers operate in Canada has been in effect since 1923. Since that time patents have been increasingly issued to foreigners. Now, more than ninety-two per cent of all patents are owned outside Canada. Furthermore, since 1923 the patent system of the United States has gradually extended into Canada. We deem the monopolistic aspects under the seventeen-year term for drug patents to be against the best interests of Canadians."

"Perhaps you are not aware, sir," Heister said, "that I am not speaking for myself alone. Every international firm in the world knows of this meeting and is prepared to take certain actions with their own governments as a result of it."

"I am aware, sir." There was now no mistaking the tightness of the lips, thin and clenched. Joseph knew the doggedness. Heister was making a mistake in speaking this way, but there was no way he could interfere.

"I am authorized to say that if you proceed with the Bill as constituted, we are prepared to withdraw all research from Canada, and in fact, to consider closing all our companies. Canada would be without medicine."

Joseph was shattered by the directness, by the arrogance, by the sheer stupidity.

"May I remind you, sir, that Canada is not the United States. A menacing attitude may work in your country where party affiliation is minimal, but the Canadian experience is quite the opposite. Cabinet government demands that a good lobbyist cannot threaten, particularly in those cases where the lobby has no large-scale following, and your industry does not. It has succeeded in alienating itself from most of the public." He then addressed Joseph. "I understand you are a Canadian, sir. While I find it distasteful to think that Canadians could be engaged in working against the interests of their own countrymen for their own gain, I am realistic enough to accept that this is more normal than not, even in political parties. But surely you should have advised your client better."

Joseph was about to respond, but thought better of it. What deceitful arrogance! Many cabinet ministers, even the prime minister, took campaign money from American multinationals. A trade-off for the good of the country? If one has the tunnel vision to equate your party with the general good. Joseph didn't buy it.

Nationality meant little to Joseph. He had been to too many places in the world, seen corruption everywhere, identified with too many peoples. He remembered Sorenson's surprise that he had remained a Canadian citizen. "You work and live in the United States and yet you haven't taken out American citizenship?"he had asked incredulously. All hail Imperial Rome, Joseph had thought. But it wasn't only Americans who

210

thought they were the greatest nation state in the world.

"It is clear to you that I represent an international industry and am speaking on their behalf," Heister repeated. It was beginning to dawn on him that he was making no headway at all and wouldn't.

"And I, sir, represent an independent country." He rose to leave indicating the interview was over. "If you are so concerned about patent protection, think what might happen if we decided one day to remove the profit aspect from the drug industry. Canada, like most western nations, is a mixed economy. Electric power is a public enterprise and we have many crown corporations. It would not be too difficult to create a crown corporation out of the drug industry. We would not have to take you over in any crass way, just compete with you. Eventually the Canadian people might decide they are entitled to health provided by drugs," he paused, "without having to pay through the nose."

After the meeting, the rest of the night disappeared in a haze of scotch. No matter how much he drank Joseph couldn't shake the ominous sense of knowing that what was about to happen he had always known would happen. They would have to flood the country with counterfeit drugs. Their main chance now of stopping the legislation was to shock and frighten the Canadian people and the politicians. For a moment Joseph felt again like chucking the whole thing . . . taking Violetta and running to Peru. But what for? It was obvious from her actions that one couldn't base life on love. Love was ancillary to everything else. An ornament only. Like religion, it had nothing to do with daily living.

The next morning Joseph was so hung over he didn't make it to his office. Heister managed to catch a three o'clock plane to New York. When finally Joseph dragged himself in, his secretary told him that Hamish Jarvis had called three times and that it was urgent. He returned the call.

"You must think I'm a complete fool, Mr. Mann. I sat here until the hearings were finished. I knew what would happen the minute they were over. I would be fired — and I was. Now you think you've got me cooled out. But there's still plenty of trouble

211

I can make when that Bill comes to Parliament. Either I'll come and see you or you'll come and see me. I don't know what Kendall has told you about me. I could have had his job, was offered it. I was a big man and then I became a drunk. But I want you to see me; you'll see I'm perfectly straight. And then I want you to get me a job."

Fool, Joseph thought, as he agreed to go to Montreal to meet him. He had to get out of the city anyway. Impossible to be here with Violetta only a half mile away. The next day he got into his Thunderbird and drove through the spring countryside to Montreal. It was only a two hour drive. And Joseph felt an ache in his body. Often when he and Violetta were driving she would squeeze his leg and he would tighten his muscles and she felt the strength of his body and it pleased her and in a primitive way made him feel like a man.

As he pulled up in front of Hamish Jarvis' expensive home, he was certain he heard the report of a rifle. Pow. Pow.

There it was again. He was aware that French-Canadian separatists had set off bombs in English-owned buildings downtown and in mailboxes in Westmount, so it was entirely possible that they were shooting up the Town of Mount Royal, another English enclave in the heart of Montreal. Another shot. He heard and then saw a large collie dash off, yelping in pain.

"You Joseph Mann?" a voice yelled from the window. And Joseph saw the barrel of a BB gun protruding from the window and then a head poking out. "Come on in."

Two things struck Joseph on entering the house—its size and cost, easily seventy-five thousand dollars, and the lifeless skin on Jarvis' face. His eyes were bright, his mouth moved, but the skin was immobile and yellowish in colour.

"Look, don't jump to conclusions. I love animals. Got two hunting dogs of my own. This air rifle just scares him. I spend a bag of money and time looking after my lawn and that goddam collie comes over every day, same time every day, and deposits the biggest turds you ever saw. I told my neighbour 'next time that damned dog comes over here I'm going to shoot him right in the balls' and by God I'm sure that's right where I got him. Let me get you a drink."

Jarvis brought back a scotch and a coffee for himself.

"I didn't need a drink, if you weren't going to."

"Now, Mr. Mann, you know I'm an alcoholic. I can't touch a drop. And I don't. You go ahead. I like seeing a man drink."

"Lovely home you have, Mr. Jarvis."

"I've been lucky in a way. I inherited some money when I got out of the war, made a few lucky stock buys, and made a packet of money. Then put the capital with a trust account which gives us an income. Fortunately, my wife put it in a joint account. Otherwise we'd be on poverty row today."

Hamish got Joseph another drink and talked about himself; he had wanted to be a doctor and flunked out, and that's when he got a job as a detail man for a large pharmaceutical company. "I've been everything in this business, drug store detail man, hospital detail man, then the big time — marketing, advertising. Hell, I've called on doctors all across this country and I can tell you they're dumb. Like plumbers. I can remember calling on a famous surgeon, this was years ago, at University Hospital here in Montreal. We had a new drug that was useful against shock as a result of an operation. That man, head surgeon if you can believe, said, 'My patients never have shock.' Selye had been writing about shock for the longest time, everyone goes into some kind of shock everytime a knife cuts, and this jerk wouldn't believe it. Of course, that's all past, the big question now is chemical scarring. It's all changed, the whole concept of medicine has changed. Doctors are like plumbers today, stupid. A detail man could sell them shit and they would prescribe it."

He got up and, still talking, fetched Joseph another scotch. It was only twelve o'clock, but Joseph had long since stopped drinking by the clock. Jarvis rambled on, his eyes and face moving, his skin dead and motionless. "Talk about doctors, and I wanted to be one . . . to help mankind. I was detailing in the town of Cobalt once, if you can believe, old silver mine town, and left this doctor and went across the street to say hello to the druggist. I always made a deal with the druggists, one way or another, to let me see all doctors' prescriptions to find out if they were prescribing medicine from our company or the competition. Don't look so shocked, everyone does. You slip the druggist something, a deal now and then, something. Anyway, the doctor came across the street with a patient in tow. 'Hey Hamish,' he says, 'I want to give this man a shot of that B12 you were telling me about.' He was a farmer who wasn't making a good recovery from an operation, as I remember. Anyway, the druggist got out the vial of B12 and the doctor gave this patient an injection and the patient fell unconscious to the floor. Now the doctor looks at me and yells, 'Hamish, you've killed my patient.' The patient was lying on the floor and everyone was stunned and blaming everyone else. The doctor had not followed instructions, had injected the stuff too quickly. It's a hell of a shock to the system. Anyway, while they were still discussing what to do, the patient came around by himself. Look, Mr. Mann, I'm not against the industry. The government is dumb. Why today, aspirin wouldn't be approved by Food and Drug. I'm for the industry. I believe in it. I've given my life to it. I just want a chance to work. And I figure that this committee and now the upcoming debate in Parliament has given me my last chance. You can see I'm not a drunk. Look." And he held out his hands. "They don't even shake any more."

"What do you see yourself doing?"

"Anything. Sure, I'd like to be a sales manager or marketing manager, but I'd start again as a detail man, even for a small company. I mean there are seventy companies in Canada that belong to the association employing fourteen hundred detail men; surely it could be fourteen hundred and one. And there are hundreds of smaller companies that the larger ones sell chemicals to. Heister, you, or Kendall could insist I work for them. I don't care where or what, I want to get back in. After that, I'll make it on my own."

Joseph sat there thinking only that he liked Hamish and that because of him he might go to jail.

Misinterpreting Joseph's silence, Jarvis' tone became threatening. "You may not realize just how much damage I can do to the industry. I'll tell Grant MacDonald my whole story.

214

About detail men, the way they sell samples to drug stores, how they steal prescription pads from doctors and forge prescriptions for amphetamines and then supply the rackets. There can't be that many legitimate sales. I'll tell him chapter and verse about price deals, about how doctors sell samples to drug stores, about the companies giving large amounts of drugs free to doctors who in turn sell them to patients so they can get good reports on the drug's therapeutic value."

Whatever sympathy and doubt Joseph had, vanished. He didn't like being pushed. And that material in Grant's hands could really hurt the whole pharmaceutical world — manufacturer, druggist, and doctor alike. "Mr. Jarvis, the minute I get back to Ottawa I will get right on this. I'll go over the lists of every manufacturer. You're absolutely right. Why can't there be fourteen hundred and one salesmen?"

Driving back to Ottawa, Joseph thought there were so many men like Jarvis, clever men who for one reason or another had hit the bottle. There were so many things a man past forty could get tripped up on and then it was usually too late to come back. Unless he were tough and ruthless or prepared to settle for twenty years of repetition, he'd get lost in the shuffle. He'd better watch his own drinking. And for the first time in years he saw his father's face clearly.

A week later, Hamish Jarvis received a call from Fred Smith and started to work for Pureco the next day. The Italian suppliers had insisted that Pureco hire Jarvis if they wanted to receive the psycho-active pills.

Hamish Jarvis was ecstatic. He couldn't believe his luck. There had been no word of Joseph Mann in the negotiations with Fred Smith, but Jarvis knew that somewhere the industry had been frightened. It proved a man couldn't let himself be kicked around.

19

Of course Violetta had known that Joseph's fragile experiment with love would end in failure if he discovered she was a member of INTEGRAL. She realized now, however, that she had blotted that reality from her mind, had not been able to project beyond the happening. For a time she believed that his rejection of her was deserved and accepted it with a fatalism, born of her life, even feeling relief that she no longer had to anticipate his discovery and its results. At least she was now living it. Yet, acceptance of blame didn't make the pain easier to endure. Many times she tried to make contact with him, but Joseph refused to see her, speak to her, acknowledge that she was alive.

Once in desperation, unable to keep herself away, she had knocked at his apartment door. "Joseph, Joseph, I know you're there. I know you're inside." She could almost feel him through the door, wanting her, but unable any longer to unlock the protective barrier with which he had surrounded himself.

He was on the other side of the door and kissed the door where he felt her mouth to be and felt her lips through the door and wanted to open it, but could not move, was too weak to cry out, and he stood there pressed against the door until he heard her leave and then he slid to the floor.

She left, knowing in her heart that if she stayed long enough he would open the door to her. Then why, why, did she not wait? Did she want to punish herself because she felt she deserved that pain, felt she had upset the delicate balance of Joseph's life, hurt him even more than Grant had? Or was it more? She had tried to reach out to him and he had failed to respond quickly enough. Was she punishing him for his weakness?

And after that, finally accepting that he was unable to open himself in the way he had, in self-protection, because she felt her own mind in trouble, she asked for and was given a leave of absence from her job. Taking Mylita out of school she went home to her mother. There, while her mother cooked and cared for Mylita, Violetta spent much time alone, in bed, in her room with the door shut, much time crying, hours of crying. She took much valium and drank much scotch and thought about Joseph Mann and thought about Violetta Norgela. So many lives. Each Violetta different from the one before. The Violetta of some not-remembered-past, before the flight. And the Violetta shrieking after her mother lying on top of that body of her father that never moved again. The Violetta of the displaced persons' camp in Germany and the Violetta of the farm in western Canada and the Violetta of the house with the rats on Spadina Avenue in Toronto. The ethnic Violetta so full of pride in her beauty, dancing in costume during the Lithuanian national holidays, singing in the choir the beautiful Lithuanian songs that were of a far-off land more in her heart than the one she lived in. And the Violetta who left school in anger when her mother wouldn't agree to send her to college, the Violetta who read *Cosmopolitan* and the horror stories and killings in the newspaper (and she felt herself blushing in embarrassment). Later, when her tastes developed, she found only an illusion of life in the editorial pages and the serious magazines, and devoted herself exclusively to medicine.

And then there was the Violetta of men. Langorous, too much make-up (oh God, that too?), not talking, keeping herself down in men's company. Decorous (did I think then?). And her first sex — with a married man who had seen her and followed her home and went into the store and introduced himself to her stepfather and asked if he could take his daughter out; of course, he didn't reveal he was married. He was thirty-five and she sixteen. She didn't love him but decided that she wanted to have sex and that he would be the man to have it with the first. It had been a good choice; he had been careful and tender, if not exciting and passionate, and when he was transferred it ended on a friendly basis. Years later she had run into him on the street in Ottawa and he had hinted that he would like to see her again and she looked at him in disbelief that he had been inside her . . . so gray and old, and ineffectual and weak. And she felt so strong.

And then Vido. Vido. Vido. Vido. The most beautiful face and body she had ever seen or would ever see. She had lusted after him. Not loved. Never loved. Never spoke to. Never knew as a human being or he her. Just lust. She had gone to him every night, and one night, finding his door locked, had climbed the fire escape to get into his room, wanting him so badly, and had seen him in bed with another woman. And yet she continued to go to him for three months after that, debasing herself. And then he broke his leg skiing, and she had to manoeuvre herself into all kinds of strange positions so he could do it and still she wanted him, until one day she went up to see him and before she had taken her coat off he said, "Come on let's fuck." To her wonderment, something about that order made her say, "No, I don't want to." And to herself, as a release, she realized she neither wanted to nor had to. And then the strangest thing happened, something she didn't really understand to this day. When she refused him, he seemed to turn green and went into the bathroom and she was sure she heard him throwing up. And while he was there she grabbed her coat and ran out and never saw him or wanted him again.

But it hadn't ended there because, as she thought about the different Violettas, she wondered whether she had married Peter, the Lithuanian boy, to erase the dirtiness she had carried with her because of Vido. Had she done that to Peter, poor Peter?

And Douglas Clark. Always planning, not able to do one thing without knowing in advance what result he wanted. Douglas, with whom sex came absolutely last, when it did. Douglas, who stayed up to prepare for the next day's meeting and made sure he went to bed on time so he would be fresh for it. And Douglas who never drank whisky during the week, so his head would always be clear. With Douglas everything was on a timetable. Nothing free. In a way, although on a much higher intellectual plane, Douglas was like her husband, Peter, completely predictable. Both also held the same view of a woman. A woman was a wife to do the cooking and have children. A woman was to serve a man. Both wanted a woman in the image they created and no other. And Joseph, would he have been the same? No, because in some non-rational way, Joseph had opened himself to her and she to him. And they were human beings, the one to the other. And there, in her mother's home, nursed back to psychic health by her mother's love, not by anything her mother said, but because she was able to be loved as a daughter simply because she existed, Violetta came to realize that Joseph had been wrong. She was not to blame. There was no reason for her to feel guilt.

If they were free and if he believed her right to live as a separate human being, then he should have realized that they came together in the middle, so to speak. She was in orbit when she met him, as was he. He should have been able to accept the situation, realize that there was nothing she could have done, unless they had both decided to discuss the problem and quit — smash their respective entrapments. But she had made a commitment and so had he, and although she knew now that such commitments were antihuman, what was one to do? In her mind she had done nothing wrong. She had not used him, had not questioned him about his work and, in fact, had always stopped him when he started to talk. The world was to have been outside their apartment, their bed, their hearts and bodies as lovers. Joseph was wrong. Egocentric. Childish. Male of the males in the society. And she no longer felt any guilt. His hurt was his responsibility, not hers.

But she loved him still. "You are my first love," she had said to him. "You will be my only love." And he had told her that souls are split in heaven before birth and they look for each other ever after to be rejoined. And in her his soul had found its other half. And when she remembered that, an aloneness that was intolerable swept over her and she went into her mother's bed.

After three weeks it was time to leave. Anyway, she thought

219

(and a pain went through her as she remembered how Joseph used to tease her for starting sentences with "anyway"), it was time to go back to living. She was a doctor and a mother. She would endure as herself, as her mother had. And with a man if necessary. Now she thought of herself as self — first. From time to time needing sustenance from her mother, returning to her mother's breast, just as she would always be there to give to her daughter when she needed her, but essentially herself. Alone. She had a capacity to love, but most likely would never love again because she would not ever want to open herself again. And that night she cried herself to sleep. Cried for herself for the last time.

20

Because of the long, cold winter, Ottawa's tulip festival was late. But now, tens of thousands bloomed throughout the city, the most thrilling mass display in the world. In gratitude for Canada's help during the Second World War, Queen Juliana of the Netherlands had made a gift of thousands of tulip bulbs, enough to make the resulting tulip festival an important tourist attraction. The festival made a lot of money for a lot of people, Joseph thought cynically. The Queen's gift could even be looked on as good marketing strategy as it focused attention on Dutch bulbs, reinforcing the idea that they were the best in the world. Still, it wasn't as commercial as the Japanese cherry blossom nonsense in Washington, co-sponsored by a shopping centre.

Sitting in the public galleries waiting for the opening of Parliament, Joseph flipped through the booklet handed everyone by the House of Commons' protective staff. "The House of Commons is the focal point of our parliamentary democracy . . . . The 265 elected representatives of the people of Canada enact legislation to carry on the nation's business". (Do they carry on the nation's business, Joseph wondered, or does business carry on the nation's politicians?) "The Speaker presides over the House, sitting in the Great Chair which is the replica of that in the Palace of Westminster destroyed by enemy bombing in 1941. Part of the Chair includes oak from the roof of Westminster Hall and from Lord Nelson's flagship, *Victory*." (That seemed the height of idiocy) "To the right of Mr. Speaker sits the Prime Minister" — he looked different than he had at Grant's party; he wasn't

221

wearing his mask then — "the Ministers and other members of the government party. To the left sit the Leader of Her Majesty's Loyal Opposition and his supporters. Further down sit the leaders of the other opposition parties . . . New Democrats, the Social Credit Rally."

Looking down at the Members below, Joseph saw sitting in front of him in the press gallery, ready to take notes, his old and beloved friend, Grant MacDonald. Grant looked around, saw him and waved. Joseph did not respond. As the public gallery, which easily seated three hundred, began to fill, he saw Violetta enter with Douglas Clark and other members of INTEGRAL. Everyone coming to hear the Bill introduced. "All the principal players are here," he said bitterly to Sorenson, his eyes unable to pull away from her, his head spinning dizzily, his chest and arms aching.

The Minister of Consumer and Corporate Affairs rose and moved the second reading of the Bill to amend the Patent Act and the Trademarks Act. He was a good-looking young man from one of the élite families in the country, a man who years before had his name romantically linked with Princess Margaret. Born with a silver spoon in his mouth, he was a man assured of his position. He would never have to worry about not having enough to eat or where he would find a job, Joseph thought enviously. Surveying the House, the Minister knew that this was his moment and he wasn't going to rush it. He was aware of the historic significance of a new Bill being presented, aware that each new Bill affected peoples' lives. At least he believed it did.

Joseph's mind drifted. It was difficult to concentrate, he had heard it all before. The Minister's words droned in and out of his consciousness. "Those who pay the largest drug bills are, because of their disability, likely to have incomes substantially below average . . . . Canadian drug prices are unduly high. No single measure by itself would bring about a significant reduction." The Minister at this point introduced a table that showed what drug costs were in different countries in the world.

"We failed," Joseph said.

"There was nothing we could have done," Sorenson assured

him.

"I wonder," Joseph said, thinking of the veiled warning he had had, of his involvement with Grant and Violetta. "I wonder." And he wondered, too, if he would ever be free from the agony of his longing for her and the hate for her because she had made a fool of him.

"The drug industry operates within a given economic framework and members of the drug industry, like rational businessmen everywhere, have responded to the profit opportunities provided by the framework."

He described the framework. "First, the demand for ethical drugs is largely by incidence of sickness and the writing of prescriptions by doctors. Because he must follow the doctor's advice, the patient is unable to purchase any but the specified drug. Ordinarily the busy physician is not price-conscious. Often he may not even know the prices of different brands of drugs and therefore he gives the factor of price little consideration when he prescribes a medicine. There is little opportunity for the consumer to switch to something else if he doesn't like the price.

"There are high barriers to the entry of newcomers who might inject vigorous competition . . . but the most important barriers arise as a result of the interaction of the Patent Act, the Trademarks Act, the Customs Tariff, the very intensive and costly program of marketing and promotion undertaken by the established firms and the requirements of the Food and Drug Act."

"It is not surprising in these circumstances that the major drug firms have not on the whole found price competition necessary and charge what the traffic can bear . . . ."

The Minister spoke for four hours straight, detailing all aspects of the Bill and the reasons behind it. As Flanagan had said, there were five parts to the Bill: removal of sales tax; modification of anti-dumping duty; programs of information to doctors regarding use of generic drugs; government support by loans for production of drugs; and amendments to the Patent and Trademarks Acts. Three were intended to reduce barriers to competition, the other two were to encourage prescribing and manufacturing of lower priced drugs in Canada. If carried (and the government had a majority so there was no doubt of that), it would be the most disastrous blow the industry had ever received from any country in the world.

After the session, walking along the corridor, Grant caught up with him. "Joseph," he said with warmth, "Come have a drink. Let's talk."

"About what?" Sorenson walked on ignoring him.

"Joey, listen. This thing is almost over" — oh no, Joseph thought, not yet it isn't — "let's have a drink. Listen, Violetta is strung out. I mean you're giving her a bad time. The girl is in love with you. Joey, you aren't right. You aren't being fair. You came here . . . an outsider. How could you expect ——"

"That's her problem," Joseph said viciously, as he walked away. Violetta loved him? Not true. Not true. Love was shit. Love cannot hide us from the world or ourselves. A woman was to fuck. Nothing more. Quoth the raven, "Nothing more," and he started to laugh out loud, not caring that people were looking at him. And yet inside, deep inside, as if inside some other's being, he heard a voice crying, "Violetta, Violetta, I love you."

As the days passed and the debate over the Bill continued, a routine medical check of the several thousand employees who worked in the Parliament buildings, including Members of Parliament, the Senate, and the press gallery, revealed two cases of tuberculosis. Due to the crowding involved in the old buildings, the medical authorities, fearing that more people might be infected — that indeed more might already have contracted the disease but it was not far enough advanced to show up — recommended that because of the importance of their work to the nation, everyone who worked in the Parliament buildings, from secretaries to the Prime Minister himself, should receive Isoniazid (INH). It was the drug of choice for the treatment of tuberculosis and for preventing the development of the disease as well.

224

"Couldn't have happened at a better time," Sorenson said. "Of course, I mean if it had to happen at all. Here they are attacking our industry and yet they have to come to us for one of the wonder drugs to help keep them from getting sick." It was always thus with politicians, he thought. The same ones who attacked the industry in order to get votes were always first in line to their doctors with every ache and pain, demanding a new wonder drug. Sorenson wished he had a hundred dollars for every politician who had phoned him personally to get a new drug for a relative. In fact, one time he had flown a new serum from the plant to New York, holding it on his knees in a box placed in ice, for the child of a Senator. One thousand bulls had been killed to get the essence of their liver for that drop of serum. And now it was synthesized, and all these bastards could think of was to accuse the industry of wasting its research money on molecular manipulation to one-up competitors' successful drugs.

"We should get a major story out on this," Kendall said to Joseph. "Or perhaps make the drug available free."

"No. That way it would seem as if we were trying to buy them. Let the medical staff of Parliament handle it in their own way. It's a big enough story that the press will cover it anyway. We might get a fact book out on the drug and distribute it to all Members. How long ago was it developed? Is it a new drug?"

"No, it's about twenty years old, I think," Sorenson said.

Three days later, one of the members of the press gallery was suspected of having tuberculosis. To Joseph's surprise, Thelma called him. "Joseph, Grant won't take that drug INH. I'm worried. He's been working so hard. He's run down, a real candidate for T.B."

"The last year hasn't been easy on any of us." He was shocked to realize that just about one year had gone by since that first meeting in Heister's office.

"I know Joseph, I know," and there was a sadness in her voice he responded to. "I thought perhaps you could talk to him. Convince him."

"Thelma, he wouldn't listen. You know."

225

"But try, Joseph. I feel a heavy foreboding. You've always been so close. And it's time to make peace. I know Grant wants to."

How curious life was. Disordered would be a better word. Man forever futilely trying to impose rationality on what was eternally and horrifyingly non-rational. On both the macro and micro level the events of the day were absurd. The Israelis and Arabs locked in mortal combat; Stalin's daughter defecting to the West, to the United States of all places; Muhammad Ali being sentenced for refusing to be inducted — or for replacing his good American slave name with an ultraforeign one? And Thelma, who had fought with him over the years, had hated him and he her, was asking him for help. And Joseph, who had felt he could never forgive Grant, was now concerned about his friend's health. For the moment, all the anger and deceit that had passed between them was of no importance. "I'll talk to him, Thelma. I'll do my best."

"Thank you. And Joseph . . ."

"Yes."

"You'll call me. You'll tell me what he says?"

"Yes."

"I knew I could count on you."

He smiled. Had it been necessary for her to say that?

The debate on the Bill continued and as Joseph listened to one of the Conservative Members he wondered how to approach Grant about taking INH.

"Mr. Speaker, I should like to congratulate the Minister on his marathon speech and for recognizing that this is a complex piece of legislation, bad in some respects, which he did his best to dress up and gild. It has a great many loopholes and I intend to deal with some of them, particularly those in respect of patents and safety, which he passed over so easily." (Joseph looked for Violetta, but she wasn't there.) " . . . a man or woman spends days, months, or years working hard and long to develop an idea into something tangible. It matters not whether the idea relates to a drug or food or an implement. Surely that person should not be cheated of the rewards of his labour, either in part or in whole.

226

This is the moral issue. Out of three thousand experiments, approximately only one comes through. A man could work in research his whole life and never come up with anything worthwhile."

After some two hours, he urged that the whole matter be sent back to the committee for further consideration.

"Not a chance," Joseph said to Sorenson. "Don't get your hopes up."

When the session adjourned, Joseph went into the "hot room." Grant was there, typing madly. He did look thinner. Joseph approached and put his hand on his shoulder. Grant was startled, his concentration total. "Joseph," he said, surprised.

"Can you take a minute?"

"Sure," he said smiling. "I wanted to talk to you the other day, remember?"

"Thelma called me."

"Is that what you want to talk about?" he said, disappointed. "She wants me to take that drug. Isoniazid."

"What can you lose?"

"I've been writing against just that kind of thing for months now. I'm opposed in principle to taking a fool drug just in case I get something else. And what about the side effects? I think the government is crazy wanting everyone to take it. I refuse."

"As I understand it, a little dizziness with some people, bowel upset with others, sometimes diarrhoea, headache, dry mouth, rashes. I've studied it, it's safe. Grant, they've been using it for twenty years."

"And maybe suppression of the bone marrow. Leave me alone with your drugs." He turned his back on him and started working on his column again.

Joseph could do nothing but leave, feeling very much a stranger, very much on foreign ground, not part of the busy activity of the press gallery when Parliament was in session. And in a way sorry he wasn't.

As promised he called Thelma, who broke down when he told her that Grant categorically refused to take the drug. He hadn't realized she was so upset, or such a hypochondriac.

227

"Joseph, can you get me that drug? Does it come in a tablet?"

"Yes."

"Does it taste?" She was cool, methodical. The tears gone. In control.

"What are you getting at?"

"You get me the drug and I'll find a way to give it to him. How long does it have to be taken for?"

"As a preventative, I think the plan is three months, or six months. I'm not sure, but I can check."

"Will you get it for me?"

"Yes," he said without hesitation, feeling easier when he put the phone down. Why? He and Grant were no longer friends. But was that true? When this was over, in a year or so, they would come together again. And if not, then that didn't matter either. Or was he doing this just to prove a point, to be able to tell Grant later that he had taken the drug? He shrugged. Too complicated.

It was an easy matter for him to get a supply and give it to Thelma with instructions. One tablet a day.

"I'll put it in his scotch before dinner," she said. And she managed to get a tablet into Grant every day for six days. Looking after her man filled her with an inner glow.

228

21

When Grant woke, he automatically looked at his watch — 7:30. Damn. Overslept. He wanted to get to the press gallery and write the column he had thought out last night before the session started.

His skin felt itchy and when he went to the bathroom he noticed his urine was a slightly different colour, a dark orange. Curious. What the hell had he eaten the night before? Beets usually made it pink. He was going to ask Thelma if she noticed anything different about herself, but the business of the morning interfered — eating breakfast, refereeing the usual bickering, making sure his kids wore clean clothes, getting them off to school. His middle son was always trying to sneak out with his favourite pair of jeans on, so thick with grime they could stand by themselves. He didn't think any more about it until he got to the press gallery and went to the bathroom again. This time his urine was dark like coca cola, and his skin was very itchy. Some allergic reaction to something, he thought. He broke into a cold sweat. Back at his desk he placed a call to Dr. Sherway. Might as well check. They had become fast friends since Sherway had appeared on his TV special on the pharmaceutical industry. Grant knew that if he had insisted on speaking to Sherway immediately, his secretary would have paged him. But when she told Grant he was lecturing over a patient, Grant just asked her to have him call when he had time.

Dr. Sherway's secretary was wrong. When Grant called, the

229

lecture had not started. Paging would not have interrupted him. Dr. Sherway, Chief of Medicine, was just entering his patient's room. And for Grant, whom he admired so much, he would have interrupted his teaching. Dr. Sherway had started out in life as Yitzhuk Shernkikovnitztky, son of a Jewish cutter who worked in the last of the sweat shops on Spadina Avenue. He had fulfilled his mother's fervent prayers and become a doctor.

And in the process, the Yitzhuk had become the English Isidore (Izzie), still too Jewish. And in the process, in disgust at the ghetto minds of his parents, he had turned his back on all things Jewish. The Izzie became Ian. Ian Shernkikovnitzky was too funny and it became Ian Sherway. And with the name he dropped all his Jewishness. His attitudes changed. His very walk and manner changed. He married an Anglican and his children were brought up eclectically. As a Jewish doctor he had developed a financially rewarding practice. But he had left that too, when, after years of further study and the achieving of a specialist's degree, he had accepted the post in a teaching hospital, with his income halved. He felt a perverse feeling of joy as if he still had to prove himself, that though he was Jewish he was not after the dollar. The image was not what they had of the Jews. For somewhere in Yitzhuk's childhood, he had accepted and believed all the things they said and thought about Jews. Jews killed Christ — guilty. Jews were all wealthy, except for his father — guilty. (His father was one of the dumb Jews who was a kike — also guilty.) Jews ate garlic — guilty. Jews jewed — guilty. Guilty. Would he ever overcome it?

"Hello sweetheart," Dr. Sherway said to his patient. "Feeling any better today?"

"Oh, yes. Yes." Her face fell. "No, Dr. Sherway. No better and we both know I never will."

Summoning a hopefulness he didn't feel, Dr. Sherway said, "We've got lots of tricks up our sleeve, young lady. You have a rare disease, systemic scleroderma. I don't deny that, but many young ladies have been cured." The trouble was, and he didn't tell her, that no one knew what cured them; since Crusio of Naples in 1752 reported the curative effects of milk baths, almost everything had been tried. And before being sent to him, she had undergone the usual therapy in an attempt to loosen the skin and joints of her fingers, hands and feet. Exercises, wax baths, and swimming in a warm pool; all to no avail.

"I'm ugly doctor." But she had combed her hair and agreed to allow him to lecture over her.

"Nonsense, you're still pretty." But not as she had been. He had seen her photo taken before her illness and her mother had corroborated the change that had taken place in the last year. She had been so vivacious, but now the skin of her face was ten years older. One year. And again, as he had for years and years, he felt total astonishment and terror at the fragility of the human body, at the inability of science to predict, prevent, or control the body's breakdown.

"My skin is like leather."

"It can be reversed." But her fiancé had broken their engagement. And that hurt could never be reversed. (Could he be blamed? There the moral question, the essential selfishness of the human that we all try to deny.) Even if there were other fiancés, she had discovered what so many women knew. Men for the most part responded only to external beauty. And that was called love.

But she had combed her hair. She had a streak of toughness. Many young girls had killed themselves when they contracted this disease. The French of the Middle Ages called it "poitrine en cuirasse," which meant the skin of the chest became like the leather vest of a medieval knight. So tight, breathing was restricted.

Five young interns entered the room and Dr. Sherway proceeded with his lecture, asking them to question the patient for symptoms, pushing them to diagnose. This was the part of medicine he liked best now, the teaching. And he never failed to warn the young men that from now until the end of their lives in medicine they were responsible for their continuing self-education. They must not be influenced by drug companies through their clever advertisements or through calls by detail men. Or by the new and dangerous gimmick — so-called medical

231

lectures by cassettes; you plugged them into your car so theoretically you could learn while driving. "Learn what?" he asked. "What drugs the drug companies want to sell." He looked at his watch. He was running behind. He had to be at a research meeting. Some young doctor had come up with an interesting idea on pericarditis.

Finishing his lecture, he hurried down the hall and saw a familiar figure. What was his name? A drug detail man. A good man as far as they went, but he objected to drug salesmen being given the run of the hospital. They were permitted to set up displays, to give lectures to nurses and interns, to see the head nurse of the operating room to sell sera, bandages, and instruments. He just didn't believe these fellows should be allowed to haunt the corridors. According to the unwritten rule, Dr. Sherway looked straight ahead as he passed the man. If the doctor had nodded or said good morning, the detail man was permitted to speak to the doctor and ask for an appointment. If the doctor looked straight ahead, the detail man was not to say anything. Sherway wondered how a man could take such an undignified job. Pay must be good.

He stopped in his office and checked the file on DMSO. Dimethylsulfoxide (90 per cent) on water (DMSO), a clear, colourless liquid with a light characteristic odour, a freezing point of 18 degrees centigrade, and a refractive index of 1.5 (25 degrees C). Its structural formula:

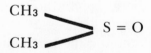

DMSO was dangerous, to the point where even the nurse applying it must be careful, spreading it with a cotton pledget directly to the leathery part. None of the drug must touch the nurse's hands as it could dangerously soften her skin. Reports were not encouraging, but he dictated a letter to Food and Drug and to the company, asking for permission to try it on his young patient.

"Do you want your calls, doctor?" his secretary asked.

"No time, I've got a research meeting," he said as he hurried out. "Anything urgent?"

She rifled through the stack of pink telephone message slips and shook her head. Part of her job was to protect him, to make his day proceed smoothly, on schedule.

In the "hot room," Grant typed his column with increasing difficulty. "In a society where the high cost of drugs is borne by those able least to afford it, the old and sick and the poor . . . " God, he felt awful. But he would finish and then head home to bed. " . . . one may be pardoned for asking why action on drugs has not had a higher priority. One answer was observed during the special committee just concluded to probe the cost of drugs. The well-heeled, monopolistic and internationally powerful drug industry mounted the most intensive lobby ever seen in Ottawa. Its effectiveness was plainly demonstrated when one M.P. was openly fed information and questions by representatives of companies and their organizations in order that he could better interrogate hostile witnesses. And we are seeing the same thing again now that the Bill is being presented.

"Representatives of the drug industry are packing the public galleries. When a difficult question arises, runners dash to the nearest phone to call the Association, where a research staff awaits to provide the answers. Members are then signalled to meet the lobbyists in the very halls of Parliament, where the information is passed to them. Within minutes this material is then being debated from the floor of the House. How much longer can we allow lobbyists, whether they are American or Canadian, to operate in such a fashion, where they seem to have the full run of the House of Commons?" He could type no more.

"Jean, Jean Baçques," he called. "Jean, I don't feel well." Jean came running over. "Help me to the bathroom."

Once there, Grant vomited. "Jean," he managed to gag, "get Luther to find Joseph Mann. Remember, you met him? Luther will know. Joey will be in the Gallery. Hurry. I have to get home."

233

Sitting in the gallery, Joseph listened to the New Democrat Member. It all seemed so tedious, the arguments, rehearsed so many times. Didn't these people know what they were doing?

Joseph didn't notice Luther signalling him and thus Luther had to work his way through to the fifth seat, difficult because of his girth. "Joey," he whispered. Startled, Joseph looked up, surprised to see Luther looming over him. But he knew instantly something was dreadfully wrong. "Grant wants you. He's sick."

"What's wrong?" he asked, aware of a horror, knowing they were all to be involved in a horror.

"I don't know, Joey. He asked for you."

That was enough. He followed Luther to the aisle, then rushed to the press gallery.

Grant was hunched over his typewriter, trying desperately to act as if nothing were wrong. "Please drive me home, Joey, I don't feel so good."

With Luther's help they got him down a freight elevator and out the back where, because of his long tenure, he was permitted to park his car.

"You'll need help, Joey," Luther said. "But I can't leave."

"We'll make it. You call Grant's home and tell his wife, Thelma, we're coming. Tell her to call the doctor."

On the way to Grant's he had to stop the car several times while Grant threw up. Then he lost control and had diarrhoea. Fouled himself in the car. "Oh Joseph, I'm sorry," The smell was awful, but more, Joseph felt for the indignity to his friend. By the time they reached his house, Grant had lost a lot of fluid, could hardly stand, and was constantly retching.

Thelma ran out. Joseph made a snap decision. "Grant must be seriously ill. It was dumb to come here. I'm going to take him to the hospital immediately."

"He was fine yesterday," she said helplessly, as if that should have made him proof against sickness today.

"Please wash me off. Please wash me before I go to the hospital," Grant managed to say.

Joseph and Thelma, working together, half-dragged him to the bathroom where they got his clothes off. He was by now too weak to help them. Joseph held him while Thelma ran the shower over him, and Joseph also got wet. They dried him and wrapped him in his kimona and then a blanket, and Joseph carried him to the car. "Thelma, I'd better drive. You sit in the back seat with Grant."

"Yes," she said, cool now, the obvious seriousness changing the semi-hysteric role she had played all her life. Joseph had wanted her to call the police, knowing the speed he would have to be driving, but chanced that if he was overtaken, it would only take a few seconds to explain. And fortunately, they met a policeman almost as they started and he led the way to the hospital, siren screaming. Joseph had not wanted to wait even the few minutes it would take for an ambulance to reach there. Or was it the knowledge of the horror that awaited, that he didn't want to leave his friend alone?

In carrying Grant to the car he felt the heat of his body even through the blanket. "Christ, he's burning up with fever."

Thelma had the sense to grab a handful of towels as they ran to the car, and despite the continuous throwing up and the steady diarrhoea — Joseph, by sheer will, keeping himself from getting sick from the smell — got Grant to the hospital.

And within minutes the organization of the hospital took over. Dr. Sherway was summoned and assumed immediate charge. Grant was put in a private room where intensive care was begun.

After what seemed an eternity, but was only an hour, Dr. Sherway came to where they were sitting. "I think Grant has hepatitis, yellow jaundice. The liver is the major storehouse of sugar along with the skeletal muscle" — he believed in detailed explanations to worried relatives and friends; it was important to assure them that the patient was receiving the best care possible — "and we've got to replace the sugar, which must be metabolized to keep other cells such as brain cells going. The first thing we must do to keep him alive is to replace his loss of fluid."

"What do you mean," Joseph almost shouted, "to keep him alive?" But he had known. They were only in the middle of the

235

horror.

"I'm sorry," Dr. Sherway spoke to Thelma. "Grant is near death."

Thelma looked at him, hearing but not assimilating the words.

And Joseph heard himself say the usual banal things. "How could it happen so rapidly? Has he a chance?"

"We'll know more in a little while," and he turned and went back to the patient.

"What day is it, Grant? Grant, what day is it?" Grant heard a voice say as if from far off.

They had decided to explore a different part of the city that day on their bikes and had gone too far. Grant had to go to the bathroom and he and Joseph debated whether to go up to a house and ask if they could use the bathroom. But they were too shy. In a park they went behind some bushes and squatted and crapped. But there was nothing to wipe themselves with. Joseph took off his underwear and they both used that and then they dug a small hole in the earth and buried Joseph's underpants.

"Extend your arms. Yes, that's right. Extend your arms and then put your wrists backwards. Can you do that?"

"He can't do it doctor. That settles it. He has acute hepatic necrosis."

"Oh God, I hope not. Extend your arms, Grant. Try."

They had found a great farm with apple trees by the road and they would go there every day and wait until the farmers were in the middle of their fields and then would load up their bicycle baskets. But one day the farmer was waiting for them and jumped from his truck and chased them. They pedalled as fast as they could, Joseph screaming, "Throw out the apples, Grant." And pedalling and holding onto the handle bars with one hand, and reaching over and throwing out the apples with the other so that there was no evidence by the time the farmer caught up with them.

"Grant, Grant. Can you write your name?" He was given a pencil and a piece of paper, but despite what was going on in his brain, only a child's scrawl appeared.

"I, Grant MacDonald of the Township of Carleton make this oath and say: This affidavit outlines in detail my association, membership and activities in the Labour Progressive (Communist) party, and my activities following the termination of my membership which will show that I have

236

been in complete opposition to the Communist doctrine, program, principle and ideology."

Flashes of scenes disconnected through Grant's head, like the flipping of television channels, looking for something that pleased. Unrelated scenes: marrying Thelma; their first child; standing in a giant crowd at a peace rally on Red Square, feeling a oneness with all the people in the world, feeling there would never be another war, that socialism was the answer; standing in church listening to the minister, his family around him, feeling that there was a God in heaven and the answer for man was to find his way to Christ; lying in bed beside Louise, feeling his body beside hers, her tongue inside the upper lip of his mouth and her mouth all over his body, and knowing that sex was the only emotion that brought peace to man.

"Grant is acutely jaundiced. If he cannot recover quickly, if the liver is unable to handle the metabolic products sent to it from the gut through the bloodstream, then he becomes stuporous." (Grant stuporous? The thought was incredible to Joseph. Grant was one of the brightest, most alert human beings he had ever known.) "The patient finally goes into coma. And he has all the symptoms. He doesn't know what day it is or who the prime minister is." (The P.M. had been at his party; of course, he knows him.) "When he held out his hand, his fingers were jerking. Our diagnosis is certain."

Joseph wondered whether he should call Louise. Louise should know.

"I wanted to tell you this. I believe you should know what is happening."

"I want to know everything," Thelma replied.

"He may also develop kidney failure. We don't know why. But fortunately it hasn't happened yet."

A nurse came and Dr. Sherway returned to Grant's room. Joseph and Thelma were alone again, although surrounded by the bustle of the hospital. "I know you think I wasn't right for him, Joseph. But I loved him, love him. He is my life. I knew about Louise and others, but I also knew he was my husband and would never leave me."

237

Joseph put his arms around her and they waited.

At that moment another patient, also a member of the press gallery, was brought into the hospital with exactly the same symptoms as Grant's.

Dr. Sherway worked, his mind like a computer, knowing exactly what was going on in Grant's body; not knowing the total why of it, but knowing what he had to do, like a battlefield general. When the liver fails to metabolize normal hormones (reason unknown), there is a marked disturbance of salt balance which is the electrolyte that affects many parts of the body. If the kidney fails, there is an accumulation of edema, or being waterlogged, particularly in the dependent portions, and the patient may stop producing urine. Uremic. Watch for hyperventilation. Compensate for the acid accumulating as the kidney is unable to excrete it.

"He's starting to tremble, doctor."

"I see."

"I'm thirsty Christ, I'm thirsty," Grant said.

And in the computer mind: no water. Adds to trouble by diluting blood too much, but if we give electrolytes, they accumulate salt. He set up the machine to wash poisonous products out of the system through the semi-permeable membrane. How to get protein into him? Aminoacids? Glutamine? A mild antibiotic in order to kill the germs in the bowel which may ferment and break down the protein, which then is unable to be handled by the liver and affects the brain? Give him repeated enemas to totally wash out all bacteria? Christ, we can't give him blood, and if I don't give him blood he'll die of shock. There was nothing, absolutely nothing Dr. Sherway could do; nothing but to wait.

Again he went into the corridor to explain to Mrs. MacDonald. "We've given him a diuretic to get around the water retention. It's a risk because one gets a potent loss of sodium and the disturbed electrolytes may throw both the liver and kidney off kilter and make everything worse, but if we don't his brain will swell."

Grant started to thrash about and the doctor was called again. He had to be restrained, physically tied. Sedative drugs can kill a liver patient. Dr. Sherway debated for only a fraction of an instant as to whether to use valium or restraint and decided on the latter. A urethral catheter was inserted into the bladder. Grant could no longer control his urine and was wetting the bed, leading to the danger of further potential infection. It also helped for the moment to control the measurement of intake and output of fluid. Dr. Sherway hoped the catheter itself wouldn't increase the infection, which could race to the kidney.

Grant's condition was one of the worst situations faced in medicine. Ideally the liver should be transplanted, a technique that had been accomplished surgically, but the patient had always rejected it and died.

The music was a groove. Marijuana was passed around. The music went through his body. Suddenly one of the musicians went into convulsions.

Thelma and Joseph were called into the room where Grant lay. He opened his eyes and saw them. He looked at Thelma and knew that for him security was with Thelma.

And he looked at Joseph, his friend, and knew that for the most part he hadn't lived the life he wanted. He tried to tell Joseph but the words wouldn't come.

The music was a groove. Marijuana was passed around. The music went through his body. To live with the music. And suddenly one of the musicians went into convulsions.

He looked at Thelma. And knew that the answer is family. And he no longer felt alone. And the music stopped.

He felt nothing.

Twenty-four hours later, the other newspaperman also died. In exactly the same way.

"Why? Why?" Joseph asked, shouted, in the corridor.

"I would like your permission to do an autopsy, Thelma," Dr. Sherway asked. Drained. This, too, now, he had to dredge out of her. Now. The death of her husband not enough.

She thought of Grant, her Grant, being cut up and she sank to the chair and managed to say,"Hasn't he suffered enough?"

There were tears in Dr. Sherway's eyes as he sat beside her and held her hand. "I admired your husband very much."

Joseph wanted to scream. Let him alone. Let him alone. Jesus, don't cut him.

"An autopsy is a surgical procedure done with as much care as if the patient were alive. If I knew I was to die the way your husband did, I would consent in advance to an autopsy. Perhaps something I could do after death would help advance medical knowledge, help other people to live. I view it that way. Seriously. As a search for truth. With love for the human that was."

"I cannot think."

"I will do it myself."

Thelma consented.

The next morning they removed Grant's body from cold storage and wheeled it to the autopsy room where they placed it naked and gray on a granite table.

Interns in white and nurses in white, gowned from head to toe, with caps and surgical masks, to watch, to learn. And two senior residents to help Dr. Ian Sherway.

Masked and gowned like the others, but with rubber vest and apron and gloves, Dr. Sherway entered, like a high priest about to officiate at some primitive ritual. Dr. Ian Sherway, Chief of Medicine, doing an autopsy. Unheard of.

Grant MacDonald who was — had been — his friend, a man he admired, lay dead and he raised his hand to plunge the knife. Grant MacDonald, like some Jesus stretched out naked on the table. Christ, Yitzhuk, Izzie, Ian, whoever you are, get hold of yourself. Don't be like that son-of-a-bitch Mann, who cried crocodile tears, but who threatened to cut off all research funds to this hospital because of the TV documentary.

Scalpel in hand, he carefully made a large "Y" incision in the front of the chest, the blade entering the skin so cold. He drew the scalpel down to the pubic bone, slitting Grant. And carefully turned back the flaps. The resident handed him heavy scissors and he tried to cut the breast bone. He wasn't strong enough and he handed the scissors back and was given bone cutters, the crack of the bone smashing through the silent room.

240

The sound of the bone reminded Sherway of the time he had broken his leg skiing. He willed himself to stop thinking. He removed the breast bone and a wave of putrefaction swept the room. A student in his final year in medicine vomited.

Dr Sherway remembered as a boy going to market with his grandmother and watching her choosing a live chicken, after much feeling and poking of the breast and legs. The *shoichet* tied the chicken's legs to a hook and while it was hanging down said a prayer and quickly slit its throat. And he had watched the life's blood drip out of the chicken into a pail. (Thou Shalt Eat No Blood.) They took the chicken home and hung it on the clothesline while everyone plucked it. Then his grandmother took it inside and opened it and reached her hand right inside and pulled out the guts — the stomach and liver — her hand going right inside the chicken, right up past the wrist, and coming out with all that stuff, bloody.

Dr. Sherway removed the lungs and heart and the portion between the lung and the mediastinum containing the windpipe, after having first cut across the windpipe at the throat in order to free the lungs from the rib cage. The whole thing came out as a piece and was carefully handled for later dissection. Some of it would later be blown up with air, sealed, and fixed in paraffin and sectioned for examination under a microscope. Dr. Sherway removed each organ, examining it with his eye, and passed it to his aides who examined it and then put it aside for later transectioning and microscopic examination.

The heart was separated and cut so that Dr. Sherway could study each chamber. Starting with the left atrium he followed the valve into the left ventricle, then he opened the right atrium and finally the right ventricle.

And up to this point nothing had seemed unusual, although you couldn't tell, until you studied sections under a microscope. But when he came to the liver, all seemed clear. There were bleeding spots on the surface of the capsule of the liver and on the liver itself. But the colour of the liver seemed to be proof of what he had thought. It was a very pale yellow. He handed it carefully to his assistant who sliced it in sections.

241

Later he joined Thelma and Joseph who were waiting in his private office. He had showered, was in a suit, and there was no longer any of Grant's blood on him.

"Was it worth it?"Thelma asked.

"We know the cause of death. His liver failed. A healthy liver is red like a beef liver. And it does not tear. Grant's liver was soft and tore readily. The colour was yellow because the liver cells had died and were not able to metabolize normally, and fat accumulated. There was also staining around it. When the liver fails, the spleen is larger and congested and red and pulpy."

"But do you know what he died from?" Joseph persisted.

"Let me explain first what we looked for and what we didn't find. We did a complete autopsy. There were no tumours, although there was a lot of blood in the gut."

"Doctor, please," Joseph said, containing the frustration and the fear that began to build in him. The horror was not over; that he knew.

"Although we will have to verify this in a few days from microscopic examination, it seems clear he died from acute hepatic necrosis, probably as a result from taking Isoniazid. The other young man died in the same way."

"That drug is supposed to be safe. Has been administered for twenty years . . ."

Sherway shook his head. "That drug is the drug of choice if a person has T.B. and if it is always administered with streptomycin para-aminosalicylic acid or another antibiotic. I've seen these deaths before, mainly in children. I've always been against it as a preventative, for many reasons. But we'll have to wait to be sure."

A wave of madness swept over Joseph. Of frustration. Of powerlessness. Of minuteness. And he left even while the doctor was talking. Got into his car and drove.

Time became confused. For years now he had lived by the clock and suddenly it didn't matter. There was no time for Grant. Time became absurd.

And he was back in his office, chuckling as he called Heister in New York. "Hey Bob," he said. "How the hell are you? Great news."

"Joseph, how are things going up there? Is it time to blow the whistle on the distribution of counterfeit drugs?"

"Not yet, Bob," he said enthusiastically. "I'm calling about Grant MacDonald. I finally stopped him."

"You're putting me on."

"No honestly. I got him."

"Are you sure. What did you do? How?"

"I killed him."

[22]

It was a nightmare, but try as he did Joseph couldn't wake up, couldn't start at the beginning again. The nightmare was real. Grant was dead but brought to lifelike reality in the funeral home, ready to die again and be covered up.

After talking to Robert Heister, time got lost and Joseph wandered through the night. The next morning he found himself knocking at Violetta's door.

Lovely flaxen-haired Mylita. Saucer-eyed Mylita opened the door and was happy to see him and called out while he walked in. Perhaps he shouldn't have just walked in like that, but it seemed so natural, so right for him to be there; seemed that that's where he should have been all along. And he wanted to touch Violetta and tell her about Grant, and be with her, flow into her. He called to Violetta and walked into her kitchen and saw her dressed in a filmy nightgown and he could see her body through it, her breasts and legs and even the darkness of her pubic hair. And sitting at the kitchen table in his trousers and shirt with no tie, why did that seem so important, that he had no tie on, like he was naked, was Douglas Clark (he had been shot down in the war — five escape attempts, or was it six?) and everything seemed to be in slow motion. Violetta had a coffee pot in her hand, was on the way to fill Douglas' cup which he had raised. And Joseph looked into her eyes and saw the panic, and looked at Douglas Clark transfixed and it was like some "B" movie and undignified and he wanted not to be there, to somehow get out of there, and he would not be humiliated and heard himself saying out of his mouth from the mouths of hundreds of movies, heard himself

244

saying to Douglas with studied politeness, "Forgive me. I didn't mean to intrude. I'm sorry." He was apologizing, somehow needing to save his dignity by apologizing, but seeing the slight smile at the corner of Clark's mouth (and in this corner and still champion of the world) he really wanted to scream and kill and smash that face and stomp on it and cut it.

Joseph turned and fled.

Violetta ran after him down the hall in her nightgown. "Joseph, it's not what you think. He stayed the night but in a different bed."

She had not decided yet where or how to live with a man, but by chance, Oh Christ Jesus, by coincidence, Douglas had come and they had drunk too much and he had stayed . . . on the sofa. Had come to her lonely, uncharacteristic for him.

She grabbed Joseph and with her arms around him slid down to the floor. "Joseph, please. It's you I love, you I want. It's not the way it looks. It's not that way."

And yet part of her revolted at what she was doing. Wondering why must she explain. By what right had he who had left her, come back, unasked, by what right to judge?

He remembered when they would take showers together and soap each other, and she would bend down and take him in her mouth for a moment to tease like a lover, but sometimes as if to say, "there, now you are clean," like a mother soaping her baby boy. And he thought of Douglas Clark sitting in possession of her kitchen, her *putyte*. And from his own ineffectuality, and from rage, and from Grant's death, and from wanting to strike at something he grabbed her shoulders and raised her and threw her down the hall. She reeled backwards and hit the wall and then the floor. He thought of Genevieve, when one day it had become too much for him and he had lashed out at her with his hand smashing her face, and that was really why she had left, taken the two children and left . . . to escape the violence that had ever been ready to surface.

"You just want to fuck," he heard himself saying. But that wasn't what he had come to say. And for a moment, perhaps thirty seconds of clarity, he said, "Violetta, Grant is dead. You'd

245

better tell Louise. I don't think I can manage that. The funeral is in three days." And he told her where Grant's body was resting.

And then she knew the fullness of his horror at seeing her with Douglas Clark. His friend — his blood brother — had died and he had come to her. Needing. And she saw in his eyes as before, the naked aloneness, naked inside. But now there was nothing she could do for him. Nothing he would permit her to do for him. Closed.

The funeral was a social and political event. Because of Grant's prominence, Thelma had been able to get the bishop of Trinity Church to read the order for the service and to deliver the eulogy.

"I am the resurrection and the life, saith the Lord: he that believeth in me, though he were dead, yet shall he live: and whosoever liveth and believeth in me shall never die."

But he is dead and won't rise. And he hated the bishop. Hated him for the way he looked, fat, well-fed. Pursed, cocksucking lips. Cocksucker, Joseph felt himself about to shout at him as he spoke during the service. Lying, cocksucking bastard. You didn't know my friend. You didn't know Grant. You saw him in costume. The costume of an elder. The costume of Thelma's husband, the costume of father. But not Grant, not Grant.

"Let your heart not be troubled: ye who believe in God, believe also in me. In my Father's house are many mansions: if it were not so, I would have told you. I go to prepare a place for you."

Dr. Sherway was there. And Violetta. And Louise in dark glasses, playing out her role to the end. (The film *Gaslight* came to Joseph's mind.) Not wailing and weeping and tearing her hair like a lover should, like a true passionate lover should; because it's over baby, none of this bullshit about afterlife, like he's dead and it's really endsville. But stone cold, and detached as if it weren't her heart and her hope lying there all cut up like a chicken and trussed back together in a mockery of life by those funeral business ghouls.

"I am persuaded that neither death, nor life nor angels nor prin-

246

cipalities nor powers, nor things to come, nor height nor depth, nor any other created thing, shall be able to separate us from the love of God, which is Jesus Christ our Lord."

Grant was heavy and Joseph was terrified he would humiliate him by slipping. Did the other pallbearers find him heavy? Sherway had given him sleeping pills and he had taken amphetamines and he was in this haze but he knew, knew he had to hold on, hold up his end. Oh funny, fucking funny.

They stopped at an open pit. A hole.

"In the midst of life we are in death: of whom may we seek for succour but of Thee, Oh Lord who for our sins are justly displeased? Thou knowest Lord, the secrets of our hearts; but spare us, O Lord most holy, O God most mighty, O holy and merciful Saviour, thou most worthy judge eternal."

How could this mockery be allowed? This hateful humiliation. Grant was a man, and he lived, and he loved, and he went to war, and he was filled with passion to help, to be with his fellows; he was a man and he died, because that's what men do. They die. And this cocksucking bishop lying priest was making him nothing.

And Thelma had said to him, "You are not to blame yourself." And destroyed that togetherness they had had for one moment while waiting for Grant to die. Who to blame if not herself and him? Who did she think she was, that she had the power to absolve? No one gets off the hook. No one.

Joseph picked up some earth and threw it into the hole on top of the casket and the sound echoed through his body and his bones and he would hear that sound for all time as long as he lived. And Grant's eldest son, Grant Jr., picked up some earth and threw it into the pit. And Thelma. And Violetta. (Oh help me, kiss me, my love, he thought, while he hated her.) And Louise picked up some and threw it on the casket, and almost stumbled. But some she kept, some of that earth, precious as blood, as Grant's semen, she kept and put her hand in her pocket, and later she would transfer it to a golden box to keep, to keep.

"For as much as it hath pleased almighty God of His great mercy to

247

receive unto Himself the soul of our dear brother here departed: we therefore commit his body to the ground; earth to earth; ashes to ashes; dust to dust; in sure and certain hope of the resurrection to eternal life, through our Lord Jesus Christ, who shall change our mortal body, that it may be like unto His glorious body, according to the mighty working whereby He is able to subdue all things to Himself."

Don't hold your fucking breath, bulbous bastard bishop.

And everyone walked away, each in his aloneness. Thelma alone. Louise alone. Joseph alone. Violetta waited for a moment for him to come with her, but he turned from her. And Grant alone. No that wasn't true. Grant simply didn't exist any more.

After the funeral they gathered at Thelma's, the relatives and friends, co-workers from the press and TV, and workers in the Parliament buildings. They ate and drank and talked of Grant and in their presence, in the thickness of the living, sustained Thelma.

"*L'chaim,*" Dr. Sherway said. "To life." And he held up his glass. Joseph hadn't realized Dr. Sherway was Jewish. And he found himself thinking of Mrs. Polovsky and the first day he had ever met Grant and Grant had let him be Tailspin Tommy.

And Thelma had taken the portrait of Grant he had painted so many years before and, carrying it in front of her, told him that Grant had always wanted him to have it — if anything happened to him. He reached out his hands to take it from her but she didn't give it to him. She asked if he would mind if she kept it for a while. They both knew that it belonged to Joseph, because that was what Grant wanted, but could she keep it? She would take it out of the study and put it over the fireplace in the living room. And Joseph was welcome to come any time he wanted to look at it or to take it, but could she just have it for a while? Even in death. Even in death. And he had nodded and mumbled something and fled.

At home on the floor of his bedroom, Joseph lay in the dark, a bottle of scotch in one hand, a flashlight in the other. Every so often he took a long drink straight from the bottle and every so often switched the flashlight on the aquarium to watch the fish swim madly about. There seemed to be a pounding in his head.

He took another drink from the bottle. The pounding was getting louder.

The pounding was a knocking at his door and someone was calling his name. Violetta, he thought. Violetta. Oh thank God, Violetta. He managed to rise although his head was swimming dizzily, and open the door. A dishevelled Louise, her hair hanging in strands, her feet and hands muddy, her dress partly wet. "I've got the grass," she said insanely, a wildness in her eyes. "Ruined my clothes, almost drowned in that goddamned swimming pool, almost fell down the goddamned stairs at Grant's, but I've got it. That bitch wasn't going to have it. I knew where he had hidden it behind the big rock outside the house. Couldn't let the bitch have Grant's grass too."

"Hey, come on in. You better get those clothes off." Joseph helped her. She was shivering and he ran a hot bath for her, dried her, and gave her his kimona.

"Want to be naked?" she said like a little girl. "Want to smoke up and be naked?"

Joseph rooted around in his drawer and found some papers and she rolled one toque and then another and then another.

"Hey, that's too much."

She rolled six. "We're going to have our own wake. A super turn-on for my Grant."

But whose Grant was Grant. Had he even been his own?

"You take off all your clothes, you're making me feel naked."

Joseph got undressed and they sat there on the bedroom floor and silently passed the joints back and forth.

"My grandfather had cancer and took nine months to die sitting up at home. He sat up in the chair in my mother's living room, smelling it up for nine months, and he was ninety-one. And Grant was forty-three. I mean why would that old man live so long? He never had one thought in his whole life. Never loved. Never created. Never did anything. I wonder if he was alive. Then if he wasn't alive in the first place, he's not dead. Probably just going on and on."

Smoking the marijuana was almost religious, a ritual. Joseph looked across and saw Louise's naked breasts, and his penis thrust itself toward her. He grabbed it with both hands and looked at it. "You can't be me when you die. Or is it you can't be you when I die?" He shone the flashlight at her pubic hairs. "Eve was made for man's pleasure. It says so in the Bible so it must be right. Your crotch was made for my pleasure."

"Christianity has destroyed women. I'll never have his child now. I wanted to have a child by him, with him, or whatever the phony phrasing is." And tears came to her eyes.

"Maybe there's one up there now," Joseph said and lay on the floor shining the flashlight up her vagina.

"How could there be? You wouldn't let him sleep with me. Had him followed by detectives."

Did I do that, Joseph wondered? Did I really do that?

"But maybe there's one from before," he said shining the light.

"It burns." She shrieked with laughter and ran around the room naked trying to escape the light, and then she ran out the door and down the hall naked. And when she came back she fell exhausted on the floor, spread-eagled. "Come on," she said.

And he got on top of her and then they both realized with horror for a moment what they were doing. But the sex lust was too strong for them to resist. "Come on, you phony," she said. "The real Grant would have laughed to see us fuck on his grave. A proper wake. Fucking is for the living. We're all animals anyway."

Would he have laughed? Joseph wondered. Would he really?

23

The debate on the Bill was almost complete, the second reading almost over. Third reading was automatic, a traditional formality. If the Bill was going to be stopped it had to be now. None of their tactics had worked. Operation 100, while worrying the Canadian cabinet, had not prompted them to withdraw the Bill. The direct threat to the Deputy Prime Minister by Heister had backfired. And while the newspapers were filled with threats of epidemics, and one or two summer flu and polio outbreaks were reported, they had had no impact. There remained only the threat of counterfeit drugs to awaken the public and the cabinet to the danger of changing the Patent Act.

"I wish we didn't have to do this," Sorenson said as Joseph dialled Heister. Still very much alive in Sorenson's head were the golden years of pharmaceutical discovery when not a month went by without a feature story about a new wonder drug — the improved penicillins; Selman Waksman's fantastic breakthrough after years, with the discovery of streptomycin; and then the discovery of aureomycin, the golden antibiotic; and the tetracyclines with the psychoactive drugs that had quieted so many mentally disturbed patients to the point where they could be treated by therapy rather than lobotomies or the horror of shock. Sorenson himself had worked on production techniques for penicillin. During the early years of the war the British were making it in milk bottles. The problem was brought to the United States and there a group of American production people found a way to produce the huge quantities that were needed during the last stages of the war — saving thousands of lives. It was one thing to discover a mould or chemical that killed bugs in a test tube, and quite another to make millions of doses in a plant covering several acres and be certain that each dose was pure and had equal therapeutic effect. As much as anything else, modern pharmaceuticals were a triumph of American engineering.

How had the industry stopped being the darling of the press? An American Congressman on a visit to England during the Heath drug probe was startled by what was revealed — dangerous drugs, misleading advertising, staggering profits. This led to the Kefauver commission and its highly exaggerated charges of the same practices by the American industry. Admittedly, Sorenson, too, had been shocked to find that even Heister laboratories had not been as careful as they might. Kefauver revealed the schism between the exigencies of science and sales. Detail men oversold so that doctors, anxious not to lose patients who had read about the miracle drugs, prescribed potent remedies for simple ailments. It was a case of overkill that led to the understanding on the part of public and scientists alike that a drug, potent enough to cure, could also harm if used wrongly. And finally the thalidomide disaster broke the love affair between the American people and the drug industry. The last years had been horrendous. The love became hate and the public actually believed that industry leaders, men like Sorenson who had dedicated their entire lives to bring relief to people, were evil and loathsome in their pursuit of wealth. Sorenson had never adjusted to the present state of public hate and suspicion. Whose fault, really? The industry's? Or the doctors', for using dangerous drugs for simple ailments. Or was it the public's demand? The public believed they had a right to a long life free of pain and disability. This had imposed an unreasonable implied demand on all the people in the industry, and they had to produce pain relieving drugs instantly for any condition. And because they couldn't, the public turned on them. Now, to save the industry, so it could continue to do good, he — Dean Sorenson — and others, had manipulated the spread of counterfeit

252

drugs. They were playing God with human lives.

Heister came on the line. "Bob, I think we'd better pull in the net now," Joseph said.

How wrong he had been, Sorenson thought, to worry as he had in the beginning that Joseph might not be able to do whatever was necessary because he was not one of them. Hard to understand, Joseph Mann. A new type of man like Heister. Not committed to anything other than the job that had to be done.

"Okay, Joseph, go ahead. Be careful. Stay clear of involvement. And good luck."

Joseph felt as if he were in some drama. That nothing that was happening or had happened — even Grant's death — was real. That he was a player. It was as if he were outside himself watching himself do these things. And what was becoming difficult to understand in the aftermath of Grant's death was time. He had always thought there was time for whatever he wanted to do. But when time had run out for Grant, Joseph had this feeling of terror that it had run out for him, too; just like it was running out for Hamish Jarvis, Fred Smith, and Tony Ferrilio. But he did what had to be done — with cold precision. He placed an anonymous call to the Food and Drug Directorate telling them that counterfeit drugs were being sold in the Montreal area and named some of the drug stores. The FDD immediately sent an inspector to investigate and discovered the obviously counterfeit Heister label on a patented tranquillizer. They assumed quite naturally, as Heister had planned, that the drug was counterfeit. The R.C.M.P. was called in and a plan was developed with François Ladouçeur, one of the druggists who had unwittingly bought and sold the counterfeit drugs.

For thirty-five years now François Ladouçeur, a slight man with a thin, black moustache, had opened his drug store on St. Henri Street, in the Verdun area of Montreal, at five minutes to eight. Except for Christmas, New Year's and St. Jean Baptiste Days the pharmacy was always open. It was a good location — on the corner across from the church. To others it might have

253

looked old-fashioned, not flashy like the modern discount stores, but to him it was home. The first thing he did every morning was to bend down, pick up the bundle of newspapers, and then open the store. Inside he would slit the cord, saving the string, and then arrange the papers on the bottom of the magazine rack. Taking the broom he would sweep into the street the dirt and litter that had gathered in the entrance. This was his pattern. But on the day of July fifteenth that pattern was changed. Waiting for him as had been arranged was Sergeant Romaine of the Royal Canadian Mounted Police.

When the R.C.M.P. had approached him several days ago his heart almost stopped. His youngest son was mixed up with those damned fool separatists, spending the night in the taverns of Old Montreal and talking revolution. With bombs exploding, who knew what his son might have done? He shook his head. Who knew what anyone might do these days?

But it was not about his son. The most incredible thing. That very respectable Mr. Jarvis, who used to call on him years ago — he didn't speak French, but never mind, they always made a good deal anyway — had sold him a counterfeit drug. Imagine that. He should have known there was something wrong with the price so cheap and all that, but Mr. Jarvis had said it was because it was a special introduction to the new firm he worked for, one that would be producing mainly less-expensive generic equivalents. Then the inspector from the Food and Drug in Ottawa had taken a sample of the drug away and now, just like on television, Sergeant Romaine had asked for his co-operation, and he had called Mr. Jarvis to order more of the drug.

"Don't worry," Sergeant Romaine said in French. "We have men posted across the street and one in the back. And the Montreal police force is co-operating. When the suspect drives up the police cars will close in. There'll be no problem."

At about that time Hamish Jarvis was finishing his third cup of coffee. He had stopped at the plant early. That was a laugh — the plant; right now it was more like a warehouse with thirty girls packaging dosage forms. But it would grow. And because of his insistence the place was clean. He filled his car. A reorder already. It felt good to be back on the road. He had worried that he would feel depressed, that it would be like starting all over again. But he hadn't, at least, not so far. He'd work his ass off.

The only thing that troubled him was the worsening of the French-English thing. Just yesterday he had walked up St. Catherine Street toward Peel (it had been a while since he had walked in the heart of the city). Ahead, an old man, obviously a panhandler approached a well-dressed man. Hamish was close enough to hear.

"Could you let me have a dime for a cup of coffée?" asked the old man.

"*Parlez français*", the other replied and walked on.

Hamish felt a sense of rage. He quickened his pace, passed the Frenchman who had refused the money, and looked at him . . . his face a picture of triumph. If it had come to that, where a respectable, middle-class French-Canadian got his kicks out of putting down an English panhandler because he hadn't asked for a dime in French, then Hamish had been deluding himself. Goddamit, his people had lived in Montreal for two hundred years. He had as much right here as they did. He shook his head. He didn't speak French. Had never learned. Would it interfere now with his ability to sell to French-Canadian druggists?

Obviously not with Ladouçeur, he thought, as he drove into Verdun. He was going to take a chance and park right in front of the store, even though it was a no parking zone, dash out and make the delivery, and dash back. But he'd better chat with the old man, see how he was doing. He found a parking meter free up the street, parked, took several packages from the back seat, and walked toward the store, whistling.

Inside, a customer was already searching the shelves.

"Mr. Ladouçeur, good morning."

"Mr. Jarvis."

"Here is the reorder you wanted. I'm amazed they moved so quickly." Then to his astonishment, the customer accosted him.

"Mr. Jarvis, I am Sergeant Romaine, Royal Canadian Mounted Police. I arrest you in the name of the Queen for suspected violation of the Trademarks Act. Are you carrying a

255

weapon?"

François Ladouçeur would never understand what went through Mr. Jarvis' head, no matter how often he went over it with his wife.

"No. No." Mr. Jarvis yelled. "You must leave me alone. I didn't know." And then he turned and ran.

"Now why would he run?" Mr. Ladouçeur asked over and over. "It's not so bad; I'm not even sure they put you in jail for that offense. Why did the man run? Surely he didn't think he could outrun the Mountie. Not till hell freezes over. They always get their man."

Waiting outside in their cruiser, the Montreal police saw Jarvis come running out of the store, with the Mountie in pursuit. One of them leaped out of the car, pulled his revolver, and shouted in French, "*Arrêtez-vous!*"

Hamish Jarvis couldn't believe what was happening. Was in a panic and could only think of the shame to his wife and children, could only think of all the things that had happened to him, all the bad things, that this was the end, there was no coming back from this. If only he had opened the packages, one package, looked at the tablet. His picture would be in the papers. How could he walk down the street again, or go to his club? How could he live? Where? He must run. Fast. Get away. He heard the command for him to stop, but he couldn't. Someone yelled to him in French to stop. He heard the order to stop, heard the blood pounding in his ears, heard the report of a revolver with the same amazement as he considered himself in flight, the same unreality.

The bullet hit Hamish Jarvis in the lower spine. He would be in a wheel chair, a paraplegic for the rest of his life.

From Ladouçeur's order forms, the R.C.M.P. learned the address of Pureco and, at exactly the same time that Hamish Jarvis was accosted, other members of the Force entered the building and began interrogating all the workers, the women, two salesmen, and a chemist. By chance they missed Ferrilio and

256

Smith, who had left their respective apartments for the plant minutes before two members of the Force knocked on their doors. Ferrilio picked up Smith and they drove leisurely and unsuspectingly to the plant. As they approached they saw the plainly marked R.C.M.P. cars and several Montreal police force cars as well.

"Son-of-a-bitch," Ferrilio cursed. "Goddam son-of-a-bitch."

"What are we going to do?" Smith asked, terrified.

"Nothing we can do but get to hell across the border as fast as we can. Once we're in the U.S., we're okay."

"But how? They'll be watching the border for sure. They'll have our names, our descriptions. Perhaps they don't work that fast." He had an idea. "We can try to make it to Rouse's Point. It's only thirty miles away."

"Can't take a chance," Ferrilio said. Instead, he made the decision to drive to the Montreal airport and fly immediately to Vancouver. Once there, with Ferrilio's contacts, they took a fishing boat and were landed on the American side. (These boats were used to ferry stock salesmen in and out from the United States, as well as various kinds of dope.) Fred Smith had been totally depressed and non-communicative throughout the entire flight and subsequent trip through the Strait of Juan de Fuca. To his surprise Ferrilio behaved as if nothing had happened. He had a few thousand dollars in his pocket, gave Smith five hundred in case they became separated, and assured him that they'd be back in business again. "We're good together. We should stick together. We owe a few bucks we got to make good, but other than that, we're okay. We got walking-around money. Listen, we'll go down to Vegas. I got contacts there."

They rented a car, drove to Portland, and stayed in a small second-class hotel. That night while Ferrilio slept Smith lay awake and reviewed his whole life. If he stayed with Ferrilio he knew he would wind up in jail again. Their escape had been pure luck. Even if they could be traced, which was doubtful, their offence was not extraditable. So if he walked away now he could begin life again, without fear. It would be a different kind of life. He would have to get a job somewhere, and live as an ordinary

257

person, no money, no fancy clothes. If he found a place to settle he might be able to begin again. He'd never be able to be a lawyer, but there were other things he could do, he was sure. He was intelligent.

As he lay there in the dark he realized that if he left Ferrilio he would give up every chance to make it big. That he would spend the rest of his life as just another jerk. If he gave up on his dreams of success, in a way he would be giving up on himself — and a chance to see his children again. On the other hand, he would be starting anew. Completely anew, with a few hundred dollars in his pocket and one suit of clothes. God, it would be hard. He'd have to take a menial job to begin with, driving a taxi or clerking, and then, by putting pennies together, in a year or two he'd be living a settled life. Then he'd see where he was. Maybe buy a little house. Maybe one by one buy and sell houses. But no wild speculations. But could he escape from Ferrilio and Ferrilio's friends? Because that's what he would have to do. There was no doubt in his mind that he was on the hook for the money the syndicate had loaned. Could he disappear from them as well? He lay in a cold sweat not knowing what to do as the night minutes ticked by.

Suddenly he was jolted by a revelation. He was not smart enough to make money dishonestly. He had been caught by the law society for doing something many lawyers did, and he had been caught in only a few months of doing what apparently many others got away with. He wasn't cut out to be in any kind of racket. Not lucky enough. And he didn't want to go to jail again. And, because of his education, he felt himself to be above the people he had associated with since he had joined Ferrilio.

Without even realizing he had made a decision, he got out of bed and dressed quietly — even though Ferrilio was two doors down the hall. He looked at his watch. It was four in the morning. He counted the money in his pocket. As they had paid in advance, Fred Smith simply walked out of the hotel, hailed a cab, went to the bus station, and took the first bus to Los Angeles. There he would lose himself for a while. Starting his life anew was as simple as that.

In the morning when Ferrilio realized Smith had left, the first thing he said was, "Chicken bastard." Then he was enraged with the thought that Smith had beat him for five big ones. But as far as setting the organization to find him, he considered Smith small potatoes and he didn't want to appear ridiculous. Ferrilio rented a car and drove to Las Vegas to make his connections.

At two o'clock on the afternoon that Hamish Jarvis was shot, to the surprise of the government, the Pharmaceutical Association called a major news conference to reveal the existence of the counterfeit ring. Ron Kendall reported not only on the dangers of counterfeit drugs in Canada, but detailed cases the world over.

What the government couldn't understand was how the Association had found out so quickly. Nevertheless, that afternoon, as newspaper and television newsmen demanded comment from the Minister of Health, there were hurried meetings of the cabinet in Ottawa. The head of the Food and Drug Directorate was called in and it was quickly ascertained that Food and Drug did not have enough men to supervise properly black market and counterfeit drug operations, which could conceivably increase under the new Bill. The Bill obviously had too many loopholes to police. Further, as only the senior men of the cabinet knew there would be both a new leadership convention in the next year, followed by an election, they didn't want to take any chances of more discoveries like this one. For the present, if it were to be a choice between patents and high prices, or all kinds of counterfeit operations, it would be better to stay with the former, or what now existed, until after the election; then, perhaps, they would come at it again.

The cabinet decided to withdraw the Bill before the second reading was completed. The reason given was that the Food and Drug Directorate needed time to complete its investigation into counterfeit drug operations in Canada and study the ramifications.

The international pharmaceutical firms had won. It was over. Joseph had won.

259

24

One day they'll put up a plaque for Isoniazid and God knows what else, Joseph thought, as he waited in the Little Museum for Heister, reading some ancient Japanese remedies: *The excreta of crickets promotes the eruption of pustules and reduces fever; that of the silkworm helps the treatment of gonorrhea; the scrapings from the hoof of an ass, horse, or deer kneaded with dough from rice is useful when applied to a wound — and the larva of flies taken from animal carcasses and burned, cures tubercular children.*

The insanity of the industry — of man — was congealed in this museum. Joseph was beginning to have difficulty shaking the periods of disorientation that swept over him and he found it almost impossible to function within the rationale of what was around him — the industry, the city, life as it was.

When he had stepped off the elevator and stopped at Roma Davidson's desk, she had raised her arm and asked him to look to her left, to where she was pointing. "At that slot in the wall. Hold it," she directed. A simultaneous click and flash blinded him momentarily as she pushed a button, her desk activating a polaroid camera hidden behind the aperture in the wall. "Security" she explained hurriedly. "We've started to keep a photo on file of every visitor to our executive offices with the date and hour of their visit stamped on it."

She rose from her desk and went to a section of the wall which opened to her touch, revealing the ever-aimed camera. "We must guard against industrial espionage, dissident shareholders, anti-vivisectionists, ultraright radicals, ultraleft radicals." And then departing from what was surely a memorized script, she said with all the sincerity she could muster, "I hope you don't mind. That you understand. Being a receptionist used to be a nice job — guest-like, you know what I mean?" and then added brightly, "I read in the *Reader's Digest* about this primitive tribe in South America who believed that a photograph stole their," she frowned, "I forget the word, but it means the same as spirit, or soul."

"Mana," Joseph offered.

"That's it," she said, impressed. "You're not afraid?" she asked archly.

"I have no soul."

"Oh, don't say that."

A buzzer signified the completion of the film processing. She opened the back of the camera and removed the photograph. "It's a good likeness," she trilled. "You're so tall, I was afraid your head would be cut off. We wouldn't want that, would we?" She handed it to him.

Joseph glanced at the photo, disinterested. After forty-odd years, he knew what he looked like — a good-looking male stud, black hair, black eyes; but the essence that was him, his mana had been transmuted into a management consultant, into the technocrat supreme. Have brain will travel. Some were tall and some were short and some had spots on their too-doo-loo.

Heister came striding out of his office wearing a white shirt, a tie, but no jacket. And his sleeves were rolled about the wrists. "Well, what do you think Joseph? What do you think of the shirt sleeve image?" Joseph thought he looked nude. "Come on in."

Heister took several photographs from a drawer in his desk, photographs showing fourteen men, all his senior executive officers, including Sorenson. Some were sitting on the edge of the desk, some around the boardroom table. None were wearing jackets, all were in white shirts with their sleeves rolled up. "This is the basic photo our public relations and advertising depart-ments are suggesting for the cover of this year's *Annual Report;* 'course they're just roughs, not everyone is in the picture yet. The idea is to show a working team of knowledgeable but not stuffy guys. You know, jackets off, sleeves rolled up, ready to

261

work. What do you think?"

"Looks good," Joseph said. But the cover of the last *Annual Report* was more accurate, a photo of the map of the world in the reception area with the words, "The Heister World," superimposed.

"Sorry about your friend, Grant. One in a million."

Did Heister know he was lying? Or was he merely lying to himself? Grant wasn't one in a million to die from Isoniazid. According to Dr. Sherway, besides being sudden and horrible, Grant's death was above all unnecessary, even absurd. He told Joseph that scientists at the Pasteur Institute in France had long ago developed a serum, Bacillus Calmette Guerin (BCG), named after the discoverers, which they offered to the world, providing no profit was derived. It had been in use for many years in France and other countries to innoculate children. When the Germans invaded France, scientists from the Institute went to Mexico and there the serum was manufactured and provided to the world, but for twelve years the drug lobby prevented its use in Mexico itself, just as it stopped its use in the United States. "Just as they have exaggerated the fear of Salk and Sabin vaccines," Sherway had claimed.

Grant's death was absurd. He hadn't been given enough time. But time was absurd and everything was time.

"Too bad about that Jarvis fellow. I read all the reports. I wonder why he ran? Sorenson's in the john. We'll wait for him before we get started. Got some good news for you."

In Heister's private washroom, an elaborate setup with shower and attached sauna, Sorenson turned on the gold-plated taps and watched the water run into the imported marble sink. He washed his hands and, noticing the bottle of vitamins and stomach powders, he took two vitamins. (An apple a day may have been good enough for your grandfather.) Not many people in the firm knew, but it had been his idea to have these placed in all employee washrooms, and in cafeterias in every one of their plants and offices throughout the world. Bob Heister's father had argued violently about the cost and the bad effect on a man getting something for nothing, but Sorenson maintained

262

that keeping employees healthy was a sure way to keep the quality of the product up. He watched himself swallowing the vitamins. In such small quantities they probably weren't worth a damn to someone his age, but you never knew.

He limped out to join Heister and Joseph. God, Joseph looked terrible. Was it just the loss of his friend, Grant, or too much alcohol and amphetamines? Well, now that it was all over, he'd get his health back quickly enough.

"Good news, Joseph," Sorenson said. "I saw a report today about the first successful immunization of humans against the most serious form of hepatitis. Do you know what that means? If a vaccine is developed, perhaps within five years the disease can be controlled. We can save people like your friend."

Was that the goods news Heister had mentioned, Joseph wondered.

"First, for the record," Heister said. "I had to pay the mafia the money they were out. They wanted a hundred thousand but I settled for sixty, which was their original loan plus ten thousand dollars. That's why I started that business of taking everyone's picture."

Joseph was stunned.

"I don't know how the word got out that we were behind everything and I don't care. I'm not declaring war on them. They work their side of the street, I work mine. Sixty thousand dollars was dirt cheap. It got the Bill stopped."

"They'll introduce a new Bill the next session."

"First there has to be an election. Who knows who'll get in and you can bet I'm going to spend money personally to defeat the little Canadian bastard — that Deputy Prime Minister. Flanagan is sure that they won't end patent protection entirely. They see the dangers themselves now. We established certain principles. In business there are never any dramatic solutions. Just a series of skirmishes. As long as you keep the interest of your shareholders paramount, keep the profits up so you can keep the dividends up, you'll always come out ahead. Remember that, Joseph."

The cost had been cheap, Heister said. Were all those casualties cheap, Joseph wondered? Louise, Lewison, Thelma, Hamish Jarvis, Fred Smith, the Canadian people. And Grant . . . and Grant. And perhaps himself. Cheap? Yet who was at fault? He couldn't even decide that. Was it his fault? Was it the industry's? Impossible for him to arrive at a value judgment. The drug industry was so complex, so interrelated with all the other systems in the society. Joseph couldn't even say, "This was wrong, this is right, this I understand, this I don't understand." But whatever the answer, the cost was not cheap.

Heister came from around his desk. "Come on, let's sit comfortable." They arranged themselves on the sofas. "Joey, I didn't show you that shirt sleeve picture for nothing. You're in it. Or you will be. That's what I called you here for. I've just completed the purchase of one of the largest deodorant firms in the United States, and you're going to be president. I told you I'd have a big one for you. A hundred thousand dollars a year with stock options." ("A feather-in-your-cap son," his mother used to say when he had done something well.) "I tell you Joey, this firm has a great range of products, but the newest idea they've got and what decided me to buy the company, is they're going to put a cunt deodorant on sale. Imagine that? Isn't that the greatest idea you ever heard of? They've got this new cunt deodorant spray. It's going to revolutionize the deodorant industry. And you're going to be president. And Joey, that's just the beginning. My plans are for you to expand the company. First thing is to make it multinational. Go everywhere that the Heister corporation is. Every country. I figure Mexico should be first. Those Mexicans want to copy Americans. Drink coke, take photos; now they can smell like Americans. And that's not all, Joey. I'm starting a ten-year program of acquisition. All kinds of products and services. I'm going to build the biggest conglomerate in the world. And you're going to be right beside me. Helping me choose the companies to acquire. Maybe stepping in and getting them in shape. You've got the training. And I know I can count on you if the going gets rough. How does that sound?"

Well, now he had it made. He really had it made. Yes sir, he'd be just as trapped as Heister. Now that was funny, for all his wealth and power Heister was a pawn too. The king pawn. And he couldn't think of a damn thing to say because he couldn't think of a damn thing to think, and so he just sat there smiling.

"Joey, you look tired. You've worked hard this last year. I want you to take a month off before you start in on this new deal. Go back to Ottawa. Clean up there and go any place in the world for a vacation. On me. Consider it a bonus."

Joseph found himself wondering if Heister could send him to heaven.

After the meeting with Heister he had to attend an important principal's conference at Daniels and Company. Checking his watch, he knew he was going to be late. How was that possible? He was always on time. All Daniels' consultants were always punctual. After much deliberation, punctuality had been defined by CAMP as being ten minutes early, no more, no less. It was a tenet of the firm. In fact, the treatise on earliness had been prepared by the firm's managing partner himself, Lionel Cole. "More than ten minutes early denotes anxiousness, unseemly ostentation, and undignified pushiness, in short, an unprofessional hunger for the assignment. Even worse, it connotes that we do not place a proper value on our time. However, later than ten minutes early contains the implication that we do not consider the assignment significant, or worse, that one of our consultants is a poor manager of time. As time is what we sell, along with our technological expertise and problem-solving capabilities, ten minutes early is perfection itself."

"Damned cross-town traffic," Joseph said.

"Don't tell me," the taxi driver said in his polygot accent. "Listen, only this morning I'm driving this coloured lady down Seventh. I get behind a truck, see, and the traffic stops for ten minutes. Ten minutes. Now when I get her to where she's going, she don't want to pay me. Like I cheated her. It was my fault the traffic was so slow. She gets out of the cab and stands there yelling at me. Now across the street there's this big black guy, must be seven feet and weighs three hundred and he thinks

265

she's hot because I don't want to take her to Harlem. You know a lot of cabbies won't take them *schvartzes* to Harlem, and he yells, 'Sister, you tell that white mother-fucker that he has to take you wherever you want to go.' Listen, they just burned down their own homes in Newark, shooting firemen, and I should go to Harlem? That crazy I'm not." The cab driver, Abraham Ribovitch according to the licence in the car, shrugged his shoulders. "What do they want from me? It's my fault they were slaves? My grandfather came to this country from Russia sixty years ago. What did he know from a coloured problem? He was running from a Jewish problem."

"I'm sorry I'm late for the meeting," Joseph seemed to be saying over and over to the principals of Daniels and Company assembled in the boardroom. Lionel Coles was speaking. "For years now the heads of divisions at our firm have been called principals; to oversimplify, of course, the problem is that as the years go by fewer and fewer people, clients, understand what the word principal means."

"Exactly," interrupted Stayner Loesser, principal in charge of marketing. "We have to adopt the marketing point of view. We have to think from the customer back and provide what he wants, not think of what we produce and try to sell it. It's time we called ourselves partners."

Joseph remembered that Stayner spent a week once with a salesman choosing the right toilet paper for the washroom, maintaining that the can was an integral part of the image of the firm.

The meeting lasted three hours because many of the men had been principals for twenty years and didn't like the idea of changing into partners overnight without proper consideration, although the proposition had been discussed off and on for a year.

After the meeting, sherry and cheese were served. Joseph didn't remember what had been decided, didn't know whether he was a principal or a partner. It was so hard to focus. But he did know that Stayner took all the cheese that was left home. Stole it, as he always did.

After the conference, Joseph went to the Athletic Club. Sitting in the steam bath he was joined by a barrel-chested, bald-headed man. "Whoa, that's good," he said. "Whoa, that's hot. Whoa, that's good. You think it's too hot or you want more? I tell you I'm wide awake. I means it's ridiculous. I don't need no sleep no more since I started to work out." He rubbed his belly, patting himself. "Whoa, that's hot. I mean that's good. Like all I need is four hours sleep a night. I mean that's day in and day out and I got a job, I can tell you, I have to be sharp. Last night I went to bed at two thirty, and this morning I'm up at seven o'clock ready to go, ready to work, you know what I mean?"

In the washroom cubicle, Joseph heard two men walk in behind him. "God, you have to go through a lot of doors in here," one said. "I mean why do they need so many doors?"

"You ever been to White Pine?" the other asked. "You have to go through four doors to get into the washroom."

Reading a trade magazine while sitting there, Joseph saw an advertisement, black and bordered. The heading in black type stated: *GOOD-BYE MURPH-*, and the obit read: *E. Gerald Murph died June 15 in New York. There are consultants on both sides of the border today who learned much from Murph. He was a pro, one of the best. Beneath Murph's hard-nosed exterior was a warmth, honesty, humour, and interest in his fellow man that makes the world a little better for his having been there. Goodbye Murph. God Bless.* It was signed, *Some friends.*

And though he had never known 'Murph,' Joseph started to cry, the tears blurring the news that that week American soldiers in Vietnam had killed 3,208 Viet Cong, "their biggest bag to date."

He took Roma out to dinner. Beside them in the restaurant he heard a young woman say, "my mother doesn't understand me. She thinks I'm a pervert. I talk to my father on the phone a lot now that I moved out. I never could before." And Roma said, "You know what my girlfriend likes doing to her husband? You'll never guess. We were at this party. This hen party, and she told us all she does is pick the lint out of his belly button. If that's marriage I don't want any part of it. Joseph, you're not

267

listening. Where were you? Penny for your thoughts, Joseph."

And, walking back to Roma's apartment, they were enveloped by dozens of people, young and old, chanting, "Hey, hey L.B.J. How many kids did you kill today?"

The next day, before catching the plane back to Ottawa, Joseph went to the storage company where all his furniture and personal belongings were that he hadn't taken with him to Ottawa. He searched inside a dresser drawer until his hand felt his old officer's pistol, neatly wrapped. The moment he touched the gun a feeling of peace enveloped him. He put it in his briefcase. Then he went to a sports store and bought a box of cartridges.

He could end the absurdity, stop time, whenever he chose. And somehow that realization made it a little easier, gave him a little happiness.

He started to whistle.

25

On the way from the airport to his apartment, Joseph had the taxi stop at a pet shop where he purchased two piranha. Carefully parcelling the fish in a special water-holding cardboard container, the salesman said, "You know, of course, sir, that you cannot put these fish in with your others. They'll eat them."

"Why do you think I'm buying them?" And he laughed.

And the salesman laughed. Because he thought Joseph was joking.

At home he unpacked and undressed and then decided to stay naked for a while. He took the gun from his briefcase, oiled and loaded it. Then he poured himself a scotch and sat looking at his aquarium for the longest time. He got up, placed the gun carefully on the chair, then scooped the piranha out of the carton with a net and placed them in the aquarium. And watched in horror as the water swirled, the fear of the other fish trying to blast out of the tank, smashing against the walls. The piranha attacked the moonfish first and within minutes had destroyed it. Joseph shuddered and almost threw up, but he quickly dipped the net into the tank, caught the piranha, and put them back in their carton.

Goddam fish had cost him a fortune. What a waste. He never was able to deal with money, always buying something he usually didn't want once he had it. He was never able to come to grips with money. It always seemed an enemy, slipping through his fingers.

Resuming his place with the gun on his lap he watched the remaining fish in the aquarium slowly return to normal, their fear vanish. And soon they didn't know there was one less in their world. Everything went on as before. Was that what was bothering him? That everything was the same? Heister was still Heister (one of the few men he encountered that he couldn't understand, couldn't get a handle on), and Sorenson would continue to work for the industry until the day he died. Ron Kendall wasn't bothered. He had taken a job as P.R. director of the Swiss firm that was building in Cornwall. And Flanagan was making plans to run for office again, hoping that he was backing the right leadership candidate so he could become a cabinet minister. Even his mother was doing fine in her bowling league. No one seemed to be bothered that Grant had died, that Hamish Jarvis was a paraplegic. That the Canadian people had been victimized.

Then what was his problem? One hundred thousand dollars a year. He had it made. Everything he had ever wanted. "I mean, goddam," he said aloud. "Joey Mann from the shabby edges of Sandy Hill, with a drunken father and a mother who had been a char, at a hundred thou a year in New York."

But it wasn't enough. Somehow it wasn't enough. Everything was worthless. But what more was there? Violetta? Love? Purpose? Impossible to continue. He felt worthless. One of the things he felt about himself was that he occupied a space, that he was a construct, concrete. But somehow he no longer fitted, or there was no space, or he couldn't feel the edges of himself that defined himself. And then he had this great idea. His last great idea. Maybe he had had it before; maybe he had always had it and that was why he had bought the piranha. He would feed all his other fish to the piranha one by one, one each day; no, two by two; well, whatever. Anyway he would kill all the fish but one, and then kill that fish and when all the fish were dead he would kill himself.

And he dozed.

With the sleeping pills and the scotch and the amphetamines, time continued confused and he was dressed and walking past his old elementary school. He had been the favourite of his grade eight teacher. One day she had called him into her office

270

and told him that he really shouldn't be playing with (he couldn't remember the girl's name), a sixteen-year-old with big boobs who should have been in high school years before, that she wasn't a nice girl, not the sort that Joseph should be playing with. Mrs. McComb wanted to protect him. And Joseph almost broke up because Luther said he had fucked that girl (what *was* her name?) and Joey had wanted to and now he wouldn't be able to because he promised Mrs. McComb he wouldn't play with her and she would be watching him. More than he wanted to fuck her, he wanted to get good grades.

Goddam it, he'd go and say good-bye to old Luther. They had all been in this thing together. Past the War Memorial and he remembered the arrival of the King and Queen in 1939, shortly before the Second World War. And then some time after the war those dates, 1939-1945, had been chiselled out, added to the date already there. And Joseph wondered how many of those young men with their periscopes made at school who had watched the first ceremony were dead by the time the second dates were added. That was a big aquarium.

"Oh, if I had the wings of an angel and the red ass of a crow, I'd fly to the Parliament buildings and shit on the people below," he sang bravely as he and Grant used to. Past Parliament and seeing himself — a six-year-old, marching beside parading soldiers, strutting right into the steel arm of a burly policeman and falling to the ground while everyone laughed. The policeman picked him up and shoved him into the crowd. "There now, you aren't hurt sonny?" he asked in his Scottish accent. But he was. He was. They had all laughed at him.

Luther wasn't there. They said he wasn't on nights and it was late at night, and only the chip-chip sound of the stone carver at work could be heard. The stone carver at his lonely work as he had been now for ten years, and another stone carver before him, and another one after, chipping away at blank granite, putting on the faces of history, until, in perhaps one thousand years, every piece of granite in the building would have something chiselled on it, and men would study their whole lives in universities, and would get their doctorates by writing books about what the carvings all meant and who was who and why. Joseph laughed. If no one knew the why of anything now, how would they know later? Judgment of history! Even now, there were faces carved who were unknown; some said that as a joke the original Italian carvers had included their own faces, with a version of the Mona Lisa smile, high up looking down, probably thinking, you idiots, paying us all that good money to carve such stupid things.

He found himself drinking in Frank Flanagan's office. Flanagan poured. "My daily exercise. Twenty-five pours a day keeps a man in the pink." He didn't look too good. Hitting the bottle pretty heavily. They decided to work out a new set of laws of life that would have meaning not only for politicians, but for everyone. They tried for a new Ten Commandments, but so far could only develop six.

FLANAGAN'S (F)LAWS FOR EVERY MAN(N):

(1) You never can tell from where you sit what least to expect the most.

(2) Expectation is in direct ratio to that which is said or unsaid, dependent on what is most expected the least.

(3) Depending upon your state of mind the eventuality of any allegation is meaningful to the extent the listener is not.

(4) Rationalization is a process of expectation which elucidates the said or unsaid in direct proportion to rationality.

(5) Proportion is the division of what may be expected to most divide the least.

(6) Listening is the art of analysis which assists justification in proportion to opinion without regard to analysis.

Joseph lost weight, couldn't sleep without a sleeping pill and a lot of scotch, and couldn't get going without amphetamines. He walked the streets, wanting Violetta but not trusting the longing within him. For days he would be conscious of all the overweight people he saw. Everyone in the whole city had layers of pig-fat on them. Like that bishop who eulogized — grunted — over Grant's body. And then he would see only bones. He seemed to see right through the flesh beneath to the bones, and the city was full of skeletons with clothes on.

And he had this continuing dream where he was walking naked carrying a long sword slicing people's arms and legs and heads off. Or sometimes he would be shooting machine guns wildly at everyone he saw. And sometimes he would be found guilty and locked up in jail and he heard the clang of the gates shut behind him and there was no way out. One hundred thousand dollars a year to sell cunt deoderant. One hundred thousand dollars a year to convince women, and men, that cunt shouldn't smell like cunt. Cunt cudnt, wudnt, shudnt smell like cunt. (*An apple a day may have been all right for your grandfather, but on-the-go America needs a cunt deoderant.*) "I'm fighting for my country. What are you fighting for?" Joseph answered, "For my right to sell cunt deoderant. Which is more important?" But now he saw it was the same thing. He must tell Grant of his insight.

Through the night, walking alone, seeing the past and unable to touch it and the buildings with all the lives congealed. And he thought of Violetta. She's done it to me, he thought. Opened me up to my sense of self and aloneness. Was it that or Grant's death? Or Jarvis being crippled? Or . . . or . . . or . . . .

Two hippies dragged a young girl along with them. She didn't cry out. Was she drugged? Faking? Street theatre. Real? And he saw the young faces with the skulls showing through translucent skin. Hollow sockets where the eyes had been. No, that was a picture he had seen of young children after some war, he didn't remember which. There'd been so many in his life. Forty-three years of man killing man, and still the world was over-populated. Oh there's a lot of fucking going on tonight, honey.

And he saw these people go by on a bus and remembered a thought he had been troubled by when he was younger and watched people on the streetcar (with a streetcar you're on the rails, you know what I mean?); it cracked by, sparks shooting from the trolley, and he could see them motionless, carried along, or their mouths moving, talking, but he couldn't hear and all these people in their own worlds, with their own families, each one thinking they were the centre of their world . . . all waiting for the big piranha in the sky.

That reminded him. The kissing gourami was next to go.

And he walked and walked, every street that had been his and Grant's life, and he thought of Violetta who was lost to him. She would marry and live in a sprawling suburb with another man, with hundreds and hundreds of houses and become a mother again, wife and mother and be happy. She would forget him, forget how they loved and how they saw into each other's souls. Then time became confused again and he was alone walking the streets in the suburbs trying to find her. And every time he saw a honey-coloured head he would feel it like a knife in his body and follow it and pass it and look back in anxious expectation. It was never hers.

Louise worried about him, and every so often there was a knock on his door and she would be there. "Joseph, you must look after yourself."

"As long as I can get it up for you baby, that's all you care about."

She became angry. "I mean it. You're cracking."

He started to laugh uncontrollably. "You want to cure me. There's an ancient remedy in Heister's museum. He's the king of ancient remedies. Look, you pretend you're the goddess Isis and I'll be Horus and you straddle me and wash my body with your pee. Piss on me baby and I'll be all better."

He didn't know how long he had dozed but was awakened by a knock on the door. Without thinking he got up, naked as he was, with the gun in his hand, and opened the door. "Hi, Louise."

"What do you think you're doing with that gun?" she screamed, frightened.

"I'm going to fuck you. You will have the distinction of being my last fuck," and he started to laugh. "Not with the gun. Come on, you bitch, my cock is sticking up in the air like a telephone pole. You'll never forgive yourself if you don't climb up and lower yourself down on it."

"Joseph, please, let me call a doctor."

He put the gun to his head, pressed against his temple. "You call a doctor and I'll pull the trigger right now. None of your middle-class shrinks, please. I'm not adjusting to their society any longer. And it sure as hell isn't going to adjust to me. So let's

274

fuck. What else can we do?"

But he could not have a climax. No matter what he did, or what she did, he could not have an orgasm. And his despair was total.

Time was still confused. Because she didn't seem to be there. He searched through his apartment. No Louise. Maybe she hadn't been there. He masturbated and had a climax. "You old cock, you haven't let me down yet," he said, delighted. "I'm going to do that again before I blow my head off. Just wait a bit," and he poured himself another scotch. "It's just you and me together now. That's complete oneness."

Brain and cock he had thought of himself. No, gun and cock. He touched the gun and his happiness was complete. The final no. There was nothing in his life he controlled, had ever controlled, or would ever control. He responded only. Events were ever moving him on. Except he could say no. That was his uniqueness.

But Louise *had* been there and had fled when he wasn't looking and she knew that unless she did something, he was going to kill himself. But what to do? Call the police and have them charge in? If he wanted to he could kill himself before they got to him. Or another time. And then there was the question of freedom. It was his right to kill himself if he wanted to. Or, sadistically, did she want to see what would happen? Would he really? She had a thrill shiver. Or did she want to punish him? But if he died, and she had not tried to prevent it, could she live with herself?

She called Violetta. Louise knew Joseph loved Violetta. She would save him, if anyone could. She telephoned Violetta realizing it was the first time she had spoken to her in such a long time and she went to see her, and they both told each other everything.

And later Violetta called Joseph. The phone rang. And rang. And rang. Violetta counted the rings with rising anxiety. Was she too late? Ten, fifteen, twenty.

"Hello."

"Joseph."

275

Tears streamed down his face.

"Joseph, are you there, are you . . ." She almost said, "Are you all right?" but she didn't. Keep control, keep it natural, she cautioned herself.

"Yes," he managed to say.

"Can you come to dinner Saturday? It's Mylita's name day. (She wished it weren't four days away, but could think of no other reason to call him — to which he might respond if he were as far gone as Louise had said.) I know it's silly, but I promised my mother I would always celebrate her name day. It's an old Lithuanian custom. Will you come?"

He thought for a moment. "Yes, I would love to come." And he put the phone down. Had he said good-bye? No matter. Yes, he would see Violetta. Once more.

Saturday. Her call had settled something in his mind. It was time to get on with it. He looked in the mirror. God, he looked awful. He took another amphetamine. Did he need a haircut? Not really, and it didn't matter now. Clothes. He must be sure to look absolutely perfect. "Clothes make the man, son." But what should he wear — his best gray or his best blue suit?

He dug out his copy of CAMP and poured over it, but there was nothing in it about what to wear on name days, or last days either. He must write a letter to Lionel Coles about that. Everything was an acronym, CAMP, INTEGRAL. He must save himself, the world, from the acronym mind. MIND. What was that an acronym for? LIFE . . . MAN . . . MANN. He would decide the scientific way. First, he got completely dressed in the gray with all the accessories and looked at himself, and then in the blue. The blue. He looked very much the successful $100,000-a-year-man in the blue. He MANN.

Gift. He must take Mylita a present. But what? He walked up and down. What could he buy her? And then it occurred to him that the best thing he could do for Mylita on her name day was to show her what life was, what it was really all about. He would bring the fish or what was left of them. He would give her his

276

whole aquarium. And he would release the piranha in it and show her what life and death were all about, so she would have no illusions. That's what a father should do. She was old enough. It would take some doing, carrying all that stuff, but it was worth-while. "If something is worth-while doing, it's worth-while doing well."

And the gun. He would do it when he returned from the party. He laughed at the thought that he'd die not too far from where he'd been born. Funny, all the travelling he'd done, during the war and then as a management consultant, to end up here. But in a way he felt he fitted here or used to before he lost his space and he certainly hadn't felt that about any other place he'd ever been in his whole life. Now that was interesting. He'd never thought about it before.

Joseph was happy as he drove through the streets of Ottawa in his red Thunderbird. He parked in front of Violetta's apartment and carefully carried the aquarium and the various cartons and bottles with fish in them. It took ten trips. He placed them on the floor of the corridor beside Violetta's door. Then he knocked.

When she opened the door, and they looked at each other, there was a moment, the first in many weeks, months, when it was as it had been, this flow between their eyes. It seemed to her that Joseph wavered for a moment. Unsteady. But not from drinking. More from lack of food. He was so very thin. Gaunt. His eyes yellow. Louise hadn't exaggerated. Joseph was very ill, physically as well as mentally. But at least he was here and seemed gay. Not shabby or unshaven. Not naked. She hadn't known what to expect.

Nor what to expect of herself. In the months since Joseph's rejection she had been with a new man, had had sex with him and was nearly shattered to discover she could have a climax with him. Even while she thought of Joseph, even while she wanted Joseph, loved Joseph, this man could bring her to a climax. And it almost led to total cynicism on her part. But she ended the affair because sex without love was too bruising to her soul. She wasn't at Louise's age yet, where friendly sex was mentally satisfying and she had long since passed the stage of being satisfied by physical sex alone. That with Vido. Unfortunately, sex lust could not replace the sex love she had had with Joseph.

"What have you brought me?" Mylita came running, interrupting their mood.

"Hi kitten," he said and kissed her.

"Can I have my present now?"

"Tell you what. I'll give you half now and half after our dinner party." He started to carry in the aquarium and the cartons. Violetta recognized it and the fish and felt a moment of terror. But Joseph and Mylita began to set it up and they worked away for half an hour having a good time, placing the coloured stones, deciding where to put the castle and other decorations. And he explained about the light, and they put the water in.

"It will have to warm up. The temperature has to be just right."

And Violetta in the kitchen preparing dinner, listening to the friendly chatter, allowed herself to relax.

Dinner was fun, not full of love like their other times but it was Mylita's day and it was too much to expect that their first time together in so long would continue where they had ended. Yet she felt Joseph, loved Joseph, and felt him loving her inside himself. And there was a peace about him.

"Why are you giving up your aquarium? Are you going away?" Violetta asked.

"Yes."

"Are you taking the Peruvian assignment?"

"Bigger and better. And farther."

"Why don't you take your jacket off, Joseph? Don't be so formal."

He removed it and was about to drape it over the back of the chair when she came over to take it. "You'll ruin it that way."

"Where are you going to put it?" he asked tensely.

"I'll hang it up in the cupboard."

"Oh, that's too far away," and he reached in the pocket and took out the gun and laid it on the table in front of him, beside his plate of roast beef along with his knife and fork. He didn't seem to know that there was anything unusual in what he had done.

278

Then he handed her the jacket. "Okay, you can hang it up now."

Then Violetta felt real terror, for Mylita as much as for herself. And for Joseph. And it increased the more normal he continued to appear. He chattered gaily and when he had finished dessert — pie and ice cream — he asked for seconds. And then dinner was over.

"Come, my blond baby," he said to Mylita. "Let us put the fish in the tank." He got up leaving the gun on the dining room table. He and Mylita caught the fish with the net and placed them carefully in the tank while he explained about each one, its name and where it came from. "I used to have more," he said. "Aren't they beautiful in their world of ferns and coloured stones? Aren't the colours lovely as they swim back and forth... endlessly... endlessly... endlessly."

"Oh yes," Mylita said delightedly. "Thank you."

Then Joseph opened up the last carton and dipping the net in fished out the piranha and put them in the aquarium. Within seconds they were flashing about, tearing chunks off the other fish, killing as they ate and the terror in the tank became the terror in Mylita and she screamed hysterically as a fish's eye popped out and sank to the bottom of the tank.

"You see, my Mylita," Joseph said quite calmly, "that is what life is about. That is my gift to you. The gift of understanding. You eat me, now I eat you, now you eat me, now I eat you, in a world that is monstrous. A monstrous aquarium where we devour each other, and kill and kill and kill and are killed." He felt himself rambling, that he wasn't really getting the point that he wanted to make. But then why try to articulate? There it was going on in front of her with the piranha saying everything.

"Stop, stop," Mylita screamed. She clung to Joseph and tried to wrench the net away from him so she could catch the piranha.

Enraged, Joseph slapped her and screamed, "Don't you like your present? Don't you understand?"

Mylita reeled backwards, the blood pouring from her mouth and nose from the force of his hand. The torn fish and the blood running down her face made her scream hysterically.

279

And Violetta, who had watched paralyzed during the sixty seconds of all this, went beserk. Had the piranha eaten at her daughter's face? Like the rooster that had pecked at her face when she was Mylita's age. Only that was blood in the fish tank and blood on Mylita's face and she grabbed the gun that Joseph had left on the dining room table and fired. The recoil jerked her hand and the bullet missed Joseph and hit the aquarium smashing it, the water and glass and bits of fish spreading on the carpet. Then she held the gun with two hands and pointed it at Joseph and pulled the trigger a second time. This time the bullet hit him.

Joseph felt himself falling. Falling. As if stuck by a pin. And very conscious. Lying on the floor. He put his hand on the right side of his chest where the pain was and looked at his hand. It was bloody. And he could feel blood flowing.

At first, the silence that followed the explosion of the pistol and the sight of Joseph falling terrified her, and she wanted to run. To grab Mylita and run. Run over the fields with her mother away from the coughing sound of the airplanes.

But then her training as a doctor made her react as a doctor. Joseph lying wounded was real. An actuality she could deal with. She put the gun down and went over to where he was lying, his eyes still open, still conscious. "Don't move, Joseph. I've shot you. Let me see the wound."

She unbuttoned his shirt carefully.

"Is it bad?" he asked.

"I don't know yet. Is there much pain?"

"No."

"Take your hand away. I must be able to see it."

He had the feeling if he took his hand away from the hole that his insides would fall out. But he did as she asked.

There was a hole in the right side of his chest about half an inch in diameter, indented with burn marks around it. Thank God it was on the right side. "I'm going to have to pull your shirt off so I can see if the bullet has come out the other side." She started to help him, "I want you to sit up a bit. Lean against the sofa."

"I'll get blood on it."

"Mylita, you will have to help me. Stop crying. Bring me my medical bag. You will be my nurse, okay?"

The little girl ran into her mother's bedroom and got her bag. Violetta opened it, took out her scissors and cut off his shirt. Fortunately the bullet had gone right through. The hole at the back was uglier, jagged, about double the size. There was a lot of blood coming out of that hole, but not a dangerous amount.

"Am I going to die?" Joseph asked, realizing with surprise that the moment he'd been shot and thought he was going to die, he didn't want to die at all. He wanted to live. Everything became clear to him. His problem was how, how could he live, how could any man live? "Am I am going to die?" He was wandering, repeating.

"No, my love," and she almost lost control of herself and broke down. "You won't die."

At that moment Violetta decided she would care for him right in her apartment. Everything went through her mind at once. First, the legal aspect. She hadn't gone through the difficulties of her life to go to jail, or risk losing her medical licence for shooting a man. Second, because of the trajectory, only one or two ribs were broken at the most, and perhaps the side of the lung, the pleura, was punctured. But there were no large vessels there and no danger of him bleeding to death. Third, she had all the instruments she needed to care for him.

"Joseph, you'll have to help. And you too, Mylita." She took Joseph under his left arm. "You must get up. Walk. Lean on me. I'm going to take you to my bed."

"That's the best offer I've had today," he said weakly.

They made it to the bed and he wanted to lie down to put his head down. He felt dizzy, his face gray, and very lazy. He just wanted to lie down, but she wouldn't let him. "Help me." And she arranged him in the Fowler position — putting pillows behind him to keep him at a 45-degree angle to prevent blood from collecting in the pleura and to avoid possible infection of that organ. She kept talking, telling Joseph what she was doing and why, although she knew he had gone into a traumatic shock

281

and that what she was saying probably wasn't registering.

Every so often he coughed and she timed them. One cough every five minutes. That's okay. He complained of pain. When she checked the mucous, it was only lined with blood, so despite his pain, nothing serious. Proof her diagnosis was correct. She would be able to care for him here. Rest. Antibiotics. And time for the holes and punctures of the skin to heal.

"Mylita, nurse, my medical bag."

The child brought it.

With clamps from her bag, Violetta carefully began to remove blood clots. Then she washed around the wound with hexa-chlorophene, covered it with gauze, and taped it. She then injected 600,000 units of procaine penicillin G.

"It hurts, Violetta."

For a moment she considered using demerol and then remembered that it was a breathing depressant. Too dangerous. She wrote a prescription for a non-narcotic pain reliever. The drug store delivered it within half an hour. And Joseph slept.

However, there was much to do. Calling her office to say she was sick, calling Joseph's office — but they hadn't expected him because he had been given a month's holiday, looking after Mylita to make sure there were no after-effects. Impossible to judge the mental scar at seeing her mother shoot a man and the terror of the piranha. Within half an hour after caring for Joseph, she had given Mylita a mild sleeping pill and she had slept for fourteen hours. In that time, Violetta had cleaned up the mess from the aquarium and thrown everthing out, pieces of glass and fish. The next morning she called a rug cleaner who had come and taken the rug away to remove the stains. The following day she made sure Mylita helped look after Joseph, and it became something of a game.

Caring for the wound would be a simple matter — involving cleaning it three times a day for three days and then every other day. More worrisome was that the next day, from his anxiety, Violetta realized that Joseph was having dangerous withdrawal symptoms from amphetamines. She wondered again whether she should take him to the hospital. There they could give him amphetamines, less and less each day, accurately measuring the exact amounts. But again she decided to do it herself.

For days she sat by his bed guarding him against the suicide attempt that could quite easily result from the depression of withdrawal from amphetamines. She sat by his bed holding his hand. She almost killed this man. She loved this man and yet she wanted to kill him. That destruction was within her. She shuddered. And dozed, and the hours and the days went by.

After five days, Joseph came round, and pulled her to him and kissed her, and it was like it had always been with them. And more days went by and he became better each day.

His thoughts were clear. He experienced a kind of wholeness — saw a coherence to things — a new awareness which would structure his life.

"The old world doesn't work for me any more," he finally said.

"I know," she said, holding back the tears.

"It's all play-acting. We're born into a world that tells us how to live and we do it. But it's not real. And it's so complex. And we're so manipulated. And the manipulators are manipulated. Even Heister. Even Robert Heister is powerless. Countless decisions are made by countless managers all over the world and the cumulative thrust of all those little decisions propels the organization *and* Heister."

"What do you *really* think of the drug industry, Joseph? I feel as if you won't be clear in your head until you either deal with it, or exorcise it, and I don't think you can do the latter until you make up your mind where you stand."

"I have. In fact I've been thinking about little else lying here."

"Do you feel like talking about it?"

"Yes — I *want* to . . . To put it as simply as I can, my view is neither Grant's nor Heister's. Neither side dealt with the real problem." Joseph stopped. He felt his perceptions were right. The words — the answers so long repressed poured forth, flooding his mind with their potential for him and Violetta.

"On one level there's no question that prescription drugs are priced too high, unconscionably high. For a knowledge- and science-based industry, the selling techniques are a joke, like huckstering at a carnival. I think, however, that there's not enough known about bio-availability, so the best thing is to stay with proven drugs rather than generic ones. If Canada feels it must let multinational corporations keep control — to provide jobs and the good life the politicians claim — then we should at least force them to develop a totally integrated production and research facility here. It's simply irresponsible for us to merely put the product into bottles. The whole medical fraternity does itself and the people of Canada a disservice by practically abdicating its responsibility in the area of pharmacology, leaving the teaching of which drugs are good for what illnesses to the drug detail men."

"You have been thinking."

"But that's only the superficial part, because I still believe that if you're sick, you want the best and safest drug, price doesn't matter; and, for the most part, the drug industry has produced miracles. My quarrel is more basic.

"A drug company's research and development decisions are made not on an understanding of man's long-term needs or on what will advance the general state of knowledge, but only on what will sell. The way managers — and that includes people as high up as Sorenson and Heister — can prove themselves to their shareholders, to their peer groups, and to themselves is to play the numbers' game; how much more of that product was produced, how much more of this product was sold? But unfortunately there are no numbers which show total social cost and benefit. There's no method of arriving at these numbers. Yet these are the numbers that really affect us — polluted air, scarred countryside, and worse, lives lived by the standards of the totality of all advertising campaigns."

Joseph paused. Violetta took his hand. "I feel as if we're entering a new dark age, one that could go on for hundreds of years, with each man and woman being lost and dark *inside*. To change it is to stop being a consuming society, to stop wanting

284

more and more of the goodies. And we both know that that is simply not going to happen. We're all too brainwashed. Therefore, man will become more and more entrapped in the technological structure he has created to provide him with the good things."

"That's depressing."

He shrugged. "I suppose I've always felt this way and not faced it. I can deal with it now. I feel twice born, as James said." He paused and continued. "No, I'm not depressed. I'm not sure what to do. I'm not sure I can be real. I have to live. Want to live. And to live I have to work. But at what? A deodorant company?" He laughed. "Impossible and still be human, don't you see? How is a man to live? How is a man to be a man and a woman to be a woman? How? That's the real question today. How to live with one's powerlessness."

"If the old world doesn't work for you, you'll have to try for a new one, won't you?"

He lifted his hands helplessly, but with a smile on his face. "Where do you start? I mean where the hell do you start? That's what I still have to figure out."

She looked at him and their eyes caught and in one of those incredible moments of transcending he knew. "With love."

"First love of self," she said.

"Then?"

"Love of the other."

"I love you."

"And I you."

And finally on the fifteenth day she said, "I think it's time you got out of bed. Come on, off your ass. Get showered. Get dressed."

"If you'll come in the shower with me," he smiled.

"You're well again. I was beginning to worry."

He laughed. "I'm well again. Better than ever."

And they showered together and the water seemed to wash the whole past off them and they were new and clean.

285

"What would you like to do my love?" he asked. "Make love, go out to eat, go dancing? Your wish is my command."

"Everything."

"Everything!"

"Let's go to bed. Then go out to eat."

"Then let's walk and look at the sky and be alive in the world, totally." One life. One life only. And it occurred to him that the essence of man lies in the beauty of his dreams. Within the process of becoming was the only reality and the only happiness.

"Can you come to Peru with me?" he asked quite unexpectedly. "The job is a three month assignment. Perhaps you could do some work in a local hospital. We could take Mylita."

"You've decided on a way for yourself."

"I think so. At least I'm going to try. It comes down to four basic choices, you know. You can lose yourself in the society as it is; you can opt out — head for Haight-Ashbury, weave mats and make candles, that sort of thing; you can become a revolutionary and try to smash it, although God knows what will be put in its place." He paused. "Or you can try to work within what exists for some social good. Technology exists. Multinationals exist. We can't wish them away. So I'm going to continue as a management consultant but use my talents only on assignments that *I* perceive to be good. Helping to manage the development of a large port so the fishermen of Peru don't lose half their catch by archaic handling methods seems to me to be a good thing. And I'll make my base in Canada. Grant was right about that. We still have a chance here to build a more human society.

"I knew you'd find a way," she said.

"You'll come with me?"

"Yes, I will. But Joseph, I won't always be able to be with you. I have my work."

"I know."

How lucky he had been to find Violetta. Perhaps the love would not last. Nothing lasted. But that didn't make it any the less for the moment. He kissed her hand. A oneness.

His life was all life, the whole contained in the minute part. North America was the best place to live; it allowed for the most

286

physical freedom, yet, like him, it had to find its humanity, reorganize, realign itself for the common good. There was nothing wrong with the machines. They just had to be used to some human purpose. If not, then disaster for everyone. But in the meantime, here, he could be anything he wanted to be. He could start again. He knew he had to live in the real world. This time it would be different. This time he would not be so alone. This time he would have help.

Joseph felt good. It was possible to be happy.

Epilogue

In time, a new Bill was enacted to amend the Patent Law, but without many of the provisions so harmful to the pharmaceutical industry. In effect, instead of having a seventeen-year monopoly, the industry was permitted eight years — more than enough time to continue exacting high prices and earning huge profits.

The new Bill changed nothing. The doctors still prescribed what drug detail men promoted, druggists followed the doctors' orders, patients took their prescribed doses — and hoped.

And no other country has since tried to do what Canada tried.